HORSE

HORSE

Geraldine Brooks

VIKING

VIKING

An imprint of Penguin Random House LLC
penguinrandomhouse.com

LIBRARY OF CONGRESS CATALOGING-IN-PUBLICATION DATA

Names: Brooks, Geraldine, author.
Title: Horse / Geraldine Brooks.
Description: New York : Viking, [2022]
Identifiers: LCCN 2021039672 (print) | LCCN 2021039673 (ebook) |
ISBN 9780399562969 (hardcover) | ISBN 9780399562983 (ebook) |
ISBN 9780593493496 (international edition)
Subjects: LCGFT: Novels.
Classification: LCC PR9619.3.B7153 H67 2022 (print) |
LCC PR9619.3.B7153 (ebook) | DDC 823/.914—dc23
LC record available at https://lccn.loc.gov/2021039672
LC ebook record available at https://lccn.loc.gov/2021039673

Printed in the United States of America
12th Printing

Set in Janson MT Pro
Designed by Cassandra Garruzzo Mueller

This is a work of fiction inspired by actual events.

FOR TONY

*It will be the past
and we'll live there together*

PATRICK PHILIPS, *Heaven*

He was as far superior to all horses that have gone before him as the vertical blaze of a tropical sun is superior to the faint and scarcely distinguishable glimmer of the most distant star.

JOSEPH CAIRN SIMPSON, *Turf, Field and Farm*

After him there were merely other horses.

CHARLES E. TREVATHAN, *The American Thoroughbred*

HORSE

THEO

The deceptively reductive forms of the artist's work belie the density of meaning forged by a bifurcated existence. These glyphs and ideograms signal to us from the crossroads: freedom and slavery, White and Black, rural and urban.

No. Nup. That wouldn't do. It reeked of PhD. This was meant to be read by normal people.

Theo pressed the delete key and watched the letters march backward to oblivion. All that was left was the blinking cursor, tapping like an impatient finger. He sighed and looked away from its importuning. Through the window above his desk, he noticed that the elderly woman who lived in the shabby row house directly across the street was dragging a bench press to the curb. As the metal legs screeched across the pavement, Clancy raised a startled head and jumped up, putting his front paws on the desk beside Theo's laptop. His immense ears, like radar dishes, twitched toward the noise. Together, Theo and the dog watched as she shoved the bench into the teetering ziggurat she'd assembled. Propped against it, a hand-lettered sign: FREE STUFF.

Theo wondered why she hadn't had a yard sale. Someone would've paid for that bench press. Or even the faux-Moroccan footstool. When she brought out an armful of men's clothing, it occurred to Theo that all the items in the pile must be her dead husband's things. Perhaps she just wanted to purge the house of every trace of him.

Theo could only speculate, since he didn't really know her. She was the kind of thin-lipped, monosyllabic neighbor who didn't invite pleasantries, much less intimacies. And her husband had made clear, through his body language, what he thought about having a Black man living nearby. When Theo moved into Georgetown University's graduate housing complex a few months earlier, he'd made a point of greeting the neighbors. Most responded with a friendly smile. But the guy across the street hadn't even made eye contact. The only time Theo had heard his voice was when it was raised, yelling at his wife.

It was a week since the ambulance had come in the night. Like most city dwellers, Theo could sleep right through a siren that Dopplered away, but this one had hiccuped to sudden silence. Theo jolted awake to spinning lights bathing his walls in a wash of blue and red. He jumped out of bed, ready to help if he could. But in the end, he and Clancy just stood and watched as the EMTs brought out the body bag, turned the lights off, and drove silently away.

At his grandmother's house in Lagos, any death in the neighborhood caused a flurry in the kitchen. As a kid visiting on school holidays, he'd often been tasked with delivering the steaming platters of food to the bereaved. So he made a stew the next day, wrote a condolence card, and carried it across the street. When no one answered the door, he left it on the stoop. An hour later, he found it back on his own doorstep with a terse note: *Thanks but I don't like chicken.* Theo looked down at Clancy and shrugged. "I thought everyone liked chicken." They ate it themselves. It was delicious, infused with the complex flavors of grilled peppers and his homemade, slow-simmered stock. Not that Clancy, the kelpie, cared about that. In the no-nonsense insouciance of his hardy breed, he'd eat anything.

The thought of that casserole made Theo's mouth water. He glanced at the clock in the corner of his laptop. Four p.m. Too early to quit. As he started typing, Clancy circled under the desk and flopped back down across his instep.

These ~~arresting~~ compelling images are the only known surviving works created by an artist born ~~into slavery~~ enslaved. Vernacular, yet eloquent, they become semaphores from a world convulsed. ~~Living~~ Surviving through the Civil War, ~~forsaking~~ escaping the tyranny of the plantation for a marginalized life in the city, the artist seems compelled to bear witness to his own reality, paradoxically exigent yet rich.

Awful. It still read like a college paper, not a magazine article.

He flipped through the images on his desk. The artist confidently depicted what he knew—the crowded, vibrant world of nineteenth-century Black domestic life. He had to keep the text as simple and direct as the images.

Bill Traylor, born enslaved, has left us the only

A movement across the street drew his eye up from the screen. The neighbor was trying to move an overstuffed recliner. It was teetering on its side on the top step as she struggled to keep a grip on it.

She could use help. He did a quick personal inventory: Shorts on, check. T-shirt, check. Working in his un-air-conditioned apartment, Theo would sometimes spend the whole day in his underwear, forgetting all about his *déshabillement* until confronted by the quizzical gaze of the FedEx guy.

He reached the other side of the street just as gravity won, prising the chair from her grip. He jumped up the step and body-blocked it. Her only acknowledgment was a grunt and a quick lift of her chin. She bent down and grabbed the underside of the chair. Theo hefted an armrest. Together, crab-wise, they shuffled to the curb.

The woman straightened, pushing back her thin, straw-colored hair, and rubbing her fists into the small of her back. She waved an arm at the ziggurat. "Anything you want . . ." Then she turned and ascended the steps.

Theo couldn't imagine wanting anything in this sadness-infused pile of discards. His apartment was sparsely furnished: a midcentury-modern desk and a Nelson sofa acquired at a thrift store. The rest of the available space was filled mostly with art books, shelved on scavenged planks and milk crates he'd spray-painted matte black.

But Theo, the son of two diplomats, had been raised by the commandment that bad manners were a mortal sin. He had to at least pretend to look. There were some old paperbacks stuffed into a beer carton. He was always curious about what people read. He reached down to check the titles.

And that was when he saw the horse.

JESS

Jess was seven when she dug up the dog. He'd been dead a year. She and her mum had buried him with ceremony, under the flowering red gum in the backyard, and they'd both cried.

Her mother wanted to cry again when Jess requested large Tupperware containers for the bones she'd just exhumed. Generally, Jess's mother was the kind of parent who would let her daughter set the house on fire if she thought it could teach something about carbon and oxygen. But she was stricken with a stab of anxiety: was digging up a beloved pet and macerating its corpse a sign that your child had psychopathic tendencies?

Jess tried her best to explain that she'd dug up Milo *because* she loved him, and that's why she had to see what his skeleton looked like. Beautiful, as she knew it would be: the swoop of the rib cage, the scoop of the eye sockets.

Jess loved the interior architecture of living things. Ribs, the protective embrace of them, how they hold delicate organs in a lifelong hug. Eye sockets: no artisan had ever made a more elegant container for a precious thing. Milo's eyes had been the color of smoky quartz. When Jess touched a finger to the declivities on either side of his delicate skull, she could see those eyes again: the kind gaze of her earliest friend, avid for the next game.

She grew up on one of the dense streets of liver-brick bungalows that marched westward with Sydney's first growth spurt in the 1900s. Had she lived in a rural place, she might have exercised her fascination on road-killed kangaroos, wombats, or wallabies. But in inner Sydney, she was lucky to find a dead mouse, or perhaps a bird that flew into a plate-glass window. Her best specimen was a fruit bat that had been electrocuted. She found it on the nature strip under the power lines. She spent a week articulating it: the papery membrane of the wing, unfolding like the pleated bellows of an accordion. The metatarsal bones, like human fingers, but lighter—evolved not to hold and grasp, but to fan the air. When she was done, she suspended it from the light fixture in her bedroom ceiling. There, stripped clean of all that could readily decay, she watched it fly forever through endless nights.

Over time, her bedroom became a mini natural history museum, filled with skeletons of lizards, mice, birds, displayed on plinths fashioned from salvaged wire spools or cotton reels, and identified with carefully inked Latin tags. This did not endear her to the tribe of teenage girls who inhabited her high school. Most of her classmates found her obsession with necrotic matter gross and creepy. She became a solitary teen, which perhaps accounted for her high place in the state in three subjects when the final public exam results were published. She continued to distinguish herself as an undergrad and came to Washington on a scholarship to do her master's in zoology.

It was the kind of thing Australians liked to do: a year or two abroad to take a look at the rest of the world. In her first semester, the Smithsonian hired her as an intern. When they learned she knew how to scrape bones, she was sent to do osteo prep at the Museum of Natural History. It turned out that she had become extremely skilled from working on small species. A blue whale skeleton might impress the public, but Jess and her colleagues knew that a blue wren was far more challenging to articulate.

She loved the term "articulate" because it was so apt: a really good mount allowed a species to tell its own story, to say what it was like when it breathed and ran, dived or soared. Sometimes, she wished she'd lived in the Victorian era, when craftsmen competed to be the best at capturing movement—a horse rearing required an absolute balance in the armature, a donkey turned to scratch its flank demanded a sculptor's sense of curvature. Making these mounts had become a craze among wealthy men of the time, who strove to produce specimens dedicated to beauty and artistry.

Contemporary museums had scant place for that. Mounting bones destroyed information—adding metal, removing tissue—so very few skeletons were articulated. Most bones were prepped, numbered, and then stored away in drawers for comparative measurement or DNA sampling.

When Jess did that work, her nostalgia for the craftsmanship of the past faded, overtaken by her fascination with the science. Every fragment told a story. It was her job to help scientists extract the testimony from each fossilized chip. The specimens might have come to the museum as the product of dumb luck or the result of days of exacting scientific endeavor. A hobbyist might have stumbled upon a mammoth's tibia uncovered by the lashings of a winter storm. Or a paleontologist might have collected a tiny vole's tooth after weeks of painstaking soil sifting. Jess made her labels on a laser printer and included GPS coordinates for where the specimen had been found. Past curators left a more personal mark, their handwritten cards in sepia-toned ink.

Those nineteenth-century preparators had plied their craft ignorant of DNA and all the vital data it would one day yield. It thrilled Jess to think that when she closed the drawer on a newly filed specimen, it might be opened in fifty or a hundred years by a scientist seeking answers to questions she didn't yet know how to ask, using tools of analysis she couldn't even yet imagine.

She hadn't meant to stay in America. But careers can be as accidental as car wrecks. Just as she graduated, the Smithsonian offered her a four-month contract to go to French Guiana to collect rainforest specimens. Not many girls from Burwood Road in western Sydney got to go to French Guiana and bounce through the rainforest with scorpion specimens pegged across the jeep like so much drying laundry. Another offer followed: Kenya, to compare contemporary species on Mount Kilimanjaro with those gathered by Teddy Roosevelt's expedition a hundred years earlier.

At the end of that trip, Jess was packing her few possessions, ready to go home to get on with what she still considered her real life, when the Smithsonian offered her a permanent position, managing their vertebrate Osteology Prep Lab at the Museum Support Center in Maryland. It was a brand-new facility and the job vacancy was unexpected. The manager who had designed the lab had been struck down by a sudden allergy to frass, the soft, dusty excrement of dermestid beetles. Those beetles were the preferred and best means of bone cleaning, so being unable to work with them without breaking into hives signaled the need for a change of occupation.

The Smithsonian's nickname was "the Attic of America." Support was the attic's attic: a sprawling twelve miles of storage that housed priceless scientific and artistic collections. Jess had thought she wouldn't want to work out in the suburbs, far from the public face of the museum. But when she walked down the vast connecting corridor known as "the street," linking the zigzag of metal-sheathed, climate-controlled buildings in which all kinds of science took place, she knew she'd arrived at the epicenter of her profession.

After her interview she and the director walked across a verdant campus flanked by the botany department's greenhouses. He pointed out a newly built storage pod, looming windowless above the greenhouses. "We just opened that one, to house the wet collection," he said. "After 9/11, we realized it wasn't prudent to have twenty-five million biological specimens in combustible fluids crammed in a basement a couple of blocks from the Capitol. So now they're here."

The Osteo Prep Lab was farther on, in a building of its own, tucked off at the edge of the campus nearest the highway. "If you get, say, an elephant carcass from the National Zoo, it's pungent," the director explained, "so we sited your lab as far from everyone else as possible."

Your lab. Jess hadn't thought of herself as ambitious, but she realized she badly wanted this responsibility. Inside, the lab gleamed: a necropsy suite with a hydraulic table, a two-ton hoist, double bay doors large enough to admit a whale carcass, and a wall of saws and knives worthy of a horror movie. It was the largest facility of its kind in the world, and a far cry from her makeshift lab in the laundry room on Burwood Road.

She loved working there. Every day brought something new in a flow of specimens that never stopped. The latest arrival: a collection of passerines from Kandahar. The birds had been roughed out in the field, most of the feathers and flesh removed. Jess's assistant, Maisy, was bent over the box of little bundles, carefully tied so none of the tiny bones would be lost.

"I'm heading off tonight to pick up that whale skull," Jess said. "You have everything you need while I'm in Woods Hole?"

"Absolutely. After these passerines, I've got the deer mandibles for DNA sampling. They're in a rush for those, so that'll keep me busy."

When Jess left the lab for the day, she was aware that she might not smell so good. She'd given up taking the shuttle bus back to DC with the other employees. She'd noticed that the seat next to her tended to remain vacant, even on a crowded bus. She'd splurged on a good bike—a Trek CrossRip with dropped handlebars—and was grateful for the bike path that ran from the Support Center all the way back into the city. She twisted her long ponytail into a bun and crammed it under her helmet.

The path was dilapidated; she swerved to dodge trash and broken pavement, ducking the profusion of new spring foliage. In Sydney, the shift in seasons had always been a subtle thing: a warming or cooling of the air, a small change in the length of day and quality of light. In Washington, the seasons slammed her—summer's soup-pot heat; autumn's extravagant arboreal fireworks; winter's iciness; spring's intoxicating explosion of bloom, birdsong, and fragrance. Even the neglected bike path erupted with lushness, and with the sun low in the west, the Anacostia River shone like polished silver.

Jess swept to the right off South Capitol, into a quiet, long-established neighborhood of tall row houses set back from the street by deep front gardens. At this time of year, tulips and azaleas painted the flower beds in a palette of magentas, corals, and purples. Jess had been reluctant to look at something labeled a basement apartment, since her Australian heart craved light. But the row house had been renovated to provide an open-plan lower floor with two large windows facing the street and a generous clerestory in back, through which sun streamed all day. All summer, the interior light had a watery green tinge from the honeysuckle and trumpet vines that spilled in a mad profusion over the back wall.

She locked her bike (double locks) and unlocked the door (triple locks). She would shower, change, pack an overnight bag, then nap for a couple of hours to let Washington's gridlocked traffic clear. She planned to pick up a truck from the Smithsonian's garage at about ten p.m. and drive through the night to the Marine Biological Lab in Woods Hole.

She was headed to the shower when her phone rang. "Sorry to call you on your private number, but it's Horace Wallis from Affiliates here. Your assistant said you were heading out for a couple of days, so I thought I'd just try to touch base before you left on a problem that I hoped you might help me with." Jess vaguely recognized the speaker's voice but couldn't put a face to him.

"Sure," she said. "What do you need?"

"It's a bit mortifying, to be honest. A researcher from the Royal Veterinary College in England is on her way here to look at a nineteenth-century skeleton of ours that she's keen to study. Problem is, we can't find it. It was at the Castle in 1878, then it went over to the American History Museum— why they wanted it isn't exactly clear. Anyway, they say they certainly don't have it now. Do you think there's any chance it might've come to you at Osteo Prep? I've scoured the database. Nothing. Your place is about the last thing I could think of."

"Articulated skeleton, I'm assuming?"

"Yes."

"We don't have any articulated skeletons with us in the lab at the moment, but Support has ninety-eight percent of the specimens in storage, so that's likely where you'll find it. You've got the accession number, right?"

"Yes, of course. It's . . ."

"Just a sec. I've got to find something to write on . . ." Jess rummaged through the papers on her desk. The margins of every document were crammed with her doodles of zygomatic arcs or cervical vertebrae. She finally found a crumpled boarding pass that she hadn't scribbled all over.

"I'll double-check my own database. If it's out at Support I'm sure I can track it down. What species?"

"*Equus caballus*. A horse."

WARFIELD'S JARRET

The Meadows, Lexington, Kentucky

1850

She was no one's notion of an easy mare. Not mean, but nervous. Which could come to the same thing if you didn't account for it.

Jarret knew how to approach her. Steady and deliberate. You shouldn't hesitate or show uncertainty, but if you were too high-handed she'd make you pay. She could snake around and have a piece of your arm or kick out and crack a shin. Dr. Elisha Warfield had bred her himself, and named her for his daughter-in-law, Alice Carneal. There were jokes around the barn about what he meant by that, and what he might've been trying to say to his son.

But Alice Carneal never hurt Jarret. No horse ever had. "Look at him," Dr. Warfield would say, lifting one of Jarret's long, skinny arms. "He's half colt himself." Jarret took it as a compliment, for what would be the use in taking it otherwise? And it was true he had a feel for horses, deep in the grain. The first bed he could remember was in a horse stall. He shared straw with the two geldings in the carriage house while his mother slept in the mansion, nursemaid to the mistress's infant. Jarret barely saw her. His first language had been the subtle gestures and sounds of horses. He'd been slow to master human speech, but he could interpret the horses: their moods, their alliances, their simple wants, their many fears. He came to believe that horses lived with a world of fear, and when you grasped that, you had a clear idea how to be with them.

Those two geldings in that carriage house had been more parent to him than his mother in the mansion could have been, or his father, Harry, who had lived across town, training racehorses for Robert Burbridge. Harry had visited Jarret and his mother one Sunday of every month. Jarret had loved those Sundays. He knew his father was special, because he arrived on a fine thoroughbred and he dressed just exactly like the marse, in a fitted frock coat and a silk cravat, and every hand in the carriage house deferred to him. He seemed old to Jarret, even then. His close-cropped hair was salt and pepper, but when he smiled at his boy all the lines and creases in his face seemed to vanish. Jarret tried to win that smile. When his father shortened the stirrups and set Jarret up on his stallion, Jarret learned quickly how to find his balance and show no hint of fear. And in truth, after that first sudden sense of being high up there, he wasn't afraid. Even though the horse was large and powerful, he was kind, and Jarret could feel the way he moved considerately, adjusting to this new, slight weight on his broad back, keeping him steady. It was something to remember: a good horse will work with you, won't mean you ill.

He had been three years old then. Two years later, his mother had sickened and died. Fear was something he'd known about that year, vulnerable as a foal without a dam to protect him. His father, Harry Lewis, had spent all his savings to pay the price of his own liberty and didn't have the money to secure his son's freedom. So he'd implored Dr. Warfield to buy his boy so that he could have him close and raise him. At first, the doctor had protested that the last thing he needed was another child about the place. But when Harry's skill led the Warfield horses to an exceptional season at the track, the doctor relented and bought Jarret from the Todds.

Now, at thirteen, Jarret slept in his father's cottage, but his waking hours were still spent entirely with horses. In the Warfield barns, he knew every horse's nature, habits, history. Every vice, every virtue. Most of the horses nickered when they saw him, snuffling warm air through velvet nostrils. They'd reach out their gleaming necks, asking for his touch.

He knew better than to expect that from Alice Corneal. Most times, she'd barely look up from her hay. But this night as he entered the barn to do the late check, she moved to the front of her stall along with the others, ears forward instead of laid flat back, gazing right at him with grave, unblinking eyes.

As soon as he went up to her, she rested her head on his shoulder. Jarret stood still for a long moment, accepting the rare gesture. Then slowly— always slowly—he rolled back her stall door and went in. "Move like the air is molasses," his father had instructed, and so he did, raising a languid hand and smoothing down her withers, fingering the fine coat that still carried some winter thickness. She leaned into him, accepting the caress, so he let his hand continue to the swell of her barrel, and when she nuzzled her damp lip into his neck, he eased down into a crouch to examine her.

As he expected, she was waxing: the fine, white, tear-shaped cobweb already formed over the teat, preventing it from leaking milk. He stood again and slowly swept his two hands back toward her croup. There, between the hip and the hock, was the mares' sweet spot. In the barn, friendly mares loved it when he curried that spot, dropping their heads and softening their gaze as if they were daydreaming. It wasn't a liberty he usually took with Alice Carneal, who might spin and stamp at the unwanted intimacy. But now she let him run his fingers deep into her tail muscles as he felt for pliability. She leaned against him even more heavily.

This amiable mare was nothing like the dervish he'd struggled to lead into the neighbor's breeding shed, rearing and bucking, just a year earlier. It was the first season Jarret had been allowed to help his father there—he'd not been strong enough before his thirteenth year. She'd fought right until the minute they finally got the twitch on her. And then, in the few minutes they waited for the stallion, you could smell the reek of fear-sweat on the men. Even the most experienced—even Jarret's father Harry—wore the sheen of it on their skin.

Violent. That's what they said about Boston, all that stallion's life; everyone from the boy who shoveled his shit to the gentleman-owner who pocketed his winnings. No one would mount him—only the enslaved boys, who had no say in it. After he bucked off one boy, and then stomped him, leaving him broken as kindling, the trainer told the owner he should get him gelded or have him shot, and that he, personally, would be happy to do the shooting. But they did neither, because when Boston chose to run, he was as fast as he was fierce. In seven years, he won forty of his forty-five starts, many over a crushing four-mile distance, and most of them without decent rest between. Plenty of men like Dr. Warfield were willing to pay the considerable fee to have him stand stud, even now that the stallion was stone blind and showing the signs of his hard usage. But his poor condition hadn't quelled his temper. If anything, it made him even more touchy and dangerous.

It was just a few minutes, there in the shed. A blur of men and ropes and a ton of lunging chestnut stallion. A thrust, a shudder. And after, as the old horse was led away, Harry mopped his brow with his sleeve and laid his hand on Jarret, who was still trembling. "What we just did in this shed is where you win or lose."

It was Harry who had proposed this particular mating. Of all the mares at the Meadows, he especially admired Alice Carneal, even though she'd won just a single race in her short career. At home at the Meadows, she was fast, but between her familiar stable and the track, she would fall completely out of condition. By race time she'd be sweating, purging, and all atremble, high strung with the crowds and the noise, almost unmanageable. Harry looked past that. He liked her combination of depth through the girth and length of hind leg that gave a horse room for powerful lungs and maximum thrust at the gallop. "Her problems are in her head end, not her hind end," he said.

He had to argue hard to justify the high stud fee in what had been a lean year. He convinced Dr. Warfield that time was short: that Boston had a bad look about him and might not make another breeding season. "Same could be true for you and me both, never mind the stallion," said the doctor with a wry grin. In his seventies and suffering from several ailments, Dr. Warfield was slowing down, breeding fewer foals each year. But Harry persisted.

They found Boston dead in his stall that winter. He'd gone down still raging at the world: the sides of his stall were painted in blood from the violence of his death throes. Alice's foal would be one of the champion's last offspring.

And now that foal was on its way. Jarret took a pitchfork and thoroughly cleaned out the stall, throwing down a deep bed of new straw. Throughout, Alice watched him calmly. He gave her a last reassuring pat. He quickly looked over the other stalls—no one cast, plenty of water in the buckets— and then he stepped out of the barn and into the spring night.

The sky was clear, the stars brittle as glass shards. No moon. If Alice were foaling in the wild, this inky sky would hide her in the quietest hours either side of midnight. Mares had the capability to slow birthing so that the foal would have the dark hours to find its feet and be ready to run from a predator by dawn. Dew lay fat and round on the new spring grass. Jarret felt the wet seeping through the hem of his overalls as he crossed the unmown field. He breathed the freshness of early violets amid the musty scent of last year's rotting leaves. When he broke into a slow jog, the light from his lantern bounced across the grass like a yellow ball.

All his best memories were here, at the Meadows. Dr. Warfield had bought this land north of the town after he'd been forced by ill health to retire from obstetrics, with its unpredictable hours. He did not regret his retirement. He raised a sixteen-room brick mansion and devoted himself to his many businesses and his first love, horses. He'd been a founder of the town's Jockey Club and overseen the building of its first proper racetrack. Before that, folk had just used Lexington's Main Street straightaway for quarter-horse racing, and sometimes you could still watch those dash races from the balcony of Dr. Warfield's town apartment, atop his busy dry goods store on Main Street.

Jarret had been glad to leave the town. He misliked the rattling metal wheels of the carriages, the hard-fronted, four-square brick buildings crowded up together, and all those people whose names he didn't know. When an errand took him there, he couldn't wait to be done and get back to the Meadows. There was a lot of call for messages and goods to go back

and forth between the Meadows and the town. Because Jarret was the least
inclined to dawdle there, he was the one most often sent, instead of the boys
who loved to go to town to gawk and dally. Life did seem to him to work like
that: contrariwise.

Jarret could see the lights flickering through the trees. They were still
dining in the big house. All those candles, and Mrs. Warfield insisting on
fresh ones every day. The part-burned stubs came down to the quarters,
and that was a boon to those who could find the wherewithal to do labor on
their own account at the end of the day's assigned tasks. Most of those were
his father's men, the stable hands and grooms. Harry was a good manager,
setting a man to the tasks he was best apt to, working him to his capacity but
not past it. He knew how folk yearned to buy themselves out, just as he had
done, so he encouraged those who wanted to hire out their skills as harness
menders or saddlemakers. Dr. Warfield never stood against it, so long as his
own place was well kept.

It was quiet in the lane, most folk already gone to their rest. But he could
hear the thump of the loom from the dark cabin of Blind Jane as her skilled
hands passed the shuttle and pounded the woof. Daylight didn't mean anything to her; she would weave until weariness claimed her.

Jarret's father liked working for Dr. Warfield, because he'd been a free
man the whole time of it, and Dr. Warfield always gave him his due on that
account and was quick to credit Harry for more than doubling their track
winnings. As the doctor grew frailer, he relied on Harry for the management
of horses, and had increased his pay to five hundred dollars a year, which was
higher than many a White trainer earned.

Harry's former position, trainer for Mr. Burbridge, had been much more
precarious. In ten years' service, Burbridge never let him forget he was "Burbridge's Harry." In the old man's last days, he'd mistaken himself for a Pha-
raoh and pulled a Bowie knife, proclaiming that Harry must accompany him
to the afterlife, to train his horses in the next world.

Jarret didn't remember any of that old business—he'd been in the Todd house then. But he'd seen his father turn ashen, recalling it. All manner of misfortune can come of a Black man and a White man in the same room with a knife, even if no drop of blood is spilled.

Their cabin was set apart, with its own dooryard, a little beyond the lane. His father must have seen Jarret's lantern, because the door opened even before he reached the gate. A column of warm yellow light rushed out toward him, followed by a rich, brown smell of fried onions and back fat.

Jarret kicked his boots on the door stoop, shaking off the damp clods of earth that had adhered to them. "Alice's foal's coming," he said. "She's waxing and she's uncommon friendly."

Harry nodded. "It takes her that way. Always has done. Well, go on ahead, wash up and eat something. She's not a one to have trouble in foaling, but you never do know, and she's an old mare now, gone fourteen years. Could be a long night."

Jarret poured the ewer of water over his hands and wrists, washing off the mellow scent of horse and replacing it with the crisp bite of lye. Then he went to the hearth. There was a pot of creamy beans on the crane and a fresh skillet of corn pone on the spider. Jarret ladled out a brimming bowl and ate ravenously, mopping the dish clean with a heel of pone.

Harry lit two of the larger lanterns and handed one to his son. As they walked back to the barn, Harry placed his free arm affectionately across his son's shoulder. He had to reach up to do it, and he took a powerful satisfaction from that. Jarret hadn't come into his full height, but he was set to grow into a good-size man.

Harry hadn't had that chance. He was only five, small for his age and slight boned, when they threw him up on his first thoroughbred. Every time he fell off he earned a beating, so he soon learned to stay on. If he gained weight, they cut his meager rations to a single turnip for dinner and a pint of milk for lunch. If those starvation portions didn't keep enough weight off, they set him to walk a ten-mile circuit at the end of his chores, and if that didn't work, they sweated him. Buried up to his chin in piles of steaming manure on the hottest days of summer, he felt his scant flesh melting. He spent his youth with an ache in his gut and a lightness in his head. When you've been famished like that, you don't forget the hurt of it, even if the hunger fattened the pile of money that later bought your freedom. Winning jockeys got cash gifts and Harry saved every one. He watched the trainers closely and learned what to do from the best and what not to do from the worst. Eventually, that knowledge made him more valuable on the ground than on the horse.

He'd resolved that his own son would never know a hungry day, no matter how well he rode. And he kept to that, even when Jarret turned out to sit a horse like boy and beast were the same creature. Jarret rode with a natural grace, even over the grueling four-mile races that tested man and horse alike, demanding speed, stamina, and strategy. There were years when every voice was nagging Harry to make his boy a jockey. But Harry set his face against it, and Dr. Warfield didn't insist. Even as a stripling, the lad had a powerful length of bone in his limbs and the doctor could foresee a spurt of growth that would likely put him out of the racing saddle just as he was getting a name in the trade. One day, as soon as he saved the money, Harry intended to buy the boy so he wouldn't have to be beholden to any other man's opinion of what his fate should be. Meantime, Jarret was well grown enough to silence all the chatter. He still rode every day, schooling the horses, and soon enough he'd be a trainer in his own right.

When they reached the barn, they found Alice Carneal strutting restless circles in her stall, her coat glistening with sweat. Harry and Jarret took their places, out of her line of sight. Harry spoke to her in a low, musical voice, almost a hum, telling her how good she was and how great her foal would be. The sound was soothing, and as the evening lengthened Jarret felt himself drifting in and out of a doze.

He came awake to the splash of the mare's water breaking. She gave a low groan and folded herself gently into the bedding hay. Harry knelt beside her as the birth sac bulged. The tiny crescents of the hooves were clearly visible through the pearly membrane, folded daintily one atop the other, soles down in the correct position for an uncomplicated birth. Sure enough, when the forelegs were out almost to the knees, a slick wet muzzle followed—the foal in perfect position, arranged like an arrowhead. "Here's the hard part," murmured Harry. The shoulders, the widest part of the foal. He hummed on, encouraging Alice. He could see the little white hooves straining at the membrane of the birth sac. Minutes later, the sac split and the foal sluiced forward. A tiny horse slipped out onto the hay like a gift from a package.

It was a bright bay colt like its dam, with a white star and snip on its face and four white feet. Harry passed a cloth from the bundle across the stall to Jarret and the two of them gently toweled the slick little body. Alice nudged them aside, licking her foal all over. After a time, Alice rose gracefully to her knees, breaking the umbilical cord. Before she could stand, the colt was up, new legs splayed and trembling.

"Never seen that before," said Harry. "The colt up on all four feet before his dam." Within minutes, Alice lay down again, nudging at her sides until the afterbirth came. Harry and Jarret sat in companionable silence, watching Alice lick and nuzzle her baby. Finally, the colt found the teat, his small wet tail swishing as he tasted the rich foremilk. After about an hour, and without straining, he excreted the sticky, rust-colored muck that signaled all was well with his innards.

Harry sat back on his heels and gave a satisfied sigh. "Our work's done now, little as it was. He's a bit weedy, but we'll see how he does."

"What about the white feet? Bad luck, ain't they?"

Harry smiled as he gathered up the rags. "Some folk hold with that foolishness. Racing folks do have a mighty faith in luck. You can use that, if you're smart about it. Push odds up, push 'em down, all with some loose talk in the backstretch. My way of thinking, a good horse has no color. It's what's inside that's worth the fret."

Harry yawned and turned to the door.

"I think I'll stay," Jarret said. "I'd like to keep a watch over him."

"Makes no mind to me, son," said Harry. "But you know to let them be now. This is the time for them to get acquainted. And get some sleep, what's left of the night. The horses'll be sleeping. Come morning they'll be fresh when you come to work 'em, so you'd best be too."

Jarret watched the foal nuzzling his mother. The barn timbers creaked. A hoof struck hard against a stall. The gentle blowing of soft lips and moist nostrils. He felt warm and light, both tired and not tired. The barn smelled of fresh hay, but also the mineral scent of recent birth. He wound down the wick on the lantern and made himself a fragrant mattress of timothy and clover, pulling the old blanket over him. He was almost asleep when he heard a scraping sound in the hayloft over his head. Barn cat mousing, he thought and rolled over. But then he heard a cough.

He jumped up, reaching for the lantern, forgetting he'd just extinguished it.

"Who's there?" he said, peering up the ladder into the dark loft.

"Just me, Jarret. Mary Barr. Please don't be angry."

"It's not me being angry you should be concerned about. Miss Clay, what you doing here? You got no business, middle of the night. There'll be hell to pay, your grandmomma learns of it."

Mary Barr Clay, eleven years old, barefoot, and in her nightdress, climbed backward down the ladder. "I thought Alice might foal tonight. She was being so nice earlier. Not like herself at all. So when everyone was at dinner, I crept on down here to see. Then, when I heard you and your daddy coming, I hid up here, and your daddy's singing to the horse put me right to sleep." Picking hay stalks out of the lacework on her nightdress, she made her way over to the stall, crossing her pale arms on the sill and gazing at the foal, squinting to make him out in the darkness. "He's sure a beauty, isn't he?"

Mary Barr thought every foal was a beauty, and Jarret wasn't about to argue with her, because he felt just exactly the same. Whatever his father said about angles of stifles, cow hocks or spavins, all horses were handsome and good. You just had to find the right use for them.

"You should know better than to come barefoot to the barn, Miss Clay," said Jarret, trying to emulate an adult's tone of censure.

"I know," she said, turning to him with a rueful look. "But I didn't want anyone to hear me. I already pulled a big old splinter out." She lifted a dirty foot and showed him the place. "You won't tell on me, will you?"

"I surely should," he said. "But I won't, so long as you go right on back up to the house this minute."

"Thank you, Jarret. And if I do get caught, I won't say you saw me."

He watched her, a slight white shape in the dark, running up the rise to the house. Instead of taking the shallow stone steps to the grand front entrance, she slipped around the side porch. As he saw the white blur disappear into the kitchen ell, he knew she'd be fine. The scullery maid, Annie, slept in an alcove off the storeroom there, where a back stairs would let the girl get on up to her room unnoticed. Jarret knew that Annie had a kind eye for the Clay girl, Dr. Warfield's granddaughter. Her father, Cassius Clay, was said to be a fearsome fellow, who would fight the wind if it came from the west when he wanted it from the east. Perhaps that was why the girl and her mother were so often at the Meadows and not at either one of their own fine homes—the big Clay estate, White Hall, or the elegant townhouse in Lexington. Mr. Clay had a newspaper that opposed slavery, and he had freed all the slaves he'd inherited. This was a strange and a rare thing in Kentucky and may have been another reason Annie had such a soft spot for the Clay girl. Jarret didn't know too much about all that, since Harry discouraged any talk of emancipationists and their doings. But Jarret couldn't help but puzzle on how a man like Cash Clay lived at odds with a world and a family that thrived on the very thing he deplored. Jarret turned back to his own nest amid the hay and drifted through the small hours in the same half-sleep, half-woke state as the horses.

When the hands arrived just before dawn to do the morning feeding, Jarret uncoiled himself and checked the stall. The foal stopped nursing and popped his head up, ears pricked and nostrils wide. Foal and mare turned as one to gaze back at him. The foal's coat had dried. Where the first light hit it, it gleamed like rubbed brass. Jarret stepped out into the pearly predawn mist. He cricked his neck from one side to the other and flexed his shoulders. Then he jogged on home for the big plate of grits and eggs he knew his father would be fixing.

THEO

Theo pressed the print key. He was pleased with the article, and he hoped his editor would be too. He'd finally managed to squirm his way out of the academic writing, like shrugging off a suit to pull on a sweatshirt. He knew the magazine needed to run the piece in advance of the Traylor show at the American Art Museum, so the deadline had been tight. But he wasn't going to email it. He'd bike over and deliver it to his editor by hand. His diplomat parents had instilled in him the value of face time: never write a memo if you can make a phone call, never make a phone call if you can meet in person. Theo was keen to get more assignments if he could. For one thing, it was refreshing to write for a general audience instead of an academic one. For another, the Smithsonian's magazine paid decent rates, and the money was a welcome supplement to his meagre TA stipend.

He stood and stretched as the pages emerged from the printer, layering into a satisfying stack. He glanced out the window. The pile of free stuff out on the curb was slowly dwindling. Passing browsers had disassembled the ziggurat, turning it into an untidy string of objects strewn along the sidewalk. Just then, a student in a GW T-shirt grabbed a gooseneck lamp.

Propped on Theo's desk was his own find: a dingy canvas in a splintered frame. Theo regarded the painting. It made sense that the one piece of art in the pile of discards was a picture of a horse. Every Saturday, the old man had sprawled on his front steps with the races blaring from the radio, beer cans and cigarette butts piling up beside him.

The painting was old, Theo believed. Possibly nineteenth century. The lower half was a murky blur, the image totally obscured by a layer of grime. But the upper half looked highly accomplished. He tilted his desk lamp so that the light fell on the image. The head of a bright bay colt gazed out of the canvas, the expression in the eyes unusual and haunting. Whoever the painter was, he clearly knew a thing or two about horses. Theo looked under the kitchen sink for a grocery bag and wrapped the picture. He'd take it with him tomorrow. The editor at *Smithsonian* magazine surely would know someone in conservation who might be willing to take a look. Maybe he could even turn it into an article—how you figure out if there's any value to a painting you've plucked from the trash.

Theo's knowledge of painting was comprehensive, but as he gazed at his find he realized that he had a big blank spot when it came to American equestrian art. The Brits—Stubbs, Landseer—he knew all about. Like many foreign-service brats, he'd been educated abroad. His parents—Yoruba mother, Abiona; Californian father, Barry—had met each other during their first posting as junior diplomats, she in Kenya, he in Sudan, when they were both taking a bit of R and R in a beachside bar in Mombasa. They managed a long-distance romance and then a long-distance marriage. Theo was four years old before they finally scored a posting together, in Canberra, and those years were the happiest he'd known. But his parents were ambitious and were soon applying for postings closer to the edgier issues of their nations' foreign policies.

When they moved to London, Theo had just turned seven. He missed everything about Canberra: the long, warm evenings, the huge backyard, the multicultural classrooms full of foreign-service kids from all over the world. Most of all, he missed Saturdays on horseback beside his dad. His father had gone to a horsey boarding school near Ojai and loved riding, so he'd bought Theo a tiny pair of Blundstone boots and got him in the saddle at the earliest opportunity. Every Saturday, they'd ride together at a sheep station a short drive from the compact city.

Hacking through a London park on a jaded pony was nothing like riding a good stock horse in the Australian bush. At first, his father talked about finding a better stable in the English countryside. But he never did. Most weekends it always seemed that there was some pressing work he had to do at the big embassy on Grosvenor Square.

Later, as he grew older, Theo realized that his father was rarely home because his parents' marriage had begun to fray. Their Mayfair mews house became a tiny prison of misery. Terse words, slammed doors. Thin lips and sudden tears. The night his parents sat him down and disclosed that they had accepted separate postings and planned to divorce, Theo felt more relief than regret. His biggest anxiety was that they'd ask him to choose between them. He needn't have worried: they'd each accepted an "unaccompanied tour"—his dad in Afghanistan and his mother in Somalia—and agreed to send him to boarding school. His father suggested his own school, back in California, but Abiona wouldn't hear of it.

"An *American* school? Where they sit in a circle and discuss their *feelings*, instead of learning coding and calculus?" His father tried forlornly to make a case for creativity and self-expression, but he'd realized early in the marriage that arguing with Abiona was futile; she'd been the champion of the Nigerian national debating team. So Theo stayed in England, boarding at the elite, all-boys school that Abiona selected.

The school treasured its traditions, which meant frigid dorms and chilly relationships. Lonely, ostracized, Theo gravitated to the stables. There, he found a tribe of pale-haired boys in Persil-whitened polo pants, possessing double-barreled names and homes that were old before Agincourt. The only time that Theo didn't feel out of place was when he was in the saddle. The style of riding he'd acquired in an Aussie paddock—the fast gallops and rollbacks—was entirely suited to polo. He was too good to be left off the team and soon he was its captain.

As a polo star from an elite school, he often frequented drawing rooms and manorial halls decked out with equestrian portraits. Even then, before he'd understood that the study of art would consume him, he'd been drawn to those paintings, drifting away from whatever postmatch event the team had been invited to. At first, staring at those works gave him something to do when he was left out of conversations. But it also developed his eye. Back at the school, in the library, he pored over art books to put the paintings he'd seen in context.

He had no idea who Stubbs's and Landseer's American equivalents might have been, but he was certain they existed. Horses were a universal subject: their images among the earliest art that human beings had created. It would be fun to find out where in that history this neglected little painting might belong. He put the wrapped parcel in his bike pannier and propped it by the door.

The next morning, a Friday, he was all the way to the Mall before he realized he hadn't put the pannier on his bike. But as it turned out, he didn't need to pitch a new idea. His editor, Lior, already had another assignment in mind for him: a profile of the Californian painter Mark Bradford. Theo was pleased: Bradford was one of his favorite contemporary artists.

That weekend, he decided his apartment could benefit from a spring clean. To get the pannier out of the way while he mopped the floor, he propped it on a shelf in the closet. By Sunday, most of the neighbor's belongings had been picked off the curb. Early Monday morning, the trash collectors hauled away the rest, including the sign saying FREE STUFF.

Without anything to remind him, Theo forgot all about the painting. The horse stayed in the closet, wrapped and neglected.

THOMAS J. SCOTT

The Meadows, Lexington, Kentucky

1850

I don't know when I've been so glad to put a town at my back. It was a
mighty relief to leave the stink and bustle of Cincinnati. Rivers of mud
and blood, a chorus of squeals. Vistas of dead pigs. I'm no stranger to
slaughterhouses. My studies of horse anatomy required my presence there.
But animal death on this industrial scale is another thing entirely. Our
coachman, who has the misfortune to live in that fetid city, calls the place
"Porkopolis." What a relief to barge across the Ohio and turn my face to the
greener shores of Kentucke.

I hardly think there is a coach ride as fine in all the country. What a pleasant thing, to find the turnpike macadamized, so one isn't tossed about like a
potato in a sack. And the weather so mild, I asked the coachman if I might sit
with him upon the box, the better to see this new place, where I hope to find
work enough to allow me to settle.

That we did not make much speed, on account of the many swine being
driven northward to their fate, could be counted a blessing, as it gave me
leisure to contemplate the immense natural park that spread itself before
me: corn farms, set where the land runs level and lush, misted with a verdant spring growth, and the small orchards bedecked in pale pink blossom.
Between the farms, fine stands of ancient oak and beech have survived the

ax, leafing out in the green gold of fresh foliage. Such homes and barns as we passed added little to the view: basic shelters, shoddily constructed, speaking poverty and want of thrift. These were the homes of first- or second-generation pioneers yet to prosper from their westward adventure. There were one or two of what I took to be slave shanties, even more ill built and sad. Man has yet to enhance the natural beauties of the place, but the undulant hills, many not yet subdued to the plow, bring a welcome drama to the scene.

As a plain, rather unattractive little village came in sight, the coachman blew his trumpet to alert the innkeeper to ready the fresh horses. I and my fellow passengers alit to take some sustenance at the unprepossessing inn, but when I saw the fare on offer I was untempted: greasy corn pone and some kind of meat boiled gray, to be washed down by coffee the color of dishwater. It was no great decision to abstain, and therefore hone my appetite for the better fare I was optimistic would await me at the table of my hosts. Just as well I so chose, for no sooner had my fellow travelers put fork to mouth than the call "Stage's ready!" went up, and all had to abandon the greater part of their repast, such as it was.

Toward the end of the second stage, the sun dipped and the hills and small holdings gave way to vast swells of grassland, tinged blue in the slanted light. As the day waned, my heart soared. It was apparent that we had come into the garden of the state, where accumulation of wealth has evidently been easy. No more slovenly little farms, but manorial estates of cost and taste perched upon knolls and, at last!—my object, my muse—the elegant blood horses agraze on rich pastures.

It has been clear to me for some long time that the turf and its pursuits are more kindly and liberally encouraged in the middle states and in the south than in the north, where a morbid dread of ruinous mischief tends to be too readily associated with the very name of horse racing. And so I have left my home with hopes of more consistent employment among these gentlemen and their splendid horses.

The temperature was dropping with the sinking sun, and a chill breeze had picked up. So when we were forced to a halt by yet another hog parade, I availed myself of the chance to reclaim my seat inside the coach. The three men aboard were obliging in making space for me. One, lifting the leather flap, said he recognized the brand upon the hogs. "Them's Cash Clay's livestock," he noted. That caught my interest, since Clay's wife was the daughter of my host for the coming night. "That driver there must be one of them slaves he done freed."

"Likely so," agreed his companion. "I heard tell he pays 'em all, lets 'em leave his service if they like. Well, at least he freed his own before he set to preaching at others to do it. Inherited quite a number, so I heard tell."

"Well, he would do, his daddy ownin' more slaves then anyone in just 'bout the entire state. I don't like an abolitionist, but I do admire a man who ain't afraid to say what he believe, and to fight for hisself when obliged to."

"A mighty fellow with a knife," concurred the man who'd recognized the Clay brand on the pigs. "I was at that speech he gave, when the fellow stood on up and shot Clay right in the chest. Another man would have gone down mewling. Instead, he came right on back at the shooter, pulled his knife, and nearly carved that man to death. Dealt him such a blow to the belly that his innards spilled right on out. It was a sight to witness. I'll never forget it." The man drew his kerchief from a pocket and wiped his brow. "I've got twenty slaves, and I went there to that speech of his to argue my rights in them, but I got to say the courage of the man impressed me. Even if you are his enemy . . ."

The man trailed off, seeming to ponder the paradox of his admiration for a person whose ideas were so uncongenial to him. I thought I might venture a question at this juncture, forewarned being forearmed. I asked if his wife's family, the Warfields, shared his radical views.

They answered with a chorus of denial. Dr. Warfield, they assured me, was a slaveholder just like themselves. "Must get hot at the dinner table, on occasion." The men chuckled, and I smiled along. I wondered if I should get the chance to observe this. I'm a free labor man myself, but I knew in coming south I'd have to keep my peace on that subject, since work, if I got any, would come from the slave-owning class, just like this doctor who had dangled the possibility of a commission before me. I thought to bleed some more information from these men while I could.

I asked if Dr. Warfield's fortune came mainly from his horses.

They replied that the horses were his pleasure, but the sources of his income were various. While he had retired from medical practice, he had a dry goods store in town, a hemp farm, banking ventures, and some few land speculations.

This was gratifying news. I had to restrain myself from pressing for further intelligence lest my interest strike the men as unseemly. In any case, the woodland pastures were beginning to give way to a thickening settlement, and before long, we passed into the town of Lexington, with its neat brick homes, tree-shaded streets, imposing university, and well-stocked shops. I got down with my trunk at the Warfield store and was immediately greeted by the carriage driver charged with carrying me the last mile or so of my journey upon the Winchester Pike, to the Meadows, where my hopes of future employment were bent, and where I wished to make a good impression.

I had seen fine homes before—many grander and certainly of more venerable lineage than the Meadows—but few that sat so happily and naturally upon its site, arranged to take advantage of the prospect of fields and gardens that embraced it. The carriage passed through handsome stone pillars and up a wide drive of crushed stone flanked by young magnolia trees, already graceful, that would be magnificent in another generation.

Alerted by the squealing of the carriage wheels, a duo of liveried boys sprang from the house to carry my rolls of linen, my easel, and my trunk up the shallow curve of flagstone steps that led between a pair of flattened columns to the door.

I was not at all certain as to whether I should be deemed a guest or some kind of upper servant, so was delighted when the doctor and his wife greeted me themselves. Mrs. Warfield took the lead in offering me much respectful salutation. Her husband, a small, retiring fellow, seemed content to let her play the host, showing me the general layout of their home and instructing yet another crisply attired dusky youth to fetch my things to "the blue guest room."

"We will be dining alone this night, and I do hope you will not think it very dull," said Mrs. Warfield apologetically. "I had thought to extend some invitations, but my husband felt it best to spare you excessive company after your journey. Or at least that is what he said." She slid her eyes at the doctor and gave a smile that hinted at a coquettish youth. "I fancy his true motive is to ply you for information about northern racing prospects, and that would be intelligence he does not wish to share with his wider acquaintance."

The doctor laughed at that, and therefore I did also. "She sees through me like a pane of glass," he said. "It's what comes of a long marriage—something you, in your bachelor state, would not have experienced."

"Perhaps that state is something we can remedy, during your stay with us," Mrs. Warfield said. "I would be glad to make introductions . . ."

I raised a hand to fend off such a suggestion. "You are too kind, but I am not sufficiently established in my profession to entertain thoughts of marriage at this time. You would do your lovely young friends no service, to promote an alliance with an itinerant painter and scribbler such as myself, who lives from canvas to canvas and on the meager pennies one may make on race reportage. Therefore, do not tempt me, I beg you!" I have found it is easier to plead frank poverty than to tell the simple truth: that matrimony, with its tight shackles to a certain hearth and the daily inanities of female conversation, does not interest me in the least degree.

"Very well then, Mr. Scott," said Mrs. Warfield. "I shall revise my object on this occasion. I will introduce you only to those who might offer commissions, rather than assignations."

Since that plan suited me very well, I went up to my fine room in good spirits to set down this account of my journey so far. I am resolved to make this diary a daily practice.

WARFIELD'S JARRET

The Meadows, Lexington, Kentucky

1850

Jarret rubbed the pungent neat's-foot oil into a stirrup leather. He ran the strip slowly through his thumb and forefinger, letting the viscous liquid penetrate the pores of the hide. Jarret took pride in even the smallest of the barn jobs, and it riled him if he saw the other hands not taking the same care. A cracked stirrup leather could cost a man his life if it snapped at a full gallop. He looked up when he heard the distinctive ring of the doctor's silver-ferruled walking stick tapping across the paving stones. There was a young man with him. Not a buyer, that was evident from the worn state of his boots and the frayed cuffs of his jacket. Good-looking though, despite that—his fair hair well barbered, his neckcloth nicely tied.

Still working the oil into the leather—Harry didn't like to see an idle hand—Jarret edged over to his father, who was waiting by the barn door for Dr. Warfield, his cap already in his hand.

"Do you know the stranger?"

"I haven't met him yet. But I know who he is. Dr. Warfield said he'd be bringing by an animal painter. He's minded to have a portrait of one of the horses."

Jarret had seen the Clay girl painting in the flower garden, making some pretty work of it, but that, he thought, was just a pastime for fancy-brought-up

young ladies. He'd also seen the pictures on the walls of the Warfield mansion, but somehow he had never conceived of painting as actual work that a
man might do for hire. "Strange trade for a grown man," he said. "And by the
looks of him not a good-paying one neither."

"Well now, I don't know about that. I got my likeness done by a Swiss-
born gentleman, back in Marse Willa Viley times. I was training his fine
horse, Richard Singleton, that time. Marse was minded to have a picture
made of that horse, so he hired the Swiss man, Troye was his name, I recall,
and when he come, he say, 'Cap'n Viley, you got this fine horse and you also
got this young jockey to ride him, and this here fine-looking trainer'—I was
a younger man then, for sure. So he have us stand about, all manner of foolishness, dressed up in our best, and he made that painting of that horse, and
me in my top hat and frock coat looking mighty fine, and the jockey and the
groom as well, and all manner of trees in back of us. I believe the man was
tired out of just painting horses, and he want to set hisself more of a job to do.
Any case, it was a good likeness, all said and done, though it took a deal of
standing still for that man while he got all of us just so and so, the way he
wanted. Marse Viley put it right in the grand parlor where everyone who
came to call could see it. Still there to this day, for all I know."

Harry tilted his head toward the two men approaching. "This youngster
coming up with Dr. Warfield, he learned the trade from that same painter,
so the doctor says. And he says this one writes as well, for the racing press
up north." Harry looked at his son with a grin. "Maybe he'll put the doctor's
name in the papers."

Dr. Warfield gave Harry a good morning. "Mr. Thomas Scott, this is my
trainer, Harry Lewis." Most of the Warfield family referred to Jarret's father
as Old Harry, even to his face, and Jarret misliked it. He appreciated that Dr.
Warfield gave Harry his proper name.

"Let's see our new foal, shall we? Should you like that, Mr. Scott?"

"I should indeed. Nothing like a new horse to brighten a day."

Harry signaled to Jarret then, and he came forward to roll back the barn door. The colt and his mother looked up in unison, Alice's ears pinned flat, her good humor toward humans swept away with the morning's muck-out.

Dr. Warfield grimaced. "Four white feet and a white nose—throw him to the crows." Then the doctor laughed. "Lot of old wives' nonsense, judging a horse by the color of his socks."

Scott stood silent, his eyes running over the foal. Dr. Warfield tapped his ferrule on the barn boards, impatient to hear his opinion. "Would you mind," asked Scott, "if I went in there with them? I'd like to examine his legs."

Harry frowned, but Warfield nodded. "Go ahead." He turned to Harry. "Mr. Scott here was training to be a doctor himself, before the paintbrush called."

Scott laughed. "Wasn't so much the paintbrush calling as the creditors," he said. "Couldn't afford to pay the fees at the medical college, is the truth of it. But I have made some study of equine anatomy, and I'd be glad of the chance to examine this colt here."

Harry nodded curtly—he could hardly do otherwise—but Jarret could see displeasure in the line of his father's mouth. Still, Scott seemed to know his business, standing motionless as Alice snaked her head at him, waiting until her ears relaxed and flicked forward. Scott let the mare sniff him thoroughly, and only when she dropped her poll did he move slowly toward the colt, easing down into a crouch. He ran his hands up the spindly legs, feeling for the relationship of bone and tendon, just as Harry had done earlier. Then he held each tiny hoof in his palm, checking for heat. Jarret glanced at his father and saw that his scowl had softened. Scott looked up, smiling. "Sound and safe, seems like," he said.

Scott stood and quietly exited the stall. "He's small, and at first, you'd say there's not a lot of Boston in his looks. But then you notice the slope of the pelvic bones, same as Boston had, and the dam here has similar. Long pasterns, prominent knees. That buck knee of the Boston family—best in the world for power. Sire and dam share a very similar anatomy. Clever of you," he said, turning to Warfield, "to inbreed so closely to form."

"That was Harry's notion," said Warfield. Jarret saw his father nod, glad of the acknowledgment. "He wouldn't let go of the idea. Kept worrying away at it till I finally assented. And just in time."

"That's right," said Scott. "There'll be precious few more Boston colts." He tilted his head and narrowed his eyes as he continued to appraise the colt. "You know the John Sartorius painting of Edward Darley's Arabian? That stallion had white feet. This colt brings that painting to my mind."

"Say you so?" said Warfield. "But that's not his descent. Male line goes back to the Byerley Turk. Female line is to the Cullen Arabian. But it's a fine association in any case, and a good-enough name. Let us call him that. Darley." Warfield tapped his ferrule again to close the matter and turned to his trainer.

"Now, Harry, let's take Mr. Scott to look at Glacier. I have a mind to commission a likeness, since Mr. Scott observed last night at dinner that painting a white horse is a great challenge."

Later that day, when Jarret was seeing to the paddock picking, he noticed Scott, his lanky frame draped over the stone fence, watching the four-year-old named Glacier. Glacier was grazing in the largest turnout, the one that ran down from the home pasture to the creek edge through some stands of white oak, and it took Jarret quite a time to pick it clean, since he was particular to remove every trace of manure. He didn't mind even this lowly job. It was one way to keep track of the health of the horses. He'd saved a horse from colic once, by noticing the state of its droppings.

He'd been at it for a good half hour before Scott finally drew out a small sketchpad. Jarret was powerfully curious to get a glimpse, so he began working his way over toward the wall. When Scott straightened and stretched, he noticed Jarret and beckoned him over. Jarret wheeled his barrow closer.

"What's he like?" Scott asked, tilting his head in the direction of the horse.

Jarret averted his eyes and scuffed the turf with the toe of his boot. It wasn't a good idea to speak without putting a deal of thought into it. Words could be snares. Less of them you laid out there, less likely they could trap you up. "Collected at the post. Fast off the start."

"No," said Scott, and Jarret winced. There you go. Less than a dozen words and he'd said the wrong ones, seemingly. But then Scott spoke less sharply. "I meant, what's he *like*? Busy mind, or a dreamer? Bossy or well mannered? I want to know how he feels about the world . . . what kind of soul he's got."

Jarret had never heard horses spoken of in that way, although it was how he thought of them in his own mind. His father knew all about how to make a horse work its best, and there was a great deal of learning to that. Dr. Warfield was a shrewd judge of when to buy and sell them. But Jarret thought both his father and Dr. Warfield treated horses like mechanical contraptions: do this, get that. Jarret disagreed, but had never said so. To speak of horses as beings with feelings, even souls—it might seem like foolishness, or even maybe sinful, in the eyes of the angry God of the White church Dr. Warfield attended. But now this man was speaking as if it were the most normal thing in the world.

Jarret tried for the first time to put his thoughts into words. "Glacier, well. He'd be a fly one," he said shyly.

"'Fly'? What's that mean?" asked Scott. "We don't have that expression where I'm from, back east."

Jarret tried to think how to explain it. "Fly means . . . smart, but quiet about it. Not a know-it-all. Not cunning neither, because that's like being crooked, and Glacier's not that way. He's a thinker, and that's good, on account of he won't do the stupid thing, like getting a hoof caught in a hole, or shying if a bird breaks out of a bush. But it's bad, too, because he's not about to do what you say just because you say it. He take his own time to think for hisself. Not all jockeys can see why a horse might be that way, so I think that how he does on the track always gone depend on who's ask him to do it. You see, now? See how his tail swings, side to side? He knows how to *use* hisself, but he don't always engage that big hind end when he's in a race. You have to know to ask him just the right way. And then back home, in the paddock, he's not one to try to be the boss horse. He don't barge in to get the feed so as to rile the others, but he don't go hungry neither. He watch, and he think, and

when the others commence to fussin' for one particular pile of hay, he go off
and find one that he can eat by his ownself without aggravation. That's fly."

Jarret took a breath. He wasn't sure he'd ever said so many words in a row
before. But then, no one had ever seemed so ready to hear his opinion.

Scott was smiling. "Thank you, that helps me a good deal in thinking how
to paint him."

Jarret wasn't in the habit of questioning his seniors, especially White people. They didn't tend to appreciate it. But he was powerfully curious.

"How do it do that?"

Scott smiled. "Why do you think men like these thoroughbreds so much?"

"Money, I guess," Jarret replied.

"Well, sometimes they make money, but hardly ever nearly enough to make
up for what most folk spend on them. So there's got to be something more."

"They're beautiful?"

"Of course, they are beautiful, and men with money like to have beautiful
things. Beautiful estates, beautiful wives." Scott smiled. "But I can tell you,
and it's a fact: many a horse-owning gentleman will pay me fifty or sixty dollars for a painting of his horse, but he'd grudge to spend half that on a portrait
of his wife, no matter how beautiful she might be."

Jarret kicked at the dirt. "Then maybe it's the races—folk get excited to
go there. All kinds of folk, high and low."

Scott nodded. "'All men are equal on the turf or under it'—that's the
saying. But the folk who own the horses, it's much more, for them, than an
exciting day out. Here's the ground of it, as I see it: a racehorse is a mirror,
and a man sees his own reflection there. He wants to think he's from the best
breeding. He wants to think himself brave. Can he win against all comers?
And if not, does he have self-mastery to take a loss, stay cool in defeat, and
try again undaunted? Those are the qualities of a great racehorse and a great
gentleman. A gentleman likes to have a horse that gives the right answers to
those questions, then he can believe that he will give the right answers too.
To do my part, I have to give a man a likeness that shows not just how beautiful the horse looks, but how beautiful it feels to him."

Scott's words struck Jarret like a bell clapper, and the truth of it rang through him. "Maybe you don't need to be no gentleman to feel like that," he said. "That Darley foal. He makes me feel—hopeful. Like the future gone matter more than it did the day before he come."

Scott nodded. "I can see that. A new horse is all promise." The two stood in companionable silence, both gazing at Glacier as he cropped the lush spring grass. Jarret wasn't used to feeling so easy in the presence of a White stranger.

"You must like the work here a great deal. Otherwise, with all these fast horses, you and your pa could just mount up and ride off. The river's not that far away, after all."

Jarret felt the blood rise into his face and a taste of sickness in the back of his throat. He didn't care one bit for this turn in the conversation. Even at the Meadows, under the hand of the Warfields—who, after all, tolerated a notorious emancipationist for a son-in-law—Jarret knew better than to be drawn into any discussion of running away. Still, he couldn't let Scott's error stand. He looked him in the eye for the first time. "My pa's a free man. He can go when and where he please, horse or no horse."

Scott gave a snort and clapped Jarret on the back. "So he is, boy. I had forgot. I don't mean offense. But it's a puzzle to me. I've known a number of great horse trainers, not free men like your father, but Colonel Johnson's Charles or Mr. Wells's Hark. Why, Charles takes the colonel's best horses all over the country, clear across state lines, and nobody thinks a thing of it. Never know where you'll meet up with him next: Virginia, Kentucky, Louisiana, even right on up in New York. He could have mounted up on any of those thoroughbreds and been off and away before a mule could kick."

Jarret picked up the handles of his barrow and turned his back. Seemed this man Scott was an addlepated ass, talking of such things right out in the open when anyone at all might happen by.

"I got work to do," he mumbled. He started the barrow in motion. The man might be a northerner but how could he not know what a man like Hark or Charles had suffered to earn the place they had, and what they would risk if they became fugitive? How would they ever get work, when turfmen south and north were thick allies? And how could they leave their families? This man might know horses, but he sure did lack any sense when it came to the men who worked them.

To Jarret's irritation, Scott followed after him, clambering over the stone wall and making his uncertain way across the churned turves of the paddock.

"Don't mind me, boy. I'm just prattling. I don't mean anything by it. Your pa is one of the very best. I know Dr. Warfield thinks the world of him. In fact—and this is just between us now—he told me he's considering offering him that Darley foal as his wages this coming year. That's something, I'd say, a colt with those bloodlines. Dr. Warfield said your pa was the one who pushed for that breeding, and then Boston ups and dies right after. He says your father deserves the credit and the profit, if any. Be interesting to see what comes of the colt. I wish him—and you—good luck with him."

His father's own racehorse. What a thing it would be. But Scott couldn't be correct. No Black man could own a racehorse. It was foolishness, just like all that loose talk about runaways. It might be one thing to throw around such ideas up north. It was another thing entirely in Kentucky, where the slave power was growing stronger than ever. Still, he could see how a man like Scott might get confused at a place like the Meadows. Life looked well enough there. It was what you couldn't see that rubbed your soul raw.

"I tell you what," Scott said. "You've been helpful, what you said, about this horse here. I could use your help some more, when I get set up to paint him. The first thing I need to do is measure him—science in the interests of art, you know—and I'd be much obliged if you'd hold him for me while I run the tape over him. In return, I'll make a painting of Darley, when he's grown some, and you can keep it for your own."

Fine, thought Jarret. No law says a Black man can't have a picture of a racehorse.

So that was the first time, but not the last, that Jarret held a horse as Scott took meticulous measurements of every bone and joint. Then Jarret groomed Glacier, currying his coat till it gleamed like the ice he was named for. Later, he stood by and watched as Scott unrolled the bolt of Irish flax, fixed it to a stretcher, and propped it on his easel. He knelt down to sketch. "A horse presents better from a low-angled view," he explained. "You want to be looking up at them a little bit, not dead-on level."

Jarret was amazed as Scott's hand moved swiftly, filling the white ground with assured strokes. He sketched the horse as if he could see right inside to the bones and muscle.

When Scott stood up to stretch and to consider the charcoal lines he'd made, Jarret risked a question.

"You learn that—muscles and such—from your time doctoring?"

"I learned it from my time butchering. I worked at the Philadelphia knack-ery for six months, carving up horse carcasses till I couldn't lift a paintbrush. But by the end of it I'd learned the nature of every bone and sinew in a horse."

Scott picked up his palette then and squeezed out a dozen small knobs of color. Jarret observed the bright spectrum formed on that ordinary piece of board, from warm shades to cool. Scott named each pigment as he coaxed the shiny worms of paint from their tubes, and Jarret learned the unfamiliar names: the burnt sienna that he'd thought of as mere brown, the French ultra-marine that he'd known simply as blue. But blue wasn't so simple to Scott. He had Prussian blue, cerulean, cobalt, teal, navy. So many complicated words for a simple thing. Jarret knew the names for horse colors—bay, blood bay, buckskin, dun, roan—but now it seemed like every other thing was just as various if you troubled to look at it closely.

Jarret's task was to keep the horse's attention, rustling a pail of grain or whistling. "What you want is tension," Scott explained. "A horse shows best with a bend in the neck. He looks more agile, more elegant."

Jarret learned that when Scott squinted, it wasn't that his eyes were sore, but that he needed to eliminate detail to find the broad areas of light and shade. He watched Scott fill his left hand with six or eight different brushes and wondered why so many, until he figured it: one brush for each small pud-dle of color to keep each tone clean and pure, unmuddied with another. He saw how Scott worked on the whole painting, not just a corner of it, dabbing here, there, farther down. Nose, back, tail. Change brush, new color. Hocks, mane, haunches. Change brush, new color. Hoof, poll, withers. Change brush, new color.

Jarret had thought of the paintings on the walls up in the Warfield house as flat things. Now he understood that they weren't flat at all, but built up in many layers, just like a stone wall. He learned that shadows weren't black or brown, but richly colored by the lilac-toned light or the greens reflected off the grass. He saw how for Glacier's white coat, Scott used barely any white at all, but pinks and mauves and lively grays in pale washes, layer after layer.

Yet in the end, a white horse stood there: Glacier, looking fly.

JESS

Jess drove across the Bourne Bridge just as the eastern sky came alive. After a few miles, she turned right down a side road toward the water and pulled over to watch the sunrise.

As she stepped out of the truck, a chill fingered its way through her thin cardigan. Spring was still a rumor up here. She leaned against the hood of the truck, grateful for the engine's warmth, and tilted her face to the stinging salt air. Jess missed this, perhaps more than anything else about her Sydney home: the sense of being at the watery edge of things, turning a corner and being confronted by a shimmer of sunlight on waves, a crescent of sand curved below a rock-ribbed headland. This beach was very different; undramatic, undulant, gentled by low dunes. As she watched, a crimson sunrise gashed the purple cumulus clouds, like slashes in an Elizabethan sleeve. A seal popped its doggy head out of the water. They gazed at each other as the sun sent a slanting beam to silver the beach grass. "What are you thinking about, eh?" Jess asked the seal, who seemed happy to stare at her and showed no urgency about swimming away. "Shouldn't you be getting on with it? Places to go, fish to catch? Me, I've got an appointment with a whale. What do you think of that?"

When the seal finally vanished into the glossy curve of a wave, Jess glanced at her watch. It was just after seven. She'd made good time and her meeting wasn't till nine. She weighed her options: attempt a nap or seek coffee. She climbed back into the truck and flicked the lever to drop the seatback. But it wasn't any good. She squirmed and couldn't get comfortable. Better to tough it out, collect and load the skull, and then find a motel for a proper rest before the return drive.

The coffee shop near the Woods Hole ferry terminal was warm, pungent with the aroma of roasting beans and fresh-baked bread. She wrapped her hands around the mug and found a seat near the window. One of the big white ferries that plied the waters between the Cape and Martha's Vineyard nosed up to the dock. She watched the two-way trudge of commuters: islanders disembarking for mainland jobs and laborers climbing the gangplank for a day's work on the Vineyard. Hoodies up, heads bent, they passed one another in silence, like monks on their way to matins. Farther down the harbor, scientific vessels bristling with research instruments loomed over net-draped fishing boats and sleek yachts. As Jess sipped her coffee, she caught snatches of conversation—a table of fishermen discussing the market price of black bass while a pair of marine biologists picked apart a journal article on the seasonal dynamics of amphipod assemblages.

She liked this place; this mix of sea dogs and scientists, the swift currents sluicing around the jigsaw squiggle of the coastline, the little drawbridge rising and falling like something from a child's train set.

The Marine Research Facility was up the hill on the Quissett campus. Jess had exchanged emails about her visit with Tom Custler, the marine mammal biologist most closely concerned with the whale skull, so she was surprised when the occupant of the office number she had been given was a tall, fair-haired woman, a slight frown creasing a pale brow, studying data on side-by-side computer screens.

"Thomasina, like the Disney cat," she explained, shaking hands firmly. "My mother's favorite movie. Stupid name: of course I shortened it. The Pilgrim Whale—that's what we've been calling it, since the carbon dating—is over in the warehouse. I suppose you're keen to evaluate it?"

As they walked the bright corridors, Tom described how the skull had been discovered. "The dunes have been eroding rapidly all along the Cape—climate change, fiercer storms. Some guest at a beachside resort in Brewster basically tripped over the edge of the thing, just after it'd been uncovered by a storm. The resort manager assumed it was a rock and sent the grounds crew to dig it up. When they realized what it actually was, they called us. At first, all we knew was that it had to be pre-1974, since that's when we started keeping records of whale strandings, and we didn't have a note about this one. The carbon dating results blew us all backward—to think it's been there, covered by the dunes, for all those centuries. The resort wanted to mount it as a decoration for the lobby." She laughed. "Should have seen their faces when I gently explained that would be illegal. One tries not to slam down one's cards like a winning hand in poker. And then, of course, turns out our hand wasn't, after all."

"Wasn't?"

"Wasn't a winning hand. You lot came up aces."

"Ah yes, Smithsonian's right of first refusal."

"Well, you've got the resources to squeeze this for data. Diet, water temperature, salinity . . ."

"How it was before we messed the oceans up."

"Quite."

They reached the warehouse. A motion sensor tripped the lights.

Jess whistled. "I'm gonna need a bigger truck."

Tom grinned at the *Jaws* reference. "Well, I hope you've got a lot of foam. A *lot* of foam."

The whale's skull was six feet wide. It weighed more than four hundred pounds. It was still on the forklift, so Jess was able to raise it to inspect the underside. As she'd expected, the bone was eroded and very fragile. She turned to Tom. "Clearly a mysticete, most like a North Atlantic right whale, to judge by the skull morphology, don't you think?"

Tom nodded. "We'll be keen for you to confirm that."

Jess spent the morning gently layering foams of varying density over the immense cranium. It was noon before she felt it was sufficiently protected to be loaded into the padded flatbed of the pickup. Then she interlaced a cobweb of netting until the skull was securely cocooned against even a millimeter of movement.

"Looks cozy," Tom Custler remarked. "Let me help you get that tarp on." The two worked in silence ratcheting the straps. "No one would ever know that you had a seventeenth-century whale skull there. Want to grab lunch before you head out?"

They jumped on the MBL shuttle and sat at the bar of Quicks Hole Tavern, eating fish tacos alongside the guys who'd probably caught the fish. Tom seemed to know the entire fishing fleet, greeting everyone by name.

"We rely on them," she said. "They know better than anyone what kind of trouble our oceans are in. The older guys have seen it all happen in their own lifetime—catastrophic collapse in fish stocks. It's changed their lives."

"Made it harder to earn a crust?"

"Make a buck, you mean? Much harder. They care. If there's a stranding or an entanglement, they're generally the first ones to help."

A youth with a full red beard and long, fair hair approached them. "Thanks for patching up Hank," he said. "He's doing great—back out with me on the boat."

"Hank's his dog," Tom explained. "Got hit by a car and broke his leg. Eric couldn't afford a vet, so I set the bone for him."

"You did?"

"Well, I'm a vet by training. I came here to work on a sedation protocol for large cetaceans when we have to cut them loose from fishing gear. Then I got obsessed with North Atlantic right whales—they've kept declining while the Southern Ocean species rebounded once the hunting stopped. We've urbanized this ocean—ship strikes, fishing gear. We've made it so noisy they can't hear to navigate—boat engines, navy sonar, sea mining. Only four hundred left, and now they're putting in offshore wind farms. We need the sustainable energy, for sure, but each of those windmills is going to sit on a pad of concrete big as a city block. Right in the migration zone. We're just not leaving enough room for them."

"Seems like we don't leave room for anything other than ourselves."

A ferry horn growled. "That's the one fifteen. Time to get back to work." They took the shuttle back to Quissett, then Jess drove the truck to a motel just past Bourne, pulled the blackout shades, lay on the bed fully dressed, and plunged into a deep sleep. On the long drive back, she resumed listening to Plymouth University's recording of *Moby-Dick*. She wondered if the Pilgrim Whale had been alive during Melville's hunts. She imagined the great creature's mighty heart pounding as it fled the harpooners. Was that worse than being entangled in skeins of fishing gear and slowly starving to death? She wondered how the Pilgrim Whale had died in the end, and whether the skull would reveal that.

As the guard waved her through the gate into the Support Center, she looked up at the looming bulk of the pods and thought of everything in there—the holotypes that provide the basis for a species identity, the specimens that are the scientific ground truth for the record of biodiversity. How many of them, she wondered, no longer existed? The pods suddenly seemed less impressive than tragic: evidence lockers for the case against humanity.

But the pods also held the things people had created—the finest examples of the artistry and the ingenuity of our own species. How could we be so creative and so destructive at the same time? She felt the hot swell of easy tears and realized she was exhausted. She was taking extra care, backing the truck up to the loading dock, when her phone rang.

"It's Horace, over at Affiliates? Just wondering if you had any luck?"

She tried to focus. Who was Horace again? Then she cursed silently. She'd forgotten all about it. The missing *Equus*. "Closing in on it, Horace. I'm just back from Woods Hole and totally buggered. Can I get back to you this afternoon?" She heard the intake of breath on the other end of the line. She had to remember not to use casual Aussie slang. Americans weren't used to it. It sounded unprofessional.

"Please, if you can, because that researcher from England will be here tomorrow."

"Okay, Horace. On it."

She went to grab a coffee—double shot—and then supervised as the crew unloaded the skull and transported it to the lab. She left Maisy to oversee the removal of the foams and rifled through her wallet looking for the crumpled boarding pass on which she'd jotted down the numbers Horace had given her. Accession No. 121040, Catalogue No. 16020, entered November 7, 1878, and by now one of about ten million recorded specimens in mammal vertebrates.

Usually all Jess had to do to find an item was to type the number and hit function F on her keyboard. But not everything was in the database, especially the oldest items. Sometimes it was still necessary to pore through ink-penned card catalogues and accession books, the faded cards in various hands, the careful calligraphy of colleagues from the past. She thought of giving the job to Maisy, so she could get home and get some sleep. But Horace seemed anxious, and she knew it would be quicker to do the search herself. She would stop at the Castle on her way home and sort it out.

Two hours later, she looked up from a yellowed ledger, pulled out her phone, and called Horace back. She'd tracked the spidery handwriting from the note of acquisition in 1878, through the first eight decades of display, to the crating of the item for storage during a reorganization in 1956, to a loan for a special exhibition in 1974. Finally, a more recent note disclosed its current location.

"We haven't got your *Equus*," she said.

"*What?* You mean to say we lost it?"

"No, no. I mean, we haven't got it in the pods at Support. I said we had ninety-eight percent of the collections, but your *Equus* is in the two percent we don't have. The good news: you won't have to drag your visitor out to Maryland tomorrow. Just go across the street to the Natural History Museum. It was in the Hall of Mammals there, then American History had it for a while—some exhibition on how you measure time, apparently. Anyway, when that closed, they seem to have been at a loss what to do with it, so they shoved it in the attic."

"That's embarrassing."

"It is, a bit. Last time I was up there, and it's been a while, it was a total mess. Take a torch—I mean, a flashlight. In fact, take two—the lighting's awful. But at least you won't have any trouble recognizing it. It'll be the thing labeled 'Horse.'"

Horace laughed nervously. "Ah, Jess. Seeing that you know your way around up there, I don't suppose . . ."

She knew what was coming. Horace's department, Affiliates, was like the diplomatic corps of the Smithsonian Institution, and its top diplomat was feeling chagrined about the possible mishandling of an artifact that another institution evidently felt was highly significant. A buck was about to be passed.

He was blathering now. Something about his daughter's lacrosse game out in Reston. Could she, would it be possible, see her way clear . . . daughter really wanted him to see her play . . .

Jess laughed quietly to herself. She let him dangle for a minute or two, and then:

"Be glad to, Horace. Wish your daughter good luck from me."

THEO

Theo read through his final draft and hit the save key. This piece had gone much more easily. He hadn't had to battle against the academic jargon. It helped to have a living subject to interview, especially one as thoughtful and funny as Bradford. Theo had started his piece with an anecdote about how Bradford used perm papers from his mom's hair salon to make his art in the years when he couldn't afford to buy paint.

He gathered his reference materials and tidied his desk. Clancy looked up, head cocked, eager for a run. Theo foraged around in his laundry hamper for a Hoyas shirt. He disliked branded, elite-university apparel, but his favorite run took him through lily-white Northwest Washington and Daniel, his best friend at Yale, had instructed him that a Black man, running, should dress defensively. Theo picked up his Georgetown ID. The dog's tail thumped the floor. He grabbed a leash, not that Clancy needed one; he was a natural heeler, but the avidity of his expression and his pointy-eared intensity could make non-dog people nervous. Theo clipped the leash to his collar with an apology. "Sorry, mate. We'll take it off when we get to the park." As he opened the door, he glimpsed the neighbor across the road pushing a shopping cart—one of those old-fashioned fabric wheelie ones. She was struggling with it. The heat was clearly getting to her. As she reached the steps to her house, she stood, leaning heavily on the gate. He asked Clancy to stay, and as he crossed the street, he recalled the last time he'd helped her. That horse painting. What had he done with it?

As Theo came up behind her and reached out to take the cart, her head shot up, alarmed. Her knuckles whitened on the handle, as if she expected it to be wrenched from her grasp. Theo felt the usual gust of anger and took a deep breath. Just a White woman, White-womaning. He stepped back, spreading his hands reassuringly. "It's me, Theo, from across the street," he said. "Just wondered if you'd like a hand with that, to get up the steps?" She squinted at him, lifted her chin in a wordless assent, and relinquished the trolley, resting a hand on the stair rail and gasping for breath. "I don't see too good up close," she rasped. He watched her labor up the few steps, following behind with the trolley. As he set it down, he glimpsed a frozen chicken. Wordlessly, she turned, put her key in the door, and vanished into the dark interior.

"You're welcome!" he called. Clancy's tail thumped the pavement as Theo crossed the street. Theo scratched between his pointy ears. They set off for Rock Creek Park. Theo ran off his anger, going hard over their usual route through the narrow southern section, past the zoo to Peirce Mill. Back home, Theo set out dog food and cold water and headed for the shower. A towel around his waist, still dripping, he rifled through the closet until he found the pannier with the wrapped painting. He took his bike down off the hooks on the wall and attached the pannier.

The magazine's office was on the sixth floor of a glassy tower that rose above the entrance to L'Enfant Plaza Metro. Theo wandered through the atrium past a dumpy café claiming "the best sushi in town." He found this boast less than credible. He braved the line at the Starbucks to get a couple of macchiatos. He'd noticed last time that his editor, Lior, was drinking one, and a little sucking up never hurt. Anyway, he liked Lior, a blunt Israeli—was it stereotyping to wonder if "blunt Israeli" was a redundancy? He hadn't had a chance to make friends in the few busy months since the move to DC. The Fine Arts Department was tiny at Georgetown and, apart from his supervisor, blindingly White. Lior was half Ethiopian. Theo hoped a friendship might develop if they kept working together.

Lior met him at the elevator, greeting him with a backslap that almost made him spill the coffee. He led the way to his office.

"Last man on earth who brings me something on paper!" As he read, his red pen scrawled editor's calligraphy on every other line.

"Is okay, is good. Will read it again and send some revisions, some questions, tomorrow." He leaned back in his chair. "What will you do for me next?"

Theo pulled out the salvaged painting and explained his idea of outlining the steps in identifying the value of such a find. "I like it. Different. I'll fix things with Conservation out at Support. Meantime, you want to get an idea where this fits in, you should maybe go to the Visible Art Storage and Study Center at our American Art Museum."

Theo left the office clutching Lior's hastily scribbled map. Outside, a lone opera singer stood amid the food trucks, belting out "E lucevan le stelle" from *Tosca*. He threw the guy a dollar. He was still humming the aria to himself as he racked his bike just across from the Museum of Natural History. Then he swore silently to himself. What was he supposed to do with the painting? He couldn't leave the pannier on the bike—that was just inviting someone to steal it. But taking a painting into an art museum wasn't a great idea either—could be hard to explain when walking out with it. He looked across at the Natural History Museum. He'd check it there, in the cloakroom, and pick it up on the way back.

Lior had explained how to find the study area, tucked away in a converted library above the galleries, a vast cache of paintings crammed frame to frame on every inch of wall. It didn't take Theo long to find the nineteenth-century section and narrow his search to equestrian themes. He passed by images of mustangs swirling in dusty corrals and battle scenes of U.S. cavalry.

Then he stopped. High on the wall, so that Theo had to crane to see it, was a small oil painting, the horse posed to show its conformation, just as in the work he'd salvaged. But in this painting, a young Black man held the horse's lead rope and gazed gravely toward the observer. The youth was finely dressed: frock coat, cravat, brocade vest. Theo peered at the label: "*Star Maris with His Groom*, Kentucky, 1857, by Edward Troye." Theo studied the deft brushstrokes Troye had used to convey the rich texture of the brocade, the crisp folds of the cravat. A gentleman's attire. Yet in Kentucky, pre-Civil War, this unnamed groom, this young Black man, was probably enslaved.

Theo went back to the catalogue and scanned the database for more paintings by Troye. There were two more in the collection. He searched the walls, guided by the catalogue numbers. One showed a horse standing in a skillfully rendered southern landscape. The other, hung so low that the frame of the large canvas almost grazed the floor, was a much more elaborate composition. It depicted a racehorse surrounded by three Black attendants— a jockey hefting a saddle; a groom in a satin vest and a linen shirt; and a third man clad in a frock coat, pinstriped trousers, and a Lincolnesque beaver hat. The title: *Richard Singleton with Viley's Harry, Charles and Lew.*

Theo sat back on his heels and regarded the painting. This man Viley, whoever he was, had commissioned a painting that showed off several of his prized possessions: his thoroughbred racehorse and three men he had enslaved. The artist, it seemed, had willingly abetted this braggadocio. A line from "Ozymandias" wafted through his mind; something about the artist *well those passions read that yet survive, stamped on these lifeless things. The hand that mocked them, and the heart that fed.*

And yet. There was no mockery here. As Theo gazed at the painting, he was struck by the individuality of the three men. Troye had portrayed them as distinct personalities. They were *presences*. He had not caricatured them— there was no exaggeration of features. He'd taken minute care with the details of their faces, clothing, bearing.

Theo's dissertation was meant to be on depictions of Africans in British art; his working title: *Sambo, Othello, and Uncle Tom: Caricature, Exoticization, Subalternization, 1700–1900*. He planned to write of Coon caricatures, Orientalist fantasies, the decorative enslaved servant in ornate livery, proffering fruit or waving peacock-feathered fans for a White master. His thesis argued that these paintings were never meant to be viewed as portraits of individuals, merely status signifiers of the privilege, wealth, and power of the White sitters. The reality of quotidian Black life didn't merit depiction. His argument mirrored Frederick Douglass's caustic essay, arguing that no true portraits of Africans by White artists existed; that White artists couldn't see past their own ingrained stereotypes of Blackness. Douglass's piece, published in *The Liberator*, mocked the caricatures that White painters produced—the broad noses, the thick lips—and asked his readers to consider if they'd ever seen, in life, an actual face that combined all these exaggerated features.

But here was a painting that challenged his thesis. In particular, the man in the top hat—the trainer, Theo supposed—had been depicted possessing a dignified authority. He actually looked irritated with the artist who was interrupting his important work. He gazed boldly beyond the painting, meeting the eyes of the viewer with a challenging glare. Theo had never seen a painting depicting an enslaved person that emphasized his authority and agency in this way.

And yet. That title.

Viley's Harry, Charles and Lew. Theo felt whipsawed. Troye may have portrayed these men as individuals, but perhaps only in the same clinical way that he exactly documented the splendid musculature of the thoroughbred. It was impossible not to suspect some equivalence between the men and the horse: valued, no doubt, but living by the will of their enslaver, submitting to the whip. Obedience and docility: valued in a horse, valued in an enslaved human. Both should move only at the command of their owner. Loyalty, muscle, willingness—qualities for a horse, qualities for the enslaved. And while the horse had two names, the men had only one. Theo let the resentment rise inside him. Then, as he'd trained himself to do, he crushed it. Just as a lump of coal, under pressure, could become a diamond bit, Theo had learned to turn his anger into something he could use.

Maybe this was a fruitful area of exploration: depictions of enslaved people in the equestrian art of the antebellum South. Through the two centuries that separated them, he stared into the eyes of the confident trainer.

Just then, discreet chimes sounded to indicate that the gallery was closing. He hadn't realized it was so late. But when he stood, the tingling in his quads told him he'd been crouched on the floor for a long time, lost in contemplation of the painting.

He gazed once more at the trainer. "Harry? Charles? Lew?" he whispered. "I don't know who you are, but if I can find out, I will."

He left the gallery at a jog, anxious to get his painting out of the Natural History cloakroom before it closed for the night. The doors were shutting as he sprinted up the stairs, and at first the attendant wasn't going to let him in. Luckily, some woman in the cloakroom was arguing with a security guard about a suitcase, so the doorman let him slip by and wait behind her.

As he walked back out into the street, the air felt layered: the stored heat from the pavement rising up to meet the cooling evening. He found a bench on the Mall and began to scribble notes. He wanted to get down his reactions to that painting, exactly what he'd noticed and his response to it. You never get a second chance to have a first impression.

WARFIELD'S JARRET

The Meadows, Lexington, Kentucky

1850

Jarret leaned against the new limestone wall. The late-May morning had turned sultry and he was glad of the cool stone on his back. The lush grasses—the Irish blade that Dr. Warfield favored for its bone-building richness—were beginning to haze over with their bluish bloom. Out of the corner of his eye, Jarret watched the girl, Mary Barr Clay. She was making a precarious way along the top of the wall, arms flung out to help her balance. Since the coping atop the wall was made of narrow stones set close to vertical, this was no easy business. Jarret plucked a bloom of honeysuckle and sucked the sweetness, smiling to himself as she swayed and dipped, striving to keep balance.

When Mary Barr reached him, she jumped down with a flourish. "Did you see? I made it all the way." She lifted a corner of her pinafore and wiped the sweat off her brow, impatiently pushing back tendrils of hair. Jarret could see that someone, probably Mrs. Warfield's own maid, had gone to a good deal of trouble with that hair—you'd call it blood bay, Jarret thought, if she were a filly—twirling it up into an elaborate French braid. Now Mary Barr raked her fingers through, loosening what was left of the arrangement and letting pins fly out onto the grass.

"You'd best pick 'em up, Miss Clay," Jarret said mildly. "Could be bad if a foal got stuck in the hoof."

She flopped down onto the grass without protest, gathering up the fallen pins and putting them in her pocket. Then she came and stood by Jarret, draping herself against the wall with one raised foot pushing against the stone.

The two lolled there, watching Darley and Alice Carneal. The painter Scott hadn't been misinformed, as Jarret had thought him. Dr. Warfield had indeed offered Alice's colt to Harry as his year's wages. The doctor would remain the owner of record in order for the horse to race, since no Black man, enslaved or free, could be admitted to the gentlemen's club of racehorse owners. But Warfield said he felt too old to be campaigning a young racehorse whose first contest was still three years distant, and since the breeding had been Harry's idea, the foal could be his, to see what he could make of it.

All that spring, Jarret tried to court the mare's good opinion. A foal will take its cues from its dam, and Jarret didn't want Darley picking up Alice's high-strung ways. Temperament was risky from both sides, with the sire Boston's violent blood. But from what Harry had told him, he inclined to think that much of the hatefulness in Boston's nature had come of ill usage. Boston, then an unbroken two-year-old, had been handed over to settle an eight-hundred-dollar gambling debt. A year later, he remained unridden, bucking off and attacking any who tried. He was sent to a notoriously hard trainer, who set several men to hold him down while another thrashed him till the welts stood red on his coat. It took more than one such beating to break the horse's courage, and when he did acquiesce it was with a bitter spirit. Eventually, Boston's gaits could be controlled, but at the cost of a temper that never would be.

Jarret was determined their Darley wasn't going to grow up that way. A furious horse isn't thinking clearly, and Jarret had a powerful idea that horses win races with their head. And then, if the colt didn't make it on the racetrack, a nice-tempered saddle horse had a lot more value than a sour one.

Jarret ambled toward the shady spot where Alice and Darley were grazing, their coats flickering and twitching as they shrugged off flies. Mary Barr followed him, but at a distance. She knew how to be around horses, not just to stand about in her riding dress waiting for a groom to fetch her mount. Jarret greeted Alice first, then Darley, who rubbed his nose affectionately on his shirtsleeve. Jarret gently pushed the little head away, requesting his space. A foal's affectionate rub was a fetching thing, but a grown stallion that didn't know his boundaries would be quite another. He dropped to his haunches and let his hands climb the foal's legs just as Scott had done that first morning. Harry had taught him to feel for heat—you didn't want to find any—then the long strings of gristle running beside each length of bone. These needed to feel not too tight, not too loose—just the perfect firmness to hold the fast-growing bones in the right place. He picked up each tiny hoof in turn, to get the youngster used to it for when he'd have to stand for the farrier, and also to check the still-tender tissues for bruising. Finally, he drew a soft brush from his back pocket and commenced to groom the foal.

"May I do that?" Mary Barr asked. Jarret nodded and made way for her. He watched approvingly as she let Alice, then the foal, smell her hands and see the brush before she began to work on him, humming as she did so.

"When can we ride him?" she asked.

"Long time yet, Miss Clay. His bones got to grow. Best let that happen in its own good time." Harry didn't hold with the newfangled idea of racing two-year-olds.

"May I ride him one day?"

Jarret smiled. Mary Barr had been allowed to follow the hunt the past season and she rode her pony with fierce concentration and good balance. But a full-size thoroughbred was another gate's business.

"Not likely, Miss. A little-bitty young lady in a sidesaddle on a thoroughbred stallion—I won't say nobody ever see it, but I don't know what Dr. Warfield would say."

"I know my daddy would not speak against it. He likes me to do hard things. And anywise, I don't have to ride sidesaddle all the time. My teacher, Madame Mentelle, doesn't."

"That so? Well, we'll see. But we need to get him weaned, first off."

The practice at the Meadows was to run all the foals and mares together. Then, when it came time for weaning, to take one mare at a time out of the paddock. Some foals ran wildly about, disoriented and off their feed for days. Others, after looking around for their own mother, decided that they were safe enough with the remaining herd.

The day they took Alice to a different pasture, Darley made one madcap dash up and down the fence line. Then he became diverted by the antics of two other colts and went to join their game. Over the weeks, all the mares were withdrawn until only the colts remained. The chestnut, Rex, was perhaps the best looking of that year's foals, and the black, Onyx, was the sprinter. But Darley had athleticism and endurance. As the youngsters gained muscle and balance, they raced one another around that field. Darley could start last, distracted by a rustle in the leaves or a cricket in the grass, then, noticing that the others were away, take off after them, running right up between his rivals, game enough to force his way through to the lead. He would wear out one colt, then the other, leaving them standing, heads down and sides heaving, as he loped around in a kind of victory dance.

When Jarret approached Darley's field, the foal's head would shoot up, scenting his friend. He would trot to the fence and wait, nickering a welcome. One morning, Jarret left a lead rope draped on the gate. Darley picked it up in his mouth and ran off with it, tossing his head so that it twirled in the air. Then he let go. The rope sailed over the fence to land at Jarret's feet.

"What you do that for?" Jarret said, retrieving the rope and replacing it on the fence. Darley dropped his head and looked at him. Then he pranced over, grasped the rope again, and repeated the twirl and throw, once again tossing the rope to land right by Jarret. This time, the boy laughed. "You made up a game, have you?"

Jarret would tell Harry about the foal's antics over supper. "Bottom and courage, sounds like," Harry observed approvingly, splitting open a biscuit and laying on a thick slice of ham. "He's shaping to be a stayer. That's what we want," he said, handing the plate across to Jarret. "No tearaway can wallop flat out for one mile, much less four, and these days all the racing world cares for is the glory of the four-mile horse."

Jarret nodded, but his attention was on the biscuit. It was still warm, steaming, with just the right soft center and crusty outer. Biscuits came from the big house, which inclined Jarret to think that Harry had been keeping company with Beth, the Warfield housekeeper. This was a business that had Jarret in two minds. Beth was a fine, smart, handsome woman whose uncommon gifts had seen her risen up from maid to housekeeper at a young age. She had the same high-cheek-boned, wide-eyed beauty that recalled his own mother to him, and a direct yet gentle manner that made it easy to like her. He wanted his pa to be happy, and visiting with Beth seemed to put Harry in a fine mood. But Jarret wasn't sure how far Harry had gone in the matter, nor how far he intended to go, and that made him uneasy. A marriage between a slave woman and a free man was difficult and risky, because it always had at least three people in it: the man and woman and the marse as well. Jarret knew his father was saving to buy him out of bondage. He wondered if the desire for a new wife might make the buying of her freedom seem the more urgent. But he kept his worries to himself, since it wasn't his place to do otherwise. His father had earned the right to do just as he pleased.

As Jarret washed and dried the dishes, Harry carried the two ladderback chairs out onto their small porch. The early fireflies were just beginning their slow, twinkling rise. "Stars in the grass," Jarret had called them when he was small, and Harry would measure his bedtime by their ascent. Once the first firefly reached the lowest limb of the big locust, Jarret had to go to his shakedown. As a child, Jarret had resisted, but now he rose so early and worked so hard that he didn't need to be ordered to his bed.

The chair scraped the porch boards as Jarret came to sit by his father. "Alice Carneal to Cullen's Arabian," said Harry. His father was indeed in a good mood, for that was an easy one. Jarret closed his eyes, rocking his chair onto its back legs so that the caning creaked in time to his recitation. "Alice Carneal by Sarpedon. First dam Rowena, by Sumpter. Second dam Lady Gray, by Robin Gray." He liked names like that, carrying a link from dam and sire to foal. "Third dam, Maria, by Melzar, who was by Medley. Fourth dam . . ." He had to pause for a moment, for no name came to him, but then he recalled that the dam's name had been lost. "By imported Highflyer." In Jarret's mind, the tree branched and twigged. "Fifth, by Fearnought, sixth by Ariel, seventh by Jack of Diamonds, eighth dam Diamond, by Cullen's Arabian." He breathed out, smiling.

"Very good," said Harry. "Now let's have Cricket to Godolphin Arabian." That was a harder one. Jarret could get only halfway before he lost the fourth dam and Harry had to remind him. He'd learned to assign each a distinctive appearance, even if his imaginary mare or stallion was nothing like the actual horse who'd once stamped and snorted and crossed oceans to stand stud or birth foals. Once, Jarret had been asked to take a message to Dr. Warfield and had found him in his library, poring over a stud book. Dr. Warfield, seeing his fascination, showed him all the leather-bound volumes that explained the descent and development of the great thoroughbred bloodlines. These English General Stud books, the doctor said proudly, were the only set west of the Alleghenies. When Jarret mentioned the books to his father, he got a terse response. "Put it in your head, boy, then you don't need to be running to no book." Harry's own memory for bloodlines was prodigious. Whenever he purchased a new horse for the Warfield stables, he would have the owner go through the ancestry once or twice as he chanted along, fitting it in with all the lineages he already held in his mind. After, he could recall it forever.

Lying on his shakedown, Jarret fell asleep with the musical names still looping through his mind. That night he dreamed of a giant tree, its massive trunk big as a mountain, its branches wide as rivers, its twigs fingering upward, filling the sky. And at the end of every twig, the most magnificent fruit: thoroughbred horses with gleaming coats and flowing manes, their mighty hooves pawing the air. In his dream, Jarret saw his own hand, grown gigantic. He reached up into the boughs and gently plucked the brightest bay: Darley, by Boston, by Timoleon. As he set the horse on the ground, all the stallions in its long lineage neighed and called to him, shaking the great tree with their chorus.

JESS

Smithsonian Museum Support Center, Maryland

2019

Jess left her lab a little after four. It was still hot when she stepped out of the air-conditioning. She stripped to her tank top, carefully folded her blouse, and put it in the pannier. Pedaling past the turn she usually took to her apartment, she stayed on South Capitol and freewheeled down the hill toward the museum, glad of the breeze. The elms had suddenly leafed out, the golden haze now a canopy of welcome shade. She locked her bike on the rack, tissued sweat off her arms and neck, and shrugged her wrinkled blouse on. She crossed the road and fought her way up the stairs against the tide of departing tourists and school groups.

She loved the deafening roar in the rotunda, excited kid voices echoing off the three-story marble halls. She liked to stand and watch for that one kid who wasn't glued to her iPhone—the one who reminded her of the kid she'd been, engrossed by a specimen.

Horace had emailed her that morning with more details on the visitor: She would be flying in to Dulles from Kentucky. She had been at the affiliate down there, the Museum of the Horse, doing some kind of research on equine anatomy. Jess was annoyed that he hadn't thought to say what she was researching. She called and caught him in a meeting, distracted.

"It was—what was it? Something about motor mechanics? That can't be right."

"Biomechanics?" Jess suggested.

"Maybe that was it. But you should ask her yourself. You'll make more of it than I could."

Jess scanned the rapidly dwindling crowd in the atrium, trying to identify the British visitor. A woman stood with patient composure, a still point in the swirl of movement. Pale hair in a soft updo, linen slacks, Liberty scarf—and a cashmere cardigan, unnecessary in a DC spring. Jess, feeling scruffy and rumpled, walked over and introduced herself.

"Dr. Morgan? Welcome to the Smithsonian." The two women shook hands. Jess noticed that despite her soigné attire, she had "lab hands"—as rough to the touch as her own.

"I'm sorry I'm not better briefed on what we can do for you, Dr. Morgan, but I'm here to help with your research in any way I can."

"Catherine, please. That's very kind. The first thing, perhaps—could you have a word with your security? My instruments—glad if you could rescue them from detention."

"Of course. I'm so sorry." Jess took Catherine's claim check and headed for the cloakroom, tugging her lanyard to free her IDs. The guard scrutinized her credentials, then shook his head.

"I think I'd better check with my supervisor."

"Oh, come on!" Jess blurted. Then she took a breath. The man was just doing his job.

She leaned across the counter, willing herself to be patient, and lowered her voice. "This equipment is the property of an eminent researcher, a guest of the Institution. Please, let's not hold up her work any further."

"Well, I don't know. There's some strange things in those cases."

"Well, I do know. This is essential scientific equipment. Here, take my ID if you like"—she pulled the lanyard over her head—"I'll take responsibility."

The attendant waved a hand. "No—that's not—I'll get them."

Jess ushered Catherine past the Hall of Mammals, up the stairs, and through the passageway to Bones and Mummies. It was the last unrenovated display area in the museum—an old-fashioned collection with no fancy interactive digital features, and Jess loved it best of all. Too bad the horse skeleton wasn't on display right there, in a nice, well-lit vitrine.

Instead, Jess led the way out of the public area to a narrow flight of metal stairs, up into the vaulted roof of the 1910 building. "I'm not sure we can get those cases up—perhaps let's just go and see, shall we, and then I can bring what you need?"

"Lucky one is wearing sensible shoes," Catherine said, glancing down at her low-heeled pumps. The metal grating rang under their tread. They had to walk across an improvised gangplank to get to the storage space. Halfway across, Jess looked down and immediately wished she hadn't. They were above a section of ceiling that had been removed to accommodate the suspension of a blue whale carcass. One false step and I'll be Jonah, she thought.

She silently cursed Horace. This really was mortifying, bringing a researcher into such a neglected space. When they reached the skeleton, the bones were coated with a fine layer of dust. The fancy mahogany platform on which the armature had been so carefully mounted now served as shelving for a clutter of elk racks, the skeleton of an okapi, and a taxidermied West Indian seal.

"This is the one you're interested in," Jess said. "I'm sorry it's being stored like this."

Catherine scanned the horse's skeleton. "What a very fine example of a late-nineteenth-century articulation. Beautifully crafted armature."

Jess nodded. "It really is in remarkable condition for such an old mount." The skull was particularly elegant, with the broad, flat plane of the forehead sloping down to the delicate spines of the nasal bones. "Amazing that even the most fragile bones have remained intact all these years."

"I'll just need my calipers and the laser gauge initially," Catherine said. "Then the portable ultrasound."

"Do you mind if I ask the nature of your research?" Jess asked as she helped Catherine carry her gear.

"One of my areas of interest is the effect of conformation on the locomotor biomechanics of the horse. Basically, I'm trying to determine what bone structure allows them to run fast while avoiding injury. To do that, I'm measuring and describing all the great thoroughbred racehorses whose skeletal remains are still available. This one will be my eighteenth."

"I'm sorry," said Jess, confused. "I must be missing something. What makes you think that this skeleton here belonged to a racehorse?"

Catherine straightened and turned to stare at Jess.

"'What makes you think?' How can you possibly not . . ."

Catherine stepped up to the exhibit label on the plinth and drew out her reading glasses. "Horse!" she read. "I can't believe it! I don't suppose you people have the *Mona Lisa* stashed somewhere, labeled *Smiling Girl?*"

She ran a finger over the terse nameplate.

"Not just Horse," she said. "*The* horse. What you have here is the greatest racing stallion in American turf history."

THOMAS J. SCOTT

The Meadows, Lexington, Kentucky

1852

I'm a free labor man, always have been. But here's the truth, though I may set it down in this diary only for my own eyes and none other: If I were in purse to buy Warfield's Jarret, I believe I would do it. And so we who think we are above enslaving our fellow man are corrupted. Only show us absolute agency over the apt and the willing, and suddenly we find the planters' obduracy that much less odious. I must guard against the rank seductions of this place.

The thing of it is, I've never had an assistant half as capable as that lad. As this day's work confirmed. When he learned that I was returning to the Meadows, he made it his business to discover which horse the good Dr. Warfield wanted me to paint so as to have it clipped and fine before I even arrived upon the doorstep. He recalled how to set up my easel and put out the colors he divined that I'd need, and hardly judged a hue amiss. I'd put the boy on the canvas if I had the skill, just as Troye did with the old man Harry. But I lack the training he had at the great European art academies. All I know is horses, their muscle and bone.

The boy can be flighty as a colt. At first, I had to watch every word. But that I know how to do. If you want to get commissions, you have to know what your clients wish to hear. You have to smother them in honey like a fresh-baked biscuit. It's a necessity of my trade and I'm not shy to say I am become a great expert at it. It's more important, sometimes, to find the right word than to sketch a true likeness. It didn't take me long to know that the boy was sensitive about his father, protective of what was due to him. And it was no difficult thing, once I grasped the lad's need, to show respect. Easy enough to drop in a word or two I'd heard from the turfmen who so relied on him. Only do that, and the boy would walk another mile for me. I remembered I'd promised him a painting of Darley, so I did a quick oil study of the colt. As sometimes happens when the stakes are small, the painting came together with an uncommon felicity. I captured the play of light on that rich bay coat and the intelligent look in the eye. The brushstrokes landed effortlessly, and I was so pleased with the effect that I considered keeping the piece myself. I was glad, in the end, that I did not, when I saw the look of joy on the boy's face. It occurred to me then that his condition afforded him few possessions he might claim as his own.

I came to understand that condition somewhat better during this present stay, when the doctor's pretty daughter Mary Jane came to dine, her infamous emancipationist husband with her. I feel compelled to set down the detail of the evening, which took many revealing turns.

Ever since that conversation in the coach on the road down from Porkopolis, I had been curious to meet Cash Clay, the notorious master of White Hall who had freed his own slaves and survived assassination attempts. All the more so since his uncle, Henry Clay, is the greatest breeder in Kentucky, and I was not above forging a connection there.

Clay was not long returned from the Mexican War, where he'd made a hero of himself, saving his men from execution after their capture, nursing the sick, putting the weak on his own horse during forced marches. His conduct had added fame to former infamy.

We were assembled in the parlor when he walked into that grand room and dominated it at once. Not just by his size, though he stood over six feet, broad chested and dense boned. A portraitist would render his face in strong planes, intense brown eyes under arched brows, bright hair swept into a flamboyant fall by a pronounced cowlick. He had a certain lift to his chest and chin, a stance like a stag, alert and dominant.

Yet you could feel the chill settle when he entered. Sometimes you can tell from the drum tap that an evening will not go well. His wife, Mary Jane, acknowledged his entrance with the barest nod. Her sister Anne turned her back to him and addressed her mother in a low whisper, the two of them pointedly ignoring him. I must set down here that those sisters were as un-alike as any two siblings I've ever met. Mary Jane had large, soft eyes, a heart-shaped face with a prettily cleft chin, and a mouth that naturally came to rest with upturned corners, giving the impression of an amiable disposi-tion. Her unfortunate elder sister Anne was a freckled, ferret-faced woman, jimberjawed, so that her beaky nose almost met up with her pointy chin. Her manner was full of the foolish affectations girls sometimes bring back from their eastern finishing academies. She folded her hands in her lap as stiffly as if they were carved of marble and slid her eyes as if to look directly was some grave breach of feminine deportment. Behind the faux demure façade, I'd heard that as a scandalmonger, she was a scourge.

Clay tried to strike up conversation with his young daughter, Mary Barr, but she would not be drawn on any topic he tried to raise. I have often heard war veterans say that they return in some measure estranged from their young children, so I thought that might be the cause. Else, perhaps, the girl was shy to speak in company, as some young fillies are. It was left to me to engage him. I thought to ask about his time in Mexico and put a question about how he'd preserved the morale of his men during their captivity.

Anne Warfield turned then and made eye contact with her brother-in-law for the first time. Perhaps the Mexican *women* had some part in that, she said with a brittle laugh. "Or one of them, in any case." The girl, Mary Barr, fidgeted in her chair. Clay's wife, Mary Jane, blushed. Cash scowled. Dr. Warfield rescued the moment by turning the topic to my latest com-mission, which was to be a portrait of his aging broodmare, Alice Carneal. Given the horse's notorious temperament, this was a commission with some challenges. I asked if I might have the assistance of his boy Jarret. The doctor frowned and asked me if another groom might not do as well, because Jarret's responsibilities had expanded since my last visit. He went on to say that he had hopes the boy would make as fine a trainer as his father, as he had an uncanny affinity with the horses.

An ugly note, then. The doctor bragged that he had paid only eight hundred dollars for Jarret and was confident he could sell him south tomorrow to a large racing establishment for double the sum. His wife hushed him, indicating with a nod the elderly Negro who stood by the wall, ready to brighten our drinks. How should it be, she whispered, if Old Harry were to get wind of such a remark? Then, in a louder voice, she declared that such a thing—selling a child south while the parent lived—would never be done at the Meadows.

"*You* may not, but such barbarous things are done every day, and by the same men you call your friends," said Cassius Clay.

Mrs. Warfield stood abruptly in a rustle of taffeta, saying she would not have such hot words in her house, and in any case it was time to go in to dinner. She turned to her son-in-law. "If you will hold your tongue, you may give me your arm."

Clay bowed and extended a velvet sleeve on which his mother-in-law rested her bejeweled hand. The doctor gave an arm each to Mary Jane and Mary Barr, and I was left to escort the unlovely Anne.

In the business of scraping chairs and flourishing napkins, I glanced from face to face, hoping to divine where next the conversation might go in this riven grouping.

On the surface, the Clay family and the Warfields seemed a perfect match: both landowning and politically influential. But there had been rifts since the beginning. I knew—as everyone knew, since he had founded a newspaper devoted to the cause—that Cash had gone off to Yale and come home an emancipationist. His argument was compelling, or so it seemed to me, having perused some issues of his radical sheet. He held that slavery was an economic burden rather than a boon. Southerners, he wrote, had enslaved Man, whereas the north had enchained the elements—the "omnipotent slaves" of waterpower and minerals. The Warfields did not care to have it pointed out that almost everything they sold in their town store was manufactured by free labor in the north. It was common gossip that Mrs. Warfield had been against the match of her daughter with such a controversial man and had set about sinking the alliance, right up to the wedding. She had given Clay a note, sent by a disappointed suitor, impugning Clay's honor. Clay, incensed, had ridden off to challenge the man to a duel, which had caused him to be late back for his own nuptials.

We were scarcely through the soup when Anne Warfield, knowing she'd drawn blood in the parlor, started plying her spur again. Her first remark seemed innocuous enough. A Negro butler had commenced carving a substantial saddle of mutton and a boy laid the plates before us. She remarked that she had heard the Mexicans flavored lamb in an outlandish manner, with copious amounts of garlic, which must be ghastly for the breath. She turned to Clay and remarked that it was as well he was not obliged to embrace anyone. Then she sank the rowel in. "Or at least anyone who had not shared your odorous repast."

This, it seemed, was too much for young Mary Barr. She rose, scraping her chair back, and fled the room. Dr. Warfield tried to cover the moment in a comment on the quality of the burgundy, and even Mrs. Warfield, seeming to grasp that things had gone too far, turned the tables and began to address her son-in-law with at least a pretense of civility. I could see the blood beating in a vein on Clay's brow, yet the notoriously hot-tempered duelist kept his countenance and answered her in kind. When dessert was passed, he turned to Mary Jane and asked in a low voice why Mary Barr had not returned to the table. I will set down their terse exchange, as best I can recall it.

—Perhaps she felt ill.

—Then you must go to her.

—No need, I'm sure.

—Then I shall go.

—I don't think that will improve her state.

—I am her father. Do you not think I have a right to be concerned?

—I'm sure it is nothing. Do not break up the gathering. Father will want you to take some port with Mr. Scott.

—And I am sure, if it were nothing, my daughter would not be so ill mannered as to retire unexcused.

He turned to me then and begged that I forgive an anxious father. As he spoke to me, he stood, bowed to his mother-in-law, nodded to Dr. Warfield, and thanked them for the fine evening. There was an awkward silence in which we heard Clay's boots creak on the hall's polished floorboards, then conversation resumed. Since it was both stilted and inconsequential, I shall put down my pen and rest my eyes against tomorrow's labor.

WARFIELD'S JARRET

The Meadows, Lexington, Kentucky

1852

When it came to starting a racehorse, Jarret had a different mind to his father. Harry had always followed the general practice, which was to throw a boy up for however long he could stick, as the young horse bucked and spun and put him on the ground. It would go on so until the horse, discouraged, grudgingly accepted a rider.

Jarret watched all this, but he saw it from the horse's point of view. The colt couldn't tell the difference between a harmless boy and a mountain lion that would rip his throat open. He could feel the inbred fear of the colt, vulnerable prey in the wild, terrified as a predator leaped up onto his back.

At first, Harry just waved him off, thinking it nothing but a child's fancy. But one day, tired and frustrated by a particularly recalcitrant horse, he allowed Jarret to try it his way. The results were so persuasive that Jarret had become the Meadows's chief horsebreaker.

He worked in the horse's own stall, where the colts and fillies were most relaxed. Jarret always started with the bridle, taking it apart so that the horse learned first to accept the headpiece over his sensitive ears and, later, the bit in his mouth. Next came the saddle pad and surcingle, tightened in slow stages. Only then, the extra weight of the saddle. Finally, he'd get one of the smaller boys to lie across the horse's back for a few minutes at a time, getting the horse used to the idea of carrying a human's weight. At every step, Jarret would pat and praise the horse, reassuring him nothing terrible was happening. When the horse stood quietly, the boy would slip a leg over and sit astride. The main thing was to keep the boy on, once he was up. A horse that learned he could throw a rider would remember and try it again.

Often young horses would buck and rear and have to be held steady by a pair of strong grooms. But Darley showed no hint of fear. He took to having a rider faster than any horse Jarret had ever worked.

"He cocks his back leg and drop his head, just like he was fixin' to take a nap," Jarret told his father that night over their meal. "So I told John to go right ahead and mount on up," Jarret continued. John Porters was Harry's favorite young jockey, with a bantam cock's courage. "He throws his leg over, and Darley picks up his head, and I swear if a horse could smile . . . he perked on up and looked at me as if to say, 'Bout time, boss. What now?' He pranced out with that boy just like he'd been doing it his whole life."

They had "dinner" now, not "supper," since Beth had moved down from the big house and become Mrs. Lewis and a free woman. She insisted that dinner must be three dishes—soup, then a meat course, then a sweet syllabub or pie. This, served in a set of flowered china the Warfields had given as a wedding gift. A wash of the hands no longer sufficed before coming to the table. Now the work overalls had to be exchanged for breeches and fresh linen shirts that Beth had sewn and clearstarched for Jarret and his father. Harry seemed to thrive on the new refinements, and Jarret was pleased for him.

"I cared for your ma, you know that's the Lord's truth," Harry had told Jarret when he broke the news that Beth was to live with them. "She was a fine young filly and I must have seemed like wore-out old crowbait to her. Anywise, she had no say-so in it, nor me neither. We both answered to the same Marse that time. He took it in his head we best be a pair. No ceremony, no preacher, nothing of that kind. Just she come stay in my quarters. And later, when he goes and sells her off to the Todd family, we had no say in that, neither. We had to be thankful she stay close by in the town and not sold south down the river like so many other folk. So we could still be man and wife, time to time, which is how you come to be in this world. When she died, I say, 'Harry, you don't marry, unless you can free that woman and marry her in law.' And now that's what I'm fixing to do."

But buying her freedom had exhausted his savings.

"I'd not be doing this if you answered to any other on this place but me," Harry said. "You young yet. We got time."

He did not say it, so as not to jinx the future, but both knew that Harry counted on Darley to earn the price of Jarret's freedom. If the horse was as good as they believed, a single season's purses would be enough, even after splitting the winnings with Warfield.

Meanwhile, for Jarret, Beth's syllabub provided some small consolation. He scooped up the last lemony mouthful, then placed his fork and spoon on his plate and mopped his lips with a linen cloth in the way she'd taught him.

Harry smiled. "Well, keep on just the same way, get him bridle wise, and then we'll see how he goes at the gallop."

With Beth in the house, Jarret and Harry no longer spent companionable evenings on the porch, going over bloodlines. Beth had first claim on Harry's nights now, so to give them some privacy, Jarret took long walks. He called these wanderings a night inspection, even though all the chores had been done and double-checked hours earlier. The evenings were closing in early and it was dark by the time he left the cottage. Jarret watched the horses in the moonlight, their dark bulk moving slowly in the sleepier rhythms of night grazing.

As he turned into the river meadow, he was surprised to see a light in the riding room. There was no cause for anyone to be there at such an hour. The ring had long since been watered and raked ready for the next day's work. Jarret quickened his pace, annoyed. As he approached, he heard hoofbeats—a fast canter. Someone was working a horse—working it hard. Annoyance turned to anger.

"Door!" he cried, and threw back the latch.

"Door!" answered Mary Barr, pulling her mare up to a tidy halt. Her face, dusty from the ring's clay footing, was smeared with tear tracks.

Jarret bowed his head. "Miss Clay, I had no—I never heard—that is, no one told us you was here at the Meadows. You should of sent word you wanted to ride. I'd a seen to it someone got your mare tacked up for you."

"I can saddle my own horse, and I don't need a slave's permission to ride her."

Jarret flinched. She'd never spoken to him like that. "I know that, Miss Clay. But it ain't safe. You ought to have someone here with you."

"I just want to be alone, can't you grasp that?" She booted the mare back into a canter, bringing her in so close by Jarret that the footing flew into his face and soiled his clean linen shirt. Jarret stood his ground. It was never a good idea to bring strong emotions up onto the back of a horse, and he wasn't going to let a thirteen-year-old girl run a Meadows mare into the ground. Even if it was her horse, he was responsible for its care. So he stood and watched as she did figures of eight and small circles, urging the mare on till her flanks foamed. Even through his irritation, Jarret had to credit that the girl had grown into a capable rider. Stellamaris was a spirited thoroughbred, but Mary Barr had her measure. She rode off a strong leg and kept the mare on the bit.

A short while later, Jarret raised a hand. "That'll do, Miss Clay. Ease on down now." Somewhat to his surprise, she followed his direction, slowing the mare to a jog and then bringing her gradually to a walk.

By the time the horse had cooled down, Mary Barr had regained her composure. Jarret held the reins as she dismounted, loosened the girth, and ran up the stirrups. "I can rub her down and put her away if you like," he said.

"Thank you, Jarret, but there's no need. I don't want to go back up to the house just yet awhile." Her eyes began to fill again. "My father is here and, well. You probably know. Seems that everyone else does."

Jarret did know. Beth was full of talk about the folk in the big house, and so Jarret was well aware that the enmity between the Warfields and Cash Clay had flared into incivility over rumors that his Mexican captivity had been made more bearable by an eighteen-year-old auburn-haired beauty named Lolu.

Jarret took the reins and led Stellamaris out of the riding house, walking ahead of Mary Barr to give her a chance to further compose herself. In the barn, he took a whisk and began to work the sweat marks out of the mare's coat. Mary Barr picked out the mare's feet. She was the only one from the big house who bothered to groom her own horse, and Jarret had always appreciated that. They worked in silence. When the mare's coat was dry, they each took a brush and swept from poll to withers in long, slow strokes. Stellamaris blew softly as she relaxed under their hands.

They brushed the mare much longer than was necessary. Jarret knew how calming it could be, to lean into the warm bulk of a horse. After a time, Mary Barr set down her brush and pushed her fists into the small of her back.

"Why does anyone marry," she said flatly. "I never will."

Jarret gazed at the floor of the aisle. If she expected an answer, he wasn't minded to give one. He surely didn't need to be inviting confidences about private family matters.

"My father calls himself an emancipator, but he makes my mother the most complete slave I know."

Jarret felt the blood rise into his face. "You know? Miss Clay, you don't know nothing. We done here." He threw the brush into the tack box.

"Jarret..."

He unhitched the horse and led her into her stall.

"Jarret? I didn't..."

He did not turn back. "'Night, Miss Clay," he murmured. Just as he reached the end of the aisle, the barn door shuddered as the timbers traveled across the rollers. Cassius Clay's shadow leaped along the length of the aisle as he raised his lantern.

"Mary Barr!" he barked. "I've been looking for you this hour or more. How dare you walk out on dinner in such a manner? And what in the Devil's name are you doing out here, with this . . ." He took a stride toward Jarret, close enough that Jarret could smell bourbon on his breath. "Who the hell are you?"

White. Angry. Drunk. Jarret fought the impulse to shy away from the triple threat.

"I'm Dr. Warfield's Jarret, Marse Clay," he murmured.

"I'm not your master, boy! Don't call me so. Look at me."

Jarret raised his eyes to Clay's dark gaze.

"You're the one they were speaking of, the trainer Lewis's boy?"

Jarret nodded.

"Then why the deuce, Jarret *Lewis*, don't you give your right name?"

"It ain't allowed, Mar—I mean, suh. Only free men can go by they name."

"Your father is a free man. I suppose when you grow to be a man you'll be wanting to be free too."

Jarret swallowed hard. "Nossir," he lied. No slave would dare to say he wished for freedom. Not to a White man.

"What the devil is wrong with you, boy? There's not a slave alive who thinks he was meant to be a slave. It's unnatural. Either you're an addlepated idiot, or you are a liar. Are you an idiot, boy?"

"Nossir."

"No, I rather thought not. Are you a liar then?"

Jarret gazed at the floorboards. A field mouse ran across his line of sight. Flattening itself like a penny, the tiny creature squeezed out through a slim crack in the barn boards and made off into the night. That mouse is freer than I am, Jarret thought.

"Answer me, boy. And don't lie. What do you think you are doing out here alone with my daughter?"

"He was doing nothing other than seeing to my safety," Mary Barr said. Jarret noted that she was tight in the muscle, quivering like a filly poised for flight. So she, too, feared this man.

"I—I decided to work Stellamaris in the riding house. Jarret was concerned that I shouldn't ride alone."

Clay, his dark bulk still blocking the barn door, looked from his daughter to Jarret. "Tarnation, girl. It might occur to you that instead of playing nursemaid to you, this boy should be taking his hard-earned rest. You heard your grandfather speak about his importance here." Then he stepped aside, sweeping an arm to indicate Jarret should pass. "Thank you for looking after my daughter, whose mother, it seems, has raised her with neither respect for her father nor consideration for her servants."

Jarret edged past Clay and stepped out into the dark. Glancing back, he saw Clay move toward Mary Barr. What should he do—what could he do—if the man raised a hand against her? He stood, paralyzed. But then Clay enfolded her in an embrace. She stood stiffly, her head barely reaching his chest. "My little girl, please do not let your mother poison you against me like this."

Jarret didn't wait to hear more. He sprinted across the meadow and down the lane until he reached his own dooryard, where his father had left a single candle burning in the window to light his way home.

Jarret took the candle from the sill to show his way to the loft, which was where he'd moved his shakedown now that Beth and his father shared the downstairs room. It was a narrow area in between the roof beams, just large enough for the shakedown. He had to go on all fours to cover the few steps from the ladder to his bed. The only ornament in the tiny space was the painting that Scott had made of Darley, and Jarret gazed at it for a few moments, as he always did, before he extinguished the candle.

In the dark, he tried to clear his mind of the encounter with the Clays. People were hard to read, no matter how well you thought you knew them. He'd led out Mary Barr on her first pony. She was like a foal herself then, unsteady on her feet. In the saddle, her dimpled legs didn't reach the stirrups. But she'd whinnied in delight up on that pony all the same. He remembered that morning, laughing with that little girl, sharing her simple joy. Now her behavior was as baffling as any stranger's. And her father, well. There was a puzzle. Talked like a northern antislaver but looked and sounded just like a marse who'd beat you bloody if you glanced at him the wrong way. Jarret tossed on his shakedown. He was pleased to know that good things had been said of him up in the big house. But it concerned him too. Being noted wasn't always safe. The tallest cornstalk could be the first one reaped. What if he became too valuable? What if Warfield sold him off?

These were not good nighttime thoughts, not if he wanted to get to sleep and be ready for the horses at sunup. He punched at the shakedown, making a comfortable hassock on which to rest his head. He could waste an hour's good sleep worrying and be no wiser for it.

Think on the horses, that was what he needed to do. He filled his mind with the day's work, running through each horse he'd exercised, saving Darley for last. The colt was turning out intelligent and strong, open to whatever was asked of him. In fact, Jarret barely had to ask. It was as if he only needed to think a thing and the horse would do it. All those hours in the pasture—those empty hours, most folk would call them—were paying back now in this bond. Jarret cast his mind forward to the next day's exercises, and to the weeks that would follow, breaking down the steps he would use to get the colt familiar with running against other horses. Jarret planned to use John Porters till the horse was full grown in the bone. Then he would take over, galloping out each day, easy for the first half mile, and then pushing forward. Over weeks, as the horse built strength, they'd go longer and harder, until Darley could handle a full morning. A gallop at full speed up a hill, then a long walk. Another, harder gallop and a slow walk home. That was how you built a four-mile horse—bone and muscle and wind.

Jarret would show Darley how to control his pace, to listen to his rider's hands when he asked him to hold back or go on. Then, with Porters's lighter weight once again in the saddle come race time, the horse would fairly fly. The most important thing was to keep Darley willing every stride of the way. They would both love the work, Jarret would make sure of it. That, thought Jarret, as he eased into sleep, is how we will win.

JESS

C atherine Morgan plied her calipers and entered measurements on her laptop, occasionally muttering to herself as she typed. "Massive backbone. Absolutely extraordinary." As she worked, Jess sat on the floor, her back against a column, reading through Catherine's file of nineteenth-century correspondence between their two institutions. It was in these aged documents that Catherine had discovered that the Smithsonian had the skeleton of the nineteenth century's most remarkable racehorse.

Britain's Royal Veterinary College, where Catherine worked, had come into being in 1792 to study the skeleton of a famous English racehorse named Eclipse, an undefeated champion popular for his thrilling speed. The file contained lively newspaper reports on Eclipse's races and his obituaries. The desire to study the bones to understand the reason for his speed and endurance led to the establishment of England's first school of veterinary medicine. Eclipse's skeleton now raced eternally through the atrium of the college's Hertfordshire campus.

Almost a century later, when the Smithsonian was offered the remains of America's most renowned racehorse, a curator wrote to the Royal Veterinary College, seeking technical advice on equine skeletons. Eclipse had been autopsied directly postmortem, but the famed American stallion would have to be exhumed. Apparently he'd been buried with some ceremony, in a custom-made coffin. A note said that General Custer, visiting the horse before his death, likened the experience to "being in the sacred presence of royalty." So the horse was apparently so famous and beloved that no one balked at the notion of digging him up and shipping the remains to Washington, DC.

Jess was happily lost in the letters between her nineteenth-century colleagues—struck, as she always was, by the elegant literary cadence of scientists in the age of Darwin. The final letter was an 1878 note from the Smithsonian curator to his Royal Veterinary College correspondent, thanking him for his counsel and attaching a cyanotype. The blue-tinted image showed the newly articulated skeleton on its wooden platform in the courtyard of the Castle, surrounded by a rather weedy garden. For years, it had occupied pride of place in the exhibition space. But as the horse's fame waned, the nature of the Smithsonian's exhibitions also changed, stressing science more than spectacles and curiosities. The skeleton went into storage. There'd been a flurry of interest during an exhibition on the history of measuring time, and the skeleton had been brought out to illustrate the invention of the stopwatch, used to accurately time horse races. When that exhibition ended, the horse went back to the attic, just one among millions of artifacts, neglected in the vast institutional bureaucracy.

Jess replaced the cyanotype and pulled out the next image. It was an actual photograph of the horse: an old stereoscopic image from the earliest days of photography. She was amazed by the unusual clarity of the image. The photographer had captured the gleaming coat, but also the tender expression of the young Black man who stood at the stallion's head. The man and the horse posed together outside a fine barn, with decorative gingerbread trim on the eaves. Jess looked closer. There was no lead rope. The man wasn't restraining the stallion. She peered at the image. His hand rested lightly on the horse's withers. He seemed to be stroking its mane. Jess didn't know much about horses, but she knew about early photography. She could imagine the photographer under his billowing black shroud, the flare of the tungsten and the loud pop as he exposed his photographic plate. Wouldn't that have startled a stallion, blurred the image? How did the man manage to keep the horse so still?

Jess stood, the laminated print in hand, and walked around the skeleton. She'd never before had an opportunity to compare an image of the living animal with articulated remains almost a century and a half old.

Catherine looked up from her notetaking. "Marvelous photo, isn't it? Beautiful detail for the time. Undated, alas, but we do know who took it. James Mullen was an army photographer with the Engineer Corps during your Civil War."

"Not my war," said Jess. "Unless you call Australia the *very* Deep South."

"Sorry. Should have recognized the accent. We're lucky to have it. Photography was only in its infancy at the very end of this stallion's life. It's interesting to have that photograph to compare with the oil portraits of the horse. There are many more of those of course, earlier, made during his racing career, for the most part. There are reproductions of all the known portraits there in the folder, most by the same two painters, Edward Troye and his pupil, Thomas Scott."

Jess's eyes moved from the photo to the skeleton, evaluating the bone structure as the nineteenth-century articulator had assembled it.

"As you said earlier, this is a very capable articulation but—just my initial impression—looking at this image as an equine vet, wouldn't you say the withers seem to be set too far above the level of the coupling?"

Catherine set down her notes, took the photograph, and studied it closely. "I believe you're right. And I'd say also, now that I'm looking for flaws—the hocks seem too angular, and the pasterns too upright. I suppose whoever did this articulation never saw the horse in life, since the articulation occurred several years postmortem."

"I could do a whole lot better."

"But you wouldn't go to the trouble, would you? I mean, disarticulating it, starting from scratch . . . ?"

Jess tilted her head. "Why not?"

"Wouldn't that only make sense if you planned to do more with the artifact? Context, history, display? I mean, it's not exactly in pride of place here."

"That's exactly why I want to do it," Jess said. "This horse shouldn't be up here in an attic."

"No, he really shouldn't. The International Museum of the Horse in Kentucky, where I was this morning, would love to have him. The director was so envious when I told him what I would be doing here. Of course, if you *did* see your way clear to do it, it would be a most marvelous research opportunity for me. We could scan the key locomotor bones. Then I could reproduce them in three-D—laser-carved resin, you know. I have the equipment for that at my college. It would make it possible to replicate the mechanics of the limbs. Immensely valuable for my study of the relationship between conformation and equine injury."

"Well, in that case, we'd have a research reason. Let's do it."

As director of the lab, Jess had wide latitude to initiate projects. Still, she felt a little clandestine. as if she were ten years old again, sneaking a dead rat past her mother so that she could articulate a *Rattus norvegicus domestica* for her bedroom display. She'd found the rat at the local dump, an environmental nightmare long since regulated out of existence: steaming, reeking hills of every kind of domestic refuse and industrial waste, like Mordor with seagulls. Other neighborhood kids went there to scavenge for discarded toys. Jess hunted for corpses. Some instinct had warned that a dead rat foraged from the dump might test her mother's tolerance. So she hid her find in the garden compost heap and let it decompose there until its rattiness was indiscernible.

No such subterfuges would be necessary to get this horse to her lab. All she had to do was make a request to the collection manager, who would probably be glad to free up some space in the attic.

As far as he knew, this *Equus* in the attic was just as good as any other *Equus*. Of course, she'd tell him all about his famous artifact.

Later.

WARFIELD'S JARRET

The Meadows, Lexington, Kentucky

1853

The spring of 1853 was a strange season, the rains that usually fell in April holding off until mid-May, and then siling down relentlessly, washing out the seedlings and drenching the peonies till their sad flounces brushed the mud. In the heat of early afternoon, there was a rich smell of rot in the air. In the pastures, the mud-caked foals looked like little clay figurines.

Jarret rode Darley every day, no matter what the weather. Rain sluiced off them as if thrown by the bucketful, but it was no match for the clods of clay heaving up at them from beneath the churning hooves. After the ride, when Jarret took off his oilskin, it stood up by itself. He had to peel the mud off Darley as if it were a second skin. The heavier the going, the more Darley seemed to like it, plunging into the muck like a naughty child who loves to make a mess.

"He's a mud lark, no swallow," observed Harry. "No cause to be afeared of the heavy track, and that is a sure thing for the Phoenix, and likely for the Citizen as well." Harry had decided that these two stakes, the first a race of two one-mile heats and the second, just four days later, a tougher test of three heats over two miles each, would be the best choices for Darley's racing debut.

No one at the Kentucky Association could know that Darley belonged to a Black man, so the horse would race in Dr. Warfield's colors—light blue cap, white jacket—as if it were his own. Harry also had to ask the doctor's help in paying the entry fee. Since these were big races, the fee for the first was one hundred dollars, and Harry had only managed to save fifty dollars since buying his wife out of bondage. Dr. Warfield was happy to split the fee, and the purse, which was a princely seventeen hundred dollars and a hundred dollars' worth of silver plate.

When the entries were posted, Dr. Warfield tottered unsteadily down to the stable to read out the dozen names to Harry. It was a list that reflected the cream of Kentucky breeding—eight of the entrants were sons of the great stallion Glencoe—the first of his get since he retired to stud. There was also a son of Grey Eagle, as well as another bay colt by Boston, who hadn't yet been given a name.

The morning of May 23 saw no letup in the driving rain. An hour before sunrise, Jarret lay on his shakedown, listening to the torrent pounding on the roof just inches above his head. He rose, put on his oilskin, and trudged to the barn through mud that topped his gaiters. He'd taken Darley the short distance to the stalls over at the Association course two days earlier, to get him settled and used to the track there. So he saddled up Timon, one of the old roans who knew the racetrack and who would be a calming influence ponying Darley to the starting line. They covered the few miles through the sleeping town and out to the Association at an easy trot. The sun, a pale disk, eased up sluggishly behind the rain clouds, turning the sky pewter.

When they arrived, Darley still dozed in his stall, one white hind leg resting lazily on the point of its pale hoof. As Jarret pulled back the barn door, the horse raised his handsome head and whinnied. Jarret led Timon into an empty stall and called for a groom to rub him down. Then he went to the feed room and dried himself off as best he could with some hessian sacking. He scooped a light race-day ration. Horses stamped and banged in their stalls as they heard the grain hit the pail. Darley emptied the bucket in seconds and eyed Jarret accusingly. "Plenty more later," he reassured, running a hand down the horse's flank, feeling the muscles twitch under the fine coat. He was in peak condition, no doubt of it. Jarret led the colt out into the aisle and put him on the crossties. He felt the horse all over, checking for soundness. Darley leaned into him, warm and familiar. For the next hour, Jarret worked in silence, buffing the horse to a gleam and then blanketing him in a light sheet.

As the dreary morning wore on with rain sheeting down, the Association grounds nevertheless began to fill. Carriages plowed through the mud and delivered ladies and frock-coated gentlemen to a makeshift boardwalk that led to the grandstand. Those without access to a dry space filled the backstretch and crowded the rails, huddling under trees or climbing up into their branches, devising pavilions out of tarps and sacking. Jarret wove through the crowd. The entirety of the town seemed to be crammed into the track precincts: judges from courts they'd just adjourned began to arrive in their carriages, the suspects they should have tried that day following behind them on foot. There were ministers who'd forsaken their churches and sinners who might have benefited from visiting them. There were rogues and bawds and cutpurses; the gentry and the eminent; the cobblers, the coopers, and the dry goods sellers whose stores all bore CLOSED signs for the afternoon. Jarret was just one dark face among many. It was a common thing for masters to reward their enslaved with time off on race days. It was equally common for youths to risk unsanctioned time and take a beating for it a day later. Through the babble of voices, Jarret listened for the shouted odds, trying to get a sense of the early betting. It soon became clear to him that one of the Glencoe colts, Garrett Davis, was a clear favorite, while Darley seemed likely to start almost unbacked. The first heat of the Phoenix was to be the day's leadoff event, so Jarret didn't linger.

Head down against the wind, he shouldered his way back toward the stable. He was obliged to stop and give way to a carriage drawn by a pair of beautiful gray harness ponies. The gentleman driver sat erect, as if unaware of the filthy weather, his high hat the same gray as his ponies. As he drove forward, he turned to Jarret and nodded down to him in courteous acknowledgment.

As soon as the carriage passed, Jarret overheard a man observe to his companion: "That's Richard Ten Broeck, up from New Orleans. He owns the Metairie Race Course down there—he'll be on the hunt for likely horses, I'll be bound."

Dr. Warfield's carriage had pulled up by the stable. Mary Barr was being handed down as Jarret came up, her maid holding an already saturated parasol high over her head. She was attending to where, in this world of mud, she could possibly place her feet, and so didn't see Jarret at once. But then she glanced up and called to him. "Is Darley going to win? Isn't this the most exciting day ever?" Her bonneted head swiveled as she took in the swelling throng—Black, White, rich, poor, the very old, and the very young. As a closely kept daughter of privilege, she had never been in a crowd so diverse. "*Everyone* is here. I begged to come. Mother didn't care to, but that young painter—the one you help—he persuaded Grandpa to bring me."

Sure enough, Thomas Scott stood with Dr. Warfield and Harry Lewis as the grooms brought out Darley. Jarret had seen his father finely dressed for the races many times, but Beth had added an extra note of distinction. The brass buttons on his frock coat gleamed from her polishing and she'd bleached and starched the high collar of his shirt to a dazzling white. Somehow, even in this sea of muck, his shoes held a mirror shine. Beside him Scott, even Warfield, looked shabby. Jarret led out Darley and gave the rope to his father as he stripped the blanket. The horse shook himself, a ripple of muscle in a sheath of satin. Scott gave a low whistle. Warfield beamed, looking from the horse to his trainer. "You've done him proud, Harry," he said. Harry nodded, accepting the compliment. Darley lifted his delicate muzzle, his broad nostrils scenting the air, puzzling the meaning of the unfamiliar crowd smells and noises. He moved sideways toward Jarret, who lay a reassuring hand on his withers. Porters, dressed in the blue-and-white Warfield silks, shivered with cold and nerves. Jarret stripped his own oilskin and put it around the boy's narrow shoulders. It fell past his ankles, engulfing him. Colts were obliged to carry 86 pounds in the Phoenix, and Porters weighed in at 90. But that was of little concern, given the times Darley had been making under Jarret's 125-pound weight.

They all stood in suspended time, waiting for the call to the post, staying dry and under cover till the last possible moment. When the call came, Jarret held Darley's head in his two hands. They stood so for a moment, the horse and the boy locked in a silent exchange. Then Jarret mounted Timon and brought him up alongside Darley. Harry threw John Porters up into the saddle and calmly wished him a good ride.

Jarret reached across to hold Darley's bridle as the two horses moved in tandem through the rain, which had become wind driven. It was hard going, getting through the undisciplined crowd. A whip-wielding steward walked ahead of them, beating back the mass of people as best he could. Jarret was relieved when they reached the track at last and could stand in their stirrups for the canter out to the starting line.

The dozen young horses plunged and fretted, twisting and sidestepping in a vain effort to take the windborne rain on their flanks and not full in the face. Jarret had to raise his voice to be heard in the commotion. "You got him, John?" he said. The boy, silks already soaked through and clinging to his narrow chest, bridged his reins, his ungloved knuckles white with tension. When he nodded, Jarret let go and backed Timon well clear of the starting area.

A liveried drummer boy stood atop a platform, waiting for the steward's signal to tap the start. The steward stood with his arm raised, ready to give the wave as soon as the jockeys pulled their mounts into a momentary alignment under the starting wire. Just as it seemed that the horses were coming into line, the wind changed direction. A sharp gust hit from behind. Darley lifted his feathery tail high in the air like his Arabian namesake and thrust forward. The colt to his left, the favorite, Garrett Davis, and the filly Madonna to his right, jumped out to follow—a churning trio of energy plunging prematurely down the muddy track.

"Pull up! Pull up!" Jarret cried. It was futile: the crowd groaned and the wind roared, drowning out his urging. The three breakaways plummeted on. Jarret slumped forward against Timon's neck and buried his face in the wet mane. All the work, all the preparation, and the race lost before it had even started. He forced himself to look up as the jockey on Madonna, and then the boy on Garrett Davis, managed to slow and turn their mounts, but Porters could do nothing with Darley. The colt was unstoppable. He plunged on, rounded the homestretch and flew past the start. It was more than two miles before Porters managed to get Darley's head, turn it into his flank, and slow him to a canter.

Jarret, disgusted, slid out of the saddle and handed Timon off to a groom. Garrett Davis's connections were huddling around their horse, worried about his condition, speaking of scratching him. Jarret pushed past them, making his way to the rails, where his father stood, stoic and expressionless. Jarret felt hot tears searing his rain-washed cheeks. "That's done it," he said, his voice breaking. "You gonna have to scratch him now." Harry glanced at him, his face impassive. He gave his head a slight shake. "He just give himself a warm-up, is all. The others still stone cold. Watch now and see something."

When the restive horses came momentarily into an approximate line, the steward's arm dropped and the drummer finally beat out the starting tap. The field leaped forward on the downbeat, a river of color surging through a world of water and flying silt.

Darley stretched out like an elastic thing, easily churning through the mud. He ran as a fox does, long, low, and level. He charged out ahead and stayed there, increasing his lead minute by minute. Porters, his arms already aching from the two-mile battle, perched high on his withers and didn't even try to hold him back. As they came under the wire for the mile mark, there were only three other horses galloping, and none of them close. Darley crossed the finish line alone. The chestnut colt Wild Irishman finished second by several lengths and the bay filly Madonna a distant third. The only other finisher was the chestnut filly Fanny Fern, who came fourth. The rest of the field—eight horses—had labored in the sticky clods and been so distanced that their riders eased them to a walk, hoping to save them for a better showing in the second heat.

Harry Lewis, who had trained many winners but never owned one, confined his visible expression of joy to a slight smile and a nod of thanks to those who crowded to congratulate him. Jarret, however, could not contain his emotion. He was glad that the rain hid the tears. He wept with relief, he wept with joy. He wanted to hug his father, but he knew that Harry's dignity would be offended by any such display. So he made for the paddock to help Porters dismount. The boy was mud from his cap to his gaiters, the colors of the sodden silks unrecognizable. Jarret enfolded the soil-encrusted little figure anyway, waving off the groom whose job it was to walk the hot horse, taking the lead line and saying he would attend to it himself. Darley blew and heaved as they walked, but he cooled out quickly, his eye on Jarret, listening as the youth told him how great he was and how he'd shown them all something, sure enough.

When the time came for the second heat, the rain had let up at last. Porters, in fresh silks, held Darley on a tight rein all the way out to the start line. But this time, the horse seemed disinclined to bolt. He seemed to understand now that he would get his head soon enough. This time, he was willing to wait for the signal.

Without the driving rain in their faces, the horses were easier to muster. They took off cleanly. It was barely a race. Darley streaked out to a lead and held it all the way unchallenged. Only two other horses even made it over the distance flag.

Jarret and Harry led the horse into the winner's circle for the garlands and the presentation of the silver plate, which of course was handed to Dr. Warfield as the putative owner. All Harry could receive, in public, was praise, but that was heaped lavishly.

Jarret left his father there, basking in the attention, and led Darley off to cool out. Later, in the stall, he scraped the mud off as the horse finally got his postrace rations. Jarret did these familiar chores with a high heart, thinking

of $850. Less the entry fee for the Citizen Stakes, which his father would not
need to split with Dr. Warfield, they would be $750 closer to the price of his
freedom. He was leaning on Darley's stall door, listening to the ravenous
horse munch through his grain, when the painter Scott entered the barn,
escorting a breathless and beaming Mary Barr.

"Wasn't that a race? I don't know when I've been so excited."

"He made a show of some fine horses there," said Scott. "I've seen one or
two of them fairly fly on a faster track."

"It ain't just the track." It was a measure of Jarret's high spirits that he felt
free to offer his opinion. "Darley never even reached for the wins today. He
could go right back on out there now and run both races again and never
feel it."

"You say so? You've no doubt he'll be ready for the Citizen in four days'
time then?"

"No doubt."

"Well then, I'd better see if I can get an advance from Dr. Warfield for my
next commission, so I can lay a wager, and soon: he's going to be the favorite
next time he runs."

"Dr. Warfield told you who he want you to paint?"

"Why yes, of course: he was so pleased with today's win that he wants me
to paint Darley. So it's been a good day for all of us, I'd say."

Jarret wondered why Dr. Warfield would want a portrait of their horse,
but then he surmised the doctor was proud of having bred such a potential
champion. He hoped he would be called on to help Scott. He looked forward
to watching how he would mix the colors to capture Darley's rich bay coat
and its golden highlights. Scott himself was clearly already thinking about it.

"You and your father have really made something of him," he said. "All
horse and no ounce of surplus." He turned then, as Harry entered the stable,
accompanied by Dr. Warfield and a slim, elegant gentleman. Jarret recognized him. It was the man who had acknowledged him politely from the
carriage.

Scott made a bow. "Mr. Ten Broeck, how do you find our Kentucky course?"

"A good deal slower than Metairie, at least today, Mr. Scott." The man spoke like a northerner, an accent similar to Scott's, if a little more clipped and formal.

"Well, we all hear about the scorching times since you took ownership. They say it's the best-kept track in the country these days."

"I thank you, and I have made improvements. But it's not all my doing. Metairie Ridge is the highest ground in our watery city, and therefore has the best drainage. Even so, it is built on a marsh. The undersoil is saturated, so it's always resilient and full of life. My jockeys call it the springboard." His eyes hadn't left the horse.

"You have a special interest in the sons of Boston, I think, Mr. Ten Broeck?" said Scott. Jarret noticed that Scott's usual easy manner had become more formal, mirroring Ten Broeck's. "I admired the portrait of Arrow that Mr. Troye made for you."

"Yes, it is fine work. Arrow is a useful horse. Great shame he was gelded before I purchased him, but they said his temper was as foul as his sire's."

"Not the case with this one," said Dr. Warfield. "He has just the temper you'd wish for—fierce on the track and kind in the barn. Would you care to have the boy lead him out, then you can judge him for yourself?"

"That would be an immense kindness"—he turned to Jarret—"if the young man would not mind."

Jarret wasn't used to this level of courtesy. Dr. Warfield was always civil, but this man's manners made others seem oafish by comparison.

"Very fine," said Ten Broeck, as Jarret led him down the aisle to a patch of brightness. "Unusual, the size of his backbone and shoulder, for a horse his size—what is he—fifteen three?"

"Exactly so. You have a good eye, sir," said Warfield.

"Abundant muscle. Admirable curve to the neck, copious room for the windpipe. Dr. Warfield, I do believe you have here the handsomest horse I ever saw."

A pink tinge colored Dr. Warfield's cheeks. He turned to Harry with a small bow. "My trainer here deserves the credit. It's he"—and then he looked to Jarret—"and his boy here who have brought him to the condition you see today."

"Well, you are a fortunate man on all counts."

A stable boy came in then to say that the carriage was ready to take the Meadows party home.

"Will you dine with us tonight, Mr. Ten Broeck? Captain Viley will be there. I believe you are well acquainted."

"Why, thank you, but I drive my own pair, and I do not know the way."

"I'll send a boy to your lodging to direct you. Or, Jarret, you might go yourself with Mr. Ten Broeck."

Harry cleared his throat. "I was fixing to have Jarret stay here with the horse," he said. "Just to be sure, you know, since the Citizen and all is just four days off . . ."

Dr. Warfield dropped his voice. "Prudent, Harry. But perhaps excessively so. One of the other grooms can remain to keep an eye."

As the gentlemen left, Harry put an arm on Jarret. "You go on with him, like your marse say to do. But I'll stay right here. Not taking chances with our Darley."

Jarret followed Ten Broeck to his carriage and handed him up, then turned to mount the rear quarter. "Come up here," said Ten Broeck, patting a gloved hand to the seat next to him. "You're supposed to be giving me directions, aren't you? I won't be able to hear a word you say if you're jouncing along way back there."

"That ain't allowed."

"I am allowing it. Get up."

Jarret was used to following instructions but schooling his own discomfort about this breach of custom was more than he could manage. He climbed reluctantly up and perched at the very edge of the bench, staring straight ahead. Ten Broeck glanced at him. "One would think these good leather seats were a bed of nettles." To Jarret's further discomfort, as they turned out of the Association gateway Ten Broeck began an interrogation. It started with the details of Darley's training, especially its less conventional aspects. "That may be why the horse is so good tempered," he mused. "Methods like yours might have saved the likes of Arrow from the gelder's knife."

Ten Broeck had taken lodging in the town. They drove there so that he could change into dinner attire. Jarret stood with the horses until Ten Broeck emerged.

The interrogations continued all the way to the Meadows, probing every facet of Dr. Warfield's estate—how many bloodstock, what kind of crops, how much did the town dry goods store contribute, how active was the doctor in the day-to-day concerns? Jarret answered with the facts that were in common knowledge and stayed mum on the rest. The man was, after all, the doctor's guest, and seemingly an important one; he did not wish to appear uncivil. But he saw no need to elaborate on matters that were the doctor's private business. "I must say, for a man of his age, the doctor has a great many interests," Ten Broeck observed. "What is he? Seventy? And still fit as a four-year-old."

Jarret wasn't about to contradict the man. But at the Meadows everyone knew the doctor's frailty and had felt his increasing detachment from the business of the estate. If not for Mrs. Warfield's firm hand, many aspects of the farm and its finances might have suffered from his inattention.

As soon as the carriage slowed to make the turn into the Meadows' drive, Jarret asked to be let down. He didn't want anyone to see him sitting up alongside Ten Broeck. He was tired in the bone, far too fatigued to saddle a horse and ride back to the Association stables, too worn out even to go to the cottage where he would have to talk to Beth. He could use a change of clothes, but that could wait till morning. He still felt shy around Beth when his father was not at home. And he knew she wouldn't be relying on him for word of the day's events; news flowed her way like a stream in spate. Instead, he turned toward the stables, where a pile of sacking in the hayloft would do just fine for the night. Darley was to have a day off the next day, and Scott had proposed using the time to make a start on the painting, so he would need to rise early enough to ready the horse.

Jarret looked back toward the house. It was still daylight, so the candles had not been lit, but he could imagine the bustle in the kitchen for the celebratory dinner.

They could have it, and welcome. All he wanted was his bed.

JESS

It was almost six p.m. when Catherine finished her work and began to pack up her equipment. Jess shook the attic dust out of her hair like a dog. She felt chagrined that this immaculately groomed scientist had been subjected to such miserable working conditions.

"Do you have plans? If not, I could make us dinner—my place is nearby. Nothing fancy, but I have some lamb chops we can throw on the grill—if you eat meat."

Catherine seemed grateful for Jess's offer of a home-cooked meal. Because of her heavy cases, Jess called a Lyft for her before heading off to retrieve her bike. "I'll probably beat you there, it's no distance. But if not, make sure the driver helps you unload these bags."

The last soccer games were winding up on the Mall. Joggers were out, taking advantage of the cooling evening. As Jess walked down the steps, she felt good about the soft air, her own little act of kindness to a stranger, and the project they would do together.

Then she saw a tall Black man bent over her bike, fiddling with the lock. Her colleagues had warned her against having a fancy bike in DC. She broke into a run.

"Hey!" she called. "What do you—"

Think you're doing? She choked back the accusing words. She didn't want to be *that* woman.

"—know? I have a bike exactly like that."

The man looked up, startled, flicking back a heavy fall of ringlets. "I'm sorry? What did you say?" His accent was English, clipped and exact, like a topiary.

"Um. Coincidence, I guess. I have that exact bike, midnight blue. I had to special order the color. Took weeks."

"Is that so?" He looked down, reaching for the tumblers on the lock.

"I have that exact lock, too."

He stood then—he was very tall—and glared at her, his eyes narrowed.

"Ma'am," he said, pronouncing it in the British fashion: "marm" as in "farm," rather than "mam" as in "ham." "This is not your bike." He glanced down the rack and raised a long-fingered hand, an elegant gesture like a dancer. "I believe you will find it over there."

Jess followed his gaze to an identical Trek CrossRip, also midnight blue, also with dropped handlebars.

She felt the blush nettle its way up her neck, spread its fever stain over her cheeks, and prickle into her hairline. She wanted to disappear into the earth. She looked up, forcing herself to meet his gaze as she stammered her apology. He had a tightness about his mouth. His eyes looked both hurt and angry. She braced for the abuse she deserved.

But then he smiled. A warm smile that reached his eyes—eyes the color and luster of maple syrup. "We both have excellent taste in bikes, clearly. Is that an Aussie accent?"

"Yes," she squeaked.

"Thought so. I lived in Canberra for a few years."

Later, she would remember that first kindness—the disciplined way he'd made the anger leave his face, the swift change of subject. It was so much more than she deserved for what had been no microaggression but blatant racism. Yet he'd let her off the hook. He raised a hand in a dismissive wave, threw a leg over his bike, and cycled away. She watched his retreating figure and felt ashamed.

Pedaling home, Jess mulled the encounter, castigating herself and imagining how it might have gone if she had taken a moment to resist prejudice. Just a moment, and she would have seen her own bike and maybe even made some polite remark about their similarity to that nice man with the beautiful eyes. They may even have got to chatting about life in Canberra. But then, who was she kidding? Why would he give the time of day to a dust-covered woman in a rumpled shirt and a faint reek of the bug room?

Jess got home just ahead of Catherine. She poured them each a generous glass of pinot and then got to work, crushing garlic, bruising rosemary, and dribbling olive oil over the chops while Catherine told engaging stories of a childhood that might've been imagined by James Herriot. Both her parents had been rural vets. In a reverse of stereotype, her mother had been the large animal person—"up to her armpit in cow vaginas, inseminating Herefords, or pulling lambs out of ewes in the middle of the night. Dad did the little fluffy terriers and the geriatric cats. For me, it was always horses. At the stables doing chores before school, back there to ride after—pitch dark, rain—I didn't care. I did everything you could do—eventing, dressage, polo—"

"Polo?" said Jess, arranging the chops on the grill. "I didn't even know women played that."

"Actually, it's one of the few team sports where women compete with men on an entirely level playing field, as it were. I was rubbish at it because I'm a lefty and they require you to play right-handed. Being a good rider only takes you so far. But I still love watching when I get a chance. Wonderful, fast, exciting game. Australians are very good at it. Lots of farmers who happen to have stock horses about the place, I suppose."

"Wouldn't know," said Jess. "I'm not much for sports. It was all anyone really cared about where I grew up, so I rebelled by being completely uninterested. Museums, art galleries, libraries—that was me. I do like horses, though—I mean, to look at. Never been on one."

"That's a shame." Catherine started breaking up the lettuce for the salad, peering in the cupboard for the balsamic and rummaging around in the fridge for the mustard. "Nothing like it really. That moment when you're sending your horse over a high stone wall and you have absolutely no idea what's on the other side—"

"Gah!" Jess interjected. "That sounds terrifying!"

Catherine smiled. "You can make a strong case that every serious equestrian is a little unhinged." She rolled up the cuff of her pants to reveal a strangely shaped shin. "Not very attractive, is it? Plates, screws, a whole hardware store—absolute havoc in a metal detector. After the second surgery, the orthopedist asked me if I'd regret not riding anymore. I looked at her as if *she* were the mad one, told her I'd be back on as soon as the sutures were out."

Jess set the dishes on the table and poured more wine. "Seems like you were destined to be an equine vet."

"Oh yes. Nothing else ever occurred to me. I mean, I'd have been quite happy mucking out stables or giving riding lessons to spoiled children if it had come to that, but I was a swot at school and when I got into Oxford my path was pretty much laid out for me."

Racing was where the money was. "So I went that way, of course. At first it was exciting—the Coolmore boys with their delectable accents, the Maktoums, even the queen—for a country girl, you know, it was suddenly a very big life. Billionaires would send their private jets to fetch me to see to their horses. It was easy to be seduced by it. Easy to talk yourself into doing things that . . ."

She trailed off, put down her fork, and lifted the wineglass. Jess noticed how flushed she was. That delicate skin showed the effects of the pinot, even though they'd only had a glass. Catherine reached for a napkin and mopped at her forehead, dabbed at her eyes.

"Loo?" she asked, standing abruptly and pushing back the chair with a scrape.

She was back in a few minutes, composed. Jess served the salad.

"I'm sorry. It must be the jet lag. I don't usually get so—it's just that think-ing about those years—not good memories. There was so much abuse of the horses, you see. I'm afraid I realized rather too late that I was abetting it. Or rather, I realized quite soon that I was integral to it, but I kept doing it anyway. 'First do no harm' applies to animals as well as people. Or at least that's what I concluded once I stopped being dazzled by all the bright, shiny objects."

"What happened?"

"Nothing unusual. Nothing illegal. Just the business itself—racing horses before they should even be ridden, wrecking their bones before they've fin-ished growing. I mean, back in the days we were talking about earlier—Eclipse, for instance, didn't see a racetrack until he was five. But now we race them at two, and train them hard before that. Pump the poor things full of bute to get them on the track when they're hurt and should be resting. So many trainers asking me to fix the horse up for just one more race. And then, if I did, and the horse managed to run well through all the pain I'd masked with steroids and analgesics, it'd be just one more after that. Finally, that same horse, that beautiful, brave animal that had given its best, would either break down catastrophically and be destroyed, or stop winning and basically be thrown away. They've been taught to go full pelt in one direction, they're sore and they're cross and few of them are suitable to be retrained for any other work. It's just so cruel—and such a wicked, wicked waste." She picked up her glass, drained it. "And all for what? So rich men can wave their dicks at each other?" She thumped the glass back on the tabletop. Her hand fluttered to her hair. "Sorry."

"Don't be," said Jess. "But . . . if you don't mind my asking, what was it that made you stop?"

"A herd of Arabian horses in the Abu Dhabi dunes," she said. She was hired for a year by the elderly Sheik Zayed, who'd led the tribes before the oil wealth, before the region was even known as the Emirates. "He was an old-time desert guy—sinewy and tough as leather, even in his nineties. Nothing like the effete Porsche-driving princelings these days. He was chagrined that all the best Arab bloodstock had gone to Europe in the nineteenth century, so he decided to do something about it. He bought back some of the best mares and stallions. He had a theory that the Arab horse does best in the desert, so he built a magnificent stable and just let them run in the dunes." Her face took on a dreamy look. "The ones he bred there in the desert, their bodies changed—or changed back, I should say. Their chests expanded from the effort of running in the sand, their eyelashes thickened to keep the fine particles out. I'd go into the dunes with my Pashtun grooms to look for the herd and they would come flying to us over the sand. They knew the grooms always had a handful of dates to give them. You'd be surrounded by these exquisite horses who were just allowed to be horses—mentally and physically sound, kind, trusting, playful. They were the best horses I'd ever seen. It was a revelation to me. I knew I'd never go back to the old work after that."

When she returned to England she went into research, determined to influence breeding practices. "It's not much, but it's the one small bit I can do for them, since we're not going to end the racing industry in my lifetime. But it's quite possible to breed for bone structure that makes them less subject to injury, especially if I can definitively show that it collaterally improves performance. So that's why I'm running around measuring old skeletons. That part is really about recovering lost knowledge. These nineteenth-century horses were stronger and healthier, capable of massive endurance as well as thrilling speed. They ran four miles, you know—heats—up to three times in a single day. They were tough. They had to be. Better for the horses, and people loved it. The races were much more fun to watch, many more tactics over a distance like that, and great rivalries. The crowds that used to turn out—crowds they'd dream of at any modern track.

"That's why your horse became such a celebrity. Hundreds of thousands of people followed him. They invented a mass-produced stopwatch because people got so interested in his record-breaking times. They even wrote poems about him. Let me see if I can . . ." She lifted her chin and clasped her hands in front in what Jess recalled as the old-fashioned eisteddfod posture. Catherine cleared her throat and began to declaim:

I've a picture, time-discolored, hanging on my chamber wall,

Taken from an old oil painting that to memory will recall

Years from now the ancient legends of those races run of old,

When the winters were of silver and the summer-times of gold,

'Tis a picture of a stallion, standing where the robins call,

'Neath an ivy vine that clambers o'er a ruined garden wall.

And the tendrils overhanging almost fall upon his back,

And I fancy he is listening for the music of the track.

Catherine unclasped her hands and reached for the wine. "There's a lot more of it, but I can't believe I remembered that much. Why do bad poems stick in the brain better than good ones? You wonder what bit of orgo chemistry you had to push out to let all that doggerel settle in there."

"True that," said Jess, laughing. "My grandmother was always getting me to learn long bush ballads by heart. I can't remember what I read in a memo yesterday, but I can still do 'The Man from Snowy River' all the way through."

"You'll have to recite it for me."

"For that," laughed Jess, "I'd need a fair bit more wine in me."

"Not tonight then," said Catherine. "I've had more than enough."

"Me too." They got up to clear the plates. "It *is* a bit amazing that people were so invested in this horse though," Jess said. "And now he's forgotten. After all those poems, paintings, newspaper articles. I wonder if your poet had an actual painting in mind when he wrote that?"

"I think he might have." Catherine went over to her bag and pulled out the file folder Jess had looked through earlier. "I think—I'm not sure—but it might be this one . . ." She drew out the reproduction. "It's rather good, isn't it? He must have been a very striking horse." She turned the page over. "That's interesting—it says the original of this painting is right here, in your collection—maybe it came to the Smithsonian in the same gift as the skeleton?"

Jess dried her hands on a tea towel and took the page from Catherine. She glanced at the reference numbers on the back of the image.

"No. It's a much later date of acquisition. But I'll look it up, find out where it's stored, and go see it."

"I've always wondered how you get a racehorse to sit for his portrait. Well, not 'sit'—but you know what I mean. They always look so quiet and calm, but it can't be anything like that. Not a racehorse, and especially not a stallion. You can't get them to stand still for a second."

THOMAS J. SCOTT

Association Grounds, Lexington, Kentucky

1853

I couldn't get a thing right this morning. My mind just wasn't on my work. I could barely look at the boy. I couldn't meet his eye.

He didn't seem to notice. Taciturn as ever, his focus was all on the horse.

He'd done his usual job, which is to say, a perfect one. The animal gleamed. He had set up my easel and stretched the linen as I'd shown him. It was all in perfect order when I arrived. The two of them were in the turnout, playing some kind of game. The boy would walk forward a few quick strides and the horse would mimic him. When he stopped, so did the horse. He would give a hand signal, twirling his arm in a circle. The horse would turn on his haunches. Then he'd get the horse to do it all again, just responding to voice commands. I watched this dance until the boy noticed me and went to fetch a lead rope.

As I started to sketch, he held the horse lightly, but there was a connection between them that transcended mere ropes and reins. The youth only had to move a shoulder or tilt his head and the horse moved in harmony with him, as if they were speaking to each other without language. I could tell he loved that colt. It was going to go hard with him, when he found out.

The easier he made it for me to do my work, the less I could accomplish. I couldn't clear my mind of Richard Ten Broeck and Willa Viley and the way they'd wrapped up old Elisha Warfield, right there at his own dining table.

I had been studying Ten Broeck. He's a northerner, as I am, but he's learned to deploy the manners of the south without falling into parody. Too many of us, striving to shed our Yankee reserve, overshoot the mark. Aping the chevaliers, we exaggerate and become, instead, ridiculous Quixotes.

Ten Broeck is a hard man to read. Which is unsurprising. You don't make a fortune at cards by showing your hand. From his reputation, I expected a louche riverboat gambler, but his manner is more in the style of a classics professor than a prince of hazard. They say he was a brilliant student, before the West Point scandal. He's cool, quiet, only medium height, slim, and yet there's an air about him. To say "menacing" would be too extravagant, yet one senses a man to be reckoned with, perhaps even feared.

And he has one thing I'll never have: the polish of privilege. His dress is immaculate but not flamboyant, typical of old money, which is what he comes from, one of the original Dutch families of New York: Revolutionary War staff officers on both sides. He was meant, they say, to follow in the family's distinguished military tradition. I've had two accounts of his West Point discharge, one from an admirer, one from a fellow he'd skinned at cards. The first said an instructor insulted him, and since a cadet couldn't challenge a captain to a duel, young Ten Broeck resigned, challenged him as a civilian, won the duel, and received an apology. The other claimed he assaulted his superior officer and was saved from an ignominious expulsion by the influence of his family. Perhaps that one is the more likely, given the estrangement that followed.

In any case, he left West Point under a cloud, his people cast him out, and he "went down the river," as they say, to make his fortune. Ten years later, he turns up in the Crescent City, a *chevalier d'industrie*, rich enough to buy the best blood horses, and then winning enough with them to buy the very track they raced on. In short, he's a man well used to getting what he wants. Old Warfield was no match for him.

At dinner, he exhibited an effortless charm. Even sour-faced Anne Warfield succumbed to him. And in his presence, her lovely sister Mrs. Clay was able to unveil the playful nature and ready wit that had been suppressed by the tensions during my previous visit. Her firebrand husband wasn't there—banished to the marital home, apparently—which worked on her demeanor most wonderfully. She was like a mare released from a twitch. And the daughter, too, who had been so high strung at that last gathering, was amiable and easy, thanking me most prettily for bringing her to the races. She was looking quite fetching in a coral silk frock that showed off a lithe figure and emphasized the russet lights in her dark hair. Ten Broeck certainly noticed her, engaging her at length as to how he might make his Metairie course more attractive to younger women like herself.

It had been an entirely pleasant evening until the hour came for the ladies to withdraw. The port came in; the Negroes went out. Ten Broeck was sly enough to wait for that, lest the matter be on the tom-toms before we rose from our chairs.

Warfield himself gave Ten Broeck the opening when he asked him about his plans for the Great State Post Stakes to be run at Metairie the following spring. Ten Broeck said he conceived the race as a national test of thoroughbred supremacy; each state invited to enter its best horse at a rich price of five thousand dollars, to make sure only the very top prospects would be included. The winner would collect the monies staked, less a consolation prize of one thousand dollars to any horse not distanced. As well as this rich purse, the winner would also gain the glory of having either bred or trained the foremost four-mile thoroughbred in the land.

I saw Ten Broeck glance toward Viley, who gave an almost imperceptible nod. "The captain and I believe your Darley colt has the speed and bottom to be just that horse," Ten Broeck said. He reached for the decanter and filled Warfield's glass. His own was barely touched.

Warfield nodded, pleased by the compliment. "I thank you both, and I do agree, that was a most promising showing today. We'll see if he sustains such a performance come Friday. I think you are aware he is entered again, in the Citizen Stakes, three-mile heats. I believe he will do just as well over the longer distance." He sipped his port, pensive, no doubt running the race in his mind's eye.

Ten Broeck reached again for the decanter and refilled the doctor's glass, though it wasn't yet half empty. "Willa and I agree. In fact, we are so certain of it we wish to buy the colt from you now, as he stands, and take the risk ourselves."

Warfield smiled. "Gentlemen, I am flattered, but you are not the first to offer. Why, Louis Smith approached me at the track today, while the distanced horses were still laboring upon the track. He wanted me to sell him Darley. He planned to take him off to his stables in Alabama—perhaps indeed with your stakes race in mind. 'Name your price,' he said. I thanked him for the offer, as I thank you. But I told him what I must also tell you; that is, I must refuse."

Willa Viley stood then, and walked to Elisha Warfield, placing a hand kindly on his shoulder. "Friend, consider. We have talked about your health, your age. You yourself have said on many occasions that you feel the need to retrench. Campaigning a young stallion of such potential on a national scale is a younger man's business, surely?"

"Exactly so. That's why I decided to give this colt to my trainer, Harry Lewis, in payment of his wages, the year it was foaled. He suggested the breeding—indeed, argued most tenaciously for it—and I do believe that very able boy of his has the skill, and the hunger, to campaign him successfully."

"Do you so?" said Ten Broeck. "That was a generous gesture, in any case. And an uncommon one."

"Generous? Perhaps. But not entirely without self-interest." Warfield was flushed now, feeling the cumulative effects of the Tokay and the port. This time, he reached for the decanter himself, refilling his own glass.

"How so?" inquired Ten Broeck, leaning back in his chair. "Since you continue to bear the costs of the horse's stabling and feed, I assume. It seems unself-interested to me."

"Ah, but I stake Old Harry half the entry and share half the purse, as happily occurred this day—a most satisfactory arrangement. In short, gentlemen, while I retain an interest in the colt, even if I wished to oblige you and sell you this horse, it is not mine to sell."

Willa Viley lifted his hand from Warfield's shoulder. "I had heard a rumor to that effect, but I did not credit it. My friend, this is a grievous business." He reached into his jacket and drew out a paper. I saw that it was a copy of the bylaws of the Kentucky Association track. "You recognize this document? You must, since you helped write it when we founded the track together as young men. What were we? Still in our twenties, I believe..."

Viley fingered through the pages with an exaggerated flourish until he reached the place where he had inked a mark. He prodded at the lines with his index finger. "And here it is, what we wrote at that time, and what has been held to ever since: 'No negro or mulatto, to make nomination in any stake, to be run over this course.'" He looked up from the paper and slapped the back of his hand against it. "There you have it, words you and I and the others agreed upon. I harbor no animus toward Old Harry. Why, as I think you know, although perhaps not Mr. Scott here"—he glanced at me—"the boy was mine at one time. He was always an able fellow and I was unsurprised when he earned his way out of bondage. But his character is not at issue here.

"Elisha, consider: if in fact he owns that horse, and you conspired with him, then I am sorry to say that you broke the Association rules. The consequences for you, should this become widely known, will be grave opprobrium. Unpleasant, no doubt. Indeed, you may never recover the reputation you hold, as the man we all look to—the arbiter, should a pedigree be in dispute; the authority, if a rule is in need of interpretation. Yet I believe your reputation upon the town is such that you will be absolved in time. The consequences for Old Harry will be far more grave. There's always sentiment against free nig—against his kind. One doesn't wish to stir it up. He might well be warned off the track, which is to say, ruined in his occupation. Or worse. Ruffians who lost money on this race may well decide to go rather far in the matter. And who can say what might become of the old man then? Surely you would not want blood on your hands."

The high color had drained entirely from Warfield's face. The folds of his cheeks hung gray and flaccid. He looked suddenly very old indeed. His hand, clutching the embossed silver knob of his cane, began to tremble.

I saw Ten Broeck's appraising gaze resting on the doctor. "Come now, Willa. Let's have no talk of such sour things." His voice was low and kindly. "We are all friends here, all gentlemen who love the turf and who live, in some measure, to promote its vast pleasures. Perhaps there was some failure of understanding between the doctor and his trainer with regard to the meaning of 'ownership.' Surely the doctor had in mind a leasehold of some kind? An agreement covering the racing properties of the horse, perhaps? Something of that nature, which would not have precluded the Negro's interest in the horse to this point, but equally would not limit the doctor should he wish to change his mind and dispose of the animal otherwise. If that were the case, I would be willing, in partnership with Captain Viley here, to offer twenty-five hundred dollars for the horse, and further, to run him next year in the Post Stakes—not for Louisiana, but as the entry for the great commonwealth of Kentucky. If he wins, we will pay you a further twenty-five hundred dollars. You would retain all the credit for his breeding and starting. Perhaps the doctor will think upon the matter and give us his answer tomorrow. And I'm sure it is time we rejoined the ladies?"

I for one was glad to extract myself, so I rose at once and turned toward the parlor. As I did, I saw a glimpse of coral silk—the girl, Mary Barr, stepping quickly across the hallway.

WARFIELD'S JARRET

Association Grounds, Lexington, Kentucky

1853

J arret had just scooped Darley's morning grain when he turned to find Mary Barr standing in the doorway, her riding habit spattered with mud.

"Early for your ride, Miss Clay?"

"I came to find you. I tried last night—I thought you were at the Meadows—I went to your father's cottage but Beth said you hadn't come home. I knew you'd be here this morning, with him." She walked forward and stroked Darley's poll. "I came as early as I could. Jarret, you should know: that man Ten Broeck is set to buy Darley. It was all the talk at dinner last night. Captain Viley was dining with us, too, and he plans to go partners with him. The two of them had cooked it up between them, the notion of making an offer for the horse."

Jarret ran a hand over his hair, trying to make sense of the girl's words. "But they can't buy him. My pa's not fixing to sell him."

"That's what I wanted to tell you," she said. "My grandpa told both gentlemen that he'd given the horse to Old Ha—to your father, but Captain Viley had a copy of the laws of the track, the rule that forbids a Negro person from racing his horse here. You know what this place means to my grandfather, and your father could be in even worse trouble if they find him out. Jarret, you have to warn him so that he does nothing rash. He's likely to be quite upset when they bring him this news."

Jarret could hardly hear the girl through the noise in his head. She was right; Harry Lewis might say or do anything if he suddenly learned he was to be plundered in this way.

He muttered thanks to the girl. Even with his thoughts disordered, he knew enough to do that. She needn't have cared enough to warn them. She was still standing by the barn door, her face pinched and anxious, as he ran off to find his father.

As Jarret expected, Harry Lewis was in the backstretch, supervising the morning gallops. His reaction to the news was not the outburst Jarret expected. Only a twitch at the corner of his mouth betrayed that he felt anything at all. He swallowed hard. "Might've knowed it," he said. "Might've knowed they'd come saying that horse too good for the likes of us."

"You—you not fixing to let them take him away from us?"

"What do you think? Horse never was in my name. We got no proof I ever owned him, so we got no choice. We got to stand and watch while the best horse I ever trained just go walking right out my stable."

"You can't," Jarret murmured. He could hardly speak. His throat was tight with anger. The thought of losing Darley—never seeing him, never caring for him, never sitting aside that powerful back and feeling the energy surge through him—it was insupportable. He didn't understand how his father could be so calm in the face of such a loss. "You can't!" This time he shouted.

Harry looked at his son, startled. The mild, quiet lad with the downcast gaze and the easy disposition wasn't recognizable in the blazing eyes and clenched muscles of this tall, lean youth. He took a step toward him, but Jarret stepped back. "Tell me you ain't gonna let this go forward."

"Son, you think I like it? Not one bit. But you tell me: how do we stand against it? Warfield and Viley, they got the town in they pocket. What have I got?"

"You got Darley. And you got me."

"I *don't* got you, boy." Harry reached up and grabbed his son by the shoulders. "Dr. Warfield got you. Could be *you* he's fixing to sell south, stead of the horse, don't you know that? And I'd a had no say in that, neither. The only way that change is by his say-so. That horse wins again, maybe, just maybe, he let me buy you out for the money ought to be come to me. You think he hear anything 'bout that if I make trouble 'bout the horse sale? This point, it gone be a miracle if I even see them winnings."

"He can't take those as well?"

"Son, they take what they want. What kind of boy I raised up who don't know these things? It's on my own head I let you come up so ignorant." He felt the boy flinch under his hands and move away from his touch. They are taking that too, he thought. Stealing his son's love, his own boy's respect.

"Well, now. You gone to go get you self a lesson in how this world really turns. Now you go on and groom that horse, before young Marse Scott get here looking for him to be ready. And you keep your mouth shut and don't go speaking foolishness to that man." His father turned away, unwilling to bear his son's furious gaze. Jarret kicked at the dirt as he strode to the stables. Dar-ley flicked his ears forward and nickered to him as he entered the shed row. Jarret felt the anger go out of him, crushed down by an anvil of sadness. He pushed past the groom who was sweeping the aisle and went into the horse's stall. He lay his head against that powerful neck and wrapped his fingers in the silky mane.

He felt the warmth of the horse's body. He breathed the familiar sour-sweet scent. He didn't try to stanch his tears. If Scott arrived and saw him, so much the worse. He didn't care about Scott, he didn't care about any of them. How could he have thought a single good thing about these men, all of their fine talk and promises. Even his pa. Not a one of them was as good as their word. Jarret wiped his nose on his forearm and reached for the brushes. Not because he cared about getting the horse ready for Scott, but because it was what he loved, and at that moment, the only thing he could think to do to quiet his agitated heart. He leaned into Darley's flank and felt the horse respond with gentle acceptance. Only horses were honest, in the end.

He brushed and buffed the horse and then led him outside to a small corral. The sun had struggled out at last. Jarret faced Darley, as he always did before removing his halter. The horse bowed his head for Jarret to lift the browband and waited, as he'd been schooled, for Jarret's signal. When Jarret clicked his tongue, the horse whinnied in reply, then he wheeled away, bucking his back legs high and shaking out his mane, feeling his physicality after a night in the confines of his box. He galloped twice around the corral clockwise, then turned on his hind end and ran the other way, bucking a few more times to loosen his back, before slowing to a trot and returning to Jarret, dropping his head for a caress. In the sun, his coat gleamed. When a mayfly landed on his haunch, his skin rippled over taut muscle.

Jarret gave him some voice commands, then some hand signals, to engage his mind before the tedious business of standing for the painter.

"He sure is magnificent. I hope I can do him justice." Jarret turned to find Scott draped over the fence rail. He narrowed his eyes. Did Scott know? If the transaction had occurred over dinner, he must. Another betrayal then. Anger burned in him as he went to unload the painter's supplies from his wagon. He had let himself like this man, but he was no different from the rest. As Scott commenced his initial sketches, Jarret tried to clear his mind of anger and grief, reaching for the intense mental connection that would give Darley an alert and handsome pose. He knew what Scott needed; he'd learned a great deal since that first day in the field with Glacier.

Then, the edge of a memory, slight as the brush of an insect's wing: he'd been angry that day too. Angry at Scott's loose and dangerous chatter. *All these fast horses, you and your pa could just mount up and ride off. The river's not that far away, after all.*

Once—and only once, in all the years he'd spent starting green horses—he'd come off a filly that was erratic and excited in the freedom of her first full gallop. She'd spun and bucked, then bucked again before he had time to recenter himself, and Jarret couldn't stay with her. The world tilted and then came up to hit him. He had not expected the earth to be so hard. It was a blow that beat the breath out of him. The force of this memory had the same effect.

Not that far away. How far was "not that far"? He didn't know. Had never thought to ask. There had been whispers in the quarters, of course, of slaves who'd run off, dogs and chains and neck rings, floggings and hacked-off limbs, men sold south along the Natchez trace to die in fever swamps and burning cane fields. It was foolishness to think on such things. He'd known that his whole life.

Not that far. Harry had told so many stories about the journeys of his younger days, campaigning Richard Singleton and Grey Eagle and the other great horses that had belonged to Burbridge and Viley. Jarret tried to recall if he'd said anything about the river. One day's ride? Two? A fit horse like Darley, who could gallop four miles, could surely make a loping pace for twenty, thirty. But he'd need to keep something in reserve, if it came to a chase and slave catchers tried to run them down. If he had to push the horse, he'd need to carry grain, and how could he do that without someone noticing?

Jarret shivered. Darley, sensing his unease, shied sideways. Jarret tried to calm himself. Focus on the horse, stop this foolish run of thinking. There was no profit in such thoughts. Jarret rubbed a hand over his head as if to brush the idea out of his mind. His hand smelled of leather and horse sweat and hay. Darley's scent. Jarret felt tears prickling his eyes.

Scott, agitated himself, was not achieving much on the canvas. He set down his charcoal. "I think perhaps that will do. Thanks, Jarret. I'm just not getting him today. Perhaps we'll try again tomorrow, early, when we're all fresh."

Jarret nodded without making eye contact. "Tomorrow, early. Fo sure."

Jarret helped Scott pack up his materials, carried them to his cart, and then went in search of his father, to tell him he would like to spend the night at the track stables, watching over Darley. Harry nodded a wordless assent. It seemed natural enough to him that Jarret wanted to spend scarce time with the horse. But he wished the boy wouldn't stare at him so.

Jarret studied his father, who suddenly seemed old and stooped. How had he not noticed the softening jowls, the deep lines, the slight tremor in his hand? Jarret gave his father a sudden embrace. "I know you tried your best," he murmured. He let go and turned quickly away.

There was a pot of grits and some corn pone for the stable help. Jarret forced down the largest helping he could. He pocketed some heels of pone for later and busied himself with chores, rolling up Darley's blanket, tending to the racing saddle. Then he went into the stall and lay down on the clean straw, resting his head against the hayrack. Darley nosed the hay, looking for the sweetest stalks. Every so often, he would lay his muzzle for a moment on Jarret's head. Jarret reached up and stroked his neck. He breathed in the scent of hay and horse, trying to quiet his racing mind. Darley, done with eating, dropped his poll and rested his large head against Jarret's shoulder. The weight was a comfort and brought a measure of peace. Jarret slowed his breathing to match the soft flare of the horse's nostrils. He closed his eyes.

When the stall door rattled open, he jumped. Darley shied, hitting the stall divider.

Jarret, angry, exclaimed. "Miss Clay, you know better than to startle—"

But then he took in her appearance: breathless, her cheeks red, hair damp. He stood, brushing the hay and shavings off.

"Miss Clay?"

"I saw your father, Jarret. He looked terrible. He told me you planned on sleeping out here and I came, I rode, I know—" She broke off. "We shouldn't speak here." She inclined her head to the stable door. "Outside."

She turned toward the door. Jarret followed her slight figure up the aisle. A boy was sponging the foam off her mare. The girl herself had sweated right through her jacket.

"You ought not ride so hard through the town, Miss Clay," Jarret observed.

"Don't you tell me what I ought and ought not do," she hissed. "Not when you have it in mind to do something far more reckless." She walked on quickly till they were alone in the tack room. She pulled the door shut and wheeled around. "They *can* kill you; you know that."

"I don't know what you mean."

"Don't," she said. "Don't you dare give me that slack-jaw face. I know you are thinking to ride that horse off tonight."

"No, miss. No such thing."

"Really?" She turned to the saddle rack and laid her hand on Darley's racing saddle. She reached into the pocket that was supposed to contain the lead weights of his handicap. She pulled out a fistful of grain. "You won't make it to the river."

"How far *is* the river?" There, he'd said it.

Mary Barr compressed her lips. "Eighty miles, on the turnpike. But you can't take the pike."

"I can if you write me a pass. Say you is Marse Warfield and I got to take his horse to Cincinnati."

"Jarret—"

"You know it ain't right, Miss Clay. You know this colt was my pa's rightful wages. Just because we went on ahead and made something special of him don't give them the right to just up and take him."

"I know that. But they won't see it that way. They'll see stolen property, a runaway slave. You could die."

"Miss Clay." Jarret dropped his voice. "I might as well be dead, if this"—he lifted both hands, palms upward, in a wide, all-encompassing shrug—"if this is how living gone be."

The afternoon was waning when Jarret led Darley out of the barn, mounted up, and turned toward the track. Mary Barr watched him until they reached the backstretch. Then she ambled over to the gate of the colts' grazing pasture and raised the latch. No one could see the handful of grain she held in her fist, but the colts smelled it. Three of them rushed the gate. Mary Barr pretended to stumble and the gate flew open. She cried out for help, and the grooms came running. In the confusion, with every eye on the loose colts, Jarret asked Darley to jump the rail, and then he asked for a gallop.

He prayed that no one saw them go.

MARY BARR CLAY

Cassius Marcellus Clay House, Lexington, Kentucky

1853

Mary Barr handed her mare to the groom and turned to the rear entrance of the town house. She was sweaty, dusty, and trembling.

"Miss Clay, you ill?" the cook exclaimed. "You do look a fright!"

"I know it, Ester. I'm not ill. It's just—nothing. A little bit ill, perhaps. Can you send some hot water to my room, please? I'm going up to change. I don't want Mama to see me like this."

"No need to worry 'bout that, Miss Clay. Your Mama dining at the Meadows tonight." Ester dropped her voice. "Your Papa in town."

"Here? Now? In the house?" Mary Barr was dismayed. She had hoped to avoid her mother but avoiding her father was a necessity. She could barely keep her composure around him in normal circumstances.

"Ester, please tell him I'm ill and won't be dining down."

"I don't know 'bout that, Miss Clay. He won't like it. He say he expecting you. He asked me to make the pie you like."

"Tell him, nevertheless," she said. "I'll take the back stairs." Ester moved aside to let the girl pass through the narrow doorway that led to the servants' staircase. On the top step, she stopped and removed her riding boots, gliding across the landing in her stocking feet, avoiding the loose board that creaked. In her room, she closed the door behind her and breathed out.

When the knock came a few minutes later, she thought it was Ester with the pitcher of warm water.

"Come," she said.

Cassius Clay opened the door. "They said you were ill—I came to see . . ." His concerned expression changed as he took in Mary Barr's dusty, sweat-stained clothing, her matted hair and high color.

"Great heavens, child. What *have* you been doing?"

"Nothing, Papa. Only riding. I—I took a tumble in the dust is all. I thought you were the maid with water for the basin. I'm really not presentable now. I'm sorry for you to see me in this state." The words tumbled out in a breathy rush. Clay's frown deepened.

"Where were you riding? With whom?"

"I rode alone. Just from the Meadows to the Association track. I wanted to see how the horse was recovering from the race yesterday. It was very exciting, Papa, you should have—"

"You were with that boy again—that son of the trainer?" His tone was jussive. Mary Barr's pulse began to race.

"I wasn't *with* him, that is to say—"

"Mary Barr. Did that boy attempt anything on your person? Did you have to struggle against him? Is that why you look as you do?"

"Of course not! Nothing of that kind. I—"

"You are lying to me. I can see it in your face. You can't even look me in the eye."

He stepped toward her and raised her chin. "Look at me, child."

With immense effort, she drew her eyes up from the floral pattern on the Turkish carpet. But she could not withstand her father's gaze and turned her head away from him.

"I ask you again. Do not try to protect him. What did he do to you?"

She was in tears now. "He did nothing to me. It was I. I did something to him, and now I fear he will likely die of it."

Clay's voice softened. "Tell me."

Mary Barr poured out the story as her father stood saying nothing. He handed her his folded handkerchief.

"You know my views on slavery, I trust. You also know I am in favor of legal and negotiated emancipation, not your abolitionists' underground railroads. But I cannot say you did wrong. Indeed, you acted bravely. But you are right to fear the consequences for that boy. They could be mortal. Getting to the river with your false pass—he may do it. He may even get across. But he won't be safe in Cincinnati, or indeed anywhere in Ohio. And he'll be conspicuous. Every person who sees them will take note of it. Every backwoods oaf who has never seen such a statuesque stallion and never will again; every garrulous townsman—" Clay paced to the window, running a hand through the thick fall of his hair. He stood, eyes unfocused, gazing into the street. Then he turned and nodded decisively.

"Since this is your responsibility, you must help me to rectify it. We shall have to ride out now and see if we can catch up with him ourselves. If I go alone he will flee from me, and on that horse I am entirely certain he would outride me. That will not do. There is nothing else for it. I will need you to ride with me to persuade him that he is safe. It's possible—barely—that if we overtake him swiftly we can cover the whole matter up. But we must go at once. Where are your boots? Get them on."

In the carriage house, Clay cursed when he saw that Stellamaris had already been given her grain. "You can't ride her on a full stomach," he muttered. "You'll have to take Ryolite." Ryolite was a speckled thoroughbred, as tough and fiery as the volcanic stone he was named for. He had been Clay's chief mount till the Mexican War, when he'd been required to buy a cavalry-trained horse named Marquis. As he mounted Marquis, Mary Barr caught sight of a pistol at his waist. Under his coat, she knew that there was, as always, a Bowie knife strapped to his back.

The horse pranced under her slight weight, unwilling at first to yield to her. She shortened the reins and urged him forward, keeping the pressure on until she felt his response. It was twilight as they set out, the last birds caroling a hectic chorus. The heavy rains had left the air rinsed and cool.

When they reached the turnpike, Clay urged Marquis to a canter, and Ryolite followed. They were free of the town within minutes, and in an hour the farms had become widely separated, their rolling meadows giving way to acres of woodland.

The last of the light was draining quickly in the western sky. Clay slowed his horse to a walk and waited for Mary Barr to draw abreast of him. "Since the boy is intelligent, I am assuming he will have stayed off the turnpike while the light lasted, so even though he had almost a full hour's start on us, his going will have been slower. I'd be surprised if he pressed the horse hard. He would keep something in reserve in case of pursuit. I judge that our best chance is to press on, if you feel able, so that we may get ahead of him and intercept him in that way." Mary Barr nodded, but her father noticed her strained expression. "Do not overtax your strength," he said. "If you need to take a rest, we can do so."

"No, Father. As you say, our best chance is to press on."

They rode for another half hour before passing through a small township. Just beyond the outskirts, Clay halted again at a small track leading off through the woods. He slid out of the saddle, then handed Mary Barr down. "Here is where we'll catch him up, I believe," he said. "My best guess is that the boy will have made use of the turnpike once it turned dark. But he will avoid the townships. This track is most likely the one he would use to rejoin the road, since it bypasses the settlement. I say we wait here. We'll know soon enough if we've judged his mind correctly. You will stay by the track in plain sight and call to him. I will take my horse into the woods so as not to alarm him. We'll have to hope he halts for you and that he listens to reason." Clay led his horse into the shadows while Mary Barr sat down on a log, straining her eyes and ears for any sign of movement on the track. The log was damp from the rains and within minutes her riding dress was soaked through. She was cold, exhausted, and scared. Was he worth it, she wondered, this reckless, angry boy? Why could he not just know his place as others seemed to do?

She heard a swoosh of wings: an owl passing, close and silent. Then the cry of a small animal, quickly stifled. The strong and the weak, she thought. Predator, prey. Nature's way. God's way. Even the Bible patriarchs had slaves. Who is Jarret to stand against it in this headstrong fashion, when even his own father, who is most injured in the business, accepts it? Why should she sit and shiver in the dark on his account?

She pulled off her gloves and worried at a broken fingernail. Her father; there was another puzzle. Why had he made it his business to intervene in such a dramatic way? To protect her, she supposed, since she had written the pass and assisted Jarret's escape. Or perhaps he acted out of animus to her grandfather—surely relations had grown strained over the last few years— anyone could see the rift between them widening.

The agitation of these thoughts was the goad that kept her wakeful despite a fatigue that weighed on her limbs. The moon rose, marking the slow course of an hour. Her fretting came to an abrupt halt when she heard hoofbeats on the macadam. Someone was coming, but on the pike, not the track. Two horses, not one, and the squeal of metal carriage wheels. She gathered up the reins and dragged her horse quickly back into the trees. Her father placed a hand on her shoulder. The carriage drew closer. Two grays, their light coats gleaming in the dark. She drew a breath.

"Ten Broeck!" She looked up at her father, her face pale. The carriage slowed. Ten Broeck pulled the horses up to a halt. He must have seen them. Mary Barr felt tears spring to her eyes. They wouldn't save Jarret now, with this man on his trail. And swift as the thought, the sudden realization that it mattered to her a great deal.

But Ten Broeck was not looking in their direction. He shook the reins gently and urged his horses forward at the walk. She heard the scraping of a flint and blinked at a sudden flare of light. Ten Broeck adjusted the wick of his lantern and held it up, inspecting the intersection of the pike and the track.

"Damnation," whispered Clay. "He is thinking the same as I am. He intends to wait for the boy right here." Marquis whinnied, challenging the strange horses. Ten Broeck turned. Clay stepped out of the woods and raised a hand in greeting. "Good evening, sir. We are not yet acquainted, but I believe you know my daughter, Mary Barr." Clay inclined his head, indicating that she should step forward.

"Indeed, Mr. Clay," said Ten Broeck, offering a slight bow. "This is an odd place to make a new acquaintance, but I confess I welcome the opportunity to know you, having heard so much of your courage in the recent war, and in the duello."

"Exaggerations, I am sure of it. Any man would do the same, who values his life, and his honor."

"Perhaps, perhaps not. I should like the leisure to discuss it with you sometime. But this, as you will agree, is not the time, not the place." Ten Broeck lifted his lantern and studied the disheveled, shivering Mary Barr. "Surely, your daughter is not well, sir. One wonders why you might subject her to a night ride in these inclement conditions."

"My daughter, sir, is my own affair." Mary Barr knew that edge in her father's voice. She feared it.

Ten Broeck bowed again. "I do not suggest otherwise. And I am sure your business is pressing. As is my own. Perhaps," and he paused, "our business is the same."

Clay did not reply, but Mary Barr saw his hand drift to the butt of his pistol.

Ten Broeck saw it, too, but he went on in the same low, measured tone. "Perhaps we might profitably join forces and increase our chances of success."

"Even if what you say is true, which I do not grant, I doubt our idea of success would be the same."

"Would it not? Perhaps you misjudge me, and I do not blame you, since we are not acquainted. If I were to say that I hope to spare two young persons the consequences of rash action, perhaps you might soften your view of me. Oh yes. I know quite well why your daughter is here. I learned long ago never to make a substantial investment without taking steps to secure it. I have had eyes on that colt from the moment I decided to buy it. Those eyes saw her forge a pass for the boy and witnessed her aid his escape."

Mary Barr gasped. Her father's grim look hushed her.

"It seems, Mr. Clay, that your daughter takes after you, in conviction and boldness. I have read your newspaper, and I am not out of sympathy with its views. I have not lived so long in the south as to forget the free-labor virtues of the north."

"Then you will let the boy go?"

"I did not say so."

"Then I fear we are at odds after all." Clay eased the pistol half out of the holster. "Please step down."

Ten Broeck didn't move. He spoke even more quietly. "I do not intend, as you say, to 'let him go.' I intend to have him come, with me, to continue to care for and train that horse he loves so much as to risk his life. I will buy him from Warfield."

"But his father plans to buy him," Mary Barr blurted.

"His father can't offer such a sum as I. Neither can he put the boy in the way of such experience as I will provide. At Metairie, he can rise in his craft. If he does so, I will allow him to buy his own freedom in due time. And if Dr. Warfield accepts my offer, as I have no doubt he will, nothing more need be said of this night's foolishness."

"And there will be no consequences for the boy? You must assure me there will be no flogging or the like barbarity."

"I do so assure you. You may also like to know that while I employ the slaves of other men for various tasks, I do not generally own them. I will do so now only for the boy's welfare, as I propose to bring him to Natchez, and they are generally hostile to free Negroes in Mississippi, as I'm sure you are aware. My present plan is to establish the horse for training for some months at the plantation of Colonel Adam Bingaman. You are acquainted, I believe; he was first in his class at Harvard and is in the party of your uncle, indeed, he is one of his chief supporters in the Mississippi legislature. His trainer, John Pryor, is, I think, the finest presently working in that profession. He will take charge of the horse's preparation for the Post Stakes, and the boy will be a valuable assistant to him."

"I believe, I hope, you are a man of your word, Mr. Ten Broeck," said Clay. He let the pistol fall back into its place. "My daughter and I stand ready to assist you."

"Father, I . . ."

"Hush, child. You are too young to remember Delia Webster, perhaps, but the fine citizens of Lexington sent her to rot in prison for helping runaways, and I've no doubt they would do the same to you, to spite me, if given the chance. You have nothing more to say in this business, except the words that will help that foolish boy see his best interest."

"But they stole his horse!"

Clay sighed. "Child. Slaves may not own property, so how in this world could it ever be his horse? Negroes cannot race a horse, so how can his father claim ownership of a horse that just now won an important race? And young women cannot engage in wild escapades without the direst consequences. That is the world as it is. If you do not like it, join me in attempting to change it. Otherwise, keep your peace. Mr. Ten Broeck is being more than reasonable here."

Ten Broeck bowed. "I am glad you see it so."

"I do. And I suggest you leave it to us to deal with the boy. If indeed he comes this way, I believe we may be able to affect the desired result without a chase that would tax your horses. But if the boy sees you, he may . . ."

"I understand. I believe you are correct. I will take leave of you. I will look for the horse in the Association stables in the morning. And Warfield's Jarret with him."

THEO

"Spit."

"Spit?"

"Yes. Great solvent. Ph neutral, slightly viscous, got useful surfactants like citric acid, and it's the right temperature. Whenever I start to clean a painting I always use spit first."

Theo scanned the lab. Millions of dollars of spectroscopes and microscopes, racks of specialized chemical solvents—and yet the conservator who bent over his painting was working with nothing but his own spittle and a cotton swab on a bamboo stick.

Theo had arrived that morning, hailing the Smithsonian employee shuttle at its stop outside the Air and Space Museum. Lior had arranged for the Smithsonian's Conservation Institute to evaluate his artwork while he observed and wrote about it. It was a chance to get some free expertise on his find and make a bit of income at the same time.

Theo got off at the security checkpoint to wait for the conservator, Jeremy Raines. "We have to sign you in, and your artwork as well," Raines explained. "Otherwise they won't let you leave with it." He asked Theo to unwrap the painting, and then he stuck a barcoded label on the back. "Now we can be sure you go out with the same painting you brought in," he said.

"Oh, and you have to sign a couple of waivers—this one says that I'm not liable for any damage to the work during my assessment, and this one that states that I don't take responsibility for any opinion I might offer." Raines smiled. "Not exactly confidence building, eh?" Theo took the papers, bemused. "All a bit much for something I pulled out of a junk pile," he said.

"Well, it's amazing what people have found in junk piles," said Raines. He attached the dingy canvas to an A-frame and put it on a wheeled cart. "We assume it's a masterpiece until we prove otherwise."

After they reached the lab, Raines spent what seemed to Theo an inordinate amount of time just gazing at the little painting. He started at the back, studying the fibers of the canvas and the wood of the stretcher. "The first thing you see is the quality of the linen—it's good, so that tells you the artist was probably a professional. Then you look at the stretcher. Amazing how much that can reveal, if it's the original one, and until pretty recently, nobody bothered to do it. A lot of old stretchers were just stripped off and thrown away. Tons of potential info lost. You can tell a lot about the history of a painting from the kind of wood they used, whether the edges are beveled by hand or by machine, if there are any labels, any accession numbers. Even the kinds of nails or tacks can say something about where the painting might've come from."

Theo scribbled notes as the conservator talked. "This is a very old stretcher. It's white pine, which was a common choice of American artists—they favored conifers. Another thing: there are iron tacks—see the corrosion?—and it's hand chamfered. Both of those things indicate it's probably early or mid-nineteenth century, before manufactured stretchers were in wide use and steel tacks became more common. But it may have been resized at some point, to fit this painting. It looks to me like it was cut and remitered. There are no labels or other markings, so no clues there, except to say that the picture probably just stayed in private hands since it was painted. Oh, hang on." He brought his face closer to the painting, squinting. "Look here"—he pulled down the magnifier—"it's very faint, very worn. In pencil. Right there on the frame edge: 'Lexington.' Probably painted in Kentucky, then."

Now the conservator was working his cotton swab on the lower half of the canvas, slowly removing the layers of dirt. "I'm sure this painting hung over a radiator. The warm air, rising, carried every speck of dust, soot, and smoke right into the fibers of the canvas. That's why the damage is so symmetrical. Previous owner was a smoker, safe to say. You can tell by the particulates coming off here—typical of tar and nicotine."

"Oh yes," said Theo. "He smoked a lot." He pictured the man slumped on his stoop on a Saturday afternoon, listening to the races, flicking butts heedlessly into a gutter that ran to a drain stenciled "Treasure the Chesapeake."

The conservator tossed a grayed cotton swab into the trash can beside him. A couple of dozen more cotton swabs and the full image started to emerge—a bright bay thoroughbred in a grassy meadow. It was painstaking work, and Theo, with nothing new to observe, shifted restlessly. The lab had a window opening onto "the street"—the wide passageway linking labs and pods. Theo watched with bemusement the strange cargoes being wheeled by—a triceratops skull, a lacquered Chinese palanquin.

He jotted down a note on this—might add some color to his article. A rap on the glass interrupted his scribbling. A woman in a white lab coat stood at the window, a frown creasing her forehead.

Raines looked up from his work.

"Come on in, Jess."

"Sorry to interrupt, Jeremy. I was just on my way to the cafeteria, but I couldn't help noticing—that painting you're working on—it's so much like one I was just studying—"

"Painting? That's a bit out of your line, isn't it?" Jeremy turned to Theo and Jess followed his gaze.

Corkscrew curls, amber eyes. Trek CrossRip from Canberra. She felt the blush creep up her neck. She hoped he wouldn't recognize her.

"Jess runs our vertebrate osteology lab," Raines said. "She's our expert in skulls and bones."

"And she has excellent taste in bikes," Theo said.

"And very bad manners," Jess mumbled. Her face was on fire now. She wanted to grab a beaker from Raines's bench and pour cold water over her head.

"You two know each other?"

"Not really," they both replied in unison. There was an awkward pause.

"I had no idea you worked out here," Jess muttered.

"I don't." Theo held up his visitor lanyard.

"Theo is on assignment for *Smithsonian* magazine, doing a piece on the Conservation Institute," Raines said. "He brought in this rather abused old painting and is going to write about how we identify and evaluate it."

"I might be able to help you with that," Jess said. "It's not likely, I know— but it is uncannily similar to paintings of the racehorse whose skeleton I'm working on."

"The skeleton?" Raines interjected. "But this painting is from at least a century and a half ago."

"So is the skeleton. Bit of a long story. But the contemporaneous paintings of it that I'm using for reference have the same color palette as that one does, and those white markings on his nose and forehead are identical. But you'll have to clean more dirt off to see if the legs are the same—my horse had four white feet."

"Well. We'll know soon enough," said Raines, reaching for a fresh cotton swab. "Jess, why don't you show Mr. Northam your lab? If you bring back the reproductions, we can compare them. This bit of the work's not that interesting, and it'll take some time." He turned to Theo. "Grab a coffee if you like—Jess'll show you where. By then we'll be able to see if there are white feet hiding under all this murk."

Theo followed Jess into the street. He dawdled to glance into each lab.

"That's the Anthros," Jess said. "They've got sound recordings of endangered and obsolete languages. And over there's the Paleos—dinosaur fossils, ancient plants. The biorepository has DNA for just about every known species. Lots of stories out here for a journalist."

"Art historian, actually. Or attempting to become one. I've just started work on a PhD. The occasional magazine gig subsidizes my lavish student lifestyle."

Jess waved down the corridor. "Pod three would be closest to your heart then. It's got collections from the Freer, the Sackler—all the Institution's art museums."

They'd reached a security door and Jess swiped her lanyard. Outside, a misty rain had started to fall.

"We'll have to make a run for it," Jess said. "Follow me." Theo watched her ponytail dance across her narrow shoulders as she jogged across the grass. He slowed his runner's stride so as not to overtake her.

"This is vertebrate osteology, where we clean specimens and get them ready for the scientists to work on," she said, punching a number into the security pad. "Want to meet my coworkers?"

She shouldered a heavy, sealed door. "This is officially known as the Environmental Suite, but we just call it the bug room."

Theo stepped inside and was hit by an unlovely stench. He wrinkled his nose.

"Beetle frass—poo, I think, is the less technical term—and decomposing flesh. These guys—dermestids—are totally unwelcome anywhere else on this property. In here, we *want* them to eat things, whereas that's considered suboptimal in museum storage areas."

"That seems a bit—primitive?" Theo said.

Jess shrugged. "Dermestids can do the delicate work of cleaning bones with less damage than any other method we've been able to come up with. Efficient too. They clean about three thousand specimens a year for us—everything from hummingbirds to an elephant that died at the National Zoo. They can clean a mouse in a day; a dolphin might take two or three weeks. Let me get them something they'll like."

She crossed over to the cold store and scanned the desiccating specimens. The Arctic wolf carcass looked ready, so she picked up the tray and carried it back to the bug room. "Watch this," she said, as she set the tray down. Within seconds, the beetles found the carcass and were all over it.

"Rugby team at a buffet table," Theo said. The munching of so many bugs was audible—a soft snap-and-crackle sound.

"Yeah, they're enthusiastic. But that doesn't mean they're not picky. They don't like their meat too fresh—that's why the carcasses have to sit in the cooler for a couple of weeks to dry out. Which doesn't help the smell. But if I leave it too long, let it get too dry, they'll lose interest. Then I've got to smear bacon grease on it to tempt their appetites." She turned to Theo and smiled. "Strange job, no?"

"Definitely unusual," he said. They stepped out of the humid bug room and into the chill of the necropsy lab.

The body of the horse skeleton, on its plinth, was uncrated, ready for Jess to disarticulate. The skull, which had been removed for transport, sat on the lab bench, still carefully wrapped in foam.

"You're looking at the most famous racehorse of the nineteenth century," Jess said.

Jess explained how she would take the skeleton apart so they could scan the bones and make precise models for movement studies. "Then I'll put him back together. Hopefully do a better job of it than the last guy—make it more accurate to the actual anatomy of the horse as he was in life."

"But how can you possibly know how he looked in life? Didn't you say he died a hundred and fifty years ago?"

"That's where the paintings come in. They had to be very accurate because they were used in stock sales and to promote stud services. More like ads than art, apparently. So I'm studying every known painting for any useful anatomical info."

Jess pulled out the folder and fanned out the reproductions on her work bench.

"I see what you mean," said Theo. "It definitely looks like the same horse. A bay with that exact snip and stripe, and Civil War era is about what I'd guessed for the age of the painting."

Jess tapped a finger on one of the images. "The original of this one is right here in DC, at the National Gallery. They're pulling it out of storage for me to look at this Saturday."

"Could I come with you?"

Jess looked up. Was it possible he was hitting on her? She immediately dismissed the idea. No way, after her stupid blunder.

"My thesis—it has to do with elements of nineteenth-century American equestrian art, so I'd be interested. And since you have the access . . ."

"Sure, of course." She scooped up the reproductions and placed them back in the file. "Shall we get that coffee, and then we can show Jeremy these and see what he thinks."

At the café, as the espresso machine hissed, Jess reached across the counter and paid the tab. Theo tried to offer her his share but she waved him off.

"Least I can do—apology for"—she tilted her head in the direction of DC—"before, you know. I was bloody rude." Theo didn't protest. Let her pay a couple of bucks if it made her feel better.

They gravitated to a table by the window.

"What on earth took you to Canberra?" Jess asked.

"You've got a good memory."

"Well, they say trauma etches the neurons, and I was traumatized by my appalling behavior."

Typical, Theo thought. He'd been accused, yet she was traumatized.

"So: Why Canberra?"

Theo unspooled a brief account of his parents. "My first real memories are from there. Good memories. I loved the place."

"Did you? I always thought of Canberra as a bit too planned and manicured, like DC. Prefer the convict-built chaos of Sydney, myself."

"If you like chaos, you'd love Lagos. I used to go there on school break, when my grandmother was still alive. My mother's there, now she's retired from the foreign service, but it's been a while since I've been back. Exhausting place. Canberra was much more my speed. We had a huge backyard with a giant eucalyptus you could climb, and every afternoon it'd be full of cockatoos—I don't need to tell you what it's like. Paradise for a kid."

"Yeah. It's easy to miss it. My parents moved from Sydney to Tasmania after my dad retired. Lovely little seaside town called Cygnet. He was a mechanic—kept the public buses running. After years of commuting to a grimy city garage, he's in heaven. He helps out on the neighbors' farms whenever they need equipment mended, and my mum's become a full-time environmental warrior. She even got herself arrested, protesting logging in the old-growth forests. It was quite a thing, this silver-haired seventy-year-old being carted off to the slammer. Made all the newspapers. The logging companies hate her. Anyway, I get back there every Christmas. We sit by the sea and drink white wine in the sun, and I wonder what the hell I'm doing living anywhere else."

"Why stay then? Did you marry—what do Aussies say—a Septic?"

Jess hadn't heard that old-fashioned bit of rhyming slang in years. "No, I didn't marry a Yank." She raised her bare left hand and wiggled her fingers. "Not married at all." Why was she in such a rush to tell him that?

Theo noted her explicitness. Was she hitting on him? He sat back and regarded her.

Face devoid of makeup, a light dusting of freckles across the bridge of her nose. A delicate bone structure, angular, almost feline. Short, unpolished nails. Hair the color of caramel swirls, with rich dark strands and brighter blond filaments, pulled back in a no-nonsense scrunchie. Theo thought of Abiona's elaborate braids—how she'd travel to Peckham once a month to the only stylist who could do them to her satisfaction. He recalled her sacrosanct weekly manicure appointments and the way she didn't want anyone, even him, to see her without makeup. He imagined her disdain for this woman's unkempt, unselfconscious beauty; her green-eyed, saltwater freshness. Then he realized he was staring and looked away, out the window, where the high masses of the pods extended over acres of ground.

"I suppose I stay because I love the work, and there aren't any labs back home—or anywhere, really—like the one I run here."

"Our tax dollars at work. For something worthwhile, for once," said Theo. "All these different labs; 'all trades, their gear and tackle and trim.'"

"That's Hopkins," said Jess. "He's one of my favorites. My mum's always quoting him: 'Wildness and wet . . . let them be left . . .'"

"'Long live the weeds and the wilderness yet.'"

They finished the line together, then grinned with embarrassment as the barista glanced over at them.

Theo checked his watch. "I better get back. I'm supposed to be rigorously observing . . ."

They bused their cups and Jess led the way back to Jeremy Raines's lab. Raines stood aside proudly to exhibit his progress. The bottom half of the picture had emerged, the four white feet now gleaming.

"It's a charming work. And I can confirm your guesses: nineteenth century, and a professional artist."

"How do you know?"

"Apart from the quality of the brushwork and so on? There's a signature. I checked the database. The artist wasn't first tier, but quite well regarded."

"I can't see a signature," Theo said.

"Well, it'll be a lot clearer when the cleaning is completed. There's a good deal more to do yet. But you can't see it because you're looking in the wrong place."

Jeremy Raines adjusted the light and pulled down the mounted magnifying glass. "Most artists sign in the right-hand corner, but here it's to the left—you see, here?" He pointed to some flecks of paint that Theo had mistaken for blades of grass. "It's an *S* right there—see the curly serifs? When we clean further the rest of the signature will be revealed, but the *S* and the *T* at the end—see there? That was enough for the database to come up with the name Thomas J. Scott."

"Scott? That *is* the name of one of the artists who painted the racehorse I'm working on. So it probably is the same horse. Quite a coincidence."

"Not as big as you'd think," Jeremy said. "Equestrian portrait art of that era was a highly specialized field and only flourished briefly—after the Civil War, photography quickly supplanted it. There were few painters of note. Troye, of course, was the master. According to the database, Scott was his student. It was a small world they moved in—wealthy turf enthusiasts, one recommending his painter to the other." Jeremy stood and stretched his back. He turned to Theo. "There's not a lot else regarding Scott, I'm afraid. Hasn't been much scholarship on him."

Theo beamed. Just what an aspiring historian casting about for a PhD thesis wanted to hear. If, like Troye, he'd painted the Black horsemen as well—

"So, now we've confirmed the artist," said Raines, "and we also have the location written on the frame—Lexington—"

"No," Jess interrupted. "Not the location. The horse. The horse was named after the city.

"The name of the horse in this painting is Lexington."

TEN BROECK'S JARRET

Fashion, *Mississippi River*

1853

Richard Ten Broeck stood at the railing of the upper deck of the steamboat *Fashion*, gazing down at the stock pens two decks below. The boy was about something with the horse, he couldn't tell what. Not grooming; the beast was gleaming. Whatever it was, the horse stood for it quietly, unperturbed by the thump of the engine or the swish of the paddle wheel, the braying of cattle or the noisome scent of the pigs. The other two horses on the boat had been driven wild by the pigs—stamping and spinning in their confinement, rolling their eyes, and foaming with sweat. On boarding, Jarret had walked the horse right up to the pigpens and let him watch and smell them until his ears flicked forward and his poll dropped. Then he led him to his stall without a fuss. Ten Broeck noted that the boy had also, without anyone's by-your-leave, swept out the moldy straw provided by the boatmen and tossed it overboard, laying down one of the several bags of fresh wood shavings he'd set onto the luggage cart before they departed the Meadows two weeks earlier. The boy had declined the bunk Ten Broeck had secured for him and slept in the pen with the horse. Ten Broeck had remonstrated with him, but the boy was unexpectedly obdurate: "Darley don't know about being on a boat," he said. "He do know he's safe with me."

Ten Broeck took satisfaction from these several things. It seemed he'd judged right with the boy. He'd overpaid, of course, to outbid the father. It had been a risk. He liked a risk better than most men, but he liked it all the more when it paid off. He flexed his shoulders and ran a hand inside his collar. The steamboat's laundress had used too much starch on his shirts. Still, his stateroom was large and comfortable, and it was good to be back on the river, especially since he traveled now without the goad of necessity in his flanks. When he looked in on the card tables, he remembered how it had been: the watchful waiting for an advantage, the brinkmanship, the nerves, the strain of staying alert late into the night as an opponent grew fatigued or drowned their judgment in drink. He'd traveled a river of risk in those years, and though the Blind Goddess had smiled on him, he was glad to be her suitor no longer.

A risk like this boy was another thing. Like picking a good horse. He felt he'd assessed both very well. The journey to Kentucky had been most worthwhile. But he was pleased to be nearing home. For one thing, he would be able to get his French linens laundered properly. The collar scraped his neck, which bristled with errant hairs. He needed a shave and a haircut. He would attend to that in Natchez.

He had not inquired as to what took place in the woods the night Clay and his daughter intercepted Jarret. He was satisfied to see the horse and the boy at the Association grounds the morning following, working through the usual training regime. He was unsurprised. Clay was a forceful man and the boy seemed bright. The hours alone, riding the horse through the woods, had no doubt acquainted him with fear and given him time enough to imagine all manner of adverse outcomes to his rash act.

Three days later, the horse had won again, in a field much reduced by the rumor of his invincibility. The Friday morning of the Citizen Stakes had dawned clear and rainless. Ten entries had scratched. Might as well have scratched the other six, Ten Broeck thought with a smile. Only Midway, a chestnut filly, and the colt Garrett Davis had even made a race of it, the other four horses distanced and disqualified. Darley once again demonstrated his long, elastic stride and won effortlessly.

Harry Lewis dug his heels in over the matter of the winner's purse. Ten Broeck and Viley had expected to receive half the winnings, but the old man wouldn't have it. "I don't know nothing 'bout no halves," he announced. "Halves was agreed with Dr. Warfield, not with all you all." Viley was inclined to press the point, but Ten Broeck counseled against. "There will be larger purses soon enough. Let the Negro keep his winnings, Willa. You and I both know that he earned them."

But Harry did not keep the money. That night, he had Beth sew the cash into the lining of a yellow brocade vest she had made for Jarret. "That's your freedom money, son. I always meant for it to be so, but now that man gone offered Marse Warfield almost twice as much."

Harry's milky eyes misted. The tremor in his hand was worse. He looked every day of his hard years. "Don't you think I didn't try. I told him he'd not find a better trainer to replace me when I'm gone. But he says he too old for racehorses now and fixing on selling down the stable. 'Harry,' he says, 'you and me done fine all this time, but there won't be work for your boy here. Let him go with this man because he'll put him in the way of a good occupation.' Ten Broeck promised him you will get seen and known by those rich folk he 'sociates with down there. That's what he says, and I couldn't make him see it no other way."

Jarret stood up, laid his hand on his father's shoulder, and said nothing. He walked out into the sweet spring night, down the lane past Blind Jane's loom and Otis's banjar picking. He would miss this place, all its familiar sounds and smells; the people who had seen him grow. And the horses, most of all. He went first to the mare's barn. Since it was a fine night, the door stood open, the low sun throwing a warm band of light down the center aisle. Alice Carneal pinned her ears at him, as usual, while all the other mares reached their rainbow necks over the stall doors, hoping for a caress. He worked his way from stall to stall, talking to each mare in turn.

He was aware of a shadow behind him. The barn boards creaked. He turned, expecting to see the groom coming to do the night check.

"Hallo, Jarret." Mary Barr stood there, already dressed for dinner in a pale organza frock. The white satin slippers on her feet were crusted with a brown rime of barnyard dust.

"Miss Clay, you got no business out here dressed like that. Look at your feet."

"That's exactly what you said to me the night Alice Carneal foaled Darley. Do you remember?"

"Course I do. You got a big old splinter that night, and you'll get a big old talking-to now, when your grandma see the state of you."

"I don't care. Jarret, I had to see you, to say goodbye, and to see if you are all right. You—you don't blame me, do you?"

Jarret dragged a hand across his scalp and looked at the girl. What did they want from him, these people? The girl's face was scrunched up like she had some kind of ague. Anyone think she was the one been sold away from her home and kin.

He shook his head. "No, Miss Clay, I don't blame you."

"Really, Jarret? You mean that?"

"Miss Clay, I don't know if this gone be a good thing or a bad thing, and I'm scared, a little. But I would be more scared if I was still being chased on across that river, or if I was in jail someplace waiting on the hangman. They would have had me for a horse thief, no matter Darley rightly my pa's. You were right and I would be a fool if I hadn't heard the truth of it."

"My father says Mr. Ten Broeck is a man of his word. He promised us he would let you buy your freedom by and by . . ." Her voice trailed off. She was balling a piece of her gown in her fist, twisting it into a tight knot. "Jarret, it's not like being sold south in the usual way—he's a northerner, after all . . ."

Like that mattered, Jarret thought. But all he said was "Miss Clay, you gone tear that dress."

"Damn the dress! Jarret, I . . ."

"Miss Clay cursing. What your mamma say 'bout that?" He smiled then, but the girl was crying. "You stop that now, you hear? Truth is, I 'spect to do well enough with this trainer Mr. Pryor. No one can get Darley to work good as me, you know that. This Pryor ain't no fool—he can't be and rise as high on up as he has—so he gone see that. Natchez is the richest town in the whole country, Marse Ten Broeck say. Might be I can do myself some good there. Now you go on and get yourself up to the house and fix them shoes before someone see you."

Mary Barr ran her thumbs across her cheeks to wipe off the tears. She managed a wan smile. "Mamma says I can go with Grandpa to the Great State Post Stakes, so I will see you there."

"It ain't goodbye, then. You be there and you'll see something, for sure. Darley and me, we plan to win that race."

On the lower deck of the *Fashion*, Jarret glanced up and saw Ten Broeck staring down at him. That man was a puzzle to him. Yet Darley had taken right to him, and that was something to consider. If the horse was calm around the man, Jarret supposed he could be easy as well. The man had been kind enough on the journey, sending good bedding when he'd refused the berth, and extra food when he ate belowdecks with the other manservants who accompanied their masters. As Jarret's fear of the unfamiliar eased, he'd come to enjoy the journey—the river's changing vistas by day; the view, at night, of other steamboats, passing by like cliffs of radiance.

Ten Broeck raised a hand and Jarret nodded up at him. Then he returned to his work. He found the slight hollow around the horse's eye socket and touched his fingers to it, running them lightly and slowly all the way along the groove by the backbone and down his nearside hind leg. When he stood to work on the other side, he was startled to see Ten Broeck suddenly at his side, leaning on the stall rail.

"Whatever it is you're doing, Lexington seems to enjoy it."

"Lexington?" said Jarret.

"Willa Viley and I decided to rename him. He's going to run for the honor of the commonwealth of Kentucky in the Great State Post Stakes next spring. We thought he should have a name that would bring attention to his home-place. One thing I've learned is that racehorse men like their rivalries. Pit one man's hometown against another man's, or his region against another's region, then men become vested, and they invest. In any case, Darley was the name of an English horse: I desire this one to be distinctly American."

"He'll always be Darley to me," said Jarret. "That's the name he got the day he was foaled."

"You call him just what you like, but the world will hear of him as Lexington. And soon enough too." Ten Broeck turned and gazed out on the Mississippi. The river was a mile from bank to bank at that point. "What do you think of the river? Not like the Ohio—no swimming across."

Jarret swallowed. Ten Broeck hadn't said a thing about his attempted escape. He stared out at the wide expanse, brown and gleaming. In places the river bulged in a smooth curve, like the well-formed quarters of a conditioned stallion. Other places, the surface rippled, carved by unseen currents like a well-muscled stifle.

"Well, boy? What do you make of it?"

Jarret looked at his feet as he replied. "Remind me of a big, powerful horse."

Ten Broeck smiled. "So it does. Indeed it does. A lustrous and potent steed that carries us where we wish to go. Are you a poet as well as a groom? Full of surprises, seemingly. In any case, we'll be in Natchez within the hour. We'll put in at the landing, Under-the-Hill, as they call it. Watch how you go there. Entirely too many boatmen with their pockets full of money, which means too many bars, gambling hells, and brothels. They say the only thing cheaper there than the body of a woman is the life of a man. I hope we will not need to linger. We're to be met by Colonel Bingaman's driver, who will bring us to the colonel's town house for the night. I trust he will be prompt. You will stay with Lexington in the carriage house and ride him to Fatherland— that's the Bingaman plantation—come the morning. It's a short distance— not four miles. If we put in on time and the horse seems well set, you may want to take the opportunity to walk about in the town, as you mayn't get back once you're settled out on the plantation."

"I reckon not. I'm not one for towns."

"Well, as you like. I, for one, will be heading to the very fine barbershop of William Johnson for a haircut and a shave and the unvarnished news of Natchez. Interesting man, Johnson. He keeps an ear to the ground for all the pomp and splendid foolishness of this place. A good friend of Bingaman, in fact; which is in itself somewhat remarkable, since Johnson was born a slave. Down here, it isn't done to call a Negro 'gentleman,' but Johnson is one, in every significant way. A businessman successful enough that half the purse-proud Whites of the town are running to him for loans, and his house sits foursquare on State Street amid the dwellings of the gentry. You might profit from meeting such a man, Jarret. He only barbers for White clients, but he will not take exception to my slave's presence."

My slave. Jarret gazed out at the river. It wasn't just Darley who had a new name. *Ten Broeck's Jarret.* That was who he was now. Not Jarret Lewis, a free man like this William Johnson. Had he done right, to turn back that night in the woods, to listen to that girl and all her preachments of the dangers he would face going forward? Perhaps he was like a horse rescued from a barn on fire, who runs back into his burning stall simply because the place is familiar. Two weeks on the river hadn't settled his mind on the matter. And why should Ten Broeck care if he met this man Johnson or not? What profit could an enslaved horseman take from meeting a free man of business in a strange town? The only way to solve that puzzle was to go with him, he supposed. "If Darley is all right, I'll go," he mumbled.

"Very good then. I shall see you at the landing."

Jarret gazed out at the passing landscape. The flats began to rise into towering loess bluffs, and as the boat rounded the final bend, the close-set brick buildings of Natchez came into view. It was late afternoon, and a heavy mist hung over the river. You could hear the port before you could see it: the uncouth cries of the boatmen cursing their laborers, the laughter and yelling from the riverside bars, the grind of hoists and carriage wheels. As the boat glided into port, Jarret could not count the number of craft lined up, jockeying for moorings. Large oceangoing liners full of European cargoes loomed over simple flatboats. There seemed to be hundreds of craft moored in a bobbing, shifting line as their crews flung curses one to the other. On the landing, bales of cotton awaiting export rose like a second cliff face. From shore, fetid scents assailed the nostrils: hemp and pitch, cooking grease and hops, human sweat and animal dung.

Jarret stood by Lexington, who flared his nostrils and flicked his ears as the boat's wooden hull scraped against the dock. Ropes flew from ship to shore and hands deftly secured them to bollards. Lexington's coat twitched with nerves and Jarret felt his own skin crawling. There was entirely too much of everything in this place. The horse sensed his fear and tossed his head. Jarret struggled to master himself, breathing deep despite the stink. He leaned into the horse and spoke to him with a reassurance he did not feel. When the crewman gave the signal, Jarret unlatched the stall and led the horse to the ramp. He put a hoof on the planking and pulled back, not liking the hollow sound. But Jarret urged him forward, slowly, step by tentative step, down the ramp and onto the teeming dock. Ten Broeck was standing beside a tall, richly belaced Black coachman in a showy livery of topcoat and velvet cape. The carriage bore the emblem of the Fatherland plantation. "You may hand walk the horse, it is no very great distance," Ten Broeck instructed. "Follow along beside. Stay close." The coachman handed Ten Broeck up into the carriage and then mounted to the velvet cushion of the box, where he sat erect, stern as an ebony statue, and flicked the horses forward down Silver Street. Jarret looked up at the houses. Young girls, loose haired, half clad, leaned out of the windows, touting for business. He'd never seen women's breasts all but bare—and White women at that. He felt the heat prickle and turned quickly away, studying the ruts of the roadway.

The hill rose steeply in hairpin switchbacks. They left the reek of the mudflats and the port behind them as they climbed. At last the land flattened out into a wide avenue flanked by grand houses with high, dense hedges and greensward gardens. In the street, they passed a pair of finely dressed young gentlemen, who stopped and exclaimed at Lexington. "That's a magnificent

horse indeed!" called one, pointing his walking cane. "Surely we haven't had
the pleasure of seeing this one in Natchez? I would have remembered him. Is
it Bingaman's newest fancy nag?"

"No, gentlemen," Ten Broeck called down. "I am the happy owner of this
beast. The colonel's Mr. Pryor is to train him for me here. But I am afraid
you will be obliged to travel to Metairie for the pleasure of seeing him run.
It will be worth the trip, I assure you. This horse is Lexington. Remember the name. He'll be running for Kentucky in the Great State Post Stakes
next spring. You should back him!" The young men laughed. The coachman
clucked the horses onward.

They turned into a shaded drive that led to a brick mansion conspicuous
for the immensity of the fluted columns that flanked the doorway. Jarret and
Lexington followed behind the coach as a brace of liveried slaves hastened
to carry Ten Broeck's bags and usher him toward the entrance. Ten Broeck
turned to Jarret. "They will show you to the carriage house. I will send for
you soon."

The carriage house stalls were of lacquered wood, the aisle scrubbed
spotless. Lexington's nostrils flared, taking in unfamiliar scents of wax and
brass polish. Jarret could see his own reflection in the burnished metal of the
water trough. He plunged a hand into the brimming hayrack and breathed
the scent of alfalfa and timothy. "We come to a fancy place," he whispered.
The horse nickered back, nudging him away from the tempting feed. Jarret
unwrapped the cloths from Lexington's legs and felt for heat, as he had done
through the journey. There was none. The horse was a good traveler. When
a boy brought the carriage horses in, Lexington called a greeting. Then he
nosed the hay and began to eat. All that was left for Jarret to do was to hang
Lexington's bridle on the brass hook by the stall door.

Ten Broeck called for him soon after. "We must go or Johnson's establishment will be closed for the evening. Your clothes," he said, fingering
Jarret's linen shirt. "Good quality, well made, but you'll need something
more in the current style. Also some in a lighter weight for New Orleans.
It can get surpassing hot there. You'll see. I shall ask Johnson to recommend

a tailor who can take your measure today and send the garments out to Fatherland."

Johnson's barbershop was large and well appointed, with leather chairs and porcelain fittings. Staff in crisp white aprons lathered, shaved, and tonsured their clients. Johnson himself sat at a finely carved desk by the door, a large crystal pen-and-ink set before him, and a leather journal open to a page almost entirely filled with script in an elegant hand.

"I've come at a busy hour," said Ten Broeck. "I see you hardly have an empty chair, and no barber free."

"That's the case at any hour, these days," said Johnson. "Happily, this town does not get poorer. And I shall be glad to attend to you myself."

Ten Broeck bowed. "I'm honored." Jarret wondered if he would ever become accustomed to the man's extravagant manners. Johnson donned a starched apron that bore his initials monogrammed in a gold silk thread.

"I hear you have acquired a fine new horse," Johnson said as he fastened a cape around Ten Broeck's neck and draped his face with steaming cloths.

"News flies to you faster than iron filings to a magnet," Ten Broeck said, his voice muffled by the towels.

"It's my currency," Johnson replied. "Clients desire it, perhaps, even more than my deft blades."

"Indeed. It's your sharp wit that attracts us. My new horse is Lexington, named for his birthplace. He will be the winner of the Great State Post Stakes next year, I assure you. I counsel you: back him early, while you may still get odds."

Johnson smiled. "I'm in debt to you for the advice. I hope I won't be in debt to the bookmaker because of it." Johnson peeled back the cloths and plied a lather-laden brush over Ten Broeck's cheeks.

"And your boy here—he's also new, I think?" Jarret, standing by the door, squirmed under the barber's scrutiny.

"Indeed. That's my Jarret, Lexington's groom. I was hoping you might suggest a tailor? I want to have him measured for some new clothes, suitable for Fatherland and later for Metairie."

"Of course," said Johnson. "Bon is a very able man, skilled with a needle and fair in his prices. His premises are quite close. I will give you his directions. But—you are to send the boy out to Fatherland?"

"Yes, with my horse, tomorrow. He's been with the horse every day since it was foaled, and he is very able, even at his young age. I'm sending him to Pryor in the hopes of forging a trainer out of him."

"Pryor? Does he know?"

"I assume he does. I made the arrangement with Bingaman. You sound surprised?"

"I am surprised. Mr. Pryor is an able trainer, of course. The best, so they say. But he's not known for taking on apprentices."

In the next chair, a large man, his face obscured by lather, guffawed. "He'd rather drink the hemlock than share the credit for a winner. Pryor's a one-man band, always has been. Jealous of the limelight. Why, he'd leave the horses out of it if he could, and just prance round the winner's circle all by hisself."

Ten Broeck's face was obscured by lather, so Jarret couldn't see how he received this information. He had worried about arriving alone at a strange stable on an unfamiliar plantation, but to arrive unwanted—perhaps even unexpected—Jarret felt sweat break out on his skin.

Later, as they walked the short way from Johnson's premises to the tailor's, Ten Broeck turned to him. "Don't be concerned about Pryor. I'll speak to Bingaman when I reach New Orleans."

"The colonel is not here in Natchez?"

"No. Neither here nor at Fatherland. Has not been for some time. You may as well know, since I'm sure the quarters will be full of talk. Bingaman resides in New Orleans. After his wife died, he set up house there with a former slave, a fine woman, I must allow, and one to whom he is most devoted. He has confided that their relationship awoke him to the real nature of union, unlike the humbug of most marriages, which are property transactions dressed up in lace bows. To make his point he has willed his fortune to his children by this woman, which will cause a fine stir one day, though he won't be here to see it. The heart will rule the head, it seems. Brilliant man, first in his class at Harvard. Handsome, a most active intellect, yet he has taken a cannonball and directed it at his own prospects." Ten Broeck walked on.

Jarret's thoughts darted. First the spectacle of Johnson in his fine establishment, now the notion of mulatto bastards inheriting the vast fortune of a White planter—this was a topsy-turvy world. How would he ever find a foothold?

Bon, the tailor, took Jarret's measurements with a brisk efficiency, turning him this way and that, lifting his arms as if he were a mannequin. He proffered various samples of cloth for Ten Broeck's approval, effusively praising his choices. "Very fashionable color this coming season. A nice hand, but a durable weave."

They walked back, silent in the gathering dusk. Violin and piano music drifted from the parlors of the fine homes. Jarret wanted to stop and listen to the singing of the strings, so different from the banjars of the Meadows evenings. But Ten Broeck paced ahead, unmoved. As they approached the iron gates of the Bingaman house, a white-gloved slave drew back the lock and ushered them inside with a low bow.

"Possibly I will not see you in the morning. I depart on the early boat for New Orleans. You may ride out midmorning with the messenger boy. He will show you the way. Your box will go ahead on the supply cart." He peered at Jarret in the dull light of the carriage lamp. "No need to look like that," he said. "Just continue to do your work, keep your attention on the horse, and mind Pryor's instructions. We have almost ten months till the Post Stakes, so there need not be any pressure. Light work, easy gallops. But Pryor will know that, and be sure, he is a gentleman of high character and integrity, and not such a dolt as to mistake your quality."

Jarret felt a little better as he turned toward the carriage house. But then Ten Broeck called sharply, "Jarret. I forgot to say—when you leave the town tomorrow, do not go toward the east. Ask the boy to take you by the south road. It is only a little longer that way." Ten Broeck turned and strode toward the house's pillared entrance. Inside the carriage house, the driver led Jarret to the tureen of soup that had been left for their supper. He offered Jarret a pallet in the room above the stalls, but Jarret declined. Instead, he set the saddle in a corner of the stall, rested his head on it, and fell into a restless sleep beside his horse.

He woke to the sound of grain hitting buckets as the stable boy measured out morning feeds. Somewhere, a rooster greeted the sunrise. "Hot oatcakes and coffee in the house—cook says you better go git some." Jarret supervised the grain ration and then made his way around the back to the pump house where he splashed his face with water before presenting himself at the kitchen door. A girl handed him a mug of coffee and a plate heaped with cakes fresh off the griddle, a generous pat of golden butter melting on top. He sat under a flowering myrtle to enjoy this and was just mopping up the last crumb when a tall youth with skin the color of cider came striding from the main house, a leather pouch slung across his chest. "I'm Ben," he said. "I'm the one gone to ride with you to Fatherland. I just saw your marse's horse. He's a fine one, sure enough." The two walked to the carriage house. Ben's mount, a large bay gelding, had been saddled by a groom and stood pawing the ground, eager to go. Jarret tacked up Lexington and swung into the saddle. He took a moment to enjoy the feeling of being mounted again. It had been two weeks on the river and he'd never gone so long without riding in his life. The horse seemed pleased too. He lifted his head and danced in place. Jarret only had to bring his hands forward on the reins and they stepped out into a showy, pistonlike trot, through the gates and down the wide avenue, turning the heads of everyone they passed. Ben seemed to know every person of color and most of the Whites, nodding to them in acknowledgment.

From the position of the sun, Jarret could tell they were heading south, as Ten Broeck had instructed. He drew abreast of Ben and asked why they weren't taking the more direct eastern road.

"The Forks is that way. We don't never go by that way. Ain't safe. And sure ain't pretty. Thousands poor souls penned up, wailing and a-crying 'bout they family being bust up. Some folk from up by where you from, most likely."

They trotted on a few furlongs. "A few of the hands we got at Fatherland come through there. You can ax them 'bout it if you are fixing to hear a sorry tale. I heard tell from one hand how he got whipped along that way more than a thousand mile." Jarret tried to imagine that journey, thinking of the distance he'd covered in the relative comfort of the steamship.

"One time, I was rubbing down a horse and the new boy helping me suddenly starts up cryin', sayin' it was the exact same thing they done to him at the Forks—stripped and rubbed down, right there in public, like a animal. The way we going, we doan need to see nothing of that kind unpleasantness. And the traders work that place, they might grab a person and sell him and by the time his right marse hear 'bout it you be gone off who knows where and they just say, 'Yo boy run off on you, nowt to do wit me' and the good lord know what happen to you then."

They rode on in silence as the dwellings thinned and the trees drew closer. Jarret's spirits lightened once they entered a stretch of tall sassafras, locust, and oak that shaded and cooled the winding road, painting the way with dapples. Festoons of Spanish moss fell in swags from the oak branches, and where the road narrowed they brushed Jarret's face. The footing was good; soft loess soil. The horse was asking to go, so Jarret let him ease up into a canter and Ben and his mount followed suit. Soon they were galloping. Jarret threw his head back and let out a hoot of sheer pleasure. Ben answered. They galloped for about a mile, slowing when the woods ended abruptly, opening onto a vast expanse of rolling upland cotton and cornfields. They pulled up the horses.

"This is Fatherland," said Ben, leaning forward in the saddle to pat his mount's neck.

"Which part?" said Jarret.

"All of it."

The scale of the place exceeded anything Jarret had ever seen in Kentucky. The cotton plants, already large leafed and lustrous, stood in ranks for what seemed to him like miles. Far off in the distance, men drove teams of mules to clear the weeds between the wide-spaced rows, while workers—men, women, and children in broad palmetto hats—moved through behind them, wielding hoes. Beyond, the sun gleamed on a creek threading between the cotton and the cornfields, which had begun to haze over in green shoots. Where the ground rose from the flats into low hills, Jarret could just make out the rows of a large orchard.

They walked on to the main gate, the reins slack on their horses' necks, as Ben pointed out the different parts of the plantation. Inside the gate, Ben halted his horse and looked off to the right. There, partly screened by a thicket of trees, were the farm buildings and livestock pens. Ben pointed to each building—the gin house, seed store, dairy, smithy, and a clapboard chapel with a cross atop. Beyond were the quarters—a long double row of cabins facing each other with doors opening into a shared laneway and vegetable gardens and chicken pens behind. At the beginning of the lane was a larger brick dwelling set in fenced grounds. "That there's the overseer house."

There was a coppice of ornamental trees—magnolia, cypress, and crape myrtle—screening all this from a white mansion that rose on a hillock at the far end of the drive. "Great big pile of stones like that and no one in it but slaves, since the marse run off to set up house in New Orleans." Ben booted his horse on and turned to the west, following a track that led up over another rise of ground. When they reached the crest, Jarret pulled up, stunned again by the scale of what lay before him. The road wound down to a full-size racetrack with its own small grandstand. Beyond a dense cluster of barns and stables, white-fenced turnouts stretched as far as the eye could see. Horses, their morning work done, grazed on lush pasture. "You see that big barn with the wind vane on top? That's where you need to go. I'll be heading right on over to the big house now, to see if they got any messages need go back to town."

Jarret rode on alone, nervous yet elated. To be a part of such a vast operation would be something. As he reached the main barn, a man came striding toward him. He was a small-built man, not much bigger than a jockey, hair the color of sand, skin pink and freckled from too much sun. He did not take his pale gaze from the horse.

Jarret dismounted. Pryor did not acknowledge him. He walked all around the horse, eyeing the conformation and nodding. When he moved in, the horse shied. As Jarret placed a hand on his neck and murmured a soothing hum, Pryor frowned. He grabbed the reins out of Jarret's hand. The horse reared. Pryor jerked the reins down hard. Trying to escape the pressure, the horse shifted sideways, rolling his eyes and pinning his ears back. Harry had said most trainers were thrashers. Jarret prayed that Pryor wasn't one of them.

Pryor snapped his fingers and a man ran up with a halter. "Henry, put him in the empty stall in the stallion barn." Jarret reached up to unbuckle the throat latch on the bridle, but Pryor swept his hand away.

"My boy will do it. You go on back over to the farm. Ask for Gossin. He'll find some work for you. I already sent the carter with your box on up to the quarters."

Jarret felt the blood drain from his face. He did not move. "But Marse Ten Broeck sent me here to work for you. I'm Darley's groom. I'm supposed—"

Pryor turned, his blue eyes narrowed. "Darley? Who in hell's name is Darley?"

"Lexington, I mean."

"Some groom, who doesn't even give his horse's right name. While it's in my stable, I will say who its groom is. Your work with it is over. Now get on with you."

Henry widened his eyes at Jarret, a look of warning. He reached up to remove the bridle. As he did so, Lexington shied again, tugging the reins from Pryor's hands. Pryor snatched the lead rope from Henry and wielded the end of it like a whip, thwacking Lexington across the shoulder. The stallion spun in a blur of hoof and mane. He was gathering himself to bolt as Jarret jumped in front of him, grabbed the loose reins, and turned his head away from Pryor, speaking soothing words. Pryor did not move, but his lips thinned. He let Jarret secure the halter before he spoke.

"It's clear you've coddled this nag. That ends today. Give the lead rope to

Old Henry and get out of here. I don't want to see you down here again unless I send for you. Do you understand?"

Jarret heard the words but couldn't register them. He put his hand on Lexington's withers and leaned his body against him.

"Do you hear?" Pryor bellowed. "Get out of my yard!"

Henry came up behind Jarret. He grasped the lead rope and leaned in close. "You go on," he whispered. "I'll find you in quarters. Later."

Reluctantly, Jarret backed away. Henry struggled to control the horse, who began to call for Jarret. Pryor moved on him then and shoved him hard.

"Do as I say!" he bellowed. "The damned horse won't settle while you're in his sight." He turned. "Zack! Abe! Where the hell are you?" Two youths ran out of the stable. "Get a rope! Help Old Henry with this damn horse!"

As the headman and the two grooms ducked and grabbed for the halter, Jarret felt his muscles clench. His fists balled. He was taller than Pryor. He imagined the rope in his own hands, lashing the man as he'd lashed the horse. But he knew his own grief and agitation were radiating back to Lexington, adding to his distress.

He moved in and the horse stopped plunging. He clipped the second lead rope to the halter and handed it to one of the grooms. "You'll be all right," he crooned. Then he turned and willed himself to walk calmly away. Only when he was out of Lexington's line of sight did he break into a sprint, desperate to outrun the sounds of the horse's cries.

On the other side of the hill, he stopped and bent over, resting his hands on his knees and gasping for breath. Then he trudged on in the direction of the farm buildings. He was almost to the quarters when he saw Ben, sitting on a stump, a chicken leg in his hand.

"What you back here for?"

"Pryor don't want me. He won't let me stay with my horse. He wants me to see someone named Gossin—"

"That's the White man manage the farm. Makes no sense, trained horseman like you. You ain't no field hand."

"It's not me I care about. It's my horse. He's not used to thrashers. I don't know what to do. My marse meant for me to care for him."

"Too bad you caint write, or you could send him a message. I got letters here for Natchez and New Orleans that I got to mail from the town to Colonel Bingaman and such—" He opened the leather pouch slung over his shoulder and showed Jarret the vellum envelopes within.

The directions inked on the letters jogged a thought loose in his head. He recalled William Johnson and his journal, written closely in his elegant hand.

"You know that barber in Natchez, Mr. Johnson?"

"Sure enough. Everyone know him."

"Ben, could you go by him—seems like he is friendly with my marse and he'll surely know how to get a word to him—can you see if he can write a line to say that they sent me away from Darley, that I ain't allowed to work with him, or even be near him. Do you think he would do that?"

Ben shrugged. "I can ax him."

"I don't know what I'll do if something bad happen to my horse."

"Well it ain't your fault if old man Pryor too swelled headed to take you on. No one gone blame you for it."

"I'm gone blame me," Jarret said, his voice breaking. "That horse about the only one thing I care for."

"All right, I'll go by the barber on my way. I'll tell him you is just wanting your marse to know what's what. No one can make any mind about that. Now you best get along to Gossin. Ax at the quarters, they'll tell you where he's at." He flung his bone away, wiped his chin, and went off to retrieve his mount.

Jarret found Samuel Gossin after a long trudge out to the fields, where he was conferring with one of his drivers as a gang of women and children wielded hoes on a harvested cornfield. As Jarret drew closer, he saw that the picturesque nature of this rich place did not extend to the people who worked it. The women were grim-faced and exhausted, their worn skirts reefed up at the hips, their legs wrapped in rags to protect them from the dry cornstalks. Jarret felt conspicuous in his good clothes. Gossin regarded him with bemusement when he introduced himself. "So Pryor didn't want

Richard Ten Broeck's handpicked Kentucky groom looking over his shoulder?" He chuckled. "Typical. But I don't think Ten Broeck will be too happy with me turning his boy into a field hand." He eyed Jarret's lean, slight build. "You sure don't look like one. Show me your hands." Jarret turned his palms over. Gossin snorted. "Little use to me, a soft stable boy. Try the forge. The smith might be glad of help with the farrier work."

So Jarret went to work for Gem, a stocky, muscular young man, coal black and shiny from sweat. Most of the work at the smithy was maintaining farm tools—wagon wheels, hoes, plows, ginning saws, and metal strapping for the cotton bales. "Pryor got his own farrier for the thoroughbreds, but I do all the farm horses," Gem said. Jarret carried in the charcoal to feed the forge and worked the bellows; he fetched water from the stream to cool the iron, and he filed and finished the hooves after Gem hammered the new shoes in place. Between the roar of the furnace and the ringing of the mallets on iron, there was no space for small talk, and that suited Jarret. Gem was glad of the help; less happy to have to fit another body into his crowded cabin.

That first day, as Gem walked him from the forge to the quarters, Jarret tried to count the people, but he soon lost track. The double row of cabins housed more than two hundred souls, Gem told him. "More folk up in the 'pendencies by the big house and over by the stables where you was s'posed to be." Hands returning from their day's tasks began their second workday, tending their plots of beans and sweet potatoes, making and mending clothes, repairing a fence, slaughtering a fowl for the pot.

Gem lived in single man's quarters with three others; two of them, Cato and Ira, were youths without kinfolk, who hadn't yet received permission to take up with a woman. Cato worked in the gin house and Ira at the mill. The third was Gem's father, Old Gem, a widower with palsied hands and an addled mind. He had been a smith but had grown too frail and forgetful for forge work, so he did light chores in the big house gardens, and no one bothered him too much when he forgot what he was supposed to be at. They shared a small cypress-floored room with cotton-filled hessian shakedowns for bedding. There was barely room for Jarret to set out his bedroll.

Old Gem kept a catfish line in the pond. Jarret helped skin, gut, and fillet the queer-looking fish while Young Gem set a trivet over the hearth and melted some lard in a cast-iron pan. He dipped the fillets in cornmeal and fried them golden. They carried stools outside and sat in the dooryard. Jarret had no appetite, but the fish was good, and he managed to eat his share. He was wiping the grease from his hands when Pryor's headman, Henry, walked up the lane.

"There you are. I said I'd come find you. Now don't you mind how Pryor spoke wit you today. It's just the way he is. Rough edge to his tongue. The minute I see you had a strong connection with that horse I knew Pryor wouldn't abide it. He like to be the only one man a horse look to."

"How's Dar— How's Lexington?"

"Restless," said Henry, scuffing the dirt with his foot. "He ain't settled down. Pacing and weaving in his stall."

Jarret dragged a hand across his head. He needed to be down there in that stall, to reassure the horse that everything would be all right in this strange new place.

"Is he eating?"

"A little grain is all. No hay to speak of."

"If you can heat some water, pour it on the hay, I do that for a special treat sometime. He likes it that way."

Henry nodded. "I can do that."

"What's the morning routine?"

Henry shrugged. "Generally we just turn a new horse out to graze by itself, let him take a look, let the others look at him."

Jarret nodded. That sounded right.

"That a fine horse you got there, any fool can see it, and Pryor ain't a fool. I know he seem harsh, but he ain't so harsh as he seem. And he sure ain't stupid. You think the colonel would trust him with all that"—he waved a hand toward the racing complex—"if the man didn't know his work?"

Jarret nodded, but he didn't feel comforted. He thanked Henry for taking the trouble to find him. He sat and fretted as the light waned, listening to the hectic complaints of the birds as they jostled for roosts and the crescendo of frogs thrumming from the creek. As the dusk gathered, fireflies began to wink on and off, low in the grass at first then slowly ascending. He waited, as he had as a child, till the first ones reached the tree boughs, then he went inside and found his place beside the others, who were settling in to sleep. Cato commenced a wet, hacking cough that seemed to have no end to it. Old Gem sat up on his shakedown, grumbling.

"Now then, Pa, he can't help it," Young Gem remonstrated quietly. "It's the cotton dust, get inside you in the gin house," he whispered to Jarret. "Every soul who works there winds up with the coughing." Cato hacked intermittently throughout the night. Jarret tossed on his thin pallet, just as, over the rise, Darley paced his stall.

He was jolted from fitful sleep by a strident clanging. It was still dark. Beside him, the men turned and groaned. Gem shuffled to the hearth and breathed the coals of the cook fire back to life. The others ladled water from the barrel and splashed their faces. Gem handed Jarret a cup of bitter chicory and a heel of pone. As the first glow kindled the veil of mist in the bottomlands, roosters commenced their loud hosannas. From the corrals, a mule complained in his half bray, half whinny as the driver hitched him to the scraper. A line of brightness lit the horizon as the first work gangs trudged to the fields.

Inside the blackened walls of the smithy, the air reeked of doused coals and iron dust. Jarret was glad to take two buckets and walk down to the brook. An iridescent-headed mallard broke cover and flew off with his mate, quacking indignantly. Jarret let the first bucket down, feeling the pull on his muscles as the water poured in and strained the rope. The grass was lush on these alluvial soils. He picked a few blades and tasted them: soft and fine, different from the sturdy, lime-enriched bluegrass of home.

Home. A place he would never see again. A heaviness settled on him that didn't lift as the long, dull days stretched on, spent in toil that offered neither mental challenge nor reward. Because it had been his whole life, Jarret had

never realized what it meant to be skilled at something that was highly valued. Now, he was merely a pair of hands, the same as any other. He yearned
for Darley—the scent of him, the silky feel of his mane. It was torment to
know he was just over the rise, but out of reach. Whenever he could, he made
his way to the hilltop and gazed down at the pastures to catch a glimpse of
the horse when they let him out to graze. He'd creep as close as he dared and
watch as long as he could before anyone noticed he wasn't at his tasks.

As the spring advanced, the air became dense and wet, like the breath of
a horse after hard exercise. The infirmary saw more souls laid out with the
saddleback fever and other ailments of the hot weather. The cotton blossoms
fell and then the fields began to froth in a white so dazzling that Jarret sometimes had to shade his eyes from the brightness.

The plantation began to gear up for picking, tell-tales set up at the end
of rows, the big wooden balers hauled out, the gin house cleaned ready to
receive the crop. Jarret wondered whether his message to Ten Broeck had
ever reached the barber Johnson, and if it had been passed on. Every day,
he awoke hoping that this would be the day word would come, reversing his
fortunes, bringing him back to the side of his horse.

But no word came, day following day. And as picking began, Jarret was
called to the fields. Everyone, other than the key horsemen and the most
senior housekeepers, was required to set aside usual tasks. Even the youngest were put to work, darting under the plants, gathering the lowest-growing
staple into the foaming clouds bulging from hessian sacks.

Jarret soon missed the dull chores of the smithy. This new labor was
relentless; the pressure from the overseers constant and cruel, pushing exhausted people to work ever faster. Jarret, slow from inexperience, and later
from the ache of strained muscles and the dozens of small, oozing cuts on his
hands, became a particular target. The first time he felt the switch sear his
back, he turned in disbelief and rage. He lunged for the man who had struck
him, but the girl working beside him grasped his arm tight, hissed at him,
and shook her head. "You gone make it worse."

If he did not run to the tell-tale when his sack was full, he would hear the switch crack the air just before the blow landed. By the end of the week, his good shirt hung in shreds and red weals bloomed across his shoulders. From before first light till full dark, the days were a blur of throbbing pain, agonized spirits. He had never known life could be so bitter.

The only respite came on Sunday. He hadn't cared for the obligatory church services at the Meadows, where the Warfields favored a stern Calvinist style of worship. There, Black worshippers were segregated up in the rear gallery, out of sight, and no one was the wiser if you just closed your eyes and drifted off during the service. Usually, Jarret would sit in the hard pew and let his mind run on barn matters.

The Fatherland chapel was a different thing entirely, built for the slaves. Somehow, the exhausted congregation found the strength for singing and witnessing, a joyful noise only briefly interrupted by the White preacher's dull sermon about the duty of obedience and the promise of reward in the next life for the hardships of this one. "This preacher say the exact same thing, just about, every Sabbath," Gem whispered. "When Uncle Jack preach, the way he tell the stories, make it seem like the Bible happened just a week or so since, right here in Mississippi. You could swear he know Abraham and Isaac and all them folk personal."

When Uncle Jack replaced the White preacher the second Sunday of the picking, Jarret understood what Gem meant. He preached out of the book of Job, and all through the following week, words from that lesson rang in Jarret's mind as he toiled. *Why died I not from the womb? Why did I not give up the ghost when I came out of the belly?* It was some comfort to know that another man, in a far-off time and a distant place, had given voice to the same despair. *I will speak in the anguish of my spirit; I will complain in the bitterness of my soul.* And yet that man had endured, according to Jack's account of how the story went. Jarret tried to hold that thought as he suffered.

He conceived, in those hard days, a renewed gratitude toward his father, who had endured hardship to rise to a measure of dignity that had extended its protective cloak over Jarret's childhood. He learned, in those fields, what he had been spared. He felt a new understanding for the folk who bore it, and an admiration for those brave enough to risk everything to run away from such a life. An empathy grew in him. He began to watch people with the sensitive attention he'd only ever accorded his horses. He observed the mother at the end of the day, no matter how tired and broken, still tender to her child; the brothers finding cause to laugh one with the other. The girl, sliding her eyes at a youth, the two of them slipping away in the dark. He would like a girl to look at him with such inviting eyes.

He hadn't had thoughts like that before. Even as his world contracted and pressed in upon him, in equal measure his heart expanded. One day, bending to the picking, he saw a snakeskin, dry and twisted, blown against the stem of the cotton plant. He wondered if the snake had to struggle to shed that constricting encasement and if it suffered before it could break free.

The translucent skin rattled softly in the hot wind. Maybe this season was his shedding. He closed his sore hand around another bole and stuffed it in his sack. He resolved that he would make it so. He would leave the boy behind, discarded in the dust of this damnable field. He didn't know how, but he had to find a way.

He would go on in the world as a man.

JESS

Jess waited for Theo on the terrace of Art and Soul, a restaurant he'd suggested as a place to grab lunch before they went to inspect the horse painting.

She recognized him blocks away by his graceful walk. He had a dog with him—a kelpie, of all breeds. The first one she'd seen since leaving Australia. She felt a pang of longing for her own dog, aging with her parents in Tasmania. She'd never considered having an American dog, because she still saw her Washington life as provisional. Eventually, she'd go home, and she didn't want to subject a dog, maybe old by then, to a long journey and the required quarantine. As Theo drew closer, she could see that he was conducting a one-sided conversation with the canine as they ambled along. She liked people who talked to their dogs.

She realized why Theo had chosen this particular restaurant. Most of the tables on the outdoor terrace were occupied by people with their dogs, and the menu included tasty items for them: frozen beef bone, sliced sirloin.

"Clancy!" said Jess, delighted, when Theo introduced them. "What a perfect name for an Aussie dog. You really are nostalgic for your childhood, aren't you?"

Theo smiled. "Every Saturday I'd watch the kelpies working at the sheep station where I rode horses with my dad. They were amazing dogs, moving a couple of hundred merinos with just the power of their stare. I couldn't get over it. I always wanted to have one of my own one day."

"But they're not common here. Yours is the first one I've seen."

"I know. I found him at the pound in New Haven when I was in college there. They had no idea what he was—had him down as a mixed breed. Who knows how he ended up in the pound, poor guy. But as soon as I got him, he made me into his job. Came with me to all my classes, waited outside the Beinecke, sat on my feet in the lecture halls. He's a very well-educated dog."

"My George did that too," Jess said. She handed Theo her phone. The lock-screen image was of a black mutt with a graying muzzle. "That's George. My parents spoil him rotten. I miss him like mad."

They ordered lunch—shrimp and grits for them, a bone for Clancy. Theo surprised her by ordering wine for both of them.

"I finished that magazine piece," he said, lifting his glass. "I think that's worth a toast."

Jess raised her drink and clinked glasses with Theo.

As he ran an index finger around the rim of his wineglass, Jess imagined the bones: the extended metacarpals and phalanges, the nubbly carpals of the wrist. His fingers were long, tapered. She pictured each bone: proximal, intermediate, distal. A bump on the back of his hand betrayed a poorly healed metacarpal.

"How did you do that?" she asked.

"Do what?"

"Break your hand." She reached across the table and touched her own index finger to the bulge below his knuckle. He made a fist and regarded the protruding bone.

"Oh, that. I was up at Oxford, polo match, came off in the first chukka, torqued my hand when I landed. It didn't seem like a big deal at the time, so I never even got it seen to. It turned purple but no one could see that under the glove, so I just kept playing."

"It must've hurt?"

"Everything hurts, most of the time, when you're playing at that level. You're one big bruise after most matches." He lifted the long ringlets falling beside his ear to expose a scar from a neat row of stitches. "Ball hit me. That's why I wear my hair like this, even though it takes a shelf of product to keep it up. No fade for this vain guy."

"Does everyone in England play polo? I mean, you're the second one I've met this month. The vet I'm working with, she used to play too. But she said she was rubbish at it."

He took a long sip from his wineglass and said nothing.

"I'm betting you weren't. Rubbish. I bet you were bloody good at it."

He scratched his head absently. "Yes, I suppose so."

"Do you still play?"

He looked down. "No."

"Is that why you stopped, the injuries?"

"No one cared about injuries. Not when you're flying down the field, you and the horse—" He was suddenly animated. "You're one being, like a centaur. The best ponies are total athletes. They find the line of the ball without you doing anything. One time I came off—my fault, not the pony's—and she went on, tearing down the field, and blocked my opponent's shot as if I were still riding her."

Jess sat back, regarding him. His expression had a fierce avidity.

"Then why stop, if you loved it so much?"

He glanced away. He could still hear the epithets: Sooty, Spook, Caca. Names tossed off as if they were just a bit of fun. It wasn't enough to be the best player, or the bravest. The price of admission also included not making a fuss. Pretending it didn't hurt, when every insult cut another slice off him.

"Everyone is bullied at boarding school," Abiona had said airily. "Even Prince Charles. It's what they do there. Make you or break you. I know you won't let them break you." After this brush-off from his mother, he was reluctant to mention his unhappiness to his father. But when Barry came to take him to Cornwall for Easter break, he could tell something was wrong. As they walked a rain-lashed beach, he had gently probed Theo for the source of his distress, leaning in against the wind to hear Theo's mumbled answers. Then he had taken him by his shoulders and enfolded him in a long hug. Theo, when he recalled the moment, could still smell the wet oilskin of his father's jacket. "You know there's a silver lining to this," Barry said. "You have to know that bigots are unwittingly handing you an edge. By thinking you're lesser than they are, they underestimate you. Lean on that. Learn to use it, and you'll get the upper hand."

Theo carried those words back to school after that break. He built himself a thick carapace and hid the hurt inside it. He watched for the dismissive remarks, the moments of underestimation, seizing each opportunity to outperform and confound expectation. The day after he'd been told his new handicap was the highest in school history, the team threw a party for him in their dorm. He was still basking in the warm feeling of acceptance the next day, when he found the message *Coon Cunt* scrawled on the inside of his jersey. He looked around the locker room. Any of them could have done it; he'd never know which one.

It was better when he went up to Oxford: he wasn't the only dark-skinned team member there. But then, at an away game, he went to the hospitality tent before he'd changed into his captain's uniform. An official swooped down on him: "Grooms not allowed." The day he heard an opposing coach from a venerable, royal-including team yelling at his players to smash that uppity black-faced fucker, he led his team to a crushing victory in a game so violent that even the umpire was assisted off the pitch with a broken rib. The next day, he resigned.

He didn't feel like going into any of it with Jess.

"I guess I loved it more than it loved me."

It wasn't his job to enlighten White people about their own racism. He'd made light of that bike incident, but it stung. Maybe she'd never used the hard R; maybe she'd even read all the way through a Ta-Nehisi Coates article. But he bet she clutched her purse when a Black guy stepped into an elevator. And if he scraped her social media feed he wondered if he'd find a single selfie with a Black friend.

Their food arrived then: Clancy's in a cute dog bowl with "Bone Appetit" written on the side. Laughing about that, Theo did what he usually did: changed the subject. Then he ordered them both a second glass of wine.

After lunch, they walked along the Mall toward the art museum. Jess noticed once again the graceful way that Theo moved: in her mind's eye she saw the perfect sphere of the femoral head rotating smoothly in the lunate surface of his acetabulum.

"You must have really strong hip flexors," she blurted.

She immediately wished she could have the stupid remark back. What on *earth* was the matter with her?

Theo looked startled. "What?"

"I'm—I—it's—" She was flustered. "You've got immense rotational flexibility—" She was making it worse. "I mean—when you work with bones all the time, you can't help seeing—I'm obsessed with how people are put together." *Stop. Blathering.* She took a deep breath. "Most people, adults, don't have a one-hundred-degree rotation like you've got, unless they started doing something like ballet before puberty."

Theo had a sudden image of his muddy-kneed, Rugby-playing schoolmates in tutus, doing the Dance of the Cygnets. He laughed. "I'm afraid they didn't go in for ballet at the kind of boarding school I went to."

He couldn't decide if his predominant feeling toward this very odd woman was bewilderment or amusement. He certainly hadn't encountered anyone quite like her. But he liked her accent, even when what she was saying was so strange. And Clancy had taken to her. Usually, those avid kelpie eyes never left Theo. But now they studied Jess as the dog weaved around her, nudging her hand for a pat.

Perhaps Clancy also had early memories. Maybe he'd been a puppy in Australia before he wound up lost in New Haven. Maybe Clancy, too, was a sucker for that accent.

TEN BROECK'S JARRET

Fatherland, Natchez, Mississippi

1853

After the last bale was pressed and strapped for shipping, Jarret was glad enough to return to the smithy. He welcomed even those dull tasks. To walk to the stream without the goad of an overseer, to labor at his own pace; these things he had not valued. The rope of the buckets bit into his raw skin. When he reached the stream, he let the cold water run across his damaged hands. Back at the smithy, the torn flesh on his back stung as he lifted each bucket and emptied it into the barrel.

He turned as he heard a horse approaching. Henry, Pryor's headman, riding hard. He pulled his mount to a sliding stop. "You, quick. Get up. Pryor wants you." Henry tossed his head, indicating his horse's rump. Jarret mounted, grabbing the cantle as the horse turned on its hind end and Henry booted it to a gallop.

They pulled up at the stallion barn. "In there." Jarret flung himself from the saddle. He was terrified of what he'd see inside.

"Here!" called Pryor. Jarret ran down the aisle. Lexington was down in his stall, eyes closed. Jarret fell to his knees beside the horse, pressing his ear to the belly. He could feel the heat of a raging fever.

"Damned if Old Henry didn't let the horse get out of his stall in the night—"

"Hush!" Jarret said. Pryor frowned, but held his peace.

"No sounds. He's colicking."

"Course he is—broke into the feed store and ate best part of a bag of corn. This happened before?"

Jarret glared up at Pryor. "We wouldn't have let it happen." Then he saw the basin brimming with blood on the floor by the horse's shoulder.

"What in tarnation you bleed him for? That ain't the cure for a colic."

"I can't get the stupid beast to take the remedy."

"How long?" Jarret barked. "How long you let him be like this?"

"Old Henry found him at sunup."

"Why didn't you come get me right then?" Pryor didn't answer.

Jarret put his hand in the mixture Pryor had prepared and tasted it.

"This ain't right. Should be linseed oil for a start."

"No matter, since the horse won't take it."

"He'll take it for me." Lexington had raised his head and draped it across Jarret's shoulder.

"I need linseed oil—a pint at least, more if you got it. I need laudanum, molasses, saleratus, warm water. A bucketful. Quick!"

Pryor felt the challenge to his authority. His first instinct was to take a crop and beat the daylights out of this arrogant boy. He did a quick calculus. If the horse died, Ten Broeck would know everything. He always did. And that was an enemy Pryor could not afford.

He turned on his heel and left the barn. Jarret did not know what to make of his wordless exit. He knew he had taken a risk. But the horse's welfare mattered more to him than his own. Gently, firmly, he eased Lexington up on unsteady legs. The horse was quivering all over, his strong muscles turned to jelly. But even in his pain, the horse nuzzled at Jarret, his nose pressing into his cheek. "I know. I know," Jarret whispered. "I missed you too." Jarret led him out and walked him slowly along the fence line. The horse dragged on the rope, tossed his head, and pawed at the ground, obviously distressed. But Jarret coaxed and cooed at him, encouraging him, praising his every step.

Before long, Pryor returned from the main house, bearing the supplies Jarret had required. Jarret mixed up the potion, hoping he was remembering the right proportions, as Harry had taught him.

Pryor had his sleeves rolled up, ready to hold the horse as Jarret dosed him. But Jarret waved him away. "You just upset him," he said. He called for Henry to elevate the horse's head as he coaxed the slippery mixture down his throat. The horse eyed him the whole time, terrified yet trusting. When he had managed to get three pints of fluid down, Jarret took the lead rope and urged him to walk again, stopping every so often to check his belly for sounds of gut movements. A tense half hour crawled by. Then the horse stopped, planted his hooves, raised his tail, and let go of a steaming pile of droppings. Jarret whooped with relief.

"All right," Pryor said tightly. "You can go on now."

"Go on?"

"Back to the smithy."

Jarret glared at Pryor. "Nossir."

"What did you say?"

Jarret stepped toward him. "I'll not leave my hor—my marse's horse— again."

"You'll do as I say."

Jarret kept his voice low so that the other grooms could not hear. "If you had of let me stay with him, he never would of been able to get out of his stall and eat hisself almost to death. Just cause he let go a load don't mean he's gonna be right from this. He'll be weak from that fool bleeding. He could have the founder."

Pryor scowled. It was true. It would be weeks before they could be sure the horse hadn't done serious damage. The effects would show first in the slow-growing horn of the hoof. If there was lethal harm done, better to keep the boy handy to shoulder the blame.

"If he founders, it'll be on you. Stay. Play nursemaid. Muck out, carry water. Fewer chores for my own boys to do."

So Jarret fetched his box from Gem's room and set up his bedroll in Lexington's stall. But that night they stayed out in the paddock so Lexington could move at will and ease muscles sore from the cramps. It was a full moon, the fields bathed in a pearly luster, almost as bright as day. Jarret pulled a stable blanket around his shoulders and rested his back against a post. He watched the horse's long shadow dart out in front as he moved across the grass.

At sunrise, he took the horse on a slow amble around the paddock and tried to tempt him with some green blades of fodder. It was a full week before he was feeding well again. Jarret mounted bareback and set out at a walk. With the gentle movement and his familiar rider, the horse gradually eased his sore body into a loose stride. They followed the line of the creek and made a slow way around the perimeter of the fields. When they came by a work gang, some hands looked up and greeted Jarret, calling out compliments about the horse.

Little by little, as the days passed and the horse gained back some weight with no apparent lingering effects of the binge, Jarret felt his own spirit begin to restore itself. Since he had no duties other than the care of the recuperating horse, his days were the easiest he'd ever known. For the first time, he had some hours of his own, with no one telling him how to spend them. This left him time for reflection. As he thought back over the events that had brought him to Fatherland, his mind kept returning to the barber of Natchez, William Johnson, and the unaccustomed sight of a Black man with a crystal inkstand and a fine vellum journal. There was a power in knowing how to read and write, he'd always felt so, despite his father's views.

That evening, he ambled over to Gem's quarters and asked if he knew anyone at Fatherland who had their letters.

Gem regarded him. "You not after running off, I hope. That don't end well round here."

"Nothing like that. I just want to learn is all."

"What for, if you not fixing to write you self a darky pass? Your horse ain't gonna run any faster if you read to him."

"I just got a powerful wish to do it," Jarret said.

"Well, if you set on it, Uncle Jack know to read his Bible. I recall he talked about setting up a Sabbath school some years back. It ain't strictly allowed, folk like us learning they letters, so he say it just gone be a Bible study. But he didn't get no takers that time. Folk just wants to rest come Sunday, or they too busy making they garden or mending they clothes. But I heard tell he teach his own boys." Gem grinned. "And they got to learn, since they don't got no say in it."

Gem directed him to Jack's cabin. A morning glory vine spilled over a narrow front porch that had been added to the plain entryway. Jack's wife, Eveline, sat there, piecing a quilt from old sugar sacks, while her two youngest boys chased each other up and down the rows of beans and tomatoes. When she stood to receive Jarret, the crimson rigolette tied about her hair almost brushed against the porch ceiling. She was a tall, handsome woman, lithe figured even after bearing four sons.

"Come by after the Sunday service," she said. "My Jack will be instructing our boys in the Scriptures that time. You can sit a spell and see if you want to join in with them. We'd be glad to have you. Everyone should be able to read the Lord's book. Then they can know for they self what is in there, and what for sure is not."

On Sunday, when Jarret came by Jack's cabin, the four boys sat crowded together at a plank table, each copying a verse of Scripture onto a piece of slate. The younger boys had verses with simple words, while the two older ones had been tasked with longer, more complicated passages.

Jarret watched for a while as each boy in turn stood and struggled to read back what he had set down, as their father corrected them. When Jack had set each a new passage, he turned his attention to Jarret. "Come on out to the porch, son, and sit down by me while we figure how we gone get on with teaching you."

They sat on the narrow bench. The air was rich with honeysuckle. "I've seen you riding about on that fine horse," he said. He closed his eyes and quoted from memory: "'There is no limit to their treasures; their land is full of horses.' That be Isaiah, two-seven. The Bible has a good many horses in it, but I don't recall any in there look like yours. We got black ones and white ones and dappled ones, but no mention of any got that brass color." He sat thinking for a moment, then opened the worn Bible on his lap and dragged a finger down the text. "I think you gonna like these verses. This here is God, bragging on how he create the horse." He cleared his throat and read aloud in a preacher voice.

> *Who gives the horse its strength*
> *or clothes his mane with thunder?*
> *Who makes him spring like a locust?*
> *His splendid snort is terror.*
> *He churns up the earth, rejoicing in his power,*
> *And charges towards the clash of arms.*
> *He laughs at fear, afraid of nothing;*
> *He does not shy away from the sword.*
> *Over him rattles the quiver, the glittering spear and blade.*
> *In frenzy he devours the ground;*
> *He cannot stand still when the trumpet sounds.*
> *At the blast of the trumpet he snorts, "Hurrah!"*
> *And from afar he scents the fray,*
> *Hears the clamor of the captains, the battle cry.*

When he finished reading, he patted the page. "I think that's mighty fine, don't you?"

Jarret ran the words through in his mind. "Clothes his mane with thunder," he repeated softly. "That's good. It makes you see the power in the neck. And the part about how he devours the ground, rejoicing in his strength. It feels just that way some time. But I don't know about being afraid of nothing. Most horses I know are afraid of plenty."

"Well, the Scripture here is talking about war horses. I guess they's trained to be brave."

"That ain't it. A cavalry horse will charge a cannon because he don't know the cannonball can kill him. All he wants is to stay close to the rest of the herd. Army just learned to use that fear they have, of being left behind."

"Well, boy, you know that this here is the Word of the Lord. We don't got no business doubting what it says here. If the Lord say the horse is brave, he brave."

Jarret wasn't about to argue with a preacher. He held his peace.

"If you want to get on and try to learn your letters, we gone have to go indoors to do it, and you can't be saying nothing around the place about it, you understand?" Jarret nodded and followed Jack inside. Jack then set about showing him how each of the letters on the page had sounds and how when you grouped some of the letters together, those sounds changed in certain ways. Jarret found it confusing, but Jack reassured him. "It gone come clear to you," he said. "You don't eat a whole loaf of cornbread all in just one mouthful. You got to break off and chew it one bite at a time." He gave Jarret a slate and pencil and made a list of simple words that he was to learn. "When you got these into your head, come back and I'll give you more."

Jarret thanked him and was back the next evening for a new list, and the same thing the day after that. Each night, before he left, he asked the preacher to read the lines of the horse Scripture to him again. As he listened, he committed the words to memory.

After a few weeks of rest and easy walks, Jarret judged that Lexington was ready to be ridden out once again. He set off for an extended canter to the boundaries of the estate. When they were far from the work gangs, Jarret began to call out the verses he'd learned, matching his rhythm to the three-beat gait of the horse.

"He churns up the earth," cried Jarret, "rejoicing in his power."

Lexington flicked his ears around, trying to catch the meaning of this new game. Then he gathered his hind end and released into a gallop. The soil fanned up, speckling the air.

"Seem like reading *do* make you go faster," Jarret laughed, lifting his weight up out of the saddle and letting Lexington have his head.

The first use Jarret made of his new letters was a short note addressed to Richard Ten Broeck. He went to Jack, to ask if he had some paper to spare.

Jack looked at him quizzically. "You sure you want your marse to know you writing? Most of them take a vast exception." Jarret hadn't thought about it. It didn't seem to him the kind of thing Ten Broeck would care about. So Jack found him a scrap of paper from an old receipt book and showed him how to pencil out each word.

I am back with Lexington. All well out here. Jarret

He gave the note to a carter who was heading into Natchez with a load of cypress for the mill and asked him to give it to the barber to forward on to New Orleans.

He was surprised, when the carter returned, to be handed a letter addressed to himself. He could not make out the flowing script, but Jack read it to him:

"'I will be sure your master gets your favor of the 4th inst'—he mean there your note—'favor' is a fancy way to say that—and 'instant' mean the date of the month. 'Mr. Ten Broeck will be glad, I am sure, of your news. I am, &c,

Wm Johnson, Natchez.'"

Jarret took the note back and gazed at the handsome blue script. What a thing it was, to be able to send and receive a letter from a person. He thought it must be worth some struggle to master this skill. He applied himself even more intently to his word lists. Soon enough, Jack said he was to join the Sunday class, "since you getting on now just about as well as my youngest."

Every day, Jarret checked Lexington's hooves for any rippling in the new-grown horn that would signal founder, and every day he was relieved when none became evident. He did not press the horse but kept to a routine of light work in the early morning. Later, they would find a place by the creek or in a coppice and Jarret would let Lexington graze in the shade while he studied his letters and scraped words on his slate. They would head back to the stables in the late afternoon, their shadow long in front of them as the egg-yolk sun at their back dropped into the hazy horizon. As fall advanced, the air lost its furry breath and freshened. Jarret wondered how long they would have before Pryor put an end to this idyll and deemed the horse fit enough to train.

Until then, Jarret avoided the kind of endurance work that would come with racing preparation. Instead, he devised playful pursuits that allowed the horse to use his mind. In the round pen, with the horse at liberty, he perfected voice commands, asking Lexington to perform a leg yield or a turn on the haunches. The horse enjoyed these sessions and was quick to divine what Jarret wanted. When he did the right thing and received praise, he would curve his neck and look down his long nose at Jarret, as if to say, "Of course I can do it. What's next?"

Jarret soon could get the horse to rear simply by saying, "Up!" or raising his palm. He set about teaching him to drop to his knees when he said, "Kneel!" Jarret then mounted him bareback. He had just asked the horse to "rise!" when, from behind him, a voice called angrily: "Is that a racehorse or a circus pony?"

Lexington shied at the unfriendly shout and spun, ears pinned, to face Pryor. Jarret moved fluidly with his horse. He felt a flare of anger—you don't come up behind a horse and yell like that, as any horseman should know. But he quickly suppressed the feeling so as not to alarm the horse further. He rubbed Lexington's neck reassuringly and said nothing.

Pryor held a letter crumpled in his hand. "Ten Broeck has sent for you. You're to go right away to New Orleans on tomorrow's night boat. Pack your things. They'll be sent on."

Jarret looked down at him, stunned. How could he leave Lexington?

"But . . . how . . . why . . ."

"Here's your darky pass," he said, throwing a paper onto the ground. "And here's the money he advanced you for the journey. I never took that man for feckless, but I guess I was mistaken. He's agreed to run the nag in a grudge match December second. Good luck getting it in shape—a horse coming off a colic who hasn't been trained, against a filly a full year older who has raced all season. He's a fool."

Jarret dismounted and snatched up the dusty paper and the bills before they could blow away. He stared at the pass. He could just make out his own name and the name "Lexington," but nothing else. He felt his heart unclench. They would go together. They would leave this place.

"But . . . I don't know the way . . ."

Pryor's back was already turned. Jarret unlatched the gate, remounted the horse, and rode to find Jack. He was overhauling the balers, oiling the pressing screws. Jarret showed him the pass. "You're to go on the boat from Under-the-Hill tomorrow. Just go back on the same road you come here on. It don't take too long to get down the river. Your marse say here he gone send someone name of—well, I can't make out the name—J-A-C-Q-U-E-S— Jake-kweez—however you say that—to meet you at the dock and bring you on out to someplace call Metairie." Jack looked up from the note. "We sure will miss you. My wife and my boys are fond of you, and I'm proud of all you learned in so little time." Jack leaned down and rummaged in the tied cloth bundle that contained his lunch fixings and his tin water cup. He pulled out the worn Bible. "You take this, and you keep on striving to learn how to read what's in it, you hear?"

"But I can't take this . . ."

"The White preacher got plenty. He gone get me another one. You take it, son. You gonna need it in New Orleans, fo sure. That is a *sinful* town. A regular Babylon, what I heard tell."

The next day, as Jarret rode out of the gate, he turned in the saddle and looked back at the plantation. He felt regret that Pryor hadn't proved to be a different kind of man. He sensed he and the horse could have accomplished a great deal if things had gone differently. Still, he wasn't sorry to have seen what he'd seen, and learned what he'd learned. Not just the book learning. He felt larger in spirit. There was a space in his soul for the suffering of people. He resolved to take account of their lives, the heavy burdens they carried.

He allowed the horse to pick up a gentle canter on the narrow way back to Natchez. He puzzled on whether there was any possible way to bring Lexington to racing fitness without overtaxing him and risking injury. He was glad the horse seemed no worse for the colic, but how to get him in form in less than a week, Jarret had no notion. He ran training plans through his head, trying to square what the horse needed to do with the number of days left in which to do it.

He couldn't see it. He would have to tell Mr. Ten Broeck so. He was fretting on that and not paying close mind to his surroundings, which is why he didn't perceive the two men and their mule cart until he rounded the bend and was upon them, still at a canter.

He breathed out, the horse slowed, and Jarret lifted the reins to signal a stop. But not before one of the men, alarmed, had dived into the bushes and landed hard on his hind end.

"Just hold up there!" ordered the other man, raising a hand to halt Jarret and reaching the other hand down to his companion, who scrambled out of the shallow ditch, cursing. "Who you think you are? Who in hell's name *are* you, anyhow, to be riding that horse, just as you like, without no by-you-leave?"

Jarret looked into the man's pinched, rodent face. Soiled, threadbare clothing. A mule so thin you could count his ribs. Men with no one to look down upon except the enslaved. Men with nothing to lose. Men to fear.

"I—I didn't see you, round that there bend in the road. I didn't mean nothing, sorry."

"Sorry? I'll make you sorry. You not from around here, boy. Can hear that from the funny way you talkin." The man took a menacing step forward. Lexington pinned his ears back and snaked his head sideways, butting the man hard in the shoulder.

The other one reached into the wagon and pulled out a pistol. "Git down."

Jarret hesitated. He could ask Lexington for a gallop and they could out-run the men, no doubt. But they couldn't outrun a bullet, if the man was any kind of shot. It wasn't worth the risk. He slid down, keeping the reins firmly in his hand. He could feel the horse quivering.

"I axed you a question, boy. Who's are you?"

"I'm Mr. Ten Broeck's Jarret."

"Ten Broeck? What kind of furriner name is that?"

"I—I—I'm coming from Fatherland, Colonel Bingaman's place. I'm hired out to Marse Pryor."

It was a necessary lie. He could see that they knew those names. And they weren't about to mess with property belonging to powerful men.

"You got a darky pass, boy?"

Jarret drew out the paper and held it out. The man with the pistol sig-naled for his friend to take it. He made a show of reading it, then turned and spat on the ground. "Seems to be in order." When he handed it back, Jarret saw that he was holding it upside down.

"You right lucky, boy. You just make sure next time we see you, you showin a deal more respect. Now get on out a here."

Jarret threw a foot in the stirrup and said nothing. He asked Lexington for a trot. And soon as he judged they were out of pistol range, he urged him up to a hand gallop and let the power of the stride hurl the tension from his body and the anger from his soul.

THEO

"He's an absolute beauty," said Theo, gazing at the painting of the glossy horse with four white feet.

Jess glanced up at Theo. It would be something, she thought, to be looked at with such close, admiring attention. Perhaps that was a thought she shouldn't be having. She turned her scrutiny back to the painting.

"Does he remind you of your pony?"

Theo turned to Jess with a puzzled expression. "My pony?"

"Your polo pony. The one you used to ride."

Theo smiled tolerantly. "I didn't have *a* pony. In polo you ride a string of them. At least six, in the course of a typical match. Sometimes maybe even eight or nine."

"*Nine?* No wonder it's such a rich man's game. I grew up in a working-class backwater when it comes to stuff like that. Girls like me didn't get to fantasize about Pony Club." Or handsome polo players, for that matter. "I really don't know anything about horses—at least, not living ones with flesh on their bones," mused Jess. "Just about the only time I saw a horse was when the mounted police rode by our place. My mum had this mortifying habit of running out into the middle of our busy road to scoop up the manure for her rose beds." Theo tried to imagine Abiona doing something like that. The image was so comical he grinned. Jess returned the smile. Was it the wine, or was she becoming infatuated with this man? In either case, she couldn't afford any more stupid remarks. There was a limit, and she was sure she'd reached it, even for someone as polite as he was.

They stood together, scrutinizing Thomas Scott's gorgeous nineteenth-century oil portrait of Lexington. A curator had located the picture at Jess's request and set it up on a small easel in a study room, along with the folder containing the museum's documentation of the piece. It was a 2 x 3-foot canvas, a bit larger than Theo's salvaged painting. The artist had depicted the horse alone by a wooden water trough, his aristocratic head turned, ears alert, as if interrupted by a sudden sound. And while Theo's painting captured a young colt, this work showed the mature horse—a magnificent stallion at the height of his powers, his early promise fulfilled.

"Amazing anatomical detail," Jess said. "The musculature, the way the painter's captured the flexion in the neck."

"And the expression in the eye," said Theo. "It's haunting. This is a beautifully unified studio portrait. I don't know why that conservator was so swift to rank this man Scott as a second-tier painter. This is a polished piece of work."

"Well, Raines is only one opinion," said Jess, picking up the file. "Scott must've been well regarded in his own time to get the commission in the first place, since the horse was already quite a celebrity when this was painted. It says circa 1860 and that Scott was born sometime between 1830 and 1832. So he's almost thirty when he painted this. He'd had some time to hone his technique."

"Does it tell you anything you can use in your work?"

"Oh sure. I'm convinced, looking at this, that the bloke who mounted the skeleton had never seen this horse alive. He just threw it together as if it were any generic horse. But this horse had an exceptional anatomy. The bones have a lot more mass than most equines, for one thing. They're super-dense, none of the bone loss you'd expect in a horse of that age. And then specific details—the withers, here"—she pointed to the picture—"see how level they are? In the skeleton, they're set way too high. And another glaring thing: the painter has the hocks much less angular—here—and the pasterns shouldn't be so vertical. There's a ton of useful information in this picture."

"Does it say how it got to the Smithsonian? Did it come here along with the skeleton?"

"No, I thought that, too, but I already checked, and it came much later. Let me look and see if there's any more about it." She rifled through the forms in the folder. The usual museum bureaucracy: transport manifests, conservation notes. Finally, she plucked out a copy of the deed of gift.

"Here it is. Seems like it came as part of a large bequest in 1980." Jess skimmed the record.

"That's odd—"

"What?"

"Well, you'd know better than me." She handed the file to Theo, pointing to the list of gifted works. "Am I right? Every other work in that particular bequest is, like, famous contemporary art, no?"

Theo scanned the document. "Oh yes, you're quite right. It's pretty much a who's who of postwar modernists—Jim Dine, Diebenkorn, Oldenburg, Gorky, Hartigan. Abstract expressionists, op artists—'Martha Jackson Memorial Collection,'" he read. "I've heard of her. She owned a gallery in Manhattan in the 1950s, when the art business was still very much a man's world. Along with Peggy Guggenheim, she really influenced the direction of the art market in New York in those key years. She was quite radical in her tastes—showed avant-garde artists from Europe and Japan—and was one of Jackson Pollock's first supporters, very deep in his circle. She was friends with his wife, Lee Krasner. I think I read somewhere that she was with her when he killed himself."

"Gah. I didn't know he killed himself."

"Well, it's not entirely clear, but it seems like it. He hadn't been painting for months. Drunk, speeding, car crash. Passenger died, too." Theo trailed off.

He was thinking of another crash. A dusty road in Helmand Province. His father, visiting a girls' school that USAID had funded. The Taliban hated the idea of girls going to school, and the delegation got warning that there might be an attack. The convoy was speeding when the SUV hit a pothole, flipped, and landed upside down in a ditch.

Theo remembered the headmaster's low voice, his terse account of the accident. He remembered shivering in his damp polo uniform, staring intently at the rivulets of rainwater snaking around the lead of the diamond-paned windows in the head's study. The bands of cold light gleaming dully on the polished desk, the Persian carpet. His awareness of mud on his boots. Struggling to control his voice as he asked, "Where's Mummy?"

"Your mother. Delegation, apparently. Key member. Negotiations with the Shabab in Addis Ababa. Delicate stage. Can't leave just now. She asked me to tell you she will phone you just as soon as she can." The headmaster turned to gaze out the window so that he wouldn't have to notice Theo's tears. There were whispered voices in the outer office. "Matron's here. She's made a cup of tea for you in the infirmary. Best go along with her now, there's a good chap."

His mother had called that night. But she hadn't come to see him, even after the Addis Ababa negotiations wound up. There was another pressing mission, he couldn't remember what. He realized then that her work had always come first and always would. Ahead of her marriage, ahead of her child. It was a harsh truth for a lonely boy, but also a liberating one. He was his own man long before any of his peers even realized that was an option. He'd embraced life as a rootless loner, at home in the world but belonging nowhere in particular. Comfortable with a wide range of people, close to very few.

He blinked and swallowed. Abiona would disapprove mightily if she saw him spending time with this haphazardly groomed White woman. And yet there was something about her clumsy, unstudied personality and her deep enthusiasm for her strange occupation. He was intrigued by her. Perhaps, as she'd said, he was overnostalgic for his childhood, those few scant years in Australia when he'd felt entirely secure, entirely loved.

Well, if so, so what? It wasn't as if he had unlimited options. He couldn't date the undergrads in his TA sections. He disliked dating apps; too many waste-of-time dates, too much ghosting. His Yale friend Daniel had set him up, just after he got to Georgetown, with Makela, a DC native who worked as a curator at the Anacostia museum. They'd hit it off at first. He liked her mix of sass and seriousness. But after a few dates, she stopped answering his texts. When he finally called Daniel to ask if he knew what had gone wrong, there was a long sigh. "You really want to hear it? She declared you 'insufficiently steeped in an experience of American Blackness.'"

"What?"

"She said she felt like she had to explain more stuff to you than she would to a White guy. She told me about the 'Dixie' incident, and I was like, 'Girl, I feel you.'"

Theo groaned. "That was the last time she went out with me." He and Makela had gone to a supermarket to get some provisions for a picnic. Some Muzak version of "Dixie" had been playing. Later, lying together on a blanket at the arboretum, Theo had absently started humming it.

Makela had sat bolt upright, as if he'd assaulted her.

"How can you hum that song?"

"Earworm, I guess?"

"Don't you have *any idea?*" She outlined its history and uses. "They stood around and sang that song at the University of Georgia while they burned effigies of the first two Black students admitted there." Theo had felt chagrined, but he hadn't realized it would prove the last straw for her.

"I can't believe she told you about that."

"Don't take it personally, man. She just wants a homeboy, is all."

Now, he gazed at Jess. If he started something with her, there'd be a very different set of issues. He'd be the one forever explaining. The thought of it was suddenly tiring. Maybe this should just stay a work thing. He tapped the binder on the table to straighten the documents. "I wonder if anyone knows what this one very traditional nineteenth-century equestrian piece is doing in that bequest, along with all those abstract expressionists."

"I can ask around. If she was that prominent, we've probably got heaps of documentation on her somewhere. Especially with such a significant bequest."

"I'll do some research too. It's intriguing."

They found Clancy snoozing where they'd left him, tied up in the shade of a planter. There was an awkward silence.

"Coffee?" said Jess.

"Why not?" Theo replied.

On the way to the coffee shop, they had to race across the street to beat a red light. Theo reached behind him and grabbed Jess's hand.

When they reached the sidewalk, he didn't let it go.

MARTHA JACKSON

Blue skeined off the end of the 3 x 4, twirling in space like a cowboy's lasso. He thrust the beam back into the can of house paint and whiplashed another huge gesture. "Clem Greenberg says I don't know color? Fuck him!" The paint sailed through the air, silky and billowing, splashing onto the canvas in an emphatic diagonal.

"I'll give him fucking color." With his left hand, he scooped up a jam jar of vodka from a card table crusted with stalactites of old paint. He swilled the drink and without looking slammed the glass back onto the table. It hit the edge, shattering. Martha flinched. Glass shards shimmered on the canvas. He crouched and ran his hand right over the slivers, grinding them into the paint. Blood now joined the riot of color coruscating over the black-primed linen: crimson drips and smears amid the yellow, the silver, the filaments of white. And slashing across it all, the march of those aggressive blue exclamations.

Martha stood pressed into the splintery wall of the shed, the full skirt of her frock tucked tightly around her in an effort to protect it from splatter. Across the studio, her friend sat coiled easily in a chair, eyelids at half-mast, relaxed as a cat. Martha noticed with surprise that she was smiling. How could Lee have learned to be so numb to this man's violent theatrics?

As the last spurt of Prussian blue hit the canvas, he stepped back and flung the beam away. It hit a shelf on its journey through the air, bringing two paint cans down. The lid flew off one. A flume of glossy liquid lapped across the barn boards in a chrome-yellow tide. Lee's face remained expressionless, watching as Pollock stood there, twanging, tense as a steel cable. Then his whole body seemed to go flaccid. Lee uncoiled herself and moved as if to catch him, wrapping herself around him from behind, so that both of them could continue to gaze at the work.

"It's good," she said. "It's great."

And it was. What had seemed out of control and random was nothing of the sort. The painting was tightly composed, a movement from the dark ground of the primer up through the agitation of color and line. Like the jazz faintly audible from the radio over in the house, the bebop with its insistent backbeat: it was improvisation within structure, the massive blue gashes like the powerful and risky high notes of a virtuoso.

Pollock folded in on himself. He knelt on the floor, kneading his face with his fists, driving his knuckles hard into his eye sockets. Lee crouched behind him, pulling his paint-crusted hands away, cradling his body as it started to shake.

Martha peeled herself off the wall and edged crabwise till she reached the door. She lifted the latch gently and stepped out into the leafy fall air. Charlie Parker's alto sax bounced its onomatopoeic rhythms. She ran lightly across the grass to the house, gathering the bag, the sweater, and the shawl she'd left on the kitchen table. There was no point in staying. There'd be no business done today, or the next day. Raging, weeping, then withdrawing. That was the way it always went with him since he'd started drinking again. And Lee would have to minister to that.

Even though the crisp edge of fall needled her face, Martha decided to leave the top of the convertible down. She wrapped the shawl around her head and shoulders, tucking it tight under the sweater. At the end of the driveway, she turned the car back toward Manhattan and hit the gas.

Lee would understand why she'd left without saying goodbye. And she'd forgive her for bringing up Greenberg, even if Pollock wouldn't. Clem Greenberg had been one of Pollock's first champions when other critics derided his work. But that didn't count anymore, not since Greenberg's remark that Pollock might be out of ideas. Making wallpaper, he'd said. Critics were fickle. Most artists accepted that. But not Pollock. All in or all out, that's how it was with him.

As a woman who'd shed two damaged husbands—the first undone by business failure in the Depression, the other by the stress of his war service—Martha vacillated between admiring Lee's fierce loyalty and feeling something like contempt for it. Martha had made a choice to leave both her marriages rather than see her life reduced to a crutch for the wounded psyches of men. Lee had made the opposite choice, and Martha witnessed the fierce toll it took on the woman and her own work.

Lee Krasner was one of the first friends Martha had made in the city, and nothing would ever change that. They'd met at art school soon after Martha moved down from Buffalo. She liked Lee right away: her sheared bangs and her sharp opinions, delivered in a proletarian Brooklyn accent. Martha admired Lee's self-confidence as an artist and wondered what more she could do if she weren't in constant thrall to that leech of a husband.

A brilliant leech. That was the trouble. When Lee had first taken her to see his work, Martha immediately felt the energy crackling off the canvas, felt it on her skin, prickly. And that was her gift: her eye for the shocking, the new, the brilliant. She felt as if she had a fifth or sixth sense for what would matter in art. When conventional tastes were busy deriding a new style, Martha could sense greatness. And though she'd come to New York City to be an artist, it hadn't taken her long to grasp that her own painting would never be great.

The truth of it hit her suddenly, like the onset of a fever. She'd arrived, as she did every morning that first year in the city, for class at Hans Hofmann's studio in a loft on Eighth Street. But when she got there, she found herself frozen at the foot of the stairs. She stood, her hand on the newel post, willing her foot to step up onto the first tread. Instead, it hung suspended, shaking.

Upstairs, waiting for her on an easel, was the canvas she'd been working on the day before. It was a landscape, inspired by the salt ponds and wind-sculpted trees of Provincetown, where she studied with Hofmann in the summer. She'd used loose brushstrokes and carved the thick impasto with a palette knife. It wasn't bad. It showed a grasp of composition, some mastery of technique. But as she stood there, with the work in her mind's eye, she knew she couldn't face that canvas. It wasn't bad, but it could not be great.

She turned and stepped back into the street, narrowing her eyes against the gritty swirl of fly ash and soot. Eighth Street was a grimy palimpsest, the old sweatshops still discernible even as they became studios, the influx of foreign painters and poets replacing the older generation of immigrant factory workers who toiled here a century earlier. She paced the block, tearing at the cuticle of her index finger with her teeth, as if to punish the hand that had made such an inferior work.

She loved her life in this city. Even the grubby streets, the cold-water tenements where her friends lived their messy, ungirt lives. She loved the opinionated newcomers from Russia, Italy, Germany; the late nights in the Cedar Tavern, arguing about pragmatism, the Fauves, and William James; the careless affairs, the unruly passions. It was fun to tumble about on a stained mattress in a Tenth Street walk-up with artists whose skin smelled of turpentine and cheap bourbon, so long as she could retreat to the Frette linen sheets in her own apartment on the Upper East Side.

But now the crowding of those images and memories embarrassed her. What was she, really? Just a well-heeled tourist, ticking off her to-do list in this foreign country of real artists. How could she ever have imagined she belonged? Tears stung her eyes and she swiped at them with the end of her scarf.

Hofmann, walking to his studio from the other direction, called out to her in his thick German accent. "Martha! Why aren't you painting?" He danced across the street, dodging cars, graceful, despite his thickset frame. He raised a hand to her wet cheek. The familiar smell of linseed oil made the tears flow faster.

"I'm sorry, I—"

Hofmann hushed her. He steered her down the block and into a diner. At a Laminex table, amid the warm fug of bacon grease and fried egg, he placed a paper coffee cup in her hand and listened as she blurted out her self-doubt and her grief at the thought of giving up the life she'd begun to make for herself. When she was done, he gently uncurled her fingers from the cup and turned her hand over, as if to read her palm.

"Perhaps you don't have a painter's hand," he told her. "I don't know for sure. But I do know this: you have a critic's eye. You can see what makes a painting good. That's also a gift."

"Is it?"

"Of course it is. How do you think artists become known? Critics, dealers—they are the people who develop the public taste. Without them, we starve."

Martha tore a packet of sugar and watched the crystals fall into her cup. "I've always had a little game I play when I go to a gallery," she said quietly. "I look around quickly and pick the three best things in the room. I feel like it's important to be able to decide what you like." Hofmann nodded. "And," she added, "I do like buying paintings."

"You've bought already?"

"Oh yes. Two or three things."

"Tell me about them." He hardly expected what came next.

"One is a gouache by Marc Chagall. That was the first thing I ever bought."

Hofmann sat back in his chair and stared. He cleared his throat. "How . . . how did you come to . . ."

"Well, it was a long time ago. I went to a show in Baltimore and the three things I really liked were a Picasso and a Seurat, as well as a Chagall. But Chagall was the only one of those three you could find to buy in this country in 1940. I paid five hundred dollars for it. And then I bought a Gorky painting from an acquaintance in Buffalo. He was having second thoughts, you see. He told me he wasn't sure why he'd bought it; he didn't know if it was any good. I did." She gave a tentative grin at the memory. "So I offered to take it off his hands."

Hofmann cleared his throat. "As I said. You have the eye." And, he thought, she must also have the means. Trust fund? Inheritance? You couldn't tell from looking at her. She wasn't any kind of show pony.

"Become a dealer then. Educate people. I will help you." And so she had taken his advice. She didn't drive hard bargains like so many dealers. Within a few years, she'd opened her own small gallery in a little town house with a storefront that she was able to afford thanks to an inheritance from her grandmother. She became known as a passionate advocate for her painters. Even the impossible ones. Even Jackson Pollock.

TEN BROECK'S JARRET

Natchez III, *Mississippi River*
1853

J arret perched by the prow of the boat as the current pushed them swiftly toward New Orleans. The bluffs of Natchez soon gave way to an unbroken flatness, green with palmetto and glossy ilex, the brief wildness interrupted by serried plantations of sugarcane and cotton. From the deck above, he could hear the voices of passengers, gambling with dice or cards or arguing loudly about politics.

Not far outside of Natchez, the trappings of wealth soon disappeared. Within an hour or so, the only dwellings they passed were the rude huts of the woodcutters who supplied fuel for the steamboats. When the boat pulled in to take on logs, the skipper yelled, "Wood!" and Jarret realized he was expected to join the crew and the other manservants to help with the loading. He noted the squalor: barefoot children with tangled hair and torn clothing, a thin cow, a few squealing pigs, a gaunt woodcutter sweating and atremble, most likely from the saddleback fever. No wonder: as the afternoon light eased into dusk, mosquitos swarmed. Jarret threw a shawl around his head to fend them off, and back on board he blanketed Lexington despite the unseasonable warmth of the evening. A bright moon rose, polishing the river surface. As the hour grew later, the voices from above became more raucous.

Jarret bedded down beside Lexington, determined to be inconspicuous.

He was bone tired, but too wary for sleep. It was precarious, traveling alone, without Ten Broeck to protect him. He thought of his father's many lone journeys, campaigning horses for Viley or Burbridge, and tried to draw courage from that. He felt a sudden yearning for home—for the creaking porch chairs, the rising fireflies, and his father's voice reciting lineages. But it would be too chilly at night for fireflies or porch sitting by now. What a thing it was, to be so far from his only kinfolk that even the weather on his skin felt different. He thought of his father, indoors by the fire, and wondered who was chopping the wood for him, who was carrying it in. He hoped Harry wasn't too proud to ask a lad to help him with the heavy chores. Surely Beth would take care that he didn't overtax himself. It came to Jarret that if his father faltered or became ill—even died—he might never know of it. This dolorous thought made his throat tighten and his eyes sting.

That was a reason to keep studying his letters. With help, he could write to Mary Barr, asking for an account of Harry. He resolved to fetch out the Bible at first light and go over the verses he knew, so that the knack of the thing wouldn't leave him. That plan brought him a little solace, so he punched the straw into an accommodating shape and tried to take some rest before the ship reached the port. When the sky lightened, he shook himself from his fitful doze and tended to the horse. Then he drew out the Bible, turning to Proverbs, which he had come to like for their many references to nature and farming. He was puzzling over an unfamiliar word and was so intent on the task that it was a moment before he registered the shadow falling on his page. Jarret looked up. It was one of the rough characters from the deck above, his cheeks dark with unshaven stubble, his clothes flecked with tobacco juice.

"That's summat I ain't seen, one of your kind with a book. Ain't that agin the law where you come from, boy? Fo sure is round here. Stand up when I's talkin to you, boy!"

Jarret scrambled to his feet. The boat lurched then, jostled by the wake of a passing steamer. The man staggered and fell hard against the hay bales. Jarret reached out instinctively to catch him, but the man flinched away.

Jarret stepped back, spreading his arms so as to show he had no intention of touching the man, who stank of unwashed flesh and the dried vomit that clung to the toe of his boot.

The Bible was still in Jarret's right hand and the man's pale, bloodshot eyes struggled to focus on it.

"That's the Word of the Lord you got there," he said, his voice suddenly less belligerent. "You some kinda darkie preacher?"

Jarret ransacked his memory for the verse the White minister at Fatherland had preached upon every Sunday. He tried to school the tremor in his voice, opened the Bible, and pretended to read: "Slaves, obey your earthly masters in everything; and do it, not only when their eye is on you and to buy their favor but with sincere heart and reverence for the Lord."

"Well amen to that," slurred the man, and staggered on to relieve himself over the side.

Whenever Jarret recalled that first morning in New Orleans, it was the noise and the smell that came back to him most vividly. Through the thicket of ship masts, he glimpsed bright ensigns of every nation fluttering in the slight breeze. Sweating men stacked bales and crates on the crowded dockside.

Carefully, he led the horse down the gangway and into a wall of sound and scent—the medley of languages that, later, he would be able to distinguish as French and Spanish, Italian and Portuguese, but that first morning blended into a musical blur. The smells were various, pungent: the tang of sassafras, the biscuit aroma of fat and flour roasting together into rich, dark roux, the intoxicating fragrance of jasmine, roses, magnolias, and gardenias, and the intense perfumes of the women—old, young, their complexions every shade from linen through honey, pecan, ebony—in expensive fabric or simple calico, clothed and ornamented with more care and style than any women he had ever seen.

Lexington held his head high, his nostrils widening to absorb the unfamiliar odors, his ears rotating to catch the strange sounds. As they picked their way through the crowded dockside, a friendly voice hailed them. A trim man, not tall, moved through the crowd with authority. Ten Broeck had sent his chief of staff, a Creole native of the city named Jacques Garmond, to collect them. "Such a 'orse!" he exclaimed. "*Celui-ci est magnifique!*"

Jarret didn't understand the words, nor, at first, the outstretched hand Jacques extended. Did he expect Jarret to hand him the lead rope? That would be unwise, in this crowd. Then, to Jarret's complete astonishment, the man grasped his hand and pulled him into an embrace, kissing the air on either side of his head. "*Bienvenue*—welcome in New Orleans. M'seiur Rishar wishes that you to come first to 'is 'ome in ze city, and *après*, we go to Metairie, where you will live, *n'est-ce pas?*"

Ten Broeck's town house was a handsome structure of claret-colored brick with three tall, shuttered doors opening onto a narrow verandah trimmed with iron lace. The carriage house behind was cramped, but well provisioned. Lexington was restive in this new stable, so Jarret took up grooming tools and set about a calming rubdown. Ten Broeck emerged from the house then, greeting him as he strode across the narrow courtyard. "Lead him out for me, will you please, Jarret?"

Jarret brought the horse out into the courtyard. Ten Broeck walked around him. "You've done well," he said. "To keep him in such fair condition after a severe colic. I am indebted."

"He's well enough, but he ain't fit for racing. Not so soon. You said he wouldn't be raced for near on a year."

"That is what I said, and what I intended. But I have such an opportunity that I may not refuse it. It's a matter of honor, in fact."

"No honor in pushing a horse who ain't fit," Jarret blurted.

Ten Broeck slowly drew his gaze from Lexington and fixed it on Jarret. He flinched under the force of it. Yet he would speak, since the horse couldn't.

"No honor, and no profit, neither, if he gone get beat."

Ten Broeck's frown deepened. He clasped his hands behind his back and tilted his head. Jarret could not go back, so he plunged forward. "He ain't never been trained to run three-mile heats. And that filly a full year older and raced all season. It's too much to ask of him, coming off a colic."

Ten Broeck's gaze was hard as basalt. Jarret struggled to meet it. He would not, could not, break and look away. In the pregnant silence, the only sound was the ring of the horse's hoof as he stamped on the cobbles, trying to dislodge a fly.

"You do not varnish your sentiment."

"Nossir."

Ten Broeck drew a linen square from his pocket and dabbed his brow. Jarret felt his own sweat—from the warming morning, but also from fear— dripping down his face.

"An uncommonly blunt young man. I could take a vast exception." He paused. Jarret clenched his hand on the lead rope, so Ten Broeck wouldn't see that it trembled.

"I could. But I don't. In fact, I am glad of this want of tact. I value your candor. Nevertheless, the horse *will* race. And since you are frank with me, I will do you the like courtesy. Mr. Louis Smith, of Alabama, offered to buy Lexington from Dr. Warfield shortly before Willa Viley and I made our offer. Mr. Smith was offended in the extreme that his prior bid was rejected and ours accepted. He was so ungentlemanly as to speak behind my back of some kind of corrupt dealing. I began to think I might be obliged to call him out, a prospect I did not relish. Unlike the hotheaded son-in-law of your former owner, I am no adherent to the code duello.

"Fortunately, he has provided another way to resolve the matter. In his animosity, he has proposed what I believe is a very unwise wager. A match race against his Sallie Waters filly in which he will put up five thousand dollars to my thirty-five hundred. Those are rich odds, I'm sure you will agree. Since this city is not above rejoicing in a grudge match, I also expect to do very well off the gate at my racecourse, whatever the outcome on the track. And there is another element, beyond money. Smith's filly beat my Arrow, another son of Boston. It was an extremely narrow win and I intend to have satisfaction for it. It will be three-mile heats, yes, but only two such races. I saw your horse break the start and run two miles at the Phoenix, then cool out in less than five minutes—yes, I timed it—and go on to distance some of the best three-year-old thoroughbreds in the country. I don't see that Lexington will be overtaxed. We do have a week yet to condition him, after all. I will be glad to have your opinion on how we might best proceed with this. You may set out your thinking for me when we ride to Metairie in the cool of this evening. In the meantime, you may like to walk about the city—" Jarret grimaced. Hadn't Jack called the place a Gomorrah? Ten Broeck noted his expression and smiled. "I recall: you said that you are not one for towns. You will see something of it this evening in any case, when we ride out. Till then, do take your rest in the grooms' quarters—I have asked that a pallet be made available to you—and avail yourself of some nourishment. I hired my chef away from a family of Creole aristos, who were most put out with me. He is a *fin gourmet*, very talented, I think. I have asked him to set aside some of what he has prepared for my own dinner, since you may like to try the local cuisine."

Ten Broeck turned and strode to the house. Jarret stood staring at his retreating back. The man was a bafflement. "Take his rest" in the middle of a working day, with the sun full up? Offered food prepared by the chef, rather than a piece of fatback handed him by a scullery maid? Life had taken a strange swerve, seemingly.

And yet, after he had seen to Lexington's hay and water, there was nothing he could do other than be in the way of those sweeping the courtyard, pumping water from the wellhead, or tending to a tidy garden of culinary herbs. He was, he realized, hungry, so he approached the kitchen door and knocked shyly.

An elderly maid, her hair tied up in an elaborate lace rigolette that matched the cuffs on her linen blouse, waved him in and indicated a place already set for him at a scrubbed deal table. She ladled a fragrant stew into a ceramic bowl and set it before him with a smile and a "Bon appétit." When Jarret plied his spoon in the steaming gravy, he could recognize neither the meat nor the vegetables. Still, the aroma was enticing, so he downed slippery oysters, tender crawfish, and glutinous okra. He found it delicious even as his mouth tingled from unfamiliar spices.

He walked back to the grooms' quarters. His plan was to keep out of everyone's way, and it seemed like the best place to do that. He would keep to his resolution and practice his reading. He had no intention of falling asleep, but his full belly and the unsettled night gathered all together and descended on him. He did not feel the Bible slip from his hand.

Ten Broeck's voice seemed to come from far away, muffled, like someone calling from the shore to a swimmer underwater. Jarret came to the surface from one of the deepest slumbers he could remember. The light had waned. It was late afternoon. He sprang to his feet, wiping a thread of drool from his mouth. What must the man think of him? He was mortified.

But Ten Broeck seemed entirely untroubled. "Good nap?" he said. "You'll feel the benefit of it later." He picked up the Bible from where it had fallen. "I was glad to learn of your interest in becoming a lettered man. I myself was schooled by a stern Hollander devoted to the birch more than the book. These are skills that will avail you. It was a good use of your time, since things with Pryor did not go as I had expected. Entirely my fault. The barber, Johnson, tried to warn me. Had I listened, you and the horse might have been spared something. Ah well." He flipped the Bible pages idly. "Not much for Scripture, myself. Prefer the pagans. The Greeks and Romans have some wonderful tales with a good deal more lovemaking than the Hebrews. I will try to find you something less edifying and more entertaining on which to hone your abilities. The groom has already tacked up for you. It's just three miles, a nice leg stretch for the horse, I think. Shall we go?"

They rode together through the narrow streets. It was slow going, picking between pedestrians and hawkers with handcarts. The city had a mood quite different from Natchez, mellower, and yet more intense than the quiet precincts of Lexington, which seemed to Jarret like a village compared with this teeming, heaving place. Everywhere, there was commerce. From a makeshift stand, a man with a strange accent hawked oranges, which Jarret had seen before, and bananas, which he had not. Nearby, a woman ran a coffee stall, the aroma of her roasting beans sharp in the heavy air. Canals carved their way between the streets and children dropped lines into the ditches. From a store selling only birds, a cacophony of parrot shrieks. Women with trays balanced on their heads called out their wares, figs nestled in fig leaves or pralines fragrant with burned brown sugar.

They passed by a large storefront, advertising men's apparel. A group of well-dressed Black men stood in a tight cluster. As they drew closer, Jarret realized the men were chained, a coffle of the enslaved being dressed up for the auction block. "They'll have those clothes off their backs again as soon as the hammer falls," Ten Broeck said, clicking his tongue and urging his horse to a trot.

At last they turned onto a wide, elevated road, its broad, pale surface crusted with pulverized oyster shells that gleamed in the low afternoon light. The shell road ran between swamps bright with iris and deep green palmetto. Ten Broeck encouraged his horse to a canter and Lexington cocked an ear back to ask permission. Jarret brushed his heel in answer, and Lexington flowed into his liquid, rocking-horse gait.

Very soon, the massive grandstand of Metairie rose in the distance. Jarret marveled at the magnificence of the structure. At the gate, the attendant bowed to Ten Broeck. He waved in acknowledgment. "This is Jarret, from Kentucky, my new deputy trainer," he said. "He is to come and go as he pleases. Offer him all assistance."

Deputy trainer. Jarret's surprise to learn of this sudden promotion was such that he accidentally gave a check to the reins. Lexington stopped midstride, waiting for the next instruction. Ten Broeck, thinking Jarret had halted to take in the scene, pulled up. He rose in his stirrups, surveying his creation. "See the Ladies' Pavilion? I'm quite proud of that. Entirely my idea. Previously, the Creole demoiselles were not allowed to attend the races. The aristocratic *mères* did not think it a suitable entertainment for young ladies. But I put down carpet, velvet chairs, silken drapes, and mirrored walls, and now *tout le monde* is happy to come here. Many a fine pair of kid gloves has been wagered in that pavilion." As they paused, a string of laborers passed in front of their horses, pushing barrows. Ten Broeck acknowledged the men with a wave. "They have been spading sand into the soil of the track. I do that before each big race. Makes for a lively footing. Our times here have been remarkable. I had to redesign the entire track. Used to be impossible to see the horses for half the race—they might as well have been running in the next parish. Let's go on. I'll introduce you to Henri Meichon, the jockey, and then one of the grooms will show you the stables, and where you are to stay. The farrier is to come in the morning, to fit racing plates."

The young jockey waited for them near the backstretch, shifting his slight frame from foot to foot. His eyes widened as he regarded Lexington, and his tense little face eased into an awestruck grin. "Creole," muttered Ten Broeck. "Talented, lot of heart on the track, little confidence off it. Not much experience. He will rely on your instruction." Dismounting, Ten Broeck, who was not a tall man, loomed over the tiny jockey.

"Good evening to you, Henri. I trust we did not keep you too late? I know you have an early start, and your *maman* will not thank me for keeping you from her good cuisine and your well-earned bed. This is my horse I told you about. You will note that I did not exaggerate his qualities. I confidently expect you to ride him to victory for me in Friday's match race. And this," he said, "is my Jarret. He knows the horse. Follow his advice in every particular, as if his instructions were my own."

As a groom led Jarret and Lexington into the large, airy barn—everything at Metairie had been rebuilt since Ten Broeck bought it—Jarret tried to ignore the dissonant clanging of Ten Broeck's words. *My horse. My Jarret.* New grandstands, new barns—did the man just buy up everything he wanted in this world? Jarret wondered how it could be possible to have so much, just from gambling on cards and horses. If a man could win all this, then maybe he could lose it. What if he decided to wager Lexington away, or the two of them? They were his property, just like the barn.

Lexington's stall was ready for him, his name already engraved on a brass plate, the bedding laid thick and the manger filled with fresh hay. There was a bunk room for the grooms in a shed row against the stables. But when Jarret, having seen to the horse, began heading that way, the boy took his sleeve and shook his head. "Trainers live up yonder," he said, indicating the ladder to the hayloft. At either end of the large loft was a room. Jarret's box had already been placed at the foot of the bed in one of these. It was spacious and whitewashed, with a window overlooking the track and the bayou beyond. There was a table and chair, a washstand with a porcelain bowl and pitcher, and a bed covered in a quilt with patterning he recognized as flying geese from one that Beth had made for Harry not long after their wedding. On the table was a newspaper. When the groom left, Jarret picked it up and sounded out the words of the masthead: *Turf, Field and Farm.* He recognized the name. It was the journal that the painter Scott sometimes wrote for. Ten Broeck must have arranged for it to be put there: perhaps this was the kind of less edifying reading he had promised.

Jarret sat down gingerly on the bed. A real mattress, not a shakedown. He fingered the quilt. The pieces were made from striped work shirts of the kind his father used to wear. Jarret wondered what Harry would think if the distance between them collapsed and he could see his son in this fine room. "I might be Ten Broeck's Jarret," he murmured to himself. "But I sure is high come up."

In the morning, the sun rose pale as a pearl. The bayou mist bloused over the paddocks. As Jarret gazed out the window, it seemed to him that the horses were suspended on clouds.

The farrier arrived with the sun—a hatchet-faced Irishman whose skinny arms and bony knees hardly fit him for his trade. With his scarred leather apron flapping against thin shins, he seemed dwarfed by the bulk of the horse. But he lifted and stretched each leg with an effortless confidence, and under his hand Lexington relaxed into a sleepy trance. Body bowed, hoof held secure between his thighs, the farrier prised off a worn shoe with a flick, sending it ringing on the flagstones. Then he worked the rasp over the horn of the hoof, exposing gleaming whiteness. With deft taps of his mallet, he secured the thin racing plate and nipped off the nail tips. Lexington stood loose in his skin, his head drooping as the farrier asked for each hoof. When the man was done, he ran his hand through the silky mane, murmuring, "There's a good lad."

Jarret wanted to work Lexington a little before the young jockey arrived, so he saddled him up and led him out onto the racecourse. He had meant to go easy, a gentle canter, but Lexington liked the unfamiliar springy track and Jarret could feel the urge for speed as he lengthened his stride. That power and willingness reassured Jarret. Perhaps he might be ready for race day after all.

When Meichon arrived, Jarret slid off and threw the boy up in his place. Lexington quivered at the unexpected lightness. Jarret wanted to see what the boy could do on his own before offering instruction, but he noticed that Meichon's hands shook as he bridged his reins. As the horse cantered out and accelerated, the boy sat low and stiff, deep in the saddle. "He's 'fraid," Jarret thought to himself. "That ain't good. Where's that heart Ten Broeck say he got?"

After a couple of lengths, Jarret signaled Meichon to the rail. "One thing you got to know: this horse wants to win. All you got to do is let him. Get on up off of his back, especially at the start. Find your own balance and let him do his work. Way you sit now, you get in his way. He likes to stretch way out—low and flat. But he can't do that if you is sitting down on him like a pile of bricks. He can't get his hind end to work. Get on up out of the saddle—yes, that's it—just like that. Now go. Show me."

By the second day's training, Henri had begun to get used to the new posture. Jarret was watching, pleased, when Ten Broeck materialized at his side. "You've turned my little Frenchman into a monkey," he said. "Ungainly look. But no matter how it looks. They don't wager on who is most elegant in the saddle."

Rain set in that night, and by morning the track was a mire. Lexington didn't care. He was gaining strength and stamina every day. He flew through the muck, sending spouts of water shooting from the sodden soil. It was still raining on the last day of training. Jarret called for only light work, for which Meichon, muddy and miserable, was grateful.

The rain eased off by sunrise on Friday, and Ten Broeck ordered a battalion of workers out to shovel water from the track, press down the divots, and drag the entire course with hessian sacking to soak up as much liquid as possible. "Lexington is a mudder, we know that, but I won't have Smith say I neglected the track in order to favor my own horse."

Carriages began arriving midmorning and risked bogging to the axles to find a good vantage in the infield. Ladies, the fine fabrics of their frocks hitched as high as was seemly, picked a precarious way across a hastily laid boardwalk to the well-appointed shelter of their pavilion. As the race hour approached, Jarret made his way among the crowd, trying to get a sense of the betting. All the money was on Smith's mare, Sallie Waters. The bettors knew her. She had been campaigned with great success all season. Just twelve days earlier, she'd easily won a two-mile heat race. The odds were 2 to 1 against this unknown, inexperienced Kentucky stallion. As far as Jarret could tell from the overheard gossip, only Ten Broeck and a few of his intimates had anything on Lexington at all.

At first, Jarret did not want to entertain the notion. But it would not leave his mind. Two to one. He pushed through the crowd back to the barn to groom Lexington for the race. When he was done, he stood in front of the horse, nose to nose. He didn't generally stand there—a horse's peripheral vision fails to encompass that spot—but he felt compelled to look Lexington in the face, being to being. In his mind, he posed the question: "Can you do it?" The horse twitched his ears forward, arched his strong neck, and inclined his head, as if to nod yes. Then he turned his head sideways, regarding Jarret with an eye whose expression clearly said, "Why ask? You know I can."

Jarret reached up and gently tugged one soft ear and then the other. The young jockey arrived, pale with nerves. Jarret handed him the brushes, even though the horse already gleamed. But nothing settled a man's spirits as well as brushing a horse, he reckoned. He took a hoof-pick from the peg on the wall and climbed the ladder to his quarters. From his box, he drew out the yellow vest. Working the hoof-pick gently under the stitching, he slit the seam and drew out the banknotes: seven hundred and fifty dollars. At 2 to 1, by the end of the day that could be one thousand five hundred dollars. The price Ten Broeck had paid for him. The price, perhaps, that could set him free.

He hurried back outside and plunged again into the crowd, which had thickened. He looked around for someone who might take his wager. All kinds of bets were being proposed: bales of cotton, hogsheads of molasses. Jarret sidled past the men wagering the produce of their plantations. He would not find a taker for a cash bet here. One man stood in his carriage, crying up the stakes for his own wager. "Prime field hands, healthy young bucks . . ." Two youths—Jarret's own age—stood beside the carriage, ankle deep in mud. They gazed ahead, rheumy-eyed and miserable, as the crowd swirled carelessly around them.

Jarret stared at the young men, their rounded shoulders, their blank faces. At that moment, one of the youths turned and looked at him. Jarret held his gaze for as long as he could stand it. Then he plunged on.

Before the cotton fields, he would have averted his eyes and passed them by. Now, he knew how easily it could have been him standing helpless in that mud. If his mother had been sold south, if Harry hadn't persuaded Dr. Warfield to bring him to the Meadows when she died—a thousand chances had to fall into his hands to put him out of the reach of a man who would bet his life away at a racetrack.

His hand tightened on the dollars in his pocket. How could he think to make a bet with men such as those? He must have been mad to even consider it. People like him were the stakes, not the stakeholders. Which of these men would take seven hundred and fifty dollars from him and not accuse him of stealing it? Even if they did accept the bet, how could he expect that they would pay out, if he won, and not plunder him? Their code of so-called honor did not extend to the likes of him. It was an entire risk. There was no one he could trust. No one he even knew, except for Henri Meichon and Richard Ten Broeck. And what did he really know of them?

Time was short. He had to be with Lexington. Heartsick, he began to make his way back to the stables. He was almost there when he heard a familiar voice call his name. He turned to see the painter, Scott, making his way toward him.

"Jarret! I was looking for you. I'm writing up the race for the *Turf.* Can I meet the young jockey? Will you take me to him?"

Jarret nodded. "He's in the stall with the horse. I can take you. But first— can you do something for me?"

"What is it?"

Jarret reached inside his jacket and pulled out the notes. Scott looked amazed, then concerned, as Jarret spilled out the history of the money and his intention.

"Jarret—no. I was just over with that filly. I tell you, when they stripped her blanket, everyone in the stable marveled at her form—she's a beautiful-made horse and in prime condition. They all say Darley—I mean Lex—isn't ready. The smart money is all on Sallie. That's a fortune you have there . . . it's not wise."

"I don't care if it's wise or not wise. I need to do it. Please. You're the only hope I got."

Scott stared past Jarret and shook his head slowly. "I don't know if I should."

Jarret, desperate, raised his voice. "I ain't got time here. I got to get back to the horse. Do this for me. I'm begging you."

Scott reached out and took the money. Jarret turned and ran to the stable. Scott looked down at the thick wad of bills in his hand, then reached into his own threadbare jacket and recovered a few rumpled notes and some coin and made his way to find someone who would be glad to take this foolish wager.

As Jarret ponied Meichon to the starting wire, he didn't hazard a glance at Sallie Waters. He could sense the energy of her, the blur of strutting, prancing movement as she tried to pull free of her own accompanying pony.

But he did not turn his head to look directly. He could not afford to lose faith, in case Lexington sensed it.

When it came time to let Meichon go on alone to the starting wire, the boy was all atremble. "Don't you worry. Just remember, he wants to win. You just got to let him do it." Meichon nodded.

The two horses plunged and turned and finally came level. The steward dropped his hand, signaling the drummer, who tapped the start. Sallie made a dash to take the track. Lexington, exhilarated by her challenge, sprang forward. The two horses matched each other stride for long, swift stride. Wet earth and sand flew up from the track, spattering the jockeys' vivid silks till horses and riders were a brown blur of mud and muscle. As they lapped to the stand, the time was a swift 2:12, remarkable in the deep mud. In the second mile, Lexington began to pull ahead. He was two lengths in front as they passed the stand a second time. The clock disclosed that Lexington had actually increased his pace, to cover the second mile in 2:10. Sallie was laboring now. The jockey plied the spur and whip unmercifully on the struggling mare, though any practiced eye could see the heat was lost. Lexington loped home an easy winner.

Jarret rushed up to take the horse. Meichon's French family clustered around him. Two of his brothers—strapping lads, unlike their tiny sibling—plucked him from the saddle and hoisted him onto their shoulders.

"*Attention!*" cried Ten Broeck amiably. "*Il a une autre course! Ne le laisse pas tomber!*"

Jarret walked the hot horse past the astonished crowd, many of whom, noting the ease of his breathing and the swiftness with which he cooled out, rushed to make new wagers. By the time of the next heat, the money was 100 to 10 in Lexington's favor.

This time Jarret did take the opportunity to look carefully at Sallie as she came up to the start. She was a magnificent mare, perfectly proportioned and beautifully muscled. But she was exhausted. Her head drooped. The jockey was plying the spur just to get her up to the line. "That ain't right," Jarret said out loud. "Where's her owner? Why don't he scratch her—save her for another day. Any fool can see she sure ain't winning today." But Jarret didn't know what Smith looked like. He scanned the crowd for Ten Broeck. He caught sight of him by the rail, surrounded by admirers, deep in conversation. Jarret called out, but the crowd noise was too much. He couldn't get his attention.

"Henri, you good?" he said. Meichon nodded, no longer trembling but confident and resolved. Jarret let him have the reins and headed toward the rail. Ten Broeck turned to him, smiling with anticipation. But when he saw the concern etched on Jarret's face, his expression became grim. "What is it? Is something wrong with the horse?" He had to raise his voice to be heard over the crowd.

"Not ours, he's fine. It's that filly. She looks bad. I think she's like to founder. They should scratch her."

Ten Broeck gazed in the direction of the filly. He frowned. "I think you're right." Then his face hardened. He shrugged. "That's Smith's business. If he wants to hand me the winnings, so be it."

"But it ain't—" Jarret didn't get to finish. At that moment, Sallie's jockey finally dragged his reluctant mount level with Lexington under the wire. The steward's hand fell, the drum tapped.

Within less than a minute, what Jarret had seen was clear to everyone. Lexington flew ahead. Soon, he was running alone, even though Sallie's jockey flogged and spurred her till her flanks ran red. Meichon, perched high on Lexington's back, rode hands down for two miles of the three-mile race. Without his jockey asking for effort, and without competition from his distanced rival, the horse pushed himself, running for the joy of it. He made the muddy three miles in 6:24:5—just one second longer than the first heat.

Lexington strutted from the track amid cries that this was the best horse ever to race at Metairie. Sallie, trembling, bright beads of blood dripping from her sides, staggered to her stall. She died there that night, broken and exhausted.

MARTHA JACKSON

When Martha opened the door to her apartment, the crisp scent of lemon oil told her that Annie, her three-day-a-week housekeeper, had been cleaning. But Saturday wasn't one of her regular days. Martha threw her keys onto the hall table and called out a greeting. "Annie? You here?"

The young woman's low voice responded from the kitchen. "Yessum. I surely can leave now if it's not convenient for you."

"That's not necessary, Annie, you go right on ahead." She walked through the paneled sitting room, noting that Annie had oiled all the woodwork until it gleamed. She was meticulous. In the dining room, she'd refreshed the flowers, removing the blown roses and rearranging the buds in a pleasing tousle.

Martha paused at the kitchen doorway. Annie stood at the sink, humming softly as she polished silverware, unaware of her employer's considering gaze. The girl was thin—too thin. With her cotton shift hanging loose on her spare frame, she looked like a wraith in a Walker Evans photograph. She claimed to be eighteen, but that seemed doubtful. She had the promise of beauty—fine bones, luminous eyes—but it was a child's beauty that hadn't yet bloomed into womanliness. Because Martha Jackson moved in the penurious circles of the art world, she was more aware of the bite of poverty than most wealthy people. Perhaps the child wasn't getting enough to eat. She would have to see to that.

"I didn't expect you today."

Annie turned, startled. The ladle she had been polishing clattered onto the drainboard.

"I'm sorry, ma'am." She glanced down. "It's just, I got myself a new client, starts Monday, so I thought I'd come do for you today since you said you would be gone the whole weekend."

"The painter I was visiting took ill. That's why I'm back early. I don't mind that you're here. But surely you're working yourself too hard. Six days a week. You need more than one day off."

"Seven days, ma'am. I took on a Sunday situation last month."

"Annie, if you need a raise, I—"

"No, no, ma'am. That ain't—isn't—it at all. You already pay more than most others I do for. It's just that I need to make a little extra right now. My brother, back in Ohio, he's fixing on going to college next year." She smiled shyly. "He aims to be a doctor someday."

"And you're helping with the cost of that?"

"Yes, ma'am."

"I hope he appreciates it."

"Oh, he does, ma'am. He works hard himself. He's been going to school by day and working as a night watchman all this year, and before that he stocked shelves for the local grocery."

"Well, that makes two diligent workers. Your parents must be proud."

"They was, ma'am. They passed. My father four years ago, and my mama just before I came on up here to the city. So it's just me and Charlie."

"I'm sorry, Annie. I had no idea. I know what it means for a girl to lose her mother. I wasn't much older than you when my mother died."

"It's all right, ma'am. My great-aunt took me in. She don't see too good, so I do for her in return for my room and board. I live with her, up in Harlem, since her boys are all grown up and left home."

Martha was vexed with herself. How could she have likened her loss to the loss of this girl? Their situations were nothing alike. Her own grief had been cushioned by resources that ensured her life changed as little as possible. The same Irish maids who had always cared for her continued to do so. She did not have to leave her home until she chose to go away—eagerly, avidly—to Smith College.

"I hate to see you working yourself to the bone. I would like to help. Financially."

"Oh, ma'am. I couldn't ask that." Annie looked down. Her hand balled around a piece of her apron. "But there is one thing—you selling paintings and all. There's this painting we got, my family, I mean to say. We always had it, all the way back to my great-great-grandma day, though no one heard tell how she came by it back then. We'd consider selling it, to help Charlie."

Martha formed a mental image of some sentimental daub, the kind of painting—maybe even a reproduction of a painting, would Annie know the difference?—that might be in the possession of a rural Black family of slender means. She quickly arranged her face. She didn't want to appear snobbish.

"Well, you know I deal in contemporary art—" Martha stopped herself. Why would the young woman know that, or care?

"Oh yes, ma'am," Annie interjected. "I come in by the gallery and spend a little while every time, on my way up here. For sure, this painting of ours isn't anything like what you got there—"

"You visit the gallery every time you come to work?"

"Oh yessum. I got into that habit just soon after I come to work for you. You had that lady's painting hanging in your sitting room—that one that was all patterns that seemed to move—and I come to like it a good deal, looking at it, so I thought I might come to like some of the other ones if I spent some time with them."

Martha smiled. She had hung a Brigid Riley for several months before the successful opening of her Optical Art show that had coined the name of a new movement and launched several promising careers. But the gallery currently featured de Kooning's exuberant, voluptuously distorted women. Even many of his fellow artists found the series provoking and distasteful.

"And do you? Like them?"

"Well—" Annie hesitated, her good manners at war with her essential honesty. "Not so many, to tell the truth."

Martha laughed. "That's all right. Not many people do. But I'm glad that you take the time to look. And in return, I will be happy to take a look at your family's painting and give you an opinion on its value, if I can. Bring it by any time."

"Oh, thank you, ma'am. We'll have to fetch it up here, but me and Charlie'd be obliged. I meant to ask you this long while."

Martha didn't want to give unrealistic expectations. "Well, you know, the art market is fickle. I'm sure your painting is very good, but even some very fine works don't fetch much money. Style of painting, even subjects—they fall in and out of fashion, you know."

Annie smiled shyly. "I guess you'll like the subject of this one, any case. I know you like horses since you got all those photographs in your bedroom. The lady in the long dress jumping that horse just as if they two can fly."

"That lady was my mother. That was her horse."

"Oh, ma'am, I'm sorry."

"Nothing to be sorry about. I keep those pictures because I like to remember her that way. She loved to ride that horse."

"That right? Well, that's something. Because the painting we got, it's of a horse. And he's got four white feet, just exactly like that one your mama's riding."

TEN BROECK'S JARRET

It was hard to watch, but Jarret couldn't turn away. The teamster slung his chains around Sallie Waters's hocks. Jarret winced as the metal bit into her fine sinews. Sallie's young groom had been helping the teamster, but now he stepped out of the barn, crying. Jarret understood how he felt. He wished there was some comfort to offer. But he couldn't think of any.

Two large draft horses stood uneasy in their traces, snorting and twitching, misliking such proximity to death. When all four of the filly's legs were secured, the teamster gave a gruff "Walk on." The draft horses moved forward, the chains clanked taut, and the corpse scraped along the barn boards. At the Meadows, Jarret had seen to the burial of several horses, and it was never an easy or pleasant duty. But they had always been older animals, spavined and spare from the ailments of age. He'd never witnessed the interment of a magnificent young thoroughbred like this one.

Lexington, in his stall, gave an anxious whinny, pinning his ears and rolling his eyes. Jarret turned away from the pitiful sight of the dead filly, her tongue, lolling from her mouth, dragging in the dust toward the fresh-dug pit. He reached up and laid a hand against Lexington's neck. "She was ill used," he whispered. "But it ain't your fault. You just did your job, is all. If it's anybody's fault, it's all those ones of us got rich off of her having the life flogged out of her."

Scott had turned up late the previous night, flushed and glassy-eyed. He'd found his way to Jarret's room, knocking too loudly and drawing abuse from the early rising grooms sleeping below. Scott was in good spirits, even in drink. He handed over Jarret's winnings with a rueful grin. "Wish I'd had a stake like yours. Double nothing is still nothing, and that's close to what I made. Ten Broeck's the one whose hands are getting tired, counting all his cash. The gatemen told me he cleared three full barrels of dollars as gate receipts, not to mention five thousand from Smith's losing wager, and whatever money he might have chanced elsewhere today, which, if you can credit backstretch gossip, was considerable. If you want to speak to him about buying yourself out, I think you'll find him in a receptive mood."

Jarret said nothing. It was just as likely, he thought morosely, that with all the cash Ten Broeck had just accumulated, his own offer might seem trifling.

Scott made an unsteady progress around the room. He stopped in surprise at the oil of Lexington as a colt. "You kept it."

"Of course." Jarret had asked Metairie's carpenter to make a simple frame for it, now that he finally had a place to hang it.

"These are good quarters," Scott said, testing the mattress. "Far nicer than many a place I've been required to lay my head down. Not sure why you're so hasty to buy your way out of it, myself."

Jarret felt a flare of anger and said nothing.

"I thought all you cared about was the horse. Seems to me, if that's the case, you're well set up here, for now. Doesn't seem like anyone is asking you to do anything other than what pleases you to do. You're not looking to get back to your folks in Kentucky, are you?"

The sudden thought of the Meadows made Jarret's throat tight. It was home, and he did miss it. But he shook his head.

"No? I didn't think so. Because the horse is staying right here to run in the Great State Post Stakes come spring, that's a certainty after today."

Scott had a point. There really was no cause to confront Ten Broeck just presently. He would wait till spring. The man would be in an even better mood when Lexington won the rich purse of the Post Stakes.

Scott noticed the newspaper lying open on Jarret's table.

"You can read that?"

"Not too much, yet. But I'm trying."

"Well, good for you. That's the paper I write for. Look for the articles signed "Prog." That's me—the name I write under. It's an old word for a vagabond. You never know, you might find yourself in a story one day."

Jarret had read enough of the paper to note that where a White jockey won a race, his name appeared amid praise for his poise or his judgment. But if a Black rider won, nothing was said. He hadn't seen mention of Black trainers either. He suspected Scott wouldn't care to hear his observations on that. When he left, Jarret took the cash and painstakingly inserted it back into the lining of his yellow vest, taking care to place the bills evenly so as not to create bulges.

After the excitement of the match race, life settled into a simple routine at Metairie. Jarret's main responsibility was the care and conditioning of Lexington, but he was glad to assist with Ten Broeck's other horses when he could. In his free time, he kept working on his reading.

With the letter he had received from William Johnson as his guide, he composed a short note in his own hand and addressed it to Mary Barr Clay, asking her to read it to his father. As he strove to form the letters, he recalled the girl as he had last seen her, the fine silk of her dress balled up in her hand, the stable dust soiling her satin shoes. So, after asking his father to send news, he added a second and a third line: "There is no need to fret over me. My life is good here." Then he dipped the pen in the inkwell and copied Johnson's formal salutation, "I am, &c, your son Jarret."

The reply came directed to Jarret in the graceful script of a ladies' seminarian. It took him much time to decipher every word, but he swiftly comprehended its main import. "We were most surprised to receive a letter from your hand," Mary Barr wrote. "I would say pleased, and yet as you will soon learn, pleasure in your accomplishment was tempered by the news I must now impart to you. When your father succumbed to the saffron fever this past month—it is proving to be a very bad winter for fevers, and several of our acquaintance, young and old, have sickened—I took a slender reed of comfort in thinking that at least you would live on in ignorance of your loss. Alas, it is now my melancholy duty to impart to you this news. He died on the 20th inst., in the early hours before dawn, and we committed his remains to the burial ground which you will well remember, under a splendid locust which is just now in bud. I can tell you that your father received every care my grandfather's medical training could render to him. I will say that my grandfather felt his responsibility most keenly, as he was not unaware of the unhappiness he had caused your father in depriving him of your presence during this time. But be assured he did have the most tender ministrations of his wife, who nursed him until his last breath. I send my condolences in these lines, and I will, I hope, have the opportunity to render them in person when we travel to the Crescent City to see Lexington win the Great State Post Stakes. I regret that I am the bringer of such dire news. The ways of Providence are inscrutable and I pray you have the fortitude to bear its sternness. Yours &c, Mary Barr Clay."

MARTHA JACKSON

East Sixty-Ninth Street, New York, New York

1955

When Annie left for the day, Martha Jackson retired to her bedroom. Even though she was alone in the apartment, she closed the door. It was an old habit. As a girl growing up in a household with four live-in maids constantly in and out of her business, she had learned to guard her privacy.

She sat down upon the bed and contemplated the three framed photographs on the wall. Watery afternoon light danced on the gelatin silver images. Each depicted her mother, airborne, clearing an impossible-looking jump on the back of a magnificent bay horse whose legs—pure white as Annie had noted—were perfectly tucked beneath him. That was Royal Eclipse, just fifteen and a half hands, yet one of the best hunters on the competition circuit. Cyrena and Royal Eclipse: winners of three national championships at the National Hunt Team competition at Madison Square Garden.

Cyrena's passion had always been horses. She was an ardent competitor, famous for her flawless rounds. Daughter of privilege, Gilded Age debutante, Cyrena Case had made what was always referred to in Buffalo by that old cliché "a brilliant match." She wed handsome Howard Kellogg, the heir to a linseed oil empire that encompassed factories, grain elevators, and tanker transports that worked the Great Lakes. Howard also liked to ride and had been drawn to Cyrena's grace and guts on the competition circuit. He remained intensely proud of her successes once she became his wife, and gladly underwrote her every expensive desire: the best instructors, travel in style on the circuit, a succession of champion warmbloods imported from top European stables. Then, Royal Eclipse: an expensive American thoroughbred of impeccable breeding. Cyrena's perfect equine partner.

As Cyrena's firstborn child and only daughter, Martha was encouraged early to swim in the bright wake of her shimmering mother and set on horseback as soon as she could sit upright. She had no memories of a time before she could ride—for her it was as unconsciously learned as walking. As she grew, she studied Cyrena's mannerisms and aped her enthusiasms, eager to attract the warm glow of her approval. She blossomed into another effervescent, golden-haired beauty, athletic and game. Every summer, the family decamped from Buffalo to the family compound, Lochevan, near Derby. It was a green paradise of white-fenced horse pastures and a large stable topped with a copper wind vane of a galloping horse. The ring had luxurious footing made from shredded broadloom carpets. Martha always had her own horse there, from the first small Shetland, through later Welsh Cobs, and then the thoroughbreds, each one a little more powerful, until the best of all of them: Fashion Eclipse, a half sister of her mother's champion horse.

She had inherited her mother's steel nerves but not her urgent competitive instinct. She enjoyed dressing up in spotless breeches and tailored jackets, braiding manes and oiling hooves, but once the competition started, her focus was the exhilaration of the jumps, not the fine calculations necessary to shave a fraction of a second off the round by precisely counting strides, adjusting lines. She watched her competitors with pleasure, rather than the gnawing rat's tooth of envy and desire that ate at her mother when another rider performed well. Cyrena was confounded by Martha's insouciant attitude. She constantly pressed her to go higher, faster. As soon as Martha began to feel some mastery at one level, Cyrena insisted on entering her in a more advanced one. "If you're not moving up you are slipping down" was Cyrena's stern motto, and Martha went along as best she could with whatever her mother required of her. Preparing for a show, she had her mother's undivided attention, and that mattered more to her than blue ribbons.

One companionable autumn afternoon, as the light began to fade, they were riding side by side, at an easy walk, heading back to the stables after a hell-for-leather race on the cross-country course. A light drizzle had been falling all afternoon, and now the soggy pastures offered a sticky footing for the tired horses. "Let's jump this fence here and take the road—the going'll be easier," said Cyrena. One after the other, the horses soared over the split rails and onto the lightly trafficked rural byway. Martha liked the ring of horseshoes on asphalt, and as they went on together at a slow trot, the percussive fall of the horses' hooves punctuated their conversation.

Martha never could recall what it was they were speaking of just before Royal Eclipse tripped. It was a tiny stumble; his hind leg giving way for a second, a momentary lurch that wouldn't unseat a novice, much less Cyrena, who had stayed on over the highest rail in a jump-off. But she was turning back to reply to something Martha had said and lost her purchase in the saddle. She slid off the back of her horse. It should have been nothing; it seemed like she would manage to land on her feet and not even soil her breeches. She was laughing at herself as she fell, Martha remembered that— a surprised, self-deprecating laugh. But as her boot landed on a patch of rain-slicked leaves, she lost her balance. She was still smiling as she windmilled her arms, trying fruitlessly to regain her footing. The back of her head hit the pavement with a sickening crack. As the blood pooled in a glossy, widening arc around her bright hair, the horse—kind, intelligent, an athlete and a competitor, her mother's perfect partner—dropped his head and laid his soft muzzle on her shattered skull. He stood there, guarding her, until the ambulance arrived and took her away.

It wasn't that her father blamed the horse. An accomplished rider himself, he understood what had happened as the freakish accident it was. Nevertheless, he had no desire to see that horse again, and sent him swiftly to the sale barn without telling Martha what he had done. By the time she thought to ask, the horse was somewhere in Canada, already the property of new owners whose names she never learned. Martha rode in competition one last time, just to prove to herself that she had the nerve to do it. But without her mother, the event seemed gray and joyless. When a nice family showed an interest in Fashion Eclipse, Martha let her go to them. She turned her back on the equestrian world with few regrets.

Now, memories crowded in. The texture of her horse's mane as she worked the strands into a show braid. The warmth of the neck when she would rest her head against it. The soft flosses of hair coming loose under the shedding blade in early spring, scuttering across the barn floor like little furry animals. She recalled the acute pleasure of her mother's approval the day she mastered a flying change, the day she made her first perfect round, the day she finally won that elusive blue ribbon.

As daylight faded, the sodium streetlights blinked on. Their orange glow warmed the silvery photographs. Cyrena's face, as she rose over the horse's neck, was euphoric. She was the only competitor Martha had ever seen who looked photogenic over the jumps. Most riders frowned in thin-lipped concentration, their faces washboarded with tension. But Cyrena—smiling, luminous—was never more beautiful than in those midair moments.

That's why Martha kept the photos; to remind herself how much her mother had loved the thing that had led to her death. She found a measure of peace in that. Annie had said she wanted to show her a painting of a horse who looked just like Royal Eclipse. "I guess you like horses," she'd said.

Martha kicked off her shoes, swung her legs onto the bed, and curled up like a nautilus. Oh, Annie, she thought. It's far more complicated than that.

THOMAS J. SCOTT

Metairie, Louisiana

1854

Ten Broeck's commission—what a boon. Modest winnings, payments for reportage—as ever, paltry and laggard—would not have kept me long in New Orleans, a city whose ample pleasures are a constant tax upon the purse.

I found much different since I last took up brush to paint the horse, even the beast's very name. The milky bayou light also added a new element, bringing out novel colors and tones in the horse's coat. Jarret, a boy no longer, came unbidden to assist me, though in his raised state he need not. He has undergone a mighty change, not just in condition but also in manner and bearing. Finally, I must allow, my own state of mind was different. I was in a condition of well-being. In Kentucky I had been fretful.

Some happy confluence of these things made the painting come together with a rare fluidity. When I laid down my brushes and stood back to appraise what I had done, I must have exhibited my gratification. Jarret asked if he might look at the work, and I stepped away from the canvas to give him a view. His smile—slow, animating his entire face—took me by surprise, and—I must set it down—gave me not a little pleasure. He so rarely smiled. I realized with some surprise that his approbation mattered to me.

I took the opportunity to quiz him about Metairie, hoping to find information for my dispatches. But in this one thing he had not changed: he is no chin-wagger. One must draw the information out as if luring game shy of the snare. At one point, to keep the flagging conversation alive, I expressed hope that Mr. Ten Broeck would put me in the way of further commissions so that I might stay in the Crescent City. The boy gave me a quizzical look. You like the city, he asked. Very much, I replied. He raised an eyebrow at that. I let the subject drop, as I could hardly explain to him my attraction.

I had liked it well enough even before I encountered Julien. I could not have encountered him in any other place. It was the city's very nature that put him in my way. This city, above all others, grants one permission to *live*. One may come and go according to whim, without dread of the frowns and finger wagging one risks elsewhere from all the fine moral folk whom I might wish to have as clients. Here, no one says it is not respectable to resort to this or that establishment or to be seen in friendly intercourse with this class of person or that one. In New Orleans, one may frequent all manner of establishments with a various clientele and encounter all classes of people.

And all colors, too, although I did not grasp that I was among members of the dusky brethren until it was too late to regret the fellowship. *Les gens de couleur libres*—how much more lightly the expression falls upon the ear than "free Black." In the dimness of the club, I did not realize that my elegant young interlocutor was a mulatto. Nothing in his dress—embroidered waistcoat, elaborate neckerchief—signified anything other than a prosperous man with means to retain a fine tailor. I was merely struck by the young man's beauty, and by the coincidence that we were both of us painters. Indeed, as we conversed, I mistook him for my superior in every respect—more financially secure and possessed of a better grasp of most subjects that we held in common interest.

It was only the following day, having accepted an invitation to visit his studio, that I found myself in a neighborhood of Negroes. To be sure, his house was a graceful, freestanding timber building, shaded by a wide verandah. A servant—he had means for that—ushered me into his studio, which was flooded with light from a high oculus set into the roof. As Julien entered, that drenching light revealed his tawny complexion.

He explained that his specialty was portraiture and that the main part of his clientele comprised wealthy men who had fathered or married beautiful young quadroons and octoroons—strange words, these, for women of such refinement as were rendered by Julien's brush. Set upon an easel was a work in progress: a delicate-featured quadroon dressed like a princess in pale silks and pearls. He had employed a subtle, shimmering palette that revealed a virtuosity I frankly envied. It would be something, I thought, to have the technical skills of my new young friend, who was able to render the luster of flesh and fabric with equal skill. I allowed that I had never had the aptitude to paint human beings.

His reply: It is not aptitude, *cher.* It is technique.

He said that his father, an English shipping magnate, was in purse to afford to send him to Paris, where he had secured a place in the atelier of Abel de Pujol. I could tell he expected me to be impressed by the name. I was abashed to admit that I did not know it. He was gracious. He explained that de Pujol was the pupil of the great classicist Jacques-Louis David, and adheres to rigorous technique. He glanced at me then from beneath his heavily lashed eyelids, and shyly offered to pass on to me some of that learning.

I will set it down: I felt the brush of the wing of Eros. I put out a hand to steady myself against the back of the chaise on which his fair sitters generally reclined. It was an invitation to more than a pedagogical relationship, I felt it. But before I ventured into dangerous waters, I had to be sure. So I began on some teasing banter about the lovely young demoiselles, and whether Julien had a special connection with any of the ladies he had painted. He divined my purpose. *Pas du tout*, he exclaimed with a laugh. "The *haut bourgeois* fathers of these girls aim higher than a mere artist for their daughters, *m'sieur.* And in any case"—and there he paused, and held my eyes for a long, assessing moment: "Well, shall we just say, *chacun à son goût?*"

So I have begun to spend many hours on Bienville Street, some of them at the easel. And Julien is, to my surprise, quite comfortable to accompany me to Metairie. It was he who first suggested it, and when I hesitated, he laughed at me for thinking he might not be accepted by the "swells" in the stands.

"You do not know our city yet, *cher*. If one's *père* is rich, and one's complex-ion is more elm wood than mahogany, you would be surprised where one may venture." Indeed, watching him move fluidly among that crowd, where many, it seemed, were acquainted with him, I realized he was more in his element than I was. Julien's elegance and ease of manner were notable even among those wealthy gentlemen. I knew how I suffered from the proximity, my apparel threadbare and behind the fashion, my northern manners not yet polished to a southern gloss.

It amused me that Julien declined to accompany me to the paddocks or the backstretch. He did not care to risk his calfskin boots to horse manure or to have flecks of hay speckle his subfusc suits. The grooms and the stable hands held no interest for him. Even when I teased him that Degas—an art-ist he knew personally and much admired—had moved readily between the *barre* and the rails, I could not entice him to join me in those precincts where I found my best intelligence.

And that was, I consoled myself, one thing I could do that Julien could not: bring a horse alive in words just as well as in a painted image.

TEN BROECK'S JARRET

Metairie, Louisiana

1854

Spring came early to New Orleans and with it came an unexpected visitor. Jarret was returning from a long conditioning ride on the levee that rimmed the lake. He thought it good for the horse to have a change from the monotony of the track. They were at an easy canter when he saw Ten Broeck emerging from the stables deep in conversation with a familiar-looking man.

"Jarret—you remember Captain Viley from Lexington, I think? Willa, this is Harry Lewis's boy, whom I bought from Warfield, if you'll recall, around the same time as we bought his horse."

Viley gave Jarret an appraising glance. "I do recall. And he looks likely. Trust you, Richard, to spot value. Boy's father was one of *my* better investments."

Jarret schooled his face. His grief for his father was still raw. He'd had no way to mourn him; no funeral, no grave to visit. To hear his name in this way was like a cudgel landing upon an unhealed wound. Jarret had dropped his guard these past months, living like a free man with a respected occupation. To be spoken of as livestock was bitter as a gallnut.

Ten Broeck cut across Viley's self-congratulation. "Jarret brought the horse up from Fatherland in time for the match race. He has been in charge of the training since then."

"He *what?* You led me to understand that Pryor was to be the trainer. That was our agreement, surely?"

Ten Broeck gave an airy wave. "Pryor proved difficult. He was unaccommodating in the matter of the December race. I was obliged to make other arrangements."

"And those 'arrangements' meant giving the training of our horse into the hands of this untried boy?" Willa Viley frowned. "And you didn't see fit to send me, your partner, word of this?"

"Willa, do not vex yourself." Ten Broeck's arm swept the air from Lexington's powerful neck to his well-muscled hind end. "You can see the horse's condition—any fool can see it."

"Do you call me a fool now?"

"Of course not—it's a figure of speech merely. I meant no offense." Ten Broeck had colored slightly. Until this moment, Jarret had never seen him show a hint of discomposure.

"The horse does look well enough, I acknowledge that. But I will take the training in hand from now until the race. I'm sure you have other duties for the boy."

A bead of sweat trickled down Jarret's neck. Would Ten Broeck speak up for him? If he didn't, Jarret would have to speak for himself. He would not hazard the horse's welfare to a stranger. Not again.

Ten Broeck spread his hands. "Actually, nothing pressing. Keep him on as a groom. Best not to chance any upset at this stage of the training—it's a foul-tempered horse, very difficult to handle." Jarret caught the hint of a wink as Ten Broeck mouthed this lie. "Best to leave it in care of a boy it knows."

Viley spread his hands. "Entirely up to you. Boy, take the horse out there and show us what he can do."

Jarret looked at Ten Broeck, hoping for an intercession, but the man just stood expressionless.

Jarret cleared his throat. "Captain Viley, he just did a ten-mile workout. I was just about to water him and put him on grass."

"Were you so? Yet supposedly you are 'training' him to belt for eight miles. Stamina, boy. Let's see if you have trained him for *that*."

Jarret turned the horse to the track. As they passed the gate, Lexington's ears swiveled, as if to say, "This isn't right." Jarret brushed up with his heel to urge him on, and Lexington responded. He started fast, and then, sinking and stretching out into his low stride, accelerated. As the wind whipped Jarret's face, he whooped with the sheer joy of it—this seemingly limitless well of power that Lexington could draw on, that he seemed to *want* to draw on.

At the two-mile mark, Viley raised a hand and cried out, "That'll do!" Jarret asked the horse to ease and did a couple of slow laps to cool him down. He dismounted and led the horse toward the fence, where Viley stood, beaming.

"That horse moves like it's made of whalebone," he said to Ten Broeck. "And you," he said, looking at Jarret, "you are your father's son, clearly. Let me outline to you what I have in mind by way of a program. I would have your frank opinion of whether it will do . . ."

Ten Broeck fell behind them on the walk to the stable, smiling slightly at the two heads, silver and jet, bent toward each other.

In the week that followed, Viley arranged for several of the best mile horses to be brought to Metairie. His idea was to have Lexington train over four miles against four very fast horses, swapping out each rival horse at the mile mark, so that Lexington would continually be pressed on by a fresh sprinter. Jarret thought it an ingenious scheme that would suit the horse's competitive spirit.

One of the horses Viley leased was named Little Flea, a gelding sired by the famous Grey Eagle and said to be the fastest miler in the country. "We'll save him up for the fourth mile," Viley declared. "That'll be a true test."

It was a test Lexington passed effortlessly. Never seriously challenged by the first three horses, Lexington streaked alone toward the three-mile mark. There, Little Flea's jockey gave the miler his head and the sprinter leaped forward and tried to cut in front of Lexington. The stallion wasn't having it. Without breaking stride, Lexington jostled the gelding out of the way and then pulled ahead in a stunning burst of speed. Little Flea finished far behind, an ineffectual pacemaker for a horse who knew how to set his own blistering pace.

While Viley, Jarret, and Meichon worked with the horses, Ten Broeck schemed to get the racing world's attention for his big race. The turf press was suddenly full of his letters, challenging breeders of every state to send their best representative for what he touted as the ultimate test of excellence, a national contest for thoroughbred supremacy. The race would be held at Metairie on April 1, two four-mile heats. As he had always purposed, owners would put down five thousand dollars each, and that would make up the winner's purse, less one-thousand-dollar consolation prizes to any entrants that were not distanced.

The former president, Millard Fillmore, just a year out of the White House, said he planned to attend. By mid-March, interest in the race had grown so intense that New Orleans declared the day a holiday. Soon, every hotel in the city was booked out. Even in distant cities like New York, punters looked forward to following the race via "the lightning," the new telegraph. The turf press warned against unscrupulous gamblers who would get the flash and then try to make wagers with those who had not yet heard news of the winner.

Around this time, Mary Barr wrote to Jarret again, confirming her family's plans to attend the exciting race. "We are to be crammed into the servants' attic of the Charles Hotel, since despite my grandfather and my great-uncle's best influences no other accommodations could be secured. We all very much look forward to seeing our Kentucky stallion carry the day."

JESS

In the green-tinged afternoon light, Jess propped herself on an elbow and traced the long muscles of Theo's thigh. "*Vastus*," she whispered, slowly running her index finger down the outside of his quadricep from hip to knee. "*Sartorius*," she murmured, stroking back up the center of his leg. "*Gracilis . . .*"

Theo rolled over and grabbed her hand as her finger grazed his inner thigh. "Not there! It tickles!" He pinned her hand to the pillow and buried his face in her neck, kissing her deeply.

Just then, Clancy, who had waited tactfully at the foot of the bed, jumped up between them, tongue lolling. Jess scratched his head. "Do you think he's hungry?"

"Probably just bored," said Theo. "We usually go for a run before it gets this late."

"If you want to take him, I could start making something for dinner . . . if you'd like to stay?"

"That would be outstanding," said Theo. "I'm starving."

"I think we forgot to have lunch."

"So we did. Mind if I . . . ?" He pointed toward the bathroom.

"Course."

Jess shrugged on a silk bathrobe and went to get some fresh towels from the dryer, stopping to glance quickly into the pantry to make sure she had dinner fixings. She hadn't planned for this. Before they'd gone their separate ways the previous weekend, Jess had casually offered to give him a behind-the-scenes tour of the Natural History Museum sometime. He'd responded that he'd like to show her some of his favorite paintings.

The next Saturday, they'd met again at the American Art Museum. Jess had always enjoyed art, in the vague way most people enjoy it. But as Theo led her from painting to painting, she began to understand that his engagement was something quite different. Art, to him, was a way of responding to and shaping social change. She was stunned by how much he knew about every artist. He spoke of their eccentricities fondly, as you would of a close friend.

He led Jess to a painting of a Black woman selling flowers. She leaned in and read the wall plate. "Frédéric Bazille, *Young Woman with Peonies*. I don't know this artist."

"He was in the outer circle of the French Impressionists. Look how she offers the bouquet to a potential client, but she doesn't seem to care if he buys them or not. She's got that little frown line between her eyes—see, there?— 'Take it or leave it, mister'—as if she's impatient that he can't make up his mind. She's not a bit ingratiating. And the peonies, of course, are Bazille's *bisou* to Manet, who was the leader of the French avant-garde at the time. Manet loved peonies, cultivated them. There's a peony at the center of the bouquet that the Black servant is offering the prostitute in Manet's *Olympia*. That painting was at the height of its notoriety when Bazille painted this one. Everyone in the Paris art world would've got the reference."

"A Black servant in *Olympia*? I only remember the scowly White nude, and how upset everyone was that Manet didn't paint her in a classical style."

Theo pulled out his cell phone and called up the image with a few taps. "Here," he said, handing it to Jess.

"Wow. I've looked at that picture dozens of times. How could I not have noticed her?"

Theo frowned. "I'd be surprised, I guess, except that I once sat through a forty-minute lecture on that painting and the professor didn't mention her. He spent more time on the black cat at the nude's feet than the interesting woman who occupies half the canvas. I call it the Invisible Man effect, or in this case, Invisible Woman. Which is kind of the whole point of my work. To say, Hey, we're here. We've always been here. Look at us. In fact, we have to go to the Portrait Gallery," he said. "I have to show you something." Jess almost had to jog to keep up with him as he found his way to the work he loved.

She gazed up at a depiction of a young Black man, wearing modern clothes while riding a rearing nineteenth-century warhorse. "It's the identical composition of Jacques-Louis David's *Napoleon Crossing the Alps*, and that's exactly what this artist, Kehinde Wiley, does—puts contemporary Black men into old masters' compositions. He's a bit of a role model for me, actually. He's half Nigerian, too, and he went to Yale."

It was midafternoon when they finally left the gallery in search of a late lunch. Deep in conversation, they let Clancy choose the direction. When Jess realized that the dog's olfactory interests had led them a short block from her place, she asked Theo if he wanted to stop in and give Clancy a bowl of water.

The rest had followed in an urgent, wordless, mutual elation.

As she handed the fresh towels around the door to the shower, Theo reached out and grasped her wrist, pulling her to him under the cascading water as her robe fell in a wet heap at their feet. He turned her around to lather her hair, his fingers strong against her scalp. She leaned back against him. Wet and glistening, they fell back onto the bed as the dog shifted his weight from one paw to the other. When they eased apart, Clancy gave a single soft whine and tilted his head.

"If he could be drumming his fingers, he would be," Jess laughed.

"Sorry, Clance. We'll go now. I mean it this time." The dog squirted away toward the front door and then writhed back, circling around Theo's feet as he dressed. Jess sat up and watched as they bounded together out the door.

She pulled on an Indian cotton shift and went to the pantry to gather ingredients. With the heirloom tomatoes she'd bought at Eastern Market, she decided she could make a puttanesca sauce. She set a big pot of water on the stove, smashed garlic, chopped the anchovies. Minutes later the apartment filled with a rich, salty aroma. She hummed as she dipped each tomato into the roiling water and then pinched off the slippery skins. Theo came back with a baguette in one hand and a good bottle of cabernet sauvignon in the other. Jess read the label and nodded approval, handing him the corkscrew. Later, as he chased the last smear of sauce with a crusty heel of bread, Jess lifted her glass and watched the ruby glow absorb the candle flame.

"Why art, and not foreign policy, or something, like your parents?"

"I could ask you: why bones?" he said. "Who knows why we do what we do?" He tilted his head thoughtfully. "I suppose, for me, it started with that one special teacher. He would take the class—the whole unruly lot of us— around the school—they had some pretty splendid paintings at that place. He'd stop at a picture and make us spend the entire period looking at it. Most of the boys thought it was a bore. But I got into it. How the more you looked, the more you gleaned. All the 'ways of seeing' that John Berger wrote about."

Jess snorted. "John Berger? They made us watch his documentaries when I was at school. You surely don't buy anything that pompous old Pom had to say."

Theo set his glass down. "Berger lived most of his life in France, actually." His voice was suddenly very clipped. "He was a part Italian, part Jewish-Marxist who despised the British upper class. Hardly a 'pompous old Pom.'"

"Whoops. 'Scuse me. Am I being an antipodean bogan?"

Theo picked up his wine and gazed at her coolly. "Bogan?"

"You know: uncouth, unsophisticated. Working class."

"In fact, I don't know."

"Well, sorry." Jess felt her own accent oozing into broad diphthongs. "I guess 'bogan' is a word that only bogans use." The sharp edge of an old chip bit into her shoulder. In her first year at university, she'd felt put down by affluent, private school kids who carried a polish and an experience of the world she lacked. Now Theo was making her feel exactly the same way. She hadn't reckoned him for a snob, despite the Oxford-Yalie background. Was that some kind of racism—because he was Black, she assumed he therefore couldn't be a pompous, upper-class twit? She felt an irrational urge to double down on what she knew was a thinly held opinion formed when she was—what—thirteen years old?

"Berger did spout the biggest bunch of seventies sexist claptrap I ever came across."

"*Berger?* Berger was an ardent critic of objectification and female passivity in Western art. He was among the first to point out the equal female agency in non-Western depictions of sex. I can't believe how thoroughly you've misconstrued him."

Jess pouted. His superior attitude was really pissing her off.

Apparently, the feeling was mutual. He stood, pushed back his chair, and flung his napkin on the table. "Well, I'm glad we discovered this cataclysmic disagreement early. This relationship clearly has no future, if we have divergent views on critical methodology among Marxist-feminist art historians."

He was frowning, drawn brows, lips thin. Then, suddenly, the frown inverted into a dimpled grin. Jess laughed.

"Bit soon for our first argument?" she said.

"At least it wasn't over who is our favorite Kardashian." He paused a beat, the dimple deepening. "Still, if it wasn't for that fabulous puttanesca sauce I might not be able to forgive you."

Jess picked up her napkin and flicked him on the wrist. "See? You are a sexist!"

"Well then, could I subject you to a bit more male gaze?" He gently pulled her up from the chair and reached for the hem of her dress.

"Only while I exercise equal sexual agency." She put the tips of her fingers against his chest and pushed him backward into the bedroom.

"Indian miniatures come to mind," Theo said. "Lots of female agency. Blue Shiva, women on top. We could try a *tableau vivant* . . ."

She shut him up with a long kiss.

He didn't leave that night. In the morning, he took Clancy out for a walk and brought back croissants and the Sunday *New York Times*. In the afternoon, they strolled back to the Mall. At the Natural History Museum, Jess led him right past the flashy interactive displays and into the research areas where the science was done. She showed him projects she'd worked on and led him down the long corridors of cabinets that contained bones prepared over a century earlier, pulling out drawers to show off her favorite specimens. She liked the way he obsessed over the improbable geometry of a shark vertebra, turning the delicate triangle of bone in his fingertips. She enjoyed the wonder on his face when she handed him the jawbone of a juvenile *Utahraptor* that had lived 125 million years ago. When they finally said goodbye, at dusk, she watched him walk off down the Mall, deep in conversation with the dog.

The next day, alone in the quotidian and decidedly unromantic precincts of the frass-scented bug room, she couldn't stop thinking about him. Theo was nothing like the other men she'd fallen for. Previous lovers had been outdoorsy types with wilderness skills and few intellectual pretensions. At uni in Australia, there'd been the lumberjack turned eco warrior who spent half a year in the crown of a *Eucalyptus regnans* in Tasmania in order to stop his ex-employers from cutting it down. During her master's, she had a brief fling with the Israeli captain of a Sea Shepherd catamaran on his way to harass whalers in the Faroes. And a year earlier, there'd been an Icelandic sniper on contract to the Smithsonian to protect scientists in the field. He'd gone off to Alaska to fire sedatives at polar bears if they threatened ichthyologists doing fish counts, and had decided to stay up there.

She'd known from the get-go that relationships with global adventurers and committed activists weren't likely to be enduring. It had suited her not to have to think long term. As she hummed her way distractedly around her lab, it became clear that for all her independent ways, she'd missed this feeling—the heightened senses, the slight sparkle of the air—even if it made it difficult to focus on the task at hand.

But she did have work to do. Catherine would be waiting on the promised CT scans and she hadn't even fully unpacked the horse's skeleton yet. She put her palms flat on the bench on either side of the wrapped skull and tried to center her thoughts. Then she began to peel back the layers of foam. She was especially careful as she drew off the last layer, which contained a cottony cushion around the delicate nasal bones. They'd survived intact this long; she didn't want to be the one to damage them.

It was only when the skull was fully exposed that Jess noticed something wrong. The left lateral, the lacrimal bone, should have been a delicate crescent swooping underneath the scoop of the eye orbit. Instead, it was a raised, lumpy knuckle.

Jess's first thought was that the skull had been damaged in the mounting; that the armature supporting the skull on the spinal column might have accidentally been pushed through the lacrimal bone and then been plastered over to conceal the error. But on closer inspection she could see that wasn't so. The marks from the armature attachment were in the correct relationship, the delicate, hand-forged brass screws typical of the nineteenth century placed exactly as they should be.

It was the bone itself that was malformed. Something had happened to this horse when it was alive. Something dreadful.

TEN BROECK'S JARRET

Jarret watched all week as cloudbursts poured rain onto Metairie's spongy track. Then, as if Richard Ten Broeck had command of the weather, the morning of the race dawned fair and cloudless. Ten Broeck had the very surface for his mudder, and a glorious spring day to tempt a big crowd to the track to watch him run.

By race time, the sodden soil exhaled a warm mist that rose and billowed over the track. Through the milky haze flickered shifting facets of brilliant color: the ruby, garnet, sapphire, and topaz of the jockeys' silks. Clouds of vapor blurred the horses into a single surge of heaving muscle as the outriders ponied the racehorses toward their positions at the starting line.

Jarret felt his skin slick with moisture. Ten Broeck had given him an embroidered banyan coat to wear, and now nervous sweat and the damp air glued the cloth to his limbs. Gripping the reins of his own horse and Lexington's both, he tried to shrug himself free of the constriction. He glanced at Meichon, who had been vomiting with nerves before mounting up for the race. The boy had sweated through his ruby silks, which now clung darkly to his birdlike bones, making him look blood drenched. Jarret stared up into the brilliant blue sky to clear away that ill-omened image. The other outriders were pulling back from their charges. Unable to delay any longer, he gave

Meichon full control of the reins, uttered a final word of reassurance, and wheeled his horse away to join the other outriders on the far rail.

As he drew close to the crowd, Jarret caught fumes of cognac and claret mingled with the aromas of ripe cheese and roasted fowl. Seeing the horses about to fall in line, spectators wrapped up the remains of their picnics and jostled each other for the best vantage points.

Richard Ten Broeck didn't seem at all troubled that only four states were represented at his great challenge. When Willa Viley posited that growing tensions over the slave issue had robbed them of any entrants from the northern states, Ten Broeck dismissed it. "Since when did a sportsman, north or south, let politics come between him and a purse? No, Willa. If they have not entered it is because they think they cannot win. And though it is not in my interest to bruit it about, I think they have seen the matter clearly."

Now he left Viley to entertain the former president in the grandeur of the stands, and moved with his usual composure through the throng, accepting greetings from the diverse crowd. Whatever happened on the track, he was already a winner on the gate receipts alone. Twenty thousand souls had descended on the racetrack, paying a dollar each for the privilege. Even as the first heat was about to start, stalled carriages still jammed the shell road, an unbroken line of them, stretching back for a mile or more. Inside the gates, young men—and some few women—scrambled into the treetops to secure a view.

As he made his way closer to the rail, Ten Broeck rehearsed the race in his mind. Three of the four entrants—Lexington, Lecompte, and Arrow—were sons of Boston, and this contest would prove which was superior. Ten Broeck had sold Arrow to Duncan Kenner, a sugar baron in Ascension Parish, since gelding hadn't settled the horse's foul temper. A nagging concern was the jockey whom Kenner had purchased to ride Arrow. Ten Broeck had been reading with some pleasure an article in the *Spirit of the Times*, detailing how the potential size of the purse offered for his Great State Post Stakes had pushed up the asking price for good thoroughbreds. But at the end of the list of horses that had recently changed hands for elevated prices, the newspaper mentioned in an aside that human property, such as "the Jockey Abe," had also seen some inflation. The paper reported that Adam Bingaman, Ten Broeck's good friend, had sold Abe Hawkins to Kenner for twenty-three hundred dollars.

Ten Broeck read this report with some chagrin. His tenuously held scruples about the slave economy did not stop him from briefly musing whether he should have himself bid for Abe Hawkins. The boy was known as the Black Prince for his ebony skin, and now he had fetched a princely ransom. Ten Broeck thought uneasily of previous races when he had watched Abe ride with nerve in come-from-behind victories, and other times when he had pushed and jostled for pole position with brutal recklessness. The young French boy Meichon would be no match for Abe if it came to such a contest.

Highlander, the four-year-old champion from Alabama, also had a tough and canny jockey, a White New Yorker, Gilbert Watson Patrick, which perhaps explained the heavy betting that had made him the favorite.

But Ten Broeck saw his chief danger in the Mississippi entrant, Lecompte, unbeaten in five starts and owned by a gentleman Ten Broeck ardently disliked, General Thomas Jefferson Wells, a planter in Rapides Parish. Wells resented Ten Broeck's swift rise in New Orleans racing society and let it be known that he considered him a parvenu, if not a blackleg. Lecompte had outstanding endurance and a blazing first burst of speed. He posed a triple threat, having more experience and being arguably out of the better mare, Reel, who had seven consecutive wins before retiring to become a broodmare. The third factor was Wells's esteemed Black trainer, Hark. An elderly man with long experience, he had risen through the brutalities of the slave system to have full command of Wells's extensive racing and breeding operation.

Now, as the horses jostled and strutted near the track, Ten Broeck gazed out and noted that Abe had dismissed his outrider. He had steered Arrow back from the fray, waiting till the last moment to bring him forward, leaning on the horse's neck as if in some kind of confidential parlay. Ten Broeck supposed it was Abe's way of containing the horse's notorious temper.

If only he had known that Bingaman was of a mind to sell the boy! Still, twenty-three hundred dollars. For a jockey who could be thrown and trampled and lose all value in a second's mischance. Once crippled, not only the investment wiped out, but then the burden of his upkeep. Better to pay a freeman, like little Meichon, whose mischance could only harm one's purse in the event, not the evermore. Perhaps, speaking of free men, he should have paid the higher fee and secured the services of Gil Patrick, whose long experience could match Abe's innate skill . . .

It was unlike Ten Broeck to waste so much time second-guessing his decisions. He was vexed with himself. He shrugged and shook off all thoughts of things that could not now be changed. He would put his faith in his own judgment. He had the best horse; he was sure of it. The rest would follow.

As he moved through the crowd, it became apparent that the betting had become feverish. Stakes were various: Women wagered their kid gloves, their lace handkerchiefs. Men, their guns, their cash, or their cotton crops. As Ten Broeck made his way to the fence to watch the start, a punter with whom he was unacquainted grasped him by the sleeve. "A plantation will change hands today," the man confided. Ten Broeck gently detached the man's fingers from his coat with a gloved hand. "Oh, more than one, sir, I assure you of it," he said, and swept on to claim his favored vantage point beside the rails as the clock ticked on toward the 3:30 starting time.

The drum tapped the start. There was a second's delay as spectators grasped that the race was on, then a cheer went up. It was a base, animal roar that began on the fence and rippled backward, gaining in volume. Even the genteel ladies in the high stands opened their delicate throats and pierced the sky with their soprano squealing.

Lexington sprang into the lead, with Arrow coming up second and the other two horses bunched together neck and neck behind. For one minute, two—minutes that stretched like rubber, pulled outside the normal human experience of time—they held that formation.

At the mile mark, beyond, still they held. Then, on the far turn, Lecompte's jockey, John, urged his mount to make a dash. The horse came up, nosing past Arrow. Abe and John turned toward each other, exchanging furious glances. Abe rose up, seeming to float out of his stirrups, and plied his whip.

There's your mistake, Jarret thought.

A horse like Arrow, lashed bloody too often in attempts to tame his temper, would be hardened to the whip and resent it. Sure enough, the horse immediately stopped giving. He dropped back, despite Abe's continued urging. For a few moments, it was a three-horse race. Then Highlander began to falter. Gil Patrick tried, but couldn't rouse him.

John moved Lecompte into the gap and drew level with Lexington. Jarret watched the two horses—the rich red chestnut and the bronze-sheened bay, so different in their style of going. Where Lexington stretched out, Lecompte rose up, gathering himself in high, arched strides. He was a bigger horse than Lexington and he seemed to expand even more as he ran. They plunged forward, nose by nose. But then, almost imperceptibly, Lecompte slipped back. Inch by inch, the bigger horse gave ground, leaving Lexington once again in the lead by a neck.

"He's just feeling you, that's all," Jarret murmured. "Don't fall for it, Henri." He worried that young Meichon might conclude that Lecompte had done his dash and, aiming to save energy for the second heat, ease Lexington too early. "Don't fall for it, Henri." Jarret was speaking the words aloud now, crying them fruitlessly into the general cacophony. "Don't fall for it, Henri! Don't you be fooled."

The horses plowed into the fourth mile, and still Lexington held a narrow lead. Spouts of soupy mud flew up from the plunging hooves, splattering the spectators who thronged the rails.

Jarret began to entertain a hope that Lecompte truly lacked the wherewithal for a further challenge. Then, as they came around the turn and into the straightaway, Jarret stared hard at John's mud-encrusted hands, positioned oddly on the reins. John was holding Lecompte, even while seeming to unpracticed eyes to be urging him. Canny and patient into the home stretch, John held Lecompte back till the last possible instant. Then he let him go, releasing the winning burst of speed this son of Boston was known for. He came up in a hail of flying clods to hold level with Lexington. Jarret stopped breathing.

But Lexington eyed his rival and decided he wasn't to be challenged. Like a machine, he changed gears. One length, two. Even as he flew past the post, a clear winner, Lexington was still surging away. In the stands, the Kentucky contingent screamed their approval. Their horse won by three lengths, ending Lecompte's undefeated streak.

Highlander finished in qualifying range and could try for redemption in the second heat. Arrow, beyond the distance post, was disqualified. He would not run again that day. Abe Hawkins wore a grimace of disgust as he left the track. He was not used to losing, much less being distanced.

Jarret rode out to Meichon, who was trembling with fatigue. He signaled the other grooms to come assist the young jockey from the saddle. He took Lexington's reins. "Don't be standing around to take compliments," he told Meichon. "We ain't won yet. You got to do this whole thing again in one short hour. Go rest now."

Jarret walked Lexington, listening to the crowd as the noise level rose with the free flow of champagne. Desperate punters cried out new odds, avid for someone, anyone, to take their bets on the wondrous stallion from Kentucky. Soon, the money was $100 to $50, Lexington against the field.

Henri Meichon, washed down and clad in fresh silks, seemed somewhat restored and a good deal calmer when Jarret ponied him out for the start of the second heat. Jarret was glad of it; he hadn't liked the gray cast to the boy's skin after his earlier win. Jarret thought of Henri as a promising colt broken too early, ridden too hard. It puzzled him that Ten Broeck, with so much at stake, put his faith in this unseasoned boy. But he pushed these feelings down and arranged his face for Henri so that all he would see there as he gave him the reins was confidence.

As Jarret pulled back from the starting line, he cast an appraising eye over the other horses. As he expected, Lecompte had cooled out well; unfortunately, so had Highlander. Speed and bottom, Jarret thought. The essential qualities of the four-mile horse. All three of these horses had them.

The tiny field made a clean start. Lexington got off first and took the rail. On the first turn, Gil Patrick urged Highlander to run around Lexington and take the track. John brought Lecompte up then and challenged Highlander for the lead, pushing Lexington back to third place.

"He won't like that one bit," Jarret muttered. Finishing the first mile, Lecompte was running easily, well clear of Lexington, but Highlander began to labor. Gil Patrick couldn't do anything, and the horse dropped back. It was once again a two-horse race as they entered the third mile. Lecompte began to draw away. Lexington seemed unable to match his speed. Soon, Lecompte was a full eight lengths in front. Lexington was, suddenly, frighteningly far behind.

"Don't give up now, Henri. Lexington won't. Don't you doubt him. Just don't," Jarret pleaded, his voice lost in the roar coming now from every throat on the course. Worse, Jarret saw a sudden lightning bolt of yellow—the Highlander jockey's silks—streaking up on the rail. Gil Patrick, emboldened, had found some reserve in Highlander and was driving his horse to take Lexington's second place.

"Here he comes—do you see him?" he cried pointlessly. The Alabama horse came up level with Lexington's hindquarters, then his withers, then his throat latch. They were paired now, as if yoked together. They plunged on, slapping through the mud, neck and neck. For an instant Highlander pushed a nose ahead.

And that, apparently, was too much for Lexington's competitive heart. He broke away from Highlander and lunged ahead. Meichon plied his crop and asked Lexington in earnest. They drew level with Lecompte and swung for home, galloping with not a hair between them.

Then, as if there had been no doubt that this had always been his intention, Lexington put forth a further burst of speed and drew away. In that final furlong, the spectators' cries gained volume, rising as the horse advanced. In the Ladies' Pavilion, women from the Kentucky contingent, heedless of decorum, stood up on their chairs and screamed with unbridled joy. One length in front, then two. The cries pitched to a roar as Lexington passed under the wire and won by four lengths.

When Jarret caught up to Lexington to lead the winner through the thronging admirers, he noticed that the horse's face remained entirely unspattered, his white blaze gleaming as though he'd never left his stable. "How'd you do that, with the other one in front of you just 'bout the whole way?"

Lexington paraded up to be admired by Millard Fillmore as Ten Broeck accepted plaudits on the horse and on the event itself, which a general consensus declared the best day of racing in the city's history. Because of the heavy track, the times had been unremarkable—over eight minutes in each heat—but everyone concurred that the slower times did not capture the excitement of the races, with the excellent and closely matched horses and the uncertainty of the victory in the final heat. Even the composed Ten Broeck allowed himself a broad smile, which was the equivalent of another man's raucous laughter.

Just when Jarret was thinking that Lexington had had enough of crowds and attention, Ten Broeck nodded to him. "Cool him down, take him to his stall, and in the morning we'll have his shoes off and put him out to pasture for the rest of the spring season. Viley and I think he'll be better off for the big fall contests if he has a few months' rest. Meanwhile, you, young man, can have your pick: a fifty-dollar purse, a month to go visiting, or a tutor at your disposal for daily schooling. No need to decide now. We'll talk tomorrow." He gave a small smile. "But do not expect me early."

Jarret led the horse away. When he had walked Lexington cool, he whisked him all over and brushed him, then fed him oats and dried apples. He was bone tired as he climbed the stairs to his loft. He opened the door, shrugging off the fancy banyan coat. He was struggling to extract himself from the tapered sleeves and didn't at first see the still figure, sitting silently on his bed in the failing light.

"Miss Clay?" he said, startled. "You don't ought to be here."

"Jarret, it seems like you have spent your whole life saying that to me, or words just like it. I think perhaps a 'Good evening,' or 'It's nice to see you after so long a time' might be a more proper greeting."

"Well, I say it because it's true. This ain't the right place for a lady, in the quarters of a—of a—"

"Of an old childhood friend? May I presume you are a friend, Jarret? I feel it to be true. I entertain a hope that it may be so."

Jarret felt his face grow hot. He hardly knew how he thought about Mary Barr. A sweet-enough child. An attentive pupil, when he taught her to ride. A pitiable girl, caught in the vise of her parents' unhappy marriage. Someone whose advice he had heeded at a fraught moment in his life. But a friend?

No, he had never thought she was his friend. And now, in just the months since he'd last seen her, she had transformed herself. The young lady who now rose gracefully from the edge of his bed was not the awkward girl he'd left in Lexington. She had a new polish, new poise, and a great deal more confidence. Jarret would have been surprised to know that Mary Barr, looking at him, discerned a similar change. The taciturn boy who had lived in his father's shadow at the Meadows was barely recognizable in this fine-looking young man who now addressed her with an air of quiet authority. "Miss Clay, you need to go."

"I came up here because it is impossible to talk to you freely anywhere else in this horde. I don't have long. Grandfather is celebrating with Captain Viley and Mr. Ten Broeck just presently, so I took the chance to slip away, saying I wished to visit Darley. To be quite frank, they are all of the gentlemen so far gone in drink that I hardly think they will recall what I said. But in any case, I will be brief. You said in your letter that things are well for you here, and I was glad to know it. And now I see for myself"—she waved an arm to encompass the room—"that in many ways it is so. But still, I am concerned for you."

"You don't need to mind about me, Miss Clay. Like you say, things are as well as they can be here. I did right to come. Especially now that my father is gone."

"And I am sorry for it, and sorry to have been the means of you learning it, with no one nearby who knew him to grieve with you. But, Jarret, you must know that tensions between the slave power and its resisters grow very great. There is even talk of secession. My father says men are ready to fight to stop the spread of slavery into the new territories."

"Miss Clay, I can't see what that got to do with me right now. What *does* got to do with me is you being here where you shouldn't. Please, you got to go . . ."

Mary Barr waved a hand to brush away his concern. "Jarret, of course it has to do with you. It has everything to do with you. Why do you think there were no northern horses running here today? The enmity is grown so great that even the turf provides no neutral ground. And you may not see it here, with your head buried in haybales, but in January this year Senator Douglas—"

Her voice had risen as she became more emotional, and Jarret raised a hand to hush her.

"Miss Clay, you really do got to go. I still don't see how Senator Douglas doings back in January have a lick to do with me. But I can tell you for sure they gonna skin me standing if anybody come by and find you here."

"I will go. But only if you will come to see me tomorrow, at the St. Charles Hotel."

Jarret nodded reluctantly. He would never get the girl out of his quarters otherwise.

"So, you *will* come. Tomorrow?"

"Tomorrow, after chores." He shooed her out as if she were a wandering hen. Then he latched his door and let the anger rise. How could she be so heedless of her own reputation and his very life?

Tired as he was, agitation robbed him of his restful sleep.

In the morning, he leaned wearily against a post as the farrier snapped the nail heads and flipped off Lexington's racing plates. He stretched the horse's legs and rasped each hoof to ensure a perfect trim. Then, as before, he ran a scarred hand through Lexington's mane. "There's me fine lad." The horse responded with an affectionate bump of his nose against the farrier's narrow shoulder.

"He don't do that with most people," Jarret observed as he unfastened the crossties.

"Ah well." The farrier bent to gather his tools. "They can tell a friend, as you'd be knowin' yerself, t'be sure."

Ten Broeck had given Jarret directions to the property close by Metairie on which Lexington was to be agisted for the remainder of the spring season. It was the farm of a widow who lived alone with a single servant and did not actively work the land anymore, making her mite by renting out her rich pastures. The spring grass had come in lush, and in the early light the new growth shimmered, damp and fragrant. Jarret untacked the horse and led him out to the meadow. As he unlatched the gate, Lexington's nose twitched in anticipation. He was half in, half out of the gate when he dropped his head to graze. Jarret had to push hard on his hind end to trouble him to move forward. "Easy now!" Jarret laughed. "You got weeks to eat all this. No need to rush." Jarret hung the bridle and lead rope by the gate and then lingered awhile, listening to the horse tear at the moist tuffets. There was an unvarying three-beat rhythm to it: a long ripping sound, like fingers playing a washboard, then two hummer-blow thumps as he masticated. Jarret found himself tapping his foot on the railing to the waltz-like percussion.

Later that day, he saddled up Ghosthawk, the gray gelding he used as his track pony, and trotted reluctantly down the shell road to the city. He supposed he must keep his promise to the Clay girl. And once she was out of his quarters, he had reflected on what she had said. It would not hurt him to hear more, although he found her notion that White folk might get up in arms for the Black man completely implausible. These were that girl's daddy's opinions, and that man always had been off in his own boat on some branch of the river no one else ever rowed on. Now it seemed to Jarret that he'd pulled his daughter on board with him. Time was, if Cash Clay had said to his daughter, Go left, she'd just as soon have gone right, just to vex him.

But what was that, to him? He gave his head a shake to clear his thoughts. Whatever was going on with that girl and her people had naught to do with him, except that he had to take time out of his day to go see her in a place he'd rather not be. But if he didn't answer her summons, as he'd said he would, the fool girl would likely land up again at Metairie looking for him. He couldn't risk that.

He was coming to the end of the shell road, the city closing around him. Too much noise, too many smells, too many people speaking too many languages. All those different words for the exact same thing. Jarret preferred the gestural language of horses. Any horse could tell you how things stood with the very same flick of the ear or a swish of the tail as any other horse. People could twist you up, saying words that seemed friendly when they weren't by any means your friend. But when a mare pinned her ears, you knew she wasn't looking to be congenial. Words set down on a page, that was a different thing. You could take your own time with them, to glean the sense. And you could skip past the foolish ones. You couldn't do that when someone was speaking nonsense right to your face.

And there she was, waiting for him. Sitting by herself on a wicker chaise on the verandah of that wedding-cake building. She was reading a book and had not seen him. He walked the horse to a place in her line of sight, waiting for her to glance up as she turned a page.

Finally, she did so, raised a hand in greeting, and set her book aside. He dismounted then and stood waiting as she lifted her hem and made her way down the steps and across the muddy street. Even though there was nothing especially remarkable in such a meeting—a young lady instructing a Black servant, as it would seem to any observers on the verandah who chanced to take note—Jarret felt acutely uncomfortable and shifted his weight from foot to foot as Mary Barr took up where she had left off, with Senator Douglas's bill that would let western settlers decide if they will have slavery or not.

"It was supposed to be settled; no slavery in the north, ever. My father expects the Senate will vote any day. He is assured that if it passes, blood will be spilt in the territories—in Kansas, in Nebraska. He says no man will listen to another's position. There may be great-souled men in both parties, my father avers it; I do not know—"

Two small pink blotches had appeared on her cheeks. Her voice rose in pitch.

"Look—since you can read—" She pulled from the pocket of her skirt a crumpled note and thrust it at him. "I had thought not to show you this, but you must know the extent of the hatred that is brimming. Read it. It was sent to my father. I took it from his desk without his knowing."

Jarret took the page. He looked around. Too many witnesses. People like him were not supposed to be reading. He handed it back. "You tell me what it says."

Mary Barr read in a shaky voice. *You may think you can awe and curse the people of Kentucky to your infamous course. You will find, when it is too late for life, the people are no cowards . . . the hemp is ready for your neck . . . plenty thirst for your blood . . .*

"That'll do." Jarret was sorry he had touched the same paper as one who could write down such hatred. And that, to a powerful White man, just because he favored emancipation. His hand traveled involuntarily to his own neck.

Mary Barr could see that she finally had his attention, so she came to her point. "I think you should come back with my grandfather to the Meadows. I have asked him, and he says he could ask Ten Broeck to sell you back, as a favor to him, on terms he can afford. Since that man has profited so well from the purchase of the horse, he will surely be in a generous mood. My grandfather will plead that since your father passed away, he needs you to manage his horses."

"You 'spect me to leave this horse? To leave Lexington, after I brought him this far?"

"But, Jarret, he's only a horse. There will be other horses—"

"There won't be. Not like him. Not to me."

"But you would be safe back in Kentucky. Here, should it come to a war, you might be impressed into any kind of dangerous service."

Jarret tried to command his voice. "Miss Clay, I know you mean for the best, and he your kin and all, but I got no cause to put trust in Marse Warfield. No cause. I'm fixing to stay here with Marse Ten Broeck. Go on back and tell your grandfather that you was mistaken and that he needs to let me be."

"But, Jarret . . ."

"Miss Clay, the only thing I need from you and your people is to leave me alone." He turned his back and lifted his weight into the stirrups. "Give my kind regards to Marse Warfield and have a safe trip home." He turned the horse and asked for a canter. The girl stood, astonished, watching his departing back.

It was near sunset when Ten Broeck sent for Jarret.

"Forgive the lateness of the hour," he said with his usual careful courtesy. "I was obliged to make many calls upon the town and"—he gave a slight smile—"as you might imagine, I did not make an early start upon them." If he had spent a dissipated night in celebration, he did not show it. He was as well barbered and dressed as ever. "I trust the farrier arrived, and the horse is now enjoying his respite?"

Jarret nodded. "He's well set. It's a fine-looking farm."

"Indeed. I am contemplating purchasing it someday, from the widow woman's heirs, who are distant connections and unlikely to require such a property. It is convenient to Metairie, after all. . . . But that's not today's business. I hear you paid some calls of your own upon the town today?"

Jarret cleared his throat. Did anything escape this man's scrutiny? He had nothing to be ashamed of, and yet he was discomfited.

"The Clay girl, that is to say, Miss Mary Barr Clay, she wanted to see me."

"Indeed, she did. Badly enough to make a most ill-judged visit of her own."

Jarret felt a flush climbing from his neck to his cheeks. "I tried to tell her that—I made her leave as soon—"

"Don't vex yourself. I know you did. She is headstrong, like her father. Fixed in her opinions. And, like her father, she has little regard for the opinions of the world. She will need to have a care there. It's one thing for a wealthy gentleman to flout convention, but society is more exigent regarding its young ladies. You did nothing wrong. Indeed, I was very gratified to learn that you expressed some degree of loyalty to me."

"Why wouldn't I?" Jarret blurted. "You treat me like a person."

Ten Broeck raised his eyebrows. "Unfortunate, that you have cause to find it remarkable." He looked down and rearranged some papers on his desk.

"The girl is not entirely wrong, you know. Neither is her father. There is a drift of things that could, ill managed, lead us into a most unfortunate schism. And I fear the political leadership is not—well, in any case—I have been thinking for some time that I would like to campaign my horses in England. I should not like to have all my interests vested in Louisiana if the national mood continues to darken in this way. I tell you this because I want you to know that there will be a place for you in my service, whatever befalls this country. Now, have you considered what you will take as my token of appreciation?"

"The tutor, if that's—"

"Very good. I had hoped you would so choose. I have it in mind to bring you up in my business, and you will need proficiency for that."

Almost a week later, Jarret was poring over a page of arithmetic when a stable hand interrupted him. "Marse Ten Broeck says to go fetch Lexington back from the farm. The farrier is on his way to put new plates on him. They fixing to race him again this Saturday coming."

"They *what?*" Jarret stood, pushing away the papers. "That can't be. That's just two days off and he's been doing nothin but getting fat on grass. Where is Marse Ten Broeck? I got to talk to him."

"He and Marse Viley in the dining room at the grandstand, but I don't think you . . ."

Jarret didn't stay to hear what the stable hand thought. He raced across the paddock and burst up the stairs that led to the gentlemen's dining room. The door was ajar. Viley's voice, agitated. Arguing the very points Jarret had proposed to make.

"They had the wit to keep their horse in training; we did not. It's folly to allow a match race with a proven champion when last week's race did nothing but improve him. Word is, Lecompte has been outperforming in his practice gallops all week. And Hark has switched riders."

"I heard. Hark advised Wells to retain the services of Abe Hawkins."

"Exactly. Kenner and Wells are Louisiana men first and foremost. They can't stomach being beaten by us—you'll always be a northerner to them. They are in a confederacy against us. Think on it, Richard. You know Wells resents your primacy—you have usurped him, in his own favored pursuit, in his own town, and now he sees a way to goad you. Wells is playing you for a fool!"

"You think?" Ten Broeck's voice was low and calm. Jarret had to struggle to hear him.

"Oh, I know. You'll get a crowd for a rematch, I've no doubt of it. But at what cost? You'll destroy the horse's reputation just as we're trying to build it. Worse, you'll break him down. Remember what happened to Grey Eagle— that noble horse, forced to a rematch within a week. Destroyed by it. I im- plore you, don't give way to this, this—unseemly lust for short-term gain. Whatever the gate receipts, they cannot be worth it."

"You mention the gate. I concede, the potential takings are not without interest to me. But consider, Willa. There is likely to be Leviathan betting on this match race. Two sons of Boston, noble kinsmen, both proven champions. It's the making of a legendary rivalry. We'll have a couple of days to see how Lexington goes in practice. We'll know which way to wager. One need not win in order to profit, after all."

"You'd—you'd bet against your own horse? That's ungentlemanly! I won't have it. I refuse this folly. I say the horse may not run."

"Say you so? How unfortunate. I fear I have already accepted General Wells's terms. Two thousand dollars for the purse, two four-mile heats, April eighth at Metairie. The telegraph is already reporting it."

"Then you must retract. I am also owner of this horse. I refuse."

"That would be dishonorable."

"Dishonorable! That's rich, coming from you. I see it now: You are what they have always said you were. You have the effrontery to assume the airs of a gentleman, to exchange salutations, even with presidents. And yet in fact you prowl among us only seeking plunder. To think I have defended you! I am embarrassed to be in partnership with you. You, sir, are nothing but a blackleg."

Jarret braced a hand against the wall. Richard Ten Broeck surely could not let stand such an insult to his honor. He waited for the inevitable explosion, the challenge that must follow. Instead, Ten Broeck's voice remained low and even.

"Well, Willa. I regret that you feel so. I will gladly relieve you of the burden of this partnership. What will you take for your interest?"

"You propose to buy me out?"

"Name your price."

Willa Viley fell silent. Jarret felt the truth of the situation. Viley would name a high price. Ten Broeck, flush with cash, would pay it. Lexington would be required to race, fat on spring grass, missing critical days of preparation. He leaned his head against the wall for a moment, despairing. Then he turned and crept down the stairs and away from the grandstand as fast as he could go. Ten Broeck must never know that another pair of ears had heard Viley's insult. There was nothing for it. He would go to fetch the horse.

An hour later, Jarret leaned against the stall door as the farrier tapped the last of the new racing plates into place. He finished up, as always, running a hand through Lexington's mane. But instead of the usual, "There's a good lad," Jarret heard him whisper: "It's a manky sort of man would ill use a grand horse like yerself."

It had not rained all week, and the dry track was fast. When Ten Broeck arrived to observe the workout gallops, Willa Viley was nowhere to be seen. As expected, the horse made sluggish times in the first several laps. Jarret called Meichon over to the fence when he'd run for just a mile. "That'll do. Don't push him too hard today. Tomorrow he'll be better." Meichon looked to Ten Broeck for confirmation. Ten Broeck raised his chin in assent. Meichon dismounted and Jarret led the horse away to cool off, certain that tomorrow would not be better at all.

Jarret couldn't sleep on Friday night. He tossed in his bed and finally descended to spend the night wakeful in Lexington's stall. In the morning, he took Meichon off for a private word. "I can't tell you not to use the stick and the spur, but I am asking you not to thrash him. He will give you what he can, you know that. Just don't ask him for more than he got."

Ten thousand spectators came to watch the race that Saturday. Some of the Kentucky delegation, on hearing of the rematch, had extended their stay in New Orleans. Jarret was relieved to see that the Warfield party was not among them. He did not want the old doctor to witness what he dreaded would be Lexington's humiliation.

Lecompte shot to the lead at the drum tap. Lexington contested hard, staying always within striking distance, but was never able to come up on the fitter horse. In the last mile, Meichon, desperate, began to lay on both whip and spur. Jarret couldn't watch. He knew the boy was punishing the horse to no purpose. Lecompte pulled away and won by six lengths. Abe Hawkins, hands down throughout the race, had not had to resort to either rowel or lash. The crowd erupted as word of the time spread from mouth to mouth. Lecompte had broken the record in a most spectacular fashion. His blistering 7:26 shaved six and a half seconds off the previous four-mile record, which had stood unchallenged for years.

When Jarret reached Lexington, he could see the horse's flanks heaving, his head drooping in obvious distress. He turned on Meichon. "What were you rowling him for?" he cried. "You could see it wasn't in him."

Meichon looked defiant. "Marse Ten Broeck say I 'ave to ride 'ard. I think—they say—he 'as bet against us, so 'e want no person to say he cheat."

Jarret threw his head back and cursed at the sky. He wanted to grab the crop from the jockey's hand and find Ten Broeck. But the horse's heaving breath brought him back to himself. He had to care for Lexington or the horse might drop from exhaustion. He shoved Meichon out of the way—the boy's chest felt flimsy as a bird's—and led the horse, gently and slowly, until his distended nostrils eased their bellows-like quest for air.

Jarret was relieved by how well the horse recovered. If he couldn't win this misbegotten contest, at least he might not be broken by it. By the time of the second heat, he seemed his usual self, dancing to the starting line. At the drum tap, Lexington shot into the lead, widening it to two lengths. Jarret was certain that Abe must be holding Lecompte back. Sure enough, at the third mile he made his move. Jarret expected to see Lecompte shoot past Lexington, but the earlier dominance wasn't there. Lexington was able to increase his pace so that the two hurtled on, nose-to-nose, with Lexington able to pull just ahead.

Only as they drew near the stand did Lecompte look like a threat, but then a voice called out, high and piercing, above the general roar of the crowd.

"Henri! Pull up your 'orse! Pull 'im up! The race is over!"

Meichon's head swiveled, searching for the source of the cry. As he lost his focus, Lecompte darted ahead.

Jarret yelled, "No! Go on!" But from his place with the outriders, Meichon could not hear him. Jarret heard Scott's voice, from the rail, crying a plaintive: "Go in and win!" Meichon turned again, looking for this new voice. Only then, several beats too late, came Ten Broeck's roar.

"Ride on, fool! Ride on!"

Meichon sat down and plied his spur. Half the crowd cheered him onward, others booed and jeered. Lexington responded and put on a blistering dash, but it was too late: Lecompte crossed the line and won by four lengths. Abe raised his crop high in the air, waving to the crowd in a victory salute.

THOMAS J. SCOTT

New Orleans, Louisiana

1854

I lost money on that race, but I made it back smartly. Dispatches on the controversy were in high demand. The New York turf papers were hot for every speculation. Generally, they took Ten Broeck's side, he being a native son of the north, but there was, as well, some measure of opprobrium for his greed in running an unfit horse. And Lecompte's record-setting time needed to be lauded with much verbosity.

General Wells, of course, had plenty to say about that on the record, while off the record he had even more to impart, of a highly slanderous nature, regarding his hated rival. Viley became his confederate in this, assiduously feeding grist to the rumor mill, making clear his disapprobation and letting it become well known that he had severed his partnership with Ten Broeck prior to the ill-judged contest.

Meanwhile, controversy broiled around the boy, Meichon, whose career took a mortal injury that day. Had someone really cried out to him to pull up, or had he been bribed to throw the race? If someone *had* yelled, was it an honest mistake or a nefarious trick? And if the latter, who was behind it—Wells or Ten Broeck?

Ten Broeck fired Meichon forthwith—he had to, if he were to plausibly distance himself from suspicion—and wrote to the turf papers. "For an owner to defend the defeat of his horse is an ungracious task," he admitted, before going on to ungraciously lay the blame for the defeat squarely on the narrow shoulders of his inexperienced jockey. He had, he said, been unsatisfied with Meichon's ride in the first heat and had another jockey already dressed to replace him in the second, but that boy's owner had refused to allow the ride at the last instant. It seems unlikely young Meichon will get other mounts of any note very soon. Yet I incline to think the youth was but a pawn in some high-stakes game.

There were rumors that Ten Broeck had bet heavily against his own horse and had planted a confederate in the crowd to confuse his callow jockey, this as an insurance in case his unfit-to-run horse managed to trounce expectations and pull ahead. But of course the man was too astute to have left a trail of bread crumbs, and even after I had interviewed every one of my connections at Metairie, all of whom had opinions but none of whom had proof, I was able to form no fixed view on that matter. I did learn, however, that Ten Broeck had secretly secured the services of Abe from Kenner, should there be a rematch. Later, I heard a further rumor that Ten Broeck had also tied up the services of Gil Patrick, which, if true, would leave Wells scrambling for a first-rate jockey.

With all this to work with, I was a busy scribe and, for once, decently compensated. Everyone wished to tell me their private theories of the case, except of course Jarret, who kept his own counsel, as always. I did note with great interest that when I saw him in company with Ten Broeck, something in the temper of their partnership had changed. Jarret barely spoke and didn't meet the man's eye. I was inclined to believe the youth was nursing a grudge over the ill usage of the horse. But I wondered if he held the evidence of a deeper corruption.

Ten Broeck, meanwhile, did not act like a man disgraced or traduced. And in the Crescent City, the matter seemed more like to prove nine days' wonder rather than ninety. A man as wealthy, connected, and presentable as Ten Broeck is unlikely to suffer long under the moral lash in any but the most Puritan circles, and in New Orleans those circles were small as motes.

His immediate reaction to Lexington's loss was to capitalize on the interest it had engendered. As soon as he had made arrangements binding the two top jockeys, he wrote an open letter to Wells, proposing a rematch later in the spring for a staggering ten thousand dollars, plus a generous share of the gate. Wells's brusque reply: *I beg leave to decline.*

If Ten Broeck felt the sting of this terse snub, he did not brood on it. He tried to rowel up Wells with another tartly worded letter to the *Spirit of the Times* that implied Wells lacked confidence in his horse and did not have the nerve to risk a rematch. Wells replied indignantly that Ten Broeck was merely trying to give his horse a "fictitious reputation" and to gain for himself a "wondrous notoriety" while at the same time tying up Wells's preferred rider, "thus being fortified against the possibility of a fair and equal challenge."

Unruffled, Ten Broeck became ingenious. If he could not get satisfaction in the usual way of a match race between gentlemen, he proposed a great innovation. He would run Lexington against the clock. If his horse could beat Lecompte's record time of 7:26, it would prove Lexington's superiority just as well as a rematch. Turfmen like novelty, so this was a tantalizing prospect. Two distinguished Virginian turfmen took up Ten Broeck's bold offer and backed Time against Lexington to the spirited tune of twenty thousand dollars. Ten Broeck, knowing how the notion of fortunes at stake increased the public fascination with a contest, gleefully accepted. Meanwhile, an enterprising clockmaker in New York devised an affordable stopwatch and advertised it as a necessary accoutrement for what was now being bruited as the Race Against Time.

The Crescent City had slumped, by then, into that summer stew in which no exertion is desired. Without fanfare—indeed, with some subterfuge—Ten Broeck sent Jarret and the horse north, where the stallion might be conditioned in a better clime. I learned of this quite by chance. One early evening, when some piece of business or other regarding an artistic commission had brought me to the track, I went to look for Jarret, thinking his lips might have loosened with the passing of weeks and that I might learn more about what had occurred in the now-infamous race. But when I went up to his quarters, I found his bed stripped and his effects gone. I then checked the stall blazoned with Lexington's nameplate and found it also empty. Try as I might, I was unable to uncover which facility had received them. Clearly, Ten Broeck was after cultivating a sense of mystery regarding the horse's training gallops. Since this, too, was fodder for a few column inches, I did not find the obfuscation ungratifying. My columns speculating on the where-abouts of the swift bay stallion kept me fed through the summer, if not on *boeuf au vin rouge*, at least on red beans and rice.

I wasn't able to discover where they spent that season until the pair re-turned, unheralded, to Metairie, very late in the fall. I came upon them just finishing off morning work. The horse had been brought to peak condition. I'd always thought the bay a splendid specimen. But now he moved into his characteristic low running posture as if he were made of silken fabric, not flesh and bone. As they came off the track, the youth dismounted and did not even bother to lead the horse by the reins. The beast followed at his shoul-der and moved left or right entirely by verbal command. I had never seen a highbred racehorse—a stallion, no less—biddable enough to do such things.

If the horse had improved, the youth had too. The months away had given him a new confidence. He was less shy with me and, when I asked, was ready to give an account of his adventures—and misadventures—in the north. I followed along as he cooled the horse off and led him to a paddock to graze. We leaned on the fence rail as he recounted how they had gone north by steamboat to Louisville and then onward with Ten Broeck's friend, Captain William Stuart, to Saratoga Springs, where they had rusticated among the fancy folk taking the waters in that spa town. After that pleasant interlude they had proceeded to New York City, to train at the new National Race Course. I assumed that he would have misliked the experience of such a large city, but when I asked, he looked thoughtful.

He said he was oppressed by the noise, which didn't stop even in dark of night, since people worked all hours. He'd roomed at a Black boardinghouse among free laborers and tradesmen, sharing a cot with a boy who made hawsers at the docks and reeked of pitch. He called that a blessing, since it was a clean stink, strong enough to overpower the fouler stenches of the place.

In the heat of late summer, Captain Stuart had fallen suddenly ill with what turned out to be the cholera. Jarret had helped to nurse him through the ghastly course of the disease until the poor man expired of it. I could tell he was still haunted by the experience. I knew something about cholera from medical school; the indignity and the terror of watching your innards leak their contents until there's naught to expel but the very stuff of your own guts. I remembered the rice-porridge look of those *in extremis* emissions. It was not a thing one could forget.

I asked him, after his grim recounting of this tragedy, what on earth he'd found *not* to dislike in that smelly, noisy, disease-ridden city. He looked at me with a frank, appraising look, as if to assess how far he could trust me with his true opinions.

He said it was the folk he came to know in the boardinghouse, every one of them with a powerful drive to work at some kind of trade, even if the task was hard, dirty, or thankless. You know why that was, Mr. Scott? he asked me. Tell me, I said. He stretched his hands out in front of him, his two palms facing up, and this, verbatim, is what he said: Their hands is their own. And that dollar that get put in those hands, that's their own dollar.

THEO

Theo's phone bleated with bright notes of the Coltrane ringtone he'd assigned to his friend Daniel. He hit answer and plopped on the sofa.

"Hey man, how's things in Chocolate City?"

Theo laughed. "How would I know? I live in Vanillatown."

"You still sulking over Makela? You haven't found some other fine woman can show you the real city?"

"Not sulking. Moving on."

"So you *have* found someone?"

Theo cleared his throat. "Actually, the woman I seem to be dating isn't from here. She's even more not-from-here than I am."

"'Seem to be dating'? Well shit, you are, or you aren't."

"She's White," he blurted.

There were a couple of seconds of dead air. Theo braced himself.

"No big. You won't be the first brother to fall for a snow bunny."

"I haven't exactly fallen for her. It's only been a couple of weeks."

"How'd you meet?"

Theo hesitated. Being tacitly accused of bike theft wasn't exactly a meet cute. "Ah, researching an article. For *Smithsonian* magazine. She runs a lab there." Best change the subject. "How's *your* new lab? How's San Francisco?"

Daniel had made a vast swerve in the middle of his sophomore year. He'd come east to Yale from his home in Baldwin Hills intending to be a music major and follow his parents into the recording industry. But he'd taken an intro genetics class to fill a science requirement and become obsessed with molecular biology targeting hard-to-treat cancers. His master's thesis, on disrupting a protein with the unlikely name of sonic hedgehog, had landed him a large grant at a biotech incubator. "The hours are crazy, but the lab's sick. Anything I want—mass spec, cryo-EM, Illumina sequencer—I just ask and boom, it's there. Bright shiny everything. But I literally step over people sleeping in the street to get into the place. The homelessness here is epic."

"It's not like New Haven was so great for poor folk."

"No, but the disparity wasn't so stark. This place is like some dystopian vision of inequality. I mean people are literally sleeping in the shadow of the Salesforce Tower. Anyway, reason I'm calling, Hakeem's been working his ass off at Stanford and Mike's sold his soul to Palantir. So we think we should all take a break—a long weekend—and hike Tuolumne Meadows. You know, see it before climate change totally fucks it. Do you think you could swing it?"

"Love to. Let me see if I can find a cheap flight."

Theo thought about the logistics as he and Clancy ran in Rock Creek Park. If he asked Jess to take Clancy for the weekend, would that imply too much? Perhaps a sitter from Rover.com would be less complicated. He looked down at Clancy, loping just a little ahead of him. The dog would be happier with Jess than a stranger, that was for sure. So why was he reluctant to risk the entanglement?

Daniel's call had made him a little later than usual starting his run. He realized he'd hit the post–private school drop-off hour. The mommies were out, running in pairs or threesomes, wearing vivid tank tops and cropped tights that showed off well-kept bodies and toned calves. They smiled as they moved over to let him pass on the narrow trail. "Cute dog!" called one. Theo turned, running backward for a few steps. "Thanks, but don't tell him that. You'll give him a big head!"

He sped up, passing the chatting groups, seeking some clear trail. Then he settled back into his favored pace, still perseverating about Jess. She was such an odd mix; supersmart in many ways, superclueless in others. He liked her self-deprecating humor and her down-to-earth comfort with her own body. She was unembarrassed by her appetites and clear about what she enjoyed, which was refreshing. She didn't expect him to read the tea leaves. And there was no passive-aggressive subtext. She just said what she felt. Also, she was the least princessy woman he'd ever been with: it didn't take her more than ten minutes to get dressed and out the door, a big contrast to some of the women he'd dated.

He probed himself for the source of his ambivalence. Daniel had seemed cool enough about it. Was it simply Abiona's certain disapproval that was nagging at him? On his personal list of things a Nigerian mother will never say, "Why don't you date a nice White girl?" was very high, right next to "You got a B-plus? That is a very good grade." It was so easy to hear her: that lilting, rich maternal voice.

It was less easy to hear his father. What would Barry have said? He had no idea who his father had dated before he met Abiona. It was the kind of man-to-man talk they'd never had a chance to have. He missed his dad every day, and even more acutely since he'd moved to America. There were so many questions Barry could've answered; so many that Theo wouldn't even have had to ask. He would've just been able to watch his father move through the world and take his cues from that. He did not regret his international upbringing: he was glad to have experienced life on three continents before moving to America, and while he loved his friends, they could sometimes amaze him with their insularity. When he'd proposed a spring break trip to Mexico, he'd been shocked to learn that Mike and Hakeem didn't have passports. But he felt sad and cheated that he'd never had time in America alongside his dad.

He was coming up on the chestnut oak where he usually stopped to stretch. He whistled to Clancy. The dog swiveled and came to heel, his panting regular as a piston. Theo leaned into the rough alligator bark of the big tree, stretching out his calves, hamstrings. Then he gave his limbs a shake, shrugging off the self-pity. He decided to go another mile. His heart beat faster as he pushed on.

Trust thyself: every heart vibrates to that iron string. Where did that come from? Emerson? Yes, that was it. That stupid essay, "Self-Reliance." Theo had been required to read it for a seminar on American Idealism. He'd written an angry screed in response, arguing that individualism to an almost infantile extreme was America's great weakness. He asserted that Emerson's insistence on allegiance only to himself and those like him, his characterization of alms to those unlike as "a wicked dollar," was the kind of thinking that underpinned the country's yawning divisions. He'd drawn a sharp contrast with the more communitarian ethos that prevailed in societies with which he'd had personal experience—Yoruba, Australia, even Britain in times of crisis.

But now, years later, a few fragments from the hated essay suddenly chimed. *Speak what you think today in words as hard as cannon balls* and tomorrow... what was it? Speak tomorrow's truth in hard words again, even if you're totally contradicting yourself. Something like that. And something about hobgoblins. He smiled and swiped at the sweat dripping down his face. *Sic transit* expensive education. He'd look up the proper quote after a nice cool shower. He turned for home.

He'd ask Jess to take Clancy, risk a little more intimacy.

Trust his heart's iron string. For now.

TEN BROECK'S JARRET

Metairie, Louisiana

1855

J arret stood by Lexington, a hand resting lightly on his shoulder, as Gilbert Watson Patrick approached for his first morning's work with the horse.

Though Jarret was sorry for young Henri Meichon's disgrace, which he believed unwarranted, he never had thought him a worthy jockey for Lexington. He was glad that Ten Broeck had engaged this veteran to ride Lexington in the Race Against Time. Gil Patrick was nearing the end of his long career, and it was whispered that this unique race might be his swan song. Jarret knew the man was as skilled a rider as any in the country. Now the question was how much he could trust him.

From a distance, Patrick looked like a boy: not quite five feet tall and thin as wire. "Little Gil" some people called him, although not to his face. His other nickname, "the Punisher," referred not to his treatment of horses, but to his ability to make a race hellish for competing jockeys if he harbored a grudge against them or the owner of their mount. At thirty years of age, the fine English complexion he'd inherited from his immigrant parents had weathered into a leathery, almost simian texture, deeply etched with lines. But it was a face that lit with admiration as he regarded Lexington.

He approached the horse slowly. Lexington's nostrils widened to take in his scent. He extended his hand and held it steady as Lexington dropped a soft muzzle, sniffing his palm. "I rode your da and your ma," Patrick said quietly to the horse. "You're a much calmer fellow than either." He turned to Jarret and rolled up his sleeve to expose a raised pink scar on his forearm. "That was from Boston, in the race against Fashion, back when I was a youngster in forty-two. He didn't like being beat by that filly. Neither did I."

Patrick offered his leg and Jarret hoisted him into the saddle. Jarret walked them out to the track, talking to Lexington in a low whisper until they reached the gate.

Patrick started with a gentle warm-up for a mile or so, then asked for speed. Jarret could see Patrick trying the horse's responses, asking him to hold back for a half mile, then give all again in a great energetic burst. For almost an hour, the two worked together, establishing a partnership. It was a flawless workout. But when Patrick brought the horse back to Jarret, his face showed none of the exhilaration that generally came with such a ride. He was frowning as he slid from the saddle and handed the reins to Jarret.

"How long?" he asked.

"How long what?"

"Don't trouble, boy. You know very well what. The reason you are always pouring out a stream of talk to this horse."

"The last three month. Not more. Maybe it begun before the last race, but I can't say for sure. I noticed his eyes were inflamed just after, but I thought I could bring that right with cold compresses. And I did, but . . ."

"Does Ten Broeck know?"

"Not yet."

"You going to tell him?"

"Are you?"

The older man looked up at the taller youth, his pale blue eyes boring into dark brown.

"I don't know."

"He can still run. Just as well—better—than he ever did."

Patrick nodded slowly. "That's true enough."

"And he'll only have the pacemaker horse. It's not like he'll be crowded out by a big field."

"That's also true."

Then Jarret blurted out his concern. "I'm afraid if Ten Broeck knows, he'll bet against him. And if he does that—" He stopped. He'd said too much.

Patrick pushed back the jockey cap atop his sparse, sandy hair. "If he does that, you are worried he might take other steps to ensure a loss?"

"I didn't say that."

"No, you didn't. But I had that boy Meichon crying in my rooms. I know what he thinks happened the last time Ten Broeck backed the rival horse."

Gil Patrick turned from Jarret and ran a hand down Lexington's flank. "He's barely sweating, after a workout like that. You have done a fine job with him." He gazed at the track, weighing his options. Then he nodded. "Very well. I'll keep your secret. Just for this one race. After that, no promises."

JESS

Jess stood back and leaned against the cool steel bench as Catherine examined the skull.

"It's not what you think."

"Not an injury?"

"Almost certainly not. I'd say this malformation had an organic cause. It might've happened over a period of years, in fact. Probably so gradually that the horse didn't even feel it."

"Well, that's good. I was imagining all kinds of hideous trauma. Somebody beating the poor animal. Or a bad fall at the racetrack. But you're saying disease?"

"Most probably. Although trauma was a reasonable assumption, given that the damage is not bilateral, and that the rest of the skeleton shows no similar morbidity. It was a sensible guess."

"So, what makes you think it has an organic cause?"

"The first thing I say to myself is, what do I know about *Equus ferus caballus*—the horse skull in its normal state?" Catherine lifted the skull and turned it. "What a beautiful, fragile, complicated thing it is."

"Thirty-four separate bones," Jess said. "Ours has only twenty-two."

"Right, and like ours, these bones serve myriad functions, apart from the obvious ones of protecting the brain and operating the jaw. There's all kinds of nooks and crannies to move blood, lymph, cerebrospinal fluid. Pathways for nerves to and from the brain. And pathways for infection. A lot can go awry in there."

Catherine set the skull back down on the bench and drew a finger along the faint suture lines. As she did so, Jess named the bones. "Occipital, parietal, nasal processes, zygoma . . . and . . ." She hesitated.

"Vomer," Catherine prompted.

"Vomer. And then the deformation, there on the lacrimal."

"It's quite a gross deformation. Sad to say, I've treated a lot of horses who had something like this—an imbalance in their cranial bones. Not as pronounced, for sure, but of course this horse is much older. I was generally called in to treat two-year-old babies, in the racing game. With the young racehorses, bone issues generally *were* a result of trauma—they'd banged themselves up in the starting gate or pulled back when tied, or some other common, young-horse foolishness."

She ran her finger over the teeth. "This horse's teeth are pretty terrible, even considering his age at death. Major dental pathology. Horses can't say when they have toothache, so things can go very bad before anyone notices."

"All I ever heard was the expression 'long in the tooth,' and that you could tell their age that way," Jess said.

"Well, you can, and most of the dental work on horses has been just about rasping away at that overgrowth. We weren't much good at equine dental care until quite recently. A horse's mouth is so deep, and its crushing strength so high, you don't want to just be sticking your head in there to look what's up. It's only since microcameras that the field has really advanced. When all they had was a rasp, they didn't get very far with complex pathologies. If your only tool is a hammer, everything is a nail, and all that."

Catherine went to the basin and washed her hands. "There is another possibility. With an older horse, one who didn't live in an era of modern veterinary practice, I'm thinking maybe Strangles. *Streptococcus equi equi.* Nasty, causes abscesses in the lymphoid tissue of the upper respiratory tract. Untreated, it's the kind of thing that could deform the bone. We could take a sample and screen for signs of infectious organisms. See if we can find any pathogens in the DNA. Depends how keen you are to know."

Jess realized that she did want to know. She'd become quite obsessed with this horse. He was, after all, the reason for her first date with Theo.

"Our lab can do it. I reckon we should try to find out everything these bones can tell us. Maybe he'll be rediscovered one day, like Seabiscuit, and people will want to know his whole story."

"I suggest we also order a CT of the skull in that case. There's a vet at my college who does equine maxillofacial surgery—he might have some insight, if I can show him scans."

Catherine had spent the day overseeing the scanning of the skeleton's locomotor bones. Jess had invited her for dinner, and at the last minute, since they had England and Oxford in common, she texted Theo to see if he wanted to join them.

She biked home via Eastern Market, getting there just before her favorite fishmonger closed. She selected some decent-looking shrimp for a fiery Malaysian sambal. By the time Catherine arrived, Jess's eyes were watering from roasting chilies. Catherine coughed as the aromatics hit the back of her throat. She mucked in as unselfconsciously as she had the first time, mincing garlic and lemongrass while Jess sautéed candlenuts and belacan.

When Theo arrived at the open front door, he reeled. "It smells fantastic in here." Clancy's nose twitched violently at the unfamiliar odors.

"I hope you like it spicy," Jess said. "I'm not making this for wimps. Theo, I'd like you to meet—"

From behind the kitchen counter Catherine, smiling, waved a garlicky hand. "I know who you are, Number Three. I was at Oxford when you were playing. Total polo tragic, I was. Never missed a match." She turned to Jess. "When you mentioned he was a polo player, I had no idea you meant this one. This man was *such* a star. We all died when he quit the team. Everyone expected he'd go professional."

"Well, it couldn't have been any less lucrative than art history," he smiled. "I'm sorry I didn't recognize you at first—"

"Oh, don't bother pretending," Catherine interjected with a laugh. "You couldn't possibly remember me. We were never introduced. I was just another girl hanging round the pony line, treading back divots at halftime." She turned to Jess. "The team had quite a fan club, especially this guy."

As Jess spooned the rust-colored sambal into bowls of rice, Theo and Catherine made small talk, comparing their Oxford experience. She was older, and already in the midst of her graduate degree when Theo came up. Polo was the only point of intersection, and Jess noticed Theo seemed resolute in not wanting to pursue that topic. Catherine, with an English sensitivity, followed his lead and steered away from it, although Jess sensed her disappointment. She clearly would have replayed every match, in detail, had Theo offered the least encouragement.

Instead, she turned the conversation to Theo's interest in equestrian art. "I live with a Stubbs, you know. Hangs just outside my office. Supposedly it's a very great painting. But speaking as a vet, I don't care for it. The anatomy is bizarre. Drives me a little bonkers, to be honest, every time I look at it. Especially since Stubbs could be a fine anatomist. His book of drawings on the subject of equine anatomy is meticulously done."

When Jess cleared the table, Catherine called up the Stubbs portrait of Eclipse. Theo read the caption aloud: *"Eclipse with a Groom.* I don't recall seeing this one. Nice composition, even if the horse anatomy is off. He did like to include the servant class in these portraits, didn't he?"

"Did he? I haven't seen enough of his work to know if that's usual."

"Oh yes, quite usual. There's often a groom or a jockey. Or both. Sometimes I think the men are included in the composition simply to aggrandize the horse, you know. The horse towers over the human, with a great arcing crest and a disdainful eye, just as the owners probably liked to see themselves in relation to the rest of the world. I don't think it a stretch to imagine the nobility identifying with their high-bred horses."

"Well," said Catherine. "There you are. Everything in England comes down to class. It wouldn't be the same here, I'm sure."

Theo leaned back, frowning. "You think not? The slave-holding classes considered enslaved people subhuman. They referred to them as 'the necessary mudsill' on which one constructed the edifice of a higher kind of society.'"

"What a distressing concept," said Catherine. "Although I'm not sure it's an order of magnitude worse than the upper-class attitude to the lower classes. I mean, not everything has to be about race, does it?"

"Perhaps not, when you're White."

"Oh, well, I didn't mean to downplay . . ."

Theo shifted in his seat. He imagined she would file the exchange away as an example of how easy it was to offend a Black person. He felt irritated and suddenly exhausted. Despite his aversion to ill manners, he let himself enjoy the release of a large yawn.

"Up too early this morning." He folded his napkin as he spoke. "Marking some very indifferent undergraduate papers on Michelangelo's Mannerist tendencies. In fact, I really should go—I have several more to finish." He got up and reached for Catherine's empty plate, carrying it with his own to the sink. Clancy padded after him. Jess stood and followed him to the door. She stepped outside into the cooling air.

"Are you okay?" she whispered.

"Quite."

"I was hoping—I thought you might stay. There's nothing wrong, is there?"

Is there? He wasn't sure. He bent and gave her a perfunctory kiss on the brow.

"I'll call you." And when I do, he thought, it'll be to say this isn't going to work.

Jess watched him walk briskly away. At the end of the street, only Clancy turned to look back.

As she closed the door, Catherine was fiddling with her wineglass. "I do hope I didn't say anything wrong." She gazed at the wine for a moment and sighed. "Hard to say the right thing, these days."

TEN BROECK'S JARRET

Metairie, Louisiana

1855

With twenty thousand dollars staked on the outcome, Ten Broeck expected a decent gate. He did not expect the throngs who turned up to watch a horse run against a stopwatch.

But there they were, crowding the shell road once again. Ten Broeck had built the public stand to hold fifteen hundred souls, but as race time approached it was jammed with many more than that. The *Picayune* had run a long dispatch that very morning, praising the "temerity of Lexington's owner in sending this challenge to the world, in the face of a recent defeat." Should success attend the effort, the paper wrote, "he will have the proud satisfaction of possessing the champion of America."

Ten Broeck smiled, thinking how reading such lines in his hometown paper surely had put Wells off his breakfast. Wells might have been better pleased by the dispatch in the *Daily Crescent*: "We believe Lexington will win his match against time, and still we don't think he will beat Lecompte." The paper took issue with the fact that the judges had agreed to allow Lexington a running, rather than a standing start, and had allowed pacemakers to run with him.

It was a fine day, though a stiff breeze pushed the drifting tendrils of moss almost sideways on the oaks. Ten Broeck noticed Jarret out on the track. He squinted in aggravation when he saw him kneel down in the dirt. What was he thinking—already dressed for the race? If he knew the price of that embroidered banyan he wouldn't be fouling it so casually.

Ten Broeck eased his way through the gathering crowd and waved to get Jarret's attention. Jarret stood, dusted off his hands, and came toward him, his face grave.

"They've stripped the track," he said, before Ten Broeck could remonstrate with him about the state of his garments. "It's smooth, as you wanted. But it's hard as rock. They've taken too much soil off."

"I said smooth and hard," Ten Broeck said. "We want a fast track."

"Well, it's like iron out there," Jarret said. "All the spring is gone from it."

Ten Broeck shrugged and waved a hand at the dirty circles on the knees of Jarret's breeches. "Do you have any others you can wear? You've quite ruined those."

"I'm worried about ruining the horse," Jarret retorted.

Ten Broeck ignored Jarret's ferocity. "I'm sure it's not as bad as all that. In any case, nothing to be done at this hour. Go and see if Gilpatrick is in want of anything, will you?" Ten Broeck had adopted the common habit of running the jockey's first and last names together. Jarret glared at Ten Broeck and stomped off to the stables. He could at least ensure that the jockey was aware of the appalling state of the track—so different to what they had trained upon.

As the hour for the race approached, grooms ponied out the two horses who would challenge Lexington to make his best time. A gelding named Joe Blackburn would start with him for the first two miles, then Arrow, brought in fresh, would take over to challenge him for the race's second half.

Gilpatrick started Lexington up the stretch, turned him at the draw gates, and was at a full gallop as they passed the judges' stand and heard the drum tap. Throughout the stands, spectators clicked the buttons atop the cases on their brand-new stopwatches.

Jarret had placed himself by the outer rail, as near as possible to Ten Broeck. As Lexington blazed through the first half mile, concern creased Ten

Broeck's face. At the mile, he glanced at his stopwatch: 1:47:25. Too fast. "He can't hold out at such a pace," he muttered. As Gilpatrick passed him he roared his instruction: "Take back! Take back!"

The disciplined jockey complied and held Lexington to just under two minutes in the second mile. Even so, the pacer Joe Blackburn couldn't keep up. Just three minutes into the race, he had dropped back so far as to be useless. Ten Broeck shouted to bring Arrow up early. The jockey spurred the fresh horse to challenge Lexington as he rounded the curve. Hearing him coming, Lexington fought Gilpatrick's pull and asked insistently for his head. Gilpatrick allowed enough extra speed to keep ahead of his challenger. The horse again passed the mile mark. Stopwatches clicked. Mile three: 1:51:5.

The effort to challenge Lexington at such a speed was too much for Arrow, so Ten Broeck waved Joe Blackburn back into the race. Neither horse could muster speed enough to be of any use. No matter. Lexington needed no competition to set his pace.

Jarret noticed that Lexington was fighting Gilpatrick all through the final mile, trying to swerve out from the rail. "He's trying to find the softer going," Jarret shouted to Ten Broeck. "He must keep him on the rail," Ten Broeck replied.

Only in the stretch did Gilpatrick give the horse his head, allowing him to finish the final quarter mile in under 25 seconds. As Lexington blazed across the finish line, spectators thumped their stopwatches. There was a momentary hush as they stared at the time in disbelief. Then a howl of thrilled approval. Lexington, running alone, had conquered four miles in a new record time of 7:19:75. He had trounced Lecompte's 7:26 record.

As Gilpatrick brought the horse back toward Jarret, it was immediately apparent that both his front shoes were loose. Jarret shouted to the jockey to dismount. Gilpatrick did so, standing by, concerned, as Jarret picked up Lexington's right leg, and then his left. Both of the thin racing plates had worked loose, rattling against the horn of the horse's hoof. One shoe had all but three of ten nails out. The remaining ones were bent and twisted.

"His feet must be stinging something terrible," Jarret said.

Gilpatrick pushed back his cap. "If his shoes had been right, he'd have shaved another four or five seconds. Just shows what courage he has, to run on, with shoes like that," he said. "I don't know another horse that would have kept giving like he gave, and not even a pacemaker in earshot of him. I think he's proved something today, for sure. Not just the fastest horse in history, but maybe the bravest one as well."

The next morning, Gilpatrick leaned over the door of Lexington's stall as Jarret positioned the horse's right hoof in the soaking tub. He spoke softly so that no one else could hear.

"You have to tell him."

Jarret stood, wiping his hands. "Still holding too much heat in that leg."

"Legs'll be just fine after a few more cold soaks. It's the other thing worries me. Should worry you."

"Course it worries me." Jarret ran his hand through Lexington's forelock. The horse leaned into his touch and didn't flinch as Jarret found the lumpy protrusion of bone encircling his eye. "Worries me every waking minute."

"You know they're about to set terms for the rematch. Old Man Wells is all but begging for it."

"Heard tell he's having vapor fits over Lexington being called the fastest racehorse in history."

Gilpatrick gave a dry laugh. "He fell right into the trap your man set for him." He leaned farther into the stall and dropped his voice even lower. "I think the only thing that will put a stop to it is if you speak up. Tell Ten Broeck the truth."

Jarret busied himself swabbing the other leg. He didn't reply.

"Jarret!" Gilpatrick's tone was jussive. "If you don't tell him, I will. You leave me no choice."

"You got a choice. You don't got to ride him."

Gilpatrick thumped a fist against the stall boards. "Damn it, you're a stubborn boy. You know how much I want the ride. But an owner has a right to know what he's agreeing to." He lowered his voice to a whisper. "He ought to know his horse can't see."

"He can see. Shadows, still."

"But it is getting worse."

Jarret straightened and finally looked Gilpatrick in the eye.

"Oh yes. Much worse."

It had started with the inflammation. But Jarret had tended that with cold compresses, and it had subsided. Then, in Saratoga Springs, Jarret had noticed that the horse was spooky in a way that wasn't usual for him. Jarret had ascribed it to the unfamiliar surroundings, the stress of the long journey north. When the horse began to trip during workouts, Jarret suspected he'd been nail-quicked by an unskilled farrier and called the man back to reshoe.

It was only when Lexington walked right into a barrow that someone had carelessly left in the midst of the paddock that Jarret began to suspect the truth. He pulled a kerchief from his pocket and flapped it. The horse leaped sideways and Jarret felt a rush of relief. But when he tried the same test on the other side, the horse made no response at all.

One eye was failing. There had been signs: a manner of tilting his head to favor the better eye, the way he dropped his muzzle to probe the ground, especially where surfaces changed suddenly from dark to light. The horse had been resourceful. In the familiar surrounds of Metairie, he'd made his own mental maps and compensated even as his world began to darken.

A blind horse has other acute senses: smell and hearing and the delicate sense of touch in the fine hairs of his face. He can travel well through his known world using these. But away from his familiar home, there was fear.

Harry had always told Jarret that Boston went blind because of a savage beating. He'd been sure that the blindness wouldn't be passed down to his foals. But now Jarret wondered if his father had been mistaken. Perhaps Boston's blindness *was* hereditary. He walked Lexington to his stall on the

Saratoga farm and examined his eyes closely. There was no discharge, no clouding. But then his fingers found the lump of misshapen bone. He felt the other side—no lump. That, at least, was good. He knew of many horses who raced just fine with sight in only one eye. But what could have happened to deform his bone in this way? Jarret had been with the horse his whole life, except for those hard weeks at Fatherland, and even there, he'd watched him from a distance and would have known if the horse had injured himself. Pryor had called on him for the colic; he would have done the same, surely, for any other crisis. He couldn't think what, besides a bad injury, could misshape a bone and rob a horse of vision in that way.

When they left Saratoga and transferred to the stables at the National Race Course in New York City, Jarret made various excuses as to why Lexington should not be turned out with other horses and why he alone should have the handling of the stallion. It was easy enough to convince the hands that the stallion had a foul temper, since so many did. They were willing to take Jarret at his word and leave everything, from the mucking of the stall to the morning gallops, entirely to him. Then, when Captain Stuart sickened and died from the cholera, the misfortune gave cover for their untimely return south. Stuart had been the one with good connections at the new course, and Ten Broeck had relied on him to create interest in a northern contest. With the death of his friend, Ten Broeck seemed to lose heart for promoting such a race, and sent word to bring the horse home, by slow stages, keeping him in condition for the Race Against Time.

Jarret had done so, taking every opportunity on that journey south to build on his strong bond of trust with the horse and to expand the range of verbal commands Lexington responded to. They had stopped for long rests at farms where Ten Broeck had connections, and in every strange place, Jarret worked from first light to last on building Lexington's confidence. He slept in the pasture so that the horse would be reassured by his familiar scent. By the end of the journey even a strange paddock held no terrors.

He had been confident Lexington would run brilliantly in the Race Against Time. He was just as certain that if he had time to heal the soreness in his feet, Lexington would defeat Lecompte. Maybe, with a worthy challenger to press him on, he would even beat his own world record.

Jarret wanted this chance. The blindness was progressing rapidly. Despite his hopes, the sight in the good eye had begun to fade. Soon, he feared, Lexington would be completely blind. And no one would risk racing a stone-blind horse.

But if Lexington beat Lecompte, he would prove himself beyond doubt the champion stallion of the age, assured of a good life as a coddled stud sire. He didn't need to see to do that.

Jarret lifted Lexington's hoof out of the soaking tub and dried each leg vigorously. Gilpatrick held the stall door as he carried the tub to the barn entrance and threw the water in a wide sparkling arc.

The two men stepped out into the warm spring morning. A grimace of vexation deepened the lines on the smaller man's face. Jarret sighed. "You really think he gone call this thing off if you tell him?"

"Yes, I think—I expect—"

"Then you don't know him. There ain't nothing gone make him do that. He plans to make this thing the race of the century. He reckons it's bigger than American Eclipse and Sir Henry back in 1823, bigger even than when you raced Boston up against that Fashion filly in forty-two."

"But there were seventy thousand people at that race! He can't possibly think—"

"But he does. That's exactly what he thinks. He saw how many folk came out just to watch a race against a clock, and now he reckons this rivalry—the two great sons of Boston—is sure to take hold of the racing press and fire up every single person ever liked a horse race—rich, poor, old, and young. That what he thinks. You, me—nothing we say is gonna stop him."

Jarret looked around, to make sure they weren't overheard. "But what you might do is rowel him up to some kind of foolishness. Just like we talked of last time. That man might do anything. You know that."

Gilpatrick stared up at the tall youth, considering. He'd raced against talented Black jockeys all his long career and ridden winners trained by expert

Black horsemen. Any notions he'd had about natural inferiority had long ago been rasped away by the evidence of his own experience. He knew Jarret's gift with horses was prodigious. But was he also a judge of the motives of men—especially of such a subtle player as Ten Broeck? Gilpatrick wasn't sure.

In the end, he said nothing, and the race date was set for April 14. The sporting press waxed enthusiastic, as Ten Broeck had predicted, hailing Lexington and Lecompte as "the great lions of the day" and proclaiming that their contest merited the "same interest and avidity as the probable fate of a nation."

Readers apparently agreed. New Orleans filled to brimming, once again, with racing fans lured by Ten Broeck's promotional flair. Wells's friends from the Red River district crowded the city, avid to see their man put the northern interloper back in his place. The Kentucky-bred horse and his New York owner could not be allowed another triumph. Wells's sister boasted that half of Rapides Parish had come to bet on Lecompte, "not only because they considered him the best horse in the world, but because he was Jeff Wells's horse."

By midday, coaches and drags packed the infield, carrying their noisy parties. As the clock eased slowly to the three p.m. race time, strolling bands of minstrels, acrobats, and Creole dancers entertained the crowd. Vendors carried trays piled high with fruits and iced drinks. Ten Broeck had ordered the stands decorated with festoons of bright fabric and soon the gaudy tiers were crammed. Trees sagged and boughs cracked under the weight of spectators. It was, the French denizens proclaimed, a "*succès fou*," even before the horses left the stable.

Ten Broeck moved through the crowd, pensive. The Red River men, it seemed, were not betting on their horse. Ten Broeck didn't know why, and for him that was an unaccustomed experience. By all measures, their horse should have been favored. For one thing, Gilpatrick was riding above his ideal weight, so Lexington would be carrying 3¾ pounds more than Lecompte. This was no trifling matter since Lexington was the smaller horse by some 160 pounds. It was not as if he had no eyes on the Wells horse. He had paid to be kept informed on Lecompte's form in training. A few days earlier, his informant had sent a message that Lecompte was looking grand and training perfectly. So why was the money going so heavily to Lexington? What was depressing wagers on the Wells horse?

Ten Broeck turned the matter over in his mind as he did a circuit of the stables, looking for the youth he'd paid. He could hardly ask after the boy by name without raising questions, but his scan of the grooms' quarters proved futile. His informant was nowhere to be seen. Vexed, he sought out Jarret, who was preparing Lexington.

"Have you heard anything that would account for a dearth of Red River money?"

Jarret shook his head. "But you might ask the painter, Mr. Scott. I know he was up in Rapides Parish this week past. He knows a good many of Hark's people and—"

Ten Broeck didn't wait for Jarret to finish. He'd seen Scott down by the rail earlier and now he forced his way through the crowd to find him. Scott, journal in hand, foot on the rail, was scribbling notes for his column. Ten Broeck touched his sleeve.

"Do you know why there's no money on Lecompte?"

Scott looked over both shoulders and dropped his voice.

"Three days ago. Sudden, out of nowhere. Severe colic. Hark insisted on drastic treatment. Got the horse on his feet, but I heard he's off his feed and dull in the gallops."

"Thanks for that. I assume you've bet accordingly."

Scott smiled wanly. "I would have, were I in purse to do so."

Ten Broeck patted his arm. "I'll place a wager for you." Before Scott could say anything, he slid away into the crowd.

In the saddling enclosure, Lexington danced with an excitement that told Jarret his feet were fully healed. Wells's grooms led Lecompte out. It was an impressive procession. The trainer Hark, in frock coat and top hat, walked on one side, Abe Hawkins in Wells's golden silks on the other. When the grooms stripped Lecompte's sheet, his chestnut coat gleamed. But once saddled, the outrider had to urge him forward toward the track. There was a coin toss, and Lexington drew the pole.

At the drum tap, the two rivals burst forward at sprinter speed. At the first turn, Abe challenged Gilpatrick for the pole position, but the veteran would not allow an inch. They came into the stretch head to head. No one had seen such early speed—both horses apparently going flat out—in the first quarter mile of a four-mile contest. Ten Broeck clicked his watch at the quarter mark and cursed. Twenty-five and a half seconds. "Suicidal. They will walk home."

Jarret wasn't so sure. He could see that Gilpatrick wasn't even asking as Lexington pulled ahead and took a lead around the upper turn. Abe answered with whip and spur, putting maximum pressure on Lecompte to close the gap.

The chestnut did his best. Hearing him move up, Gilpatrick nudged Lexington a single time and the horse answered instantly, widening the lead to several lengths as Lecompte labored and showed his distress under Abe's pitiless thrashing. When Jarret saw Lecompte's tail droop and fall, he knew the great horse's spirit had surrendered. Ahead of him, Lexington's tail streamed high, like a plume of triumph. Gilpatrick tried to hold Lexington back, worried he couldn't sustain this blistering speed. But as they passed the stands, the crowd's wild cheering seemed to inspire the horse. Gilpatrick, for all his wiry strength and skill, could not check him. He broke away and hurtled to the wire.

The time was 7:23. Lexington pulled up so fresh it was clear he could have beaten his own record if Lecompte had pressed him.

Lecompte, however, was head down and heaving, lathered and bloody. Wells's grooms swarmed the course carrying damp cloths and fans to cool him.

Within the half hour, Wells had accepted Hark's verdict: the horse could not recover for the second heat. To ask him might be fatal. He would be withdrawn. While the Red River contingent filed out, chagrined and defeated, most of the crowd stayed to watch and cheer as the now unrivaled champion did a leisurely strut around the course to secure a walkover victory and the indisputable title: greatest horse of the era.

THEO

Georgetown, Washington, DC

2019

Theo's day began as it always did: the press of a whiskery muzzle against his cheek. He was aware of damp, metallic breath. Clancy didn't nudge or fidget, just rested a cold nose gently on Theo's face. If he kept his eyes closed and tried to stay asleep, Clancy would give a small sigh and rearrange himself across the top of Theo's head like a large furry crown. He would doze there for as long as it took until Theo decided to stir. That usually wasn't long, since it was hard to sleep with thirty pounds of kelpie pressing on your head.

"Good morning, alarm clock," yawned Theo, reaching up a hand to rub Clancy between the ears.

Theo was well aware that there are people who don't have dogs in the house, much less on the bed, much less sharing their pillow. His mother, for one. It wasn't that Abiona disliked dogs, but she didn't see the point of them, either, unless they were guard dogs like the ones who patrolled the high fences of her compound in Lagos. Theo's father had been an animal lover but not to the point of confronting Abiona.

Confronting Abiona. Something he would have to do if he carried on with this new relationship and let it get serious. But Abiona was five thousand miles away, so he didn't have to think about that just now. Which was good, because in the lazy, sensuous moments between sleep and wakefulness, he'd rather think about Jess.

He'd left her place angry, walking off his annoyance in a brisk half jog down the length of the Mall. In retrospect, he shouldn't have accepted the last-minute dinner offer, since he'd been in a foul mood long before he stepped into the apartment.

First had come the news that he had to cancel the weekend with his friends in Yosemite. "Seems like climate change got there before us," Daniel said. "The Cali wildfires are making the air 'undesirable' for serious hiking. Anyway, Hakeem's supervisor was giving him shit about taking a long weekend away from the lab. You know how it is, Black man gotta work at least twice as hard."

Theo was dispirited, and not just because the cheap ticket he'd bought was nonrefundable and money he couldn't afford to waste. He'd longed to reconnect with his friends. Now, who knew when they'd be able to hatch another plan?

And then he'd had a meeting with his thesis adviser that hadn't gone well. She was the only tenured professor of color in the entire department, a po-co specialist with a particular interest in the art of the African diaspora. Theo had admired her writing and thought her background—Côte d'Ivoire, University of Bordeaux—would make for a unique perspective. He'd expected West African warmth but encountered, instead, an icy crust of French *froideur.* By then, however, it was too late to make a change. Invitations to graduate programs in his field weren't exactly growing on trees.

He'd hoped that she might warm up a bit as she got to know him better and read more of his work. But almost six months into their relationship, she remained excruciatingly reserved. He tried to put himself in her shoes (which, he noted, were elegant, strappy things that emphasized her slender ankles). It couldn't have been easy to rise as she had—a Black immigrant woman in academia's chauvinist ivory towers.

He held on to that thought as she gave him the silent treatment, gazing down at the document on her desk while he sat and squirmed. He couldn't guess her age. Though her CV made it clear she must be in her fifties at least, she looked much younger. She wore clingy boat-neck sweaters that showed off a long neck and slender, expressive arms. She wore her glossy, straightened hair swept up in an elaborate chignon. His revised proposal was on her desk. She always used a Mont Blanc pen and now she tapped it on his manuscript.

"Well, Tay-oh"—she pronounced his name as if it had an acute accent over the *e*—"this strange swerve in your topic. It is, I think, a little bit disappointing. A little bit . . . niche, no?"

Theo wanted to say that PhD theses were by definition "niche." But he restrained himself. "How so?"

"These artists you propose to study, these"—she paused and dropped her voice—"White males. They are not so *intéressant*, I think. Not so important."

"Well, it is actually the Black subjects that I—"

She tapped her pen harder and cut him off. "And also I am not so sure about your dialogical principles of cross-cultural interaction." She pushed her glasses up the bridge of her nose with a long, manicured forefinger. "What really is at stake? The subjects are Black, the painters White, yet you want to argue *against* objectification in this case? What can you usefully say about the aesthetics of hybridity and transculturation if you take such an approach? It's a choice, I think, a little bit perverse, no? Why must you illuminate these cases, where enslaved people are *not* depicted in a dehumanized and stereotypical way? It's rare and exceptional."

"Well, professor. You have answered for me. Because it is rare and exceptional."

She leaned back in her chair, lifted her narrow shoulders, and turned her hands up in a slow-motion Gallic shrug. "Per'aps. If you must. But I think you chose for yourself a very 'ard road."

Theo strode out, irritated. He'd wanted to be in Washington for the wealth of connections he could make for potential future employment at so many exceptional museums. But the Fine Arts Department was small, the PhD program quite new. And now he was stuck with an adviser hostile to his work. He'd been chewing on all that before he even got to Jess's place. And then, that English vet. Banging on about his aborted polo career. Bringing all that old misery back up to the surface. The last thing he'd needed: a reminder of the road not taken. No wonder he'd essentially stormed out, insofar as someone with his impeccable manners *could* storm.

But as he'd kept walking beyond the Mall, into the backstreets of Georgetown, he thought about the hurt, puzzled look on Jess's face when he'd left. By the time he stepped into his apartment, crawling into bed with his dog suddenly felt like a poor decision. He looked into Clancy's eyes, luminous on the pillow. "All right then. Don't stare at me like that."

He reached over the side of the bed, groping for his phone. He'd text her before he fell asleep. *See you on the weekend?* She immediately texted back: *Sure.* He rolled onto his back and exhaled.

"You like her, too, don't you, Clance?" he said, as the dog wriggled into place beside him. Clancy's answer was a long sigh, as if to say, "That's obvious."

In the morning, Theo swung out of bed and into a pair of running shorts, put on water for coffee, and plopped a handful of dog food into Clancy's bowl. He took a few sips of espresso as Clancy chased the bowl around the floor, hoovering up every last speck of kibble. They ran for more than an hour. Theo wanted to give them both a good workout before he headed to the Library of Congress for the day to research Scott, Troye, and any other nineteenth-century equestrian painters who might have depicted Black horsemen.

At the library, he was pleased to find that works by both Troye and Scott had been reproduced prolifically as engravings and published widely in the turf press of the day. In a very old *Harper's New Monthly Magazine*, he came upon an intriguing reference to a Scott painting. The painting wasn't reproduced, but it was described in detail, and the subject was the horse Lexington.

One of the best portraits of him was painted by Scott, representing him led by Black Jarret, his groom.

Was this, perhaps, the same Black groom as in that early photograph that Jess had shown him? Theo wrote down the name and underlined it.

The head is turned outward, and we have a full view of the dull, sightless eyes. The right fore-foot is thrown out haltingly, as if feeling for clear and firm ground upon which to place it. The whole form of the horse speaks blindness, and one can not gaze upon the picture, and recall the brilliant triumphs of the past, without a shade of sadness.

Blindness. That was interesting. Explained why the horse's racing career was so short. He must ask Jess about that. As he read on, Theo learned that this painting had been unanimously declared the best that Scott had produced, his masterpiece. In 1866, it had hung at the offices of the newspaper *Turf, Field and Farm* in New York City. But that paper had faded as the national passion for racing ebbed, and it had gone out of business in 1903. Where then was that painting now?

Theo turned to the only catalogue of Scott's work, published in 2010. Unsurprisingly, the painting that he'd plucked from the trash wasn't listed. But two other portraits of Lexington were. One was the fine work from Martha Jackson's bequest that they'd viewed at the Smithsonian. The other—the last, supposedly the best, the one with the Black groom named Jarret—was listed in the catalogue with a dispiriting note: *Has not been found.*

TEN BROECK'S JARRET

Metairie, Louisiana

1855

Jarret did not hear Ten Broeck approach the corral. He was focused on the horse, working on voice commands. For a moment or two Ten Broeck stood silently behind him, one foot on the fence rail.

"Did you think that I, also, am blind?"

Jarret spun around.

More than a week had passed since the walkover win against Lecompte. Ten Broeck, hosting lavish celebrations in the city, hadn't been seen at Metairie. Those idle days following Lexington's triumph should have been joyful ones for Jarret. Instead, a growing unease ate at his soul. He had accomplished his goal: the little foal with four white feet had become acclaimed as the greatest racehorse in the country. He had written to Ten Broeck and asked to buy himself out of bondage. What better time?

But no response had come. And every day, it was clear to Jarret that Lexington's blindness was worse. To Jarret, who knew, it was apparent that the left eye—the worst one, the one where the bone felt lumpy—had begun to lose its luster and its roundness. Other grooms had noted the horse's odd behavior. Jarret had begun to fret about how Ten Broeck would react when he learned the truth.

Now the question hung between them in the misty morning air.

"Well?"

Jarret blinked. The silence swelled. Ten Broeck turned abruptly. "Come to my office. Now."

Jarret followed his retreating back over the rolling sward of grass still scuffed and torn from the boots of the crowd. Ten Broeck strode into his office and stood at the window, his back to Jarret, his gaze held by an exercise rider breezing a horse around the track.

"Close the door," he said. He did not turn. "We have not been acquainted very long, and yet I find myself strangely vexed that you know me so little. Did you really think you had concealed such a grave matter? I have known the horse was losing his sight almost, I imagine, as long as you have. No, I am not blind. Far from it. I have eyes in my employ in every place where I have a significant asset." He turned and glared at Jarret. "I am astonished that you did not have the wit to realize that. Why do you imagine I abandoned the idea of a New York contest?"

"I thought—I believed it was because of Captain Stuart . . ."

"His death? It was unfortunate, even tragic. But I had means to arrange the contests without his help. No. It was because I did not choose to run a horse with failing sight in a field the size and nature of which I could not control. Not before he had won the Race Against Time for me. So I brought you both home to Metairie, expecting every day you would come to me and lay out the ground of what you knew to be true. That you did not do so disappointed me. I believe I know the motive, and I feel no obligation to one who both deceives and mistrusts me. So I must deny your request. You may not buy yourself out of bondage at this time. In fact"—he looked down at his walnut desk, shifted some papers—"I have sold you."

Jarret's vision blurred. He reached out a hand and grasped the edge of the desk. Ten Broeck regarded him coldly.

"For a very fair price, I must say. But not as rich as the price I will receive for Lexington."

Jarret felt his throat close.

"You—you've sold our horse?" he whispered.

"I have a vague idea that Lexington is my property, and the prevailing opinion in this country is that a man may dispose of what he owns as and when he chooses. So yes. I have sold *my* horse. For fifteen thousand dollars. Which is, I am pleased to note, the highest price ever paid for a thorough-bred in this country. A tidy profit on the amount I paid for him. I have had the lion's share of his purses, plus my winning wagers, plus the gate. A happy sum. So it has been an extraordinarily successful partnership, all told."

The thought of all that money seemed to have a mellowing effect on Ten Broeck's temper. His face lost its angry cast and he took his seat behind the desk. Jarret's stomach heaved. He forced himself to swallow the sickness that rose up in his throat.

"For pity's sake, boy, sit down."

Jarret sank into a bentwood chair.

"Before I let you go, it is important that you grasp the extent of your folly. I am going to set it out for you. As I have said, I harbor grave concern that the present regional tensions in this country will escalate. Accordingly, I intend to establish myself in England. I will be the first American owner to travel there with a string of fine American horses, and I hope to elevate the position of the American turf to rival its ancient counterpart. This is an event that the sporting world has been anticipating with interest for many years. I had intended that Lexington would be the lynchpin of my strategy. However, that is not now possible. In the event, Lecompte will do." Jarret's head shot up at that. "You are surprised? So was I. Yet it is true: Wells has sold him to me. I believe he did not wish to have the source of his humiliation linger-ing to remind him of it. I will also take Stark, Pryor, and Prioress, since all of them have been running well. I had intended that you would accompany me as trainer, and Gilpatrick as my jockey. As you may know, there is no longer a condition such as yours in England, so at the moment you set your foot down on that soil you would have been free to stay in my employ or not, as you liked. And to keep whatever monies I must now assume are in your possession, since you have proposed to buy your own manumission. For the service you have rendered to me, I will not confiscate those funds, although as you know, since slaves may not legally hold property, it is within my right to do so."

Ten Broeck paused and regarded Jarret. His face softened. The stricken look on the youth's face stirred him to a modicum of compassion.

"The short of it is, I am sending you back to Kentucky with the horse. In the course of exploring my options in England, I made the acquaintance of Mr. Robert Alexander, owner of an estate in Scotland and now also of lands adjacent to the Vileys. Despite your recent lack of candor, I spoke to him in your favor. I told him he'd be well advised to have you continue to manage the horse as he transitions to the breeding shed. You are to transport Lexington to him and assume whatever general duties he assigns to you."

Jarret barely heard what Ten Broeck next said. His mind reeled and whirled. He could stay with Lexington. As that thought took hold, he found he could breathe again.

Ten Broeck was still talking. Jarret struggled to pay attention. "Alexander's reputation is, as far as I know, impeccable. In fact, he has become, in very short order, the most successful breeder of fine livestock in the country. Thoroughbreds, sheep, cattle—his interest is in producing the finest thing of its kind. Which is why he desires to have Lexington as a stud sire. He has it in mind for Lexington to cover broodmares sired by Glencoe. An interesting notion. You should gather your possessions. You will leave with the horse on the morning's packet. That painter, Scott, will accompany you. He will be undertaking commissions for Mr. Alexander, whose man will meet your boat in Louisville. That will be all. I do not expect that we will meet again."

JESS

Catherine called Jess from London with the results from scans she had carried back with her.

"Craniofacial infection leading to malformation of the bone. That's the official diagnosis. As you know, the bone over the sinus is very thin, so it's easily distorted by disease. The scan shows the teeth interacting abnormally with the sinus complex. So, the hypothesis is that a dental infection caused the outbulging."

"Poor horse," said Jess.

"Indeed," said Catherine. "Though it might've all started with a pleasant binge at the feed bins."

"Huh?"

"Just a theory. The horse may have got loose and gorged himself. Food went where it shouldn't have and caused an occult abscess in the lining of his sinus. Result: erosive osteomyelitis. It's probably what caused the blindness—the infection damaged the optic nerve."

"But why would he have gone totally blind? The malformation is only on one side."

"It doesn't need to get to the other eye. There's a sympathetic response in the 'good' eye, and that inflammation causes the damage. But you know, it may have even been a blessing in its way. Otherwise he'd probably have been shipped to England and raced till he broke down."

"England? Why England?"

"I've been reading up on the man who owned him. Turns out there's quite an English angle to the story. Ten Broeck—strange name, Dutch, I think—the one who owned Lexington at the height of his racing career, went on to become quite a celebrity over here. He was the first to bring American horses; at the time the press called it 'the American Invasion.' He won some big races and palled about with the Prince of Wales and the Duke of Edinburgh and miscellaneous European royals for about thirty years. Then he managed to lose his fortune entirely. Died alone and penniless in a bungalow in California. The man who found his body had come to buy his racing trophies—they were all he had left to sell, apparently.

"But I digress. The point is, he didn't take Lexington on account of the blindness. Lecompte became his star horse. But Lecompte suffered during the sea voyage and died soon after his first English race. That might have been Lexington's destiny. Instead, your horse was having a leisurely life at stud. It wasn't like it is now. Now they treat the poor stallions like machines, making them stand three times a day sometimes, all year long. No winters out to graze these days. They even ship them about to the Southern Hemisphere when the mares go into heat down there. But in those days, they'd only have to cover a few dozen mares in the springtime and then they'd have the rest of the year off."

"Not a bad life then."

"Not bad at all."

ALEXANDER'S JARRET

Woodburn Stock Farm, Woodford, Kentucky

1861

J arret could see his breath. He rose from his desk in the corner of the broodmare's barn and crouched to open the door of the woodstove. The metal hinges whined their complaint. He added a log and stood back as the coals flared. Outside, pastures glittered under a hard frost and a Union Jack snapped in an icy January wind. The clang of the halyard against the pole had grown louder as the wind picked up strength. When the kettle atop the stove began to hiss, Jarret made himself a pot of strong English tea. He'd developed a taste for it in the six years he'd spent at Woodburn.

The Belland boy came in, clutching the morning newspaper in fingers blue with cold. He had been breaking the ice on the horses' water troughs. Jarret poured him a mug of tea. "Sit a minute and warm yourself," he said, pushing a stool closer to the stove. The boy took the tea but didn't approach the fire. Instead, he stood by the drafty window, gazing out at the flag rattling on its halyard. Jarret supposed this was not such a cold morning for a Quebecois. He spread the newspaper on his desk and scanned the front page. The Clay girl had been right, all that time ago: the war she had predicted now seemed inevitable. Everyone was choosing sides.

"Well, Napoleon, our county has voted. Says here we're going to stand by the Union."

"Is good or is bad?"

Napoleon Belland understood English quite well but he was shy about speaking it with his heavy accent. He reminded Jarret of himself as a youngster, more comfortable with the language of horses than people. Jarret liked the boy. He was a gifted rider and a hard worker, and since he had lived in Kentucky for less than a year, he hadn't yet acquired the antagonism that other White employees showed in the face of Jarret's authority.

Jarret spread his hands and shrugged. "Kentucky's in three minds on this thing: some for the Union, some for the secesh, and a whole lot in the middle who say we shouldn't take sides at all."

Wedged between slave states and free states, Kentucky's counties were divided, its families were divided. Jarret suspected that not a soul in their county had voted to stand with the Union in order to end slavery. On the contrary, they stood with the president-elect because he was canny enough to assure them that they could keep their slaves if they stayed loyal.

"It's good news for the Union to have one more Kentucky county take their side. But for the farm, who knows? You chose a side, you also chose an enemy."

Napoleon tipped his head in the direction of the flag, the sharp blue and red stripes blurred by the wavy glass of the barn window. "He thinks *that* will help us?"

"He wants the Rebs to know this is a British man's farm, since the British are siding with them." Jarret thought a bit of flapping cloth unlikely to mean much when it came to irregular bands of horse thieves. He was more reassured by the fact that Mr. Alexander had gone off to Illinois to buy land, in case it became necessary to have a safe place to move the horses. Jarret hoped the North's superior power could crush the rebellion long before it came to that.

Belland went out to begin his exercise riding, and Jarret set his attention to assigning the rest of the day's chores. When it came to the thoroughbreds, Jarret answered only to Alexander himself and the farm manager, Dan Swigert. He was in charge of more than seventy broodmares, five stallions, and forty-four colts, fillies, weanlings, and yearlings. Doctoring them, exercising them, breaking them, preparing them for the spring sales.

Six years earlier, Robert Aitcheson Alexander would have been hard-pressed to put a name to the groom who had come north bringing Lexington. Alexander set the broad goals for his breeding operation, hired sound management, and did not overly trouble himself with the daily details. Jarret was, to him, just one among scores of laborers.

That had changed on a quiet Sunday afternoon. Alexander came across Jarret leaving the stallion barn and noticed that he was carrying a book. He waved Jarret over. "You can read?" He held out his hand for the battered volume. It was missing a cover and spine. "Where on earth did you get this?"

"I found it in the kindling basket."

"You saved it?"

"I don't burn books."

"You can comprehend this?"

"Not every word. But most."

"Most of it? Can you so?" Alexander smiled doubtfully. "And might you share some particular passage that you find worthwhile?" He handed Jarret the book.

"Well," said Jarret, "there's this, that the prince says." Jarret flipped the pages and read: "I will not trade my horse for any that walks on four legs. When I sit astride him I soar, I am a hawk. He trots on air. The earth sings when he touches it."

Alexander took more notice of Jarret after that day and instructed the farm manager to advance him beyond barn chores to small clerical tasks. Before long, Jarret was preparing the entries for the catalogue of stallions and broodmares. Later, when Alexander learned what a prodigious memory he had for pedigrees, he made Jarret responsible for meticulously recording the lineage of every horse brought to the farm for breeding. Now, Alexander consulted him to determine which horses should be bought and which sold.

When Jarret had given out the necessary instructions for that day's tasks, he pushed away from his desk and shrugged on a heavy felted jacket. Outside, the frost crunched under his boots. As he approached the stallion barn, he felt the knot in his head begin to loosen.

He loved this hour, the best in his day. As he rolled back the heavy door, Lexington caught his scent and raised his head, ears forward. He shifted his weight from hoof to hoof, as if dancing in pleasure. Jarret gave his usual three-note whistle and the horse answered with a nicker. A groom had already tacked him up, so Jarret signaled the boy to open the stall door. Lexington stood until he gave the voice command. Then the stallion walked out, confidently finding his way down the aisle and outside to the mounting block. He dropped his nose, measuring the exact place, and stopped, waiting for Jarret.

"Where will we go this morning?" Jarret asked. "Mares, foals? You decide."

At eleven years old, Lexington remained in peak condition. The blindness that prematurely ended his racing career also had saved him before the strain of grueling four-mile contests took a toll on his joints. Even in the cold, his gait was springy and forward. And though the wind surely interfered with both his hearing and scent, his trust in Jarret was such that he readily picked up the trot, just as he would on a still day when his ears and nose worked hard to map his known world.

Lexington's race record stood unbroken. Yet he looked set to become even more famous in the breeding shed. As a stallion, he had proven virile and fruitful. Jarret had soon realized that there was no need for a teaser stallion. As soon as a mare in estrus scented him, she signaled her readiness. And he'd got foals on an unprecedented number of the mares he covered, at a stud fee of one hundred dollars each. In 1859, his first crop of seven foals won ten races. The following year, twelve of his get raced and won thirty-seven times, enough prize money to rank him second that year as stud sire. Jarret was entirely confident that he would lead the list in the coming year.

Jarret shaded his eyes against the dazzle of the frost-crusted ground. He often wished the horse could see the place they'd come to. Even in the dead of winter, Woodburn was a magnificent prospect: four thousand acres of rolling fields marked off by neat fences and stone walls, containing what must be some of the richest soil in the world. In the nearest field, the farm's large flock of Southdown sheep—seven or eight hundred—clustered together for warmth. In the far field, fat Durham cattle stood apart, all facing into the wind, attentive as an audience attending a concert. Mature trees, bark lacquered black, fingered upward. The twigs formed fine black traceries against the white sky. They reminded Jarret of pencil lines on snowy canvas.

There was always an artist in residence at Woodburn: Alexander needed images of his fine livestock for his sale catalogues. The Swiss painter, Mr. Troye, had been a recent guest, staying more than three months to complete just two portraits. Jarret had to listen to the complaints of Swigert, the farm manager, who with his pregnant wife had to play host to Woodburn's guests during Mr. Alexander's absences. He'd been vexed by the artist's rapid depletion of his employer's good cellar—"and at the end of it, the portrait of Belmont was no likeness, for all his fussing with it."

Jarret had watched the Swiss artist at work on the unsuccessful Belmont painting, and more happily, on that of another horse, Woodford, where he had produced a fine portrait. It was clear to him that Troye's technique was more polished than Thomas Scott's, but Jarret admired the vigor of the younger artist, and his ability to get the job done without revising and fretting over every detail.

Troye had recommended Scott to Alexander when the Woodburn commissions grew too numerous for him. Alexander, abroad in England when he purchased Lexington from Ten Broeck, particularly wanted a portrait of his new acquisition and Troye was unavailable. So Scott had traveled with Jarret and the horse north from New Orleans.

Jarret had helped the painter, as always, keeping the blind horse calm in his unfamiliar high-walled turnout. Scott's first effort had captured the horse superbly, but he was unsatisfied with the background. Knowing that Alexander was used to Troye's rich finishes, he decided to try a second time. He presented this work to Mr. Alexander. The other, he gave to Jarret. "If Lexington is a success at stud like he was on the track, you'll find a buyer for it someday. Think of it as payment for all the help you've given me these years."

Now Jarret wondered if he would see Scott again: he'd said, as he left Woodburn, that if it came to war he intended to enlist.

"Which side?"

"Why, North, of course. How can you need ask?"

"Hard to tell what side anyone is on. Families being split right down the middle and all."

"Maybe so. But just because I work for these Southerners doesn't mean I hold with slavery."

Might not hold *with* it, Jarret had thought. But don't mind holding the cash that comes *from* it.

Jarret eased Lexington to a walk as they circled Alexander's residence. The house was a plain two-story clapboard with a wide front porch. Wings had been added, built to accommodate the guests who came to buy livestock.

Jarret kept Lexington on a loose rein, letting him choose their direction. As they approached the broodmares' turnout, the horse raised his head, scenting. The past spring, Lexington had mated successfully with two daughters of the great Glencoe, Nebula and Novice, both exceptional mares. Jarret had already chosen the name for Nebula's foal. He would call it Asteroid, which sounded fast and powerful, and would do for either a colt or filly.

Scott's painting hung over the mantel in Jarret's cottage. It was the first thing he saw when he came home of an evening; that honey-toned painting over the welcome hearth, where May would already have a fire going and something good simmering in the crock. She'd look up from her needlework and smile in that shy, slow way that made him feel warm inside. Her boy, Robbie, would run and throw his plump arms around Jarret's knees, wanting to be lifted high in the air and spun round. Jarret was the only father he knew.

When Jarret first came to Woodburn, he had noticed May, the laundress and seamstress for Mr. Alexander. The manager, Dan Swigert, had noticed him noticing and warned him off. "Never mind that one," he said. "She's married abroad to Robert, the carpenter over by Hawthorne's farm. In fact, she's with child by him, so you'd best not be looking that way."

The baby wasn't even weaned when Hawthorne sold Robert to traders profiting on the growing labor demands of the southwest expansion. Mr. Alexander had been sympathetic to May, but that sympathy did not extend to buying her husband, as she begged him to. "I already have a carpenter, May. I have no call for another. However, if you wish, you may travel to Frankfort to say goodbye to Robert, before he commences his journey from this state." Alexander asked Jarret to select a quiet horse for her and to provide an escort.

They managed to find Robert just as he was being herded into a cart, roped at the neck and stapled by the arm to the other unfortunates on their way west. May ran beside the cart and was able to catch hold of his hand. She stumbled along, clinging to him, until she could run no farther. She felt his hand slip from her grasp until just their fingertips touched. He continued reaching out to her as she slumped on her knees in the dust.

Jarret brought the horses up and stood by her as she keened. When it seemed the right time, he lifted her and put her on the horse, carefully placing each foot in the stirrups. As he threaded the leather reins through her limp fingers, something in his own heart broke open. He was overwhelmed with tender feelings for her, an urge to protect her and her baby.

In the weeks that followed, he had written letters, seeking word of Robert's ultimate destination. After almost a year and no word in reply, May told Jarret that her hope was extinguished. "I might meet him again in heaven, but not on this earth."

A few days after that, Jarret gently broached the subject of her taking up with him. She agreed to think on it. But days passed and he did not see her. He worried that he had offended her and that she was keeping out of his way. Then one evening he came in from the barns to find his cottage scented with fresh-baked bread. When May walked toward him shyly and took off his barn coat, he felt a contentment he'd never known.

She had decided to come to him because she thought it best for her boy and because Jarret was able to provide her with a safer place, away from the many travelers who passed through the Woodburn mansion. To the worst of them, she had been just another piece of Mr. Alexander's choice livestock, and her pallet, in an alcove off the laundry room, had afforded her no lock or door bar. Since then, she and Jarret had managed to live in the precarious intimacy that is the only kind possible when one partner still ardently loves another.

When Jarret sat by his hearth under the oil painting of Lexington, gazing at her lovely face in the firelight, he tried to forget that. As he tried to forget that it wasn't a legal marriage and that, for all his authority at Woodburn, he was still enslaved.

MARTHA JACKSON

MJ Gallery, 32 East Sixty-Ninth Street, New York, New York
1956

I t had rained in the night. A long finger of dawn light silvered the wet asphalt of East Sixty-Ninth Street all the way from the East River to Central Park. Martha blinked in the reflected glare, glad of the huge glass frontage on her new gallery. Natural light flooded the space and invited—demanded—attention from passersby.

Not that there were many people on the street at that hour. Martha was expecting delivery of some large works for a Hepworth show, and the art carriers preferred to unload before rush hour clogged the streets. As she descended the sweeping metal staircase that connected the four floors of exhibition space, she wished again that she could have moved into this building when it was first offered for rent. If she had, she felt sure she would be representing Pollock and Kline and the other big names whose potential she'd seen years earlier than others.

But she hadn't had the money then. Banks wouldn't lend to a woman, especially not for such a speculative business. Even her own father had shown scant faith in her. "You've got no business plan, you've got no track record," he complained. And she knew, even though it remained unstated, that he didn't really believe a woman could be any good in business. The robber barons who built Buffalo hadn't included any baronesses.

Martha had been forced to live within her means, and that meant her first gallery had been a small town house with rent she could afford, barely, thanks to her grandmother's bequest. She'd forsaken her nice apartment on Sutton Place to cook on a hot plate and sleep in an alcove as she converted the house to a gallery. The paint was barely dry on the newly white walls when she mounted her first show of American watercolors. She'd sold half. From there it was a new show every month. The abstract expressionists out on Long Island got used to seeing her in their studios. If she couldn't get American painters to show with her, she looked abroad and brought unfamiliar names with radical visions.

This fast pace and wild ambition drew notice. The takings from one show just managed to fund the next, and she kept up that frantic tempo for two years. At her openings, the cramped interior of the little town house meant that people spilled out into the street, giving an urgent excitement to the works inside. She would move among the crowd, constantly pouring cheap wine into mismatched thrift-shop glasses, brainstorming how to build her mailing list, scouring names from donor acknowledgments in museum catalogues, and begging friends for their contacts. And then, when the East Sixty-Ninth Street place became available again in 1955, she could just manage to scrape up the funds to secure the lease.

The sigh of air brakes signaled the arrival of the truck. The back ramp clanged onto the asphalt. Brawny men wrestled with the crated sculptures. Within seconds, a cacophony of horns erupted as drivers realized they'd have to edge around the truck. Martha, preoccupied with directing the men to the freight elevator, didn't at first see Annie, waiting tentatively in the street. She was clutching a brown paper parcel. Martha waved at her to come in.

"You're early today," she said.

"Yessum. This just came up with my kin from Ohio last night. We didn't want to trust putting it in the mail, and I had a powerful urge to bring it right here to you."

"Is that the picture you want me to value?"

"Yessum."

Martha had almost forgotten the conversation about the painting. It had been some months, and Annie had not mentioned it. If the thing was worthless, as she expected, she hoped the girl hadn't gone to a lot of trouble getting it from Ohio to New York.

"Well good, then. Come on back to the office and let's take a look."

As the girl struggled with the knots in the string, Martha saw that her hands were shaking. Poor kid, she thought. They must be desperate for this money. Whatever comes out of that brown paper, I'm going to have to buy it from her for at least a hundred dollars.

Annie smoothed back the wrapping and stepped aside. Martha drew a sharp breath. Her mother's horse. The bright bay coat, the luminous eye, the intelligent, white-blazed face. The four white feet.

"Royal Eclipse!" she whispered. Even as she said the name, she knew it couldn't be so. The painting was too old—certainly from the last century.

"'Scuse me, ma'am, but that's not this horse's name. The horse named Lexington, like the city, so we always been told in the family."

"Lexington?"

"Yessum."

"This is a painting of *Lexington*?" Martha's voice had gone up in pitch. Annie looked alarmed.

"Yessum. 'S far as we been told."

"Lexington was the great-grandsire of Royal Eclipse."

"Great-grandsire?"

"Like a great-grandparent . . . your grandfather's father."

"But I don't rightly know who was *my* grandfather's father. How come you know that about a horse?"

Martha smiled. "Not just a horse, Annie. Lexington was the greatest thoroughbred stud sire in racing history. No horse has ever surpassed him. For sixteen years, his foals, when they came to race, won more prize money than any other horses that raced those years. I'm sure you've heard of some of them—Preakness was one. Even today, people pay thousands of dollars for horses in Lexington's bloodline. My father paid a fortune for Royal Eclipse."

Martha gazed at the painting. She was so excited by the improbable as-sociation that she had barely noted the quality of the art. Now she saw it was a highly competent oil. Uneven, perhaps, in the refinement of the horse com-pared with the sketchily rendered background. The water trough, the stone wall, the tufts of grass—these seemed to have been dashed off, while every detail of the horse's anatomy and expression had been finely executed. She peered at the signature. The name Scott meant nothing to her—nineteenth-century representational art had never been an interest.

She wanted the painting. She knew the girl would be more than satisfied with what she would offer. But her conscience would not let her take advan-tage. She knew someone who could—who almost certainly would—pay far more.

"I'm no specialist in nineteenth-century equestrian painting, but I know someone who is."

"You think it might be worth something?"

"Oh yes, Annie. It's worth something."

THOMAS J. SCOTT

Stones River, Tennessee
1863

Cher Julien,

I was most pleased to have a letter from your hand after so many months, and to learn from its direction that you are safely in New York and far from the fighting. Even so, your note carried with it the scent of linseed oil, the hush of paintbrush against canvas—memories of the long, warm afternoons at work in your studio.

Here, the only canvas is the stained, wet stuff that provides our poor shelter; the only scents are of unbathed flesh, damp wool, and the occasional gust from a latrine that might better have been dug some way farther from this bivouac. I am serenaded by a chorus of moist coughing—many men are ill. My ears are dull, still, from the clangor of the last affray. After so many cannons, I do not think that I will hear again so well as I was used to do.

We are a weary, footsore, ragged army taking our needed rest after fifty-six straight days of fighting. I will not write to you of battles: no doubt you read of them in the New York press. They say we are winning this war. They say it, and yet that word does not carry the same meaning to me as it once did. This does not feel like winning, even when the cannons fall silent and I stand up with my head ringing in the midst of shattered trees and shattered bodies and can count more of us alive and more of them dead. I will not write further details of this here. Instead, I will tell you something of the personalities who are become central to my present life.

I will begin with the first in importance, another Thomas, who is our chaplain. When we met, we seemed to share no point of sympathy one with the other, save that name we held in common.

This young man of the cloth had decided he disliked me from the first moment we mustered. I could tell he thought I didn't belong in his company of well-to-do Lexington lads. They had most of them been schoolfellows together. To him, I was an unwelcome stranger who uttered oaths and had made my living from what he considered the disreputable trade of horse racing. It was all too evident he didn't want me in his mess.

Well, as you know of me, I do enjoy a challenge. I decided I would make an ally of young Parson Gunn before our 21st Kentucky Volunteers struck camp. That night, I waited until he had placed his bedroll, and then unfurled my own exactly next to it. When he saw this, he shot me a disgusted look, turned on his side, stuck a candle stub in his bayonet, and set it in the ground. I perceived he intended to read from his Testament. There I saw my first chance.

I rose on my elbow. "Parson Gunn," I said, loud enough for all sixteen men in the tent to hear me. "Read that Testament aloud, would you? There's not one of us in here but needs to hear it more than you."

I could see his callow face flush in the candlelight. "Certainly," he said, "if the rest are agreed."

"Of course they are, well-bred, God-fearing sons of Lexington!" I exclaimed. "Are you not, gentlemen?"

There were murmured ayes of small conviction. So the chaplain read for some while from the Gospel of John. When he closed the book at last and turned to douse the light, I asked: "Are you meaning to pray now? If so, might I ask that you do so aloud, as we all of us need prayers more than you do."

At this I heard some muffled sighs as men shifted on the hard earth. But the young chaplain intoned the Lord's Prayer for us and then some words of entreaty for our safety in the coming fight. The next day, I saw him watching me with a specula- tive eye. My cause was helped when our regiment commander, the noted surgeon Ethelbert Dudley, said that on account of my pharmacy training and my brief time as a medical student, I was to be steward of the field hospital. I took this news to Gunn and begged for his prayers for the men who would be our joint charge—he to salve the spirits of those whose bodies I could not save.

That night, I again prevailed on the chaplain to read his Testament aloud, then I asked if he would enlighten us as to his own journey to the Gospel. I have observed that there is nothing a man is more pleased to do than speak of his own life, and this turned out to be the case for the chaplain, who related his journey south to Clarksville, Texas. Not yet twenty-one and directly from college, he had won an appointment as vice president at a school there. The pupils were some two hundred rascals, as he described them, who had been sent to be "broken in and learn discipline" through what he called "a wise combination of prayer and the rod."

The whole school gave over one hour every day to visit a large and shady grove in which the boys were instructed to read their Scripture aloud. It was in that place, he said, that the conviction grew in him that it was his duty to become an ambassador of the Lord Jesus Christ. Alas, his heavenly musings were interrupted by the rude mutterings of war. On the day of Mr. Lincoln's election, the Stars and Stripes was pulled down without proper ceremony at his school and up in place went the Lone Star and the Rattlesnake flags.

Evidently, this line of talk held more interest for my tentmates than his waxing on the Gospel, for they began to stir and question Gunn as to how it had gone on for him in that nest of Texas traitors. He was happy to oblige their curiosity. It had rapidly became clear to Gunn that his Union sympathies might put him at some risk there.

Nevertheless, for a time he remained open in his opinions. But then a preacher in a nearby town was hanged simply for being an ardent Union man. Others of like mind were marched to jail. Gunn began to keep his loyalties more private, only worrying that he might betray himself to his bedfellow by talking in his sleep.

In February, Texas seceded and Gunn's school was ordered to become a military academy and prepare troops for the rebel army. Before the weapons arrived for these new cadets he fled, arriving home just in time to rush to arms. His mother, instead of gainsaying him, quite pushed him out the door: "If God has a mission for you on earth," she told him, "he will preserve you to fulfil it."

Our mission, in those early days of war, did not seem especially God-given. We did little all day but drill: marching, wheeling, marking time, and complaining bitterly that we had none of us enlisted in order to be trotted to death.

Kentucky, as you must know, was supposed to be neutral at that time. But secesh sympathy was strong and all over the state irregular guerrilla bands were forming to fight for Jeff Davis. The news of this emboldened that fool to dispatch his troops to seize the bluffs at Columbus. This galvanized those of uncertain opinion. There was rage at the violation of our supposed neutrality. As you will know, Kentucky voted then to join the Union cause and our orders came to march south.

The ladies of the Lexington Bible Society presented us with a Testament each, and a band played us on our way along the Nicholasville Pike. Some of the men had to bear the sight of wives, mothers, lady friends, and young children, in carriages or on foot, all bathed in tears. At that moment, I was glad that you were not in Lexington, and that I had no ties of affection to be so publicly displayed.

We expected to go all the way into Tennessee but got no farther than Green River Bridge, which we were charged to guard. We spent the winter there, in hand-to-hand combat with measles, scarlet fever, diarrhea, and much discontent from men eager for a proper fight.

They might not have been so eager had they known what lay ahead. I will not revisit it here, except to confess to you that no matter how dreadful the experience of battle, there was always in me, before a fight, that same deep excitement as I felt at a race when waiting for that drum tap.

But oh, after. All was a blur as we tended the injured, amputating limbs, dressing wounds, writing last letters, washing and burying the dead. Gunn was my inseparable companion in this labor. The first time I asked him to give the chloroform, the poor man fairly swooned. I shook him and told him to have a good nerve. It didn't help that the patient, as the chloroform took hold, kept crying to his new bride: "Oh Lamira, Samuel is coming back to you with one arm—this hand has done its last ploughing." He was right in that. The arm was fully flayed as if it were an anatomy lesson, and the bones cracked into wandering shards. Later, when he awoke, he insisted we bring the severed member so that he might see it one last time. Since he would not settle until we did so, Gunn retrieved the grisly thing from the bin.

Samuel took hold of his own now-stiffening fingers and cried: "Farewell until the Resurrection."

I saw tears in Gunn's eyes at that, and he took the arm away and gave it a proper burial. He was full of such small kindnesses. I would sigh to him of some poor boy gone past help and urge him: "If you've a word to say to him, say it now." For my part, all I could give was my small store of skill, and when that ran dry, some measure of tenderness. It breaks me when I see a man a second time, having saved his life by some drastic measure after one battle, to find him some months later back in my care again. If the second wound proves mortal, I try to stay at that soldier's side until death claims him.

Julien, I am sick and tired of carnage. I must set down this pen now as my hand aches from the effort of writing so much. My nails have gone soft, my fingers are tender from constant steeping in the blood of others. I would fain set down my surgeon's saw and pick up, once again, my painter's brushes.

They say that day will come soon, that the South is like a man who has received his mortal blow and only staggers feebly toward an inevitable extinction. I will join my friend, Chaplain Tom, in praying that it not be long.

Yours, etc . . .

MARTHA JACKSON

125 East Seventieth Street, New York, New York

1956

Martha Jackson was annoyed with herself. As the butler ushered her into Paul Mellon's library, she felt a flutter of nerves. Her grandfather's mansion had been grand enough. But this was a different kind of rich.

The five-story edifice felt more like a French château than a Manhattan town house. Morning light spilled through three French doors that opened onto the courtyard. Outside, a team of gardeners snipped the topiaries edging the reflecting pool. The stone pavers had been chosen for their patina; the mature boxwoods looked like they had been in place for years. Only the modest circumference of the young tree trunks gave any sign that this expansive garden was new.

Martha felt as if someone were looking at her. When she turned, a portrait of a young girl gazed down with confident amusement, her terrier balanced casually on a cocked, red-sashed hip. Martha gazed back at the painting, her brow creased. She felt she had seen it before.

"It's John Singer Sargent," said Paul Mellon, crossing the hall from his study. "The one painting my father ever gave me. They were packing it up with all the masterpieces he was giving to the National Gallery. He turned to me and said, 'You like terriers, you ought to have that one.' He never let me have an actual dog, you see."

Well, thought Martha, that was an odd introduction. She had never met the bookish billionaire, who had started his own art collection only recently, under the influence of his second wife. His first, Mary, had been more enthusiastic about his equestrian interests, and the couple had stayed mostly on their estate in Virginia. Even after Mary's physician warned her that horses exacerbated her asthma, she refused to give up riding at Paul's side in the hunts. It was an attack at the end of one such ride that killed her. Bunny, Mary's friend, quickly jettisoned her own husband to console her bereaved neighbor, and now was happily spending his money on her favored French painters: Renoir, Matisse, Cézanne, and Monet.

The Mellon taste did not run to edgy contemporary art and had not brought them to either of Martha Jackson's galleries. Bunny favored Impressionist landscapes; Paul's interest was equestrian art. Martha's research had disclosed that the first painting he bought was a racehorse portrait—George Stubbs's *Pumpkin with a Stable-Lad*. Martha knew he'd also recently bought Degas and Lautrec racing scenes.

The modest picture she'd carried uptown was not in that league, or that price range. It would normally have been beneath his interest. But Martha knew that this work would have an attraction for him that might cause him to look beyond the relative obscurity of the artist.

Mellon gestured toward a highly polished library table. Martha set the painting down and began to unwrap it. Once again, she was vexed with herself. Her hands were shaking, just as Annie's had been, a week earlier. Really, why should she be so invested in whether this man liked the work or not? She was just doing her maid a favor, after all. Mellon would likely never be her client. Still, she fumbled with the string until Mellon drew a mother of pearl letter opener from his desk and severed the twine.

"I've done some research into this artist, since you called. Not of the first rank. Troye, perhaps, would be of some interest to me, but—"

And then he stopped and drew a breath.

He stepped back.

"Well. I see."

"Exactly," said Martha, in equal parts gratified and relieved by his re-action.

Paul Mellon loved his racehorses. Since buying Rokeby Stud in the 1930s he'd been acquiring horses with multiple Lexington bloodlines, hoping to breed winners with the champion's speed and heart. Martha Jackson had guessed he would be tempted to own a portrait of his future champions' great progenitor.

"It's really quite accomplished, as a painting. I'm interested. What will you take for it?"

Martha had given some thought to this question. Paul Mellon was famous for his refusal to haggle. He thought it ungentlemanly. If he didn't like the first price, he wouldn't say so, he just wouldn't buy. For Annie's sake, and her brother's, she didn't want to undersell the painting. But she didn't want to overplay her hand and risk losing the sale.

"Why don't you keep it for a week, think about it, do some more research, if you like. Then you can tell me what you believe it is worth." She had reasoned that a man used to paying French Impressionist prices might find his way to a higher figure than she would dare suggest.

Mellon's thin lips gave a hint of a smile. He knew a canny move when he saw one. He looked at Jackson with new interest. She might be a dealer worth knowing. "Very well. I will need to show it to my wife, in any case. We make these decisions jointly, you see. She has excellent taste."

"Of course," said Martha. "Her gardens, in particular, are highly re-garded."

"I envy her. It's a passion she has nurtured since she was five years old. Not many of us find our métier at such a young age. Shall I have Christopher fetch you a cab?"

"Oh no. I'll walk, thanks. My gallery is rather close by. Perhaps you and Mrs. Mellon will visit, someday."

"Perhaps we will," he said and rang the bell for the butler to show her out.

Back at her apartment, she sat on her bed, staring at the empty wall where the Lexington painting had hung.

She'd put it up next to the photos of her mother while she waited for her appointment with Mellon. It had given her pleasure, seeing it there. Now, her eye traveled to the blank space. The black-and-white photos of Royal Eclipse seemed duller, lifeless. She got up and walked restlessly to her desk and drew out the leather journal in which she noted her income and expenses. It was a lean ledger, as always. Without the quarterly payments from her trust, she would barely be solvent. She put the journal away. It wasn't like her to form a sentimental attachment to a picture. And yet, she had. Half of her hoped for a large offer from Mellon, half of her hoped he'd offer only a low sum, one that she could easily match.

From the other room, she heard Annie singing as she went about her work. The main thing was helping her. She had to keep that in mind.

She could sell the sports car. She'd barely driven it all winter. Last time she was out on Long Island, Pollock had offered to trade her a painting for it. With spring just around the corner, perhaps he'd be tempted by a convertible. Maybe she could bargain him up to two paintings—it wasn't like his new work was exactly leaping off the gallery walls. In fact, he was barely painting. Perhaps the car would improve his mood. If she got two paintings for it, she could keep one as an investment, and sell one. That'd allow her to give Annie a decent price for the Scott picture, *and* keep the gallery lights on for another month. But what would Lee say? Maybe she wouldn't want him to have a sports car, if he was drinking heavily again. They weren't getting on well, Martha knew that much. She'd heard that there was another woman. After all Lee had put up with, all she'd done to support him. She should definitely ask her friend's opinion before she broached the subject of the car with Pollock.

The week passed with no word from Mellon. Another week. Then a month. She didn't want to harass the man, but she could tell that Annie was anxious. And every time Martha entered the bedroom, the blank space on the wall continued to draw her eye. Damn it, if he wasn't going to buy it, she wanted it back. She decided to advance Annie some money ahead of the potential sale. When Martha handed her the envelope, the young woman could barely hold back tears.

It wasn't considerate of Mellon to keep her waiting in this way. She resolved that if the week ended and he had not called, she would call him, as unsavory as she found the thought.

At a quarter to five on Friday, Martha sat staring at the telephone. It was four fifty-one when she steeled herself, placed her finger in the rotary, and dialed the number.

As she expected, Paul Mellon's English secretary answered. The woman had a voice as chilly as a January evening. Martha's own voice suddenly sounded very upstate as she explained the reason for her call.

"I see," the icicle replied. "I must tell you that Mr. Mellon is not accustomed to being dunned."

"'Dunned?' I'm hardly dunning him! I'm merely asking. Our understanding was that I would leave the painting for his consideration for one week. That is now six weeks ago. I believe that is ample time."

"Well, I am afraid Mr. and Mrs. Mellon have gone to Paris."

"When do you expect their return?"

"Not for some weeks. My understanding is they intend to spend the spring there."

"And when do you expect to speak with him?"

"I cannot tell you with certainty."

Martha sat seething at the other end of the line. She felt her spine straightening. She tilted her head to the left and right, easing the tension that had accumulated in her neck.

"In that case," she said, "would you be kind enough to have the butler—Christopher, I think?—ready the painting. I will send for it first thing tomorrow morning."

"I see," said the icicle again, but Martha caught the note of surprise that had slipped into her voice. "And what may I tell Mr. Mellon?"

"Tell him I have another buyer, who has already been quite patient, and since you say the delay on your end may be indefinite . . ."

"In that case, perhaps I *could* place a call to Mr. Mellon in Paris . . ."

"Don't trouble. I'm sure it's a matter of indifference to him. I would not want him disturbed. Goodbye." Before the flustered assistant could reply, she depressed the button on the cradle with a decisive click.

As Martha replaced the handset, she smiled. She had never expected that blowing up a millionaire client would be so very gratifying.

ALEXANDER'S JARRET

Woodburn Stock Farm, Woodford, Kentucky

1865

J arret trudged wearily from the stallion barn to his cottage. He'd been up most of the night helping with a troublesome foaling, and as often happens when one is least equipped to deal with it, the day had been nothing but one problem after another. A colic in the mare's barn, mold in the hay, a fall by a new exercise rider that had caused a broken wrist.

He was yearning for the comfort of his wing chair, of the boy crawling into his lap, all hugs and small confidences, of May's soft smile as she helped him ease off his boots and brought him some good warm thing to eat.

But May was not smiling when she opened the door. Her lovely face was pinched. It looked as if she had been crying. The boy, who usually jumped into his arms, cowered and clutched her skirt, his eyes wide.

"Why May, honey, whatever is—"

As Jarret reached out to caress her brow, she flinched and drew away from him.

A tall man in Union blue, one arm in a sling, came forward and stood behind her. "Jarret, it's Robert," she said quietly.

Jarret took a step backward into the dooryard. Struggling to master himself, he closed his eyes, took a breath, stepped back inside the cottage, and closed the door behind him.

"Hello, Robert."

"Hello, Jarret."

It was an awkward supper. There were long silences, interrupted only by the scrape of spoons on the bowl and the fall of logs in the fireplace. Eventually, Jarret learned that Robert Hawthorne, as he now styled himself, had been sold into Louisiana. He had worked as a carpenter on a cotton plantation until he heard news that Union forces were closing in. He escaped and fled to a contraband camp and volunteered for the army. He had been in Tennessee, building breastworks, when a minié ball shattered his left arm. "Look like the war ended for me that day," he said. "But I still got my good arm so I can do some kind of work with that."

May got up to clear the bowls and put Robbie to bed.

Through the thin wall, Jarret could hear her singing softly to the boy.

"Why did you not send a message?" Jarret said quietly. "You've done May—all of us—a great wrong."

"I know it. I am sorry. Truth is, I didn't want to say anything to May until I could say what I came here to say today. That I have saved my army pay, and been to Marse Alexander, and he done said yes to what I could give for the both of them. So, May and the boy free to come with me, if that her choice."

Jarret swallowed hard. "And . . . is it?"

"She ain't give me an answer yet. She say she need to talk to you, first off." The two men sat in silence, staring into the embers. "I know you give her and the boy a good life here. I'm thankful to you."

Maybe, thought Jarret. But he had never been sure that May felt good about the life they shared. Even though no law on the books recognized a slave marriage, that didn't make it less real to two people who loved. In his bed, May never initiated lovemaking, and never looked him in the face during the act. Jarret couldn't shed the conviction that she was thinking of Robert. This caused a waning of his own desire. Now, he thought, it was fortunate that their lovemaking had been infrequent and that there was no baby of their own.

Jarret knew what her answer would be. She would go with Robert, even though it was uncertain how well he could provide.

"Where will you go?"

"Head up north to Ohio. One of the freedmen in my unit say we could go to his family—they got a small hog farm outside Ripley. His momma widowed and all alone there. He say she could use help since he and his brother still in the fighting."

Although he longed to hold May in his arms for one last night, Jarret left the cottage, making the excuse that he was needed again at a foaling. He went, instead, to the stallion barn and spent the night on the floor of Lexington's stall, his heart soothed by the horse's steady breathing.

In the morning, at first light, May came to find him. She knew exactly where he would be. He took her by the hand and walked with her into the privacy of the woods. Tears glazed her eyes and ran down her cheeks. He softly wiped them away with his two thumbs.

"No need of that," he said gently. "You've been good to me, but you weren't never mine. I know that."

"Jarret, I—"

"Hush now," he said. "Robert is your boy's rightful pa. No one should stand between a good man and his son. And he see to it you two gone be free, no matter which way this war goes on." He drew her to him and kissed her for the last time.

They walked back to the cabin, side by side but not touching. As May went to pack her things, Jarret took the painting of Lexington down from above the mantel, removed it from the frame, and rolled it in a piece of sacking. He handed the package to May.

"That's the painting of Lexington that Mr. Scott gave to me some while back."

"Jarret, I can't take this."

"Sure you can. I still got the old picture he painted for me when I was a boy and Lexington but a colt. I can put that one here on the wall. You take this one, and if you ever need money for the boy, you sell it. Don't you take less than ten dollars for it. Someone might even give twenty, if they know what horse it is."

MARTHA JACKSON

Springs, Long Island, New York
1956

L ee Krasner flung another sweater into the open suitcase on her bed. Her plum-colored bathrobe swirled around her. She cinched the sash on the robe.

"Give him the goddamned car. What do I care?"

It was a cold, bright February day, the sun low and silvery on the pond. Martha, dressed in a woolen jacket and slacks, felt chilly just looking at her friend. But Lee's cheeks were pink with restless agitation. Her internal fires seemed to be protecting her from the drafts rattling the poorly glazed windows.

"I just thought—I didn't want to do it if you would worry—"

"About him driving drunk? Honestly, Martha, I've worried about him long enough. I can't keep carrying him. Everything I've done to protect him has just turned him against me. That's why I'm going to Paris. If the Big Game Hunter thinks she can get him sober and painting again, then let her try. I won't be in the way."

Everyone in New York knew about Pollock's new lover, an art student half his age with movie-star looks and an appetite for famous men. One account said she'd gone after Pollock, asking a friend to draw her a map of where he sat at the Cedar Tavern. Another rumor claimed she was there with

someone else, and that Pollock had been the one who'd fallen all over *her*.
Either way, it hardly mattered. Bloated, balding, without a significant piece
of work in three years, Pollock had been easy to seduce.

Lee slammed the suitcase and pressed down hard to snap the clasps. "In
Paris I might be able to get my own work done, for a change."

"Your work is wonderful."

"I'm glad you think so. No one else does."

"That's not true, Lee. It's just always harder for women."

Lee flopped on the bed. The pink in her cheeks became blotchy. She
swiped at her eyes. Martha rose from her chair by the window and crossed
the room to sit by her friend.

"This thing won't last. You know that. By the time you get back from
Paris he'll be sick of her and desperate for you."

Lee sighed. "That's what I tell myself. But you've seen her. What man
wouldn't want that? You know he's never stopped telling people how plain
I am. Now he's finally got the glamour girl he thinks he deserves."

"Oh, Lee," said Martha. "It's not true. He adores you. He's going to remember that."

Lee ran her paint-stained fingers through her hair, took a deep breath,
and changed the subject.

"What paintings did he offer to trade you?"

"Two of the black enamels from fifty-one. The one I always liked—
number five—you know, the one I call Elegant Lady."

"You know he hates it when you give them names."

"I don't do it in front of him. The other one is twenty-three—I think I'll
call it Frogman—but don't tell him."

Lee gave a snort. "Never," she laughed. "Or maybe I will, just to
annoy him."

One week later, back in the city, Martha Jackson handed over the keys to
the convertible to Pollock. It wasn't even noon, but he was already slurring
his words. She watched him walk unsteadily out of the gallery and climb
into the car. The woman was waiting for him. She slid across the bench seat,

flipping back a glossy fall of dark hair and thrusting her hand between his thighs. Martha glimpsed full lips, dark eyes. Young, luscious. Poor Lee. She heard the gears grind as Pollock inexpertly threw the stick into first. She winced. Rubber screeched as they sped off down Sixty-Ninth Street.

Then she shrugged. You couldn't live everybody's life for them. You just helped where you could. She got out her checkbook and wrote:

Pay to the order of Annie Hawthorne. One thousand dollars only.

It was a lot of money. But Annie said her brother aimed to become a doctor; he would need every penny. And with the Pollocks in hand, Martha could afford it.

The two enamels leaned against the gallery wall, their energetic lines of bold black calligraphy commanding her eye. She gave a sigh of satisfaction. She picked up the modest old painting she'd just overpaid for and climbed the wide staircase from the gallery to her apartment.

In the bedroom she hung the portrait of Lexington back on the wall between her mother's photographs and laughed at a stray thought.

"Martha Jackson, when you die, and the vultures start circling over your collection, they're all going to look at this painting and say, What the hell is *this* one doing here?"

ALEXANDER'S JARRET

Woodburn Stock Farm, Woodburn, Kentucky

1865

J arret bought May a pair of mules for the journey north. He made sure they were sound animals with steady tempers. When they got to the farm in Ohio, they could sell one and use the other to work the land.

Jarret couldn't clear his mind of the last sight of them, May and the boy atop the mule and Robert Hawthorne in his Yankee-blue uniform walking alongside, leading the other animal with the rope in his good hand.

So on the morning Jarret looked up and saw a Union soldier standing in the barn door with the light behind him, Jarret thought it was Hawthorne, returned. He felt a rush of joy and dread. Hoping to see May again, fearing that something had befallen her. Then his rational mind overrode his emotions. The figure in the doorway was much slighter, and as he stepped out of the glare Jarret saw clearly that he was White. It was a few more moments before he recognized him.

Three years of war had aged him. Scott's army uniform hung off his spare frame, and his face, once so open and youthful, had fallen into haggard folds. Scott, for his part, barely recognized the sleek figure who rose from his desk, his brow creased in puzzlement as he tried to align the image of the man he had known with the one who now stood before him.

"Mr. Scott . . . ?"

"Private Scott, Jarret. The infantry owns me now."

"Infantry? Why, I thought you'd join the cavalry for sure."

Scott shrugged. "You need a mount for that. I only paint horses; I can't afford to own any."

"It's good to see you, still standing on two legs. But what brings you here?"

"Well, for some addlepated reason, I just reenlisted. So they gave me a furlough, and since my regiment is encamped nearby, Mr. Alexander was kind enough to invite me to take my rest here, which offer I was more than glad to accept. I've heard all about what you've accomplished here, Jarret. I saw General Grant's mount, Cincinnati. That's a grand horse. You bred something special with that one."

"Lexington's get are most all turning out to be something special," Jarret said. "Last year was his third in a row as leading stud sire, this year will make it four—and that's with half his colts and fillies not racing but going off to the army, just like Cincinnati."

"Well, Grant loves that horse, and he's a man who knows horses. The only other soul he lets ride him is the president himself."

"President Lincoln rides Cincinnati? That's a fine thing to know." Jarret wished he could tell his father that he'd bred a horse fit for a president. Harry Lewis would be proud.

"You want to see Lexington?"

"You know I do."

On the way to the stallion barn, Scott, muscle-weary and worn to a raveling, found it hard to keep pace with Jarret's springy step. "You've fared well enough here, during the war?"

"We've had a good amount of luck," Jarret said. "Bushwhackers been through some nearby farms, snatching whatever horses they want. But seems like the secesh count on Mr. Alexander as a sympathizer, on account of his British raising. On the Federal side, they paid for the horses they got from us—including Cincinnati. Course now you told me where that horse ended up, I got to hope the rebels never get word we're mounting Union generals."

They found Lexington turned out in the paddock, grazing under his favorite tree, a wide beech. Jarret whistled. Lexington's fine head shot up, ears swiveling. Jarret whistled again and the stallion collected himself and cantered to where they stood by the rails. His nostrils widened, taking in Scott's scent, then he dropped his head for Jarret's caress.

"I thought it then, and I think it still. This is the handsomest horse I ever saw."

"You fixing to paint him again, while you're here?"

"I wish I could; I don't have my things."

"Mr. Troye left a good amount of his paints and linens and such, the last time he was here. He was planning to return, but I doubt we'll see him while this war goes on."

Scott flexed his fingers. It would feel good, he thought, to have a brush in his hand, to lose himself again in a painting. He regarded the sightless horse, his head resting on Jarret's shoulder. After his studies with Julien, Scott no longer shied from the idea of figure drawing. It struck him that it would be something, to capture the bond between Jarret and the horse. The stallion was still glorious, but there was a vulnerability to the champion now; it would be a challenge to see if he had the skill to convey that.

That afternoon, he asked Jarret to pose with the horse. Jarret felt awkward as Scott stared at him. His mind churned with all the many tasks that would fall neglected while he stood there. Nevertheless, days later, when he looked at Scott's finished canvas, he realized Scott had caught both Lexington's grandeur and his defenselessness. Jarret had not spent any large part of his time considering his own appearance, so he barely recognized himself in the slender young gentleman that Scott had depicted. Scott had asked him to pose in his shirtsleeves, saying that the soft whites and creams of the linen would look well against the bright bay of the horse's coat. He had painted Jarret gazing pensively at the horse, his face in three-quarter profile, his arm, holding the lead rope, raised in a graceful arabesque. Somehow Scott had conveyed, in that gesture and that gaze, the current of affection and trust that flowed between horse and man.

"I think it might be the best one you done. And I don't say that just cause

I'm in it." Jarret paused, trying to express what he meant to say. "This time, you set down who Lexington *is*."

Scott gazed at his own work and felt the rightness of Jarret's words. It *was* his best picture. He would send it on to Julien in New York, where it could be put on public display and help to build his reputation.

He was grateful to Jarret. What a journey it had been, since that day in Warfield's paddock. That shy boy shoveling manure had traveled a long way, given the foul system that constrained him. As they walked to the stallion barn, Scott lowered his voice and placed a hand on Jarret's arm.

"You know, you could come with me when I leave this place."

"What do you mean?"

"You know the Union Army is enlisting colored soldiers now—which means you'd be emancipated. I could go with you to the colored's unit, introduce you to the officer in charge."

Jarret stopped in his tracks so suddenly that Scott almost tripped over his own feet.

"What makes you think you know what's best for me?"

"Well, don't you—"

"Want to be free? Course I do. But a soldier ain't free." He thought about May's husband, his shattered arm, his uncertain future. "I respect the men who joined your army, I do. But I've been taking orders all my life, and now I'm giving them. I good as run this place, Mr. Scott. And I get paid to do it." He saw the surprised look on Scott's face. "Mr. Alexander commenced to pay us wages right after the president's proclamation. What makes you think I'd give that up to take orders from some White officer, a stranger, who don't care if I live or if I die? Just another massa, is all I see. We suffered enough on account of slavery already. I don't plan on laying my life down to end it. You folk who made this mess, I reckon you owe us to clean it up."

Jarret strode off. Scott watched his retreating back. He couldn't fault the logic.

Scott was invited to dine with Alexander and Dan Swigert. He set about making himself as presentable as his meager wardrobe allowed. Someone had already placed a pitcher of warm water on his washstand. As he shaved, he stared at his reflection in the speckled glass. He felt much older than his thirty-two years. He had lost flesh and couldn't help but imagine, as an anatomist will, the skull beneath his tired skin. He lifted a cheek with his index finger, trying to find his way to the younger man's face he had worn not long ago.

Why had he reenlisted? He surely had no further appetite for fighting. Partly, he acknowledged to himself, it was his bond with the men. Almost the entire unit had reenlisted and he was needed by them. He was more useful in the army than he had ever been in his life—more useful than he ever likely would be again. Because of him, men lived who would have died. That was something.

And this, also: He had come to ardently believe in the rightness of his side. It was a conviction that had grown in him far beyond the common loyalty to birthplace and nation that had first prompted his enlistment. In the beginning, he had spent much time with the prisoners. It was his duty, if they were wounded, to tend to them. At first, he was kindly disposed to these men, young as they were, skinny, sometimes shoeless rural boys, most from farms too poor to afford slaves. It had seemed to him an evil fate, a geographical accident, that had forced them to take up arms in what was, to him, a war to secure the rich man's wealth. Beyond what was strictly required for their care, he would talk to them, to better know their minds. But after a time, he had stopped seeking such dialogue. They were, all of them, lost to a narrative untethered to anything he recognized as true. Their mad conception of Mr. Lincoln as some kind of cloven-hoofed devil's scion, their complete disregard—denial—of the humanity of the enslaved, their fabulous notions of what evils the Federal government intended for them should their cause fail—all of it was ingrained so deep, beyond the reach of reasonable dialogue or evidence. Scott had become convinced that a total obliteration of their rebellion was the only way forward. And since the drift of things was strong in that direction, he would see it through to the end.

As he shook out his one clean shirt, he felt a certain heaviness about the coming dinner. He was in two minds about his canny host. Surely Alexander was wise to safeguard all he had built and all those who depended upon him for their sustenance and their safety. And yet to portray yourself as in some kind of sympathy, or even neutrality, with the slavers' cause seemed to him a moral bridge most hard to cross. He buttoned his uniform jacket, wondering how he might, in the next few days, show an appropriate gratitude to his host for the kindness of this respite while not blurting out the grave reservations of his heart.

As it happened, he need not have concerned himself.

When he entered the dining room, there was the bell-like chime of fine crystal as Alexander lifted the stopper from the wine decanter. He turned from the sideboard to greet Scott. But the words never left his mouth. A kitchen girl, wide-eyed, plunged into the room, shrieking.

"They here! They here! Rebels in the barn, stealing horses."

"In broad daylight, Sara? That seems un—"

As Alexander spoke, a heavy tread pounded down the long hallway from the kitchen and Swigert burst into the room. "They're in the training stable—eight or ten of them, and I think—I'm pretty sure—it's that mongrel Quantrill in the lead, and those bloody-handed James boys with him. They've already got Lexington's Asteroid and Bay Dick. I don't know which others."

"Secure the house. Bolt the windows." Alexander strode across the room and flung up the lid of his writing desk. He crammed a pistol into his waistband and took another, cocked, in his right hand. He turned. "Mr. Scott, are you armed, sir?"

"No, not presently."

"Could I suggest you attend to it?"

Scott took the stairs to his room two at a time. He had heard of the notorious William Quantrill. The brute had led a dawn massacre against antislavers in Lawrence, Kansas. They'd killed everyone—old men, boys, an entire encampment of unarmed Black recruits. They'd looted and burned the town. His unit had been warned that the brigand might have slipped into

Kentucky with a small band of his most desperate killers. He felt his skin prickle and his heart pound. He hadn't cleaned his gun in days. He was not ready for this fight.

Alexander had gone out through the front door to confront the raiders. He stepped right into their path as they rode into the kitchen yard, raised a hand, and cried "Halt! What will you have, gentlemen?"

Scott crept out by the rear door and made a way behind the house till he reached the cover of a copse of trees. He went stealthily, tree by tree, to the rear of the barn. Scott wanted to take the measure of this party so as to determine how many men they may be up against. Bushwhackers were like quicksilver—they'd come together for a big operation and then split apart into small units, the better to hide from Federal pursuit. It was a strategy that had kept the killers at their blood-soaked trades throughout the war.

He could see now how they had the gumption to travel in daylight. They were clad in Federal blue. But as he crept closer, the motley nature of their disguise revealed itself. They wore an ill-assorted selection of clothing, probably pillaged from the bodies of soldiers they'd murdered. Most of them had the long, unkempt hair favored by ill-disciplined, bloody-handed bush-whackers. He peered at the strange collar around one man's neck and it came to him with a sickening jolt that the necklace was made of human scalps. He felt a dreadful heaviness—had they come upon his own unit's encampment? Surely not—they were opportunists who preyed on the weak. They would not hazard a fair fight with a large, well-armed force.

He crept closer and flattened himself against the barn. Through a broken piece of board he was able to sight his gun on the guerrilla leader. Quantrill was a handsome youth, dark haired, with defined brows and generous lips that turned down at the corners in a kind of permanent sneer. His smooth, unlined face belied the hellish things he was said to have done. But his victims—the few left alive to speak of him—had always reflected in aston-ishment on his youthful appearance.

Scott made a grim calculation. He could take the shot and wipe that sneer off for good and all. But he was an indifferent marksman. He might miss.

Even if his shot was true, Quantrill's men would surely fall upon Alexander and everyone else in the place.

Alexander gazed up at the mounted Quantrill, who had just given the name "Marion" and was persisting in the threadbare fiction that he led a Union detachment, sent to press good horses for cavalry mounts.

"Then let me see your orders," said Alexander calmly.

At this, pretense fell away. Quantrill raised his gun, and all his men did likewise.

"*These* are our orders."

Alexander remained cool. He tilted his head. "Well, I suppose if you are bound to have the horses there is no need for a fight about it. But if you are bound to have a fight, I have armed men here and we will give you the best fight we can."

Quantrill gave a hand signal at that, and one of his raiders led up a sagging figure, mounted on what looked like a child's pony. The man was slumped over on the horse's withers, his face shadowed by a hood. Quantrill flicked his head and the raider drew off the hood to reveal Willa Viley, gagged, bound, already bruising from a beating.

"You recognize your friend?"

Alexander, for the first time, seemed discomposed. "For pity's sake, unbind my neighbor. He's an old man who should not be treated in this way."

"I will unbind him when you give me the horses, march out the armed men you brag on, and deliver up your arms."

"I will not, sir."

Quantrill reached over and violently tore the gag from Viley's mouth. A trickle of fresh blood ran into his silver beard.

"Tell him, old man."

Viley's voice rasped. "For pity's sake, Alexander, give him what he wants. They burned the depot and the freight cars at Lair Station last night. I tried to stop them. I—" His voice broke. "They'll torch this place if you don't."

Quantrill nodded. "I will. Now, where are the horses? I will have Lexington."

"But you must know Lexington is blind! He's unridable. Let me give you—"
Quantrill raised his hand.

"I heard you got a boy here can ride him just fine. I'll take him too."

"But why—I can give you two of the best cavalry mounts you could find—"

"I already have a buyer for your blind hero. But since you offer, I'll also take the two cavalry mounts."

"Whatever you expect to be paid for Lexington—I can match it."

"Bring out the cash then and we'll see. And those arms you mentioned."

"But I'm giving you the horses. I need arms for my own protection. I will order my men to stack them until you leave, if you let Captain Viley go."

Scott, pressed flat against the barn boards, measured the distance from his hiding place to the stallion barn. He would try to get across the yard and warn Jarret. He might make it, while the two men haggled. He eased himself away from the barn, into the gathering shadows. Quantrill's men had their guns fixed on Alexander, their attention on the parlay. If only they do not turn . . . He placed his feet carefully into soft leaf litter, trying to avoid a twig whose crack might draw an eye his way.

"Fetch the arms out here then, and if one shot is fired I'll torch the place."

"If one shot is fired it'll be your men who do it."

Alexander turned on his heel and strode to the house. His mind raced with possibilities. But as he opened the kitchen door, he found himself face-to-face with one of Quantrill's guerrillas. The man was molesting Daniel Swigert's young wife. He spun round as Alexander burst in and cocked his pistol against her temple. Her little daughter, not yet three, clutched at her skirt, howling.

This was more than Alexander could stomach. Impulsively, he swung at the man, knocking the pistol away from the girl and her child. The raider lunged and the two men fell, grappling, onto the gritstone floor. The pistol discharged. Alexander brought his knee, hard, into the raider's groin. The raider bellowed like a castrated calf and folded up on himself, retching. Alexander struggled to his feet and pushed the girl and the child into the corridor, bolting the door behind them. Then he ran outside.

Dusk had gathered but flames leaped from a fire by the training barn, and he could see four of Quantrill's men leading out several horses. Then he saw Scott, hog-tied, helpless on the ground.

From every direction, raiders converged with loot—candlesticks, paintings—anything small enough to carry off. Someone had raided Jarret's cabin and shoved the portrait of Lexington into his saddle bag. Another threw one of Alexander's prize calves onto the dirt next to Scott, pressing its head under his knee. The beast bawled as he plunged a knife into its heaving throat. A bright spurt of vermilion arced through the air, splattering Scott's uniform with warm blood.

Quantrill wheeled his mount and pointed his pistol at Alexander. "Harboring this filthy Federal on your farm, you damned traitor. All our bargains are off. Lead the way to Lexington or I'll shoot this scum as he lays."

Alexander, impotent and furious, strode toward the stallion barn. Someone, he saw with satisfaction, had padlocked the door. Two of Quantrill's men bashed at the barn boards with a piece of fence rail. Inside, the horses squealed. The timbers shivered and gave.

Alexander stepped over the broken boards and into the gloom of the barn. Lexington's stall gaped empty.

"Jarret?" he called. No answer. Alexander allowed himself a small smile. But Quantrill's rage made his gladness brief. "Take whatever's here," the guerrilla barked. "Bring the Federal and the old man."

He turned his horse. His raiders followed. One threw the steaming, half-butchered calf carcass across his saddle. They galloped for the gate, taking Scott, Viley, and a dozen thoroughbreds with them.

Through dense trees, half a mile down the road, Jarret watched them hurtle past. He let them get just far enough ahead, and then he asked Lexington to follow.

THEO

"But she threw it out. She gave it away."

"I know."

"You don't have an obligation—"

Theo poured wine and handed Jess a glass. "I know." They sat on the sofa, regarding the freshly cleaned painting propped up on his desk. Jess leaned her head on Theo's shoulder. Clancy turned three circles and then collapsed with a sigh across their feet.

A very young Lexington—not even one year old—gazed from the canvas with a lustrous eye, scanning the landscape of the Meadows. "It's such a lovely painting, now that you can see all of it."

"Yes, and it's probably been years since anyone *has* seen it—properly." He took another sip of wine. "There's an energy to the brushstrokes that's a bit unusual for the style of the era. You feel that the painter must've been having a good day, like he didn't need to labor over this work."

"That's why I don't think you should give it back. She didn't appreciate it."

Theo played idly with a strand of Jess's hair. "She's old, Jess. A widow. And poor, from the looks of it. She didn't know how valuable it was. Fifteen thousand dollars is a lot of money to someone like that."

"Fifteen thousand dollars is a lot of money for a grad student too. You were the one who recognized that it might have value—you're the one who found out that it did. You should be the one who benefits, not her."

He shrugged. "I got a thousand dollars for writing the *Smithsonian* piece. I think that's a pretty good return on something I picked up off the curb. Plus it inspired my thesis topic. And I've been able to put a new work in Scott's catalogue raisonné—that's a big deal, you know, in art history circles. It's the kind of thing that gets people like me up in the morning—adding our little dash of spice to the historical stew." Theo had emailed the art historian who had compiled the catalogue of Scott's known work, to tell her about his find and send her a high-resolution image. A week later, she'd called Theo with an offer for the painting from a buyer in Kentucky.

"It's tremendously exciting when we find a new work," she'd said. "And especially one with such a sound authentication." She said that Scott had become collectible ever since 2010, when she mounted the first one-man show of his work. Since then, his paintings had been selling over estimate. "If you send it to auction you might get even more—a new Lexington portrait might set a record," she said. But Theo would need to pay the commission and hassle with insurance and transport, whereas in a private sale he'd get the full amount. "I'm not advising one way or the other. Let me know what you decide."

Theo had known, as soon as he heard the figure, that he would give the painting back. He ran his fingers through Jess's hair. He liked the way every strand was a slightly different color, like grains of sand on a beach.

"I'm not desperate for that money, Jess. I inherited some from my father. Not a lot, but more than some people have. More than she has."

"But you said she was a bigot."

"Jess." He spoke more sharply. "Whatever *she* might be, it doesn't mean that *I* won't do what I know to be right."

Jess sighed, defeated, and smiled at him. "You're just a better person than me, I guess. When are you going to take it over there?"

"Maybe tomorrow morning? I was hoping you'd stay the night and come with me before you head to work. I think she'll be more relaxed if there's a White woman at her door, rather than just me."

"That's awful."

He felt a flare of anger. "You think I don't know that?"

"I'm sorry."

He took her face between his hands. He'd thought her eyes were green, but he'd come to realize that they were more than that. All the colors of the forest were there—flecks of umber, bronze, and gold. "It is what it is," he said. "But I can't let it change what I am. You do get that, right?"

"Of course I do." *And that's why I'm falling in love with you.* She wanted to say it. But he was gently extricating himself.

"I'm going for a quick run before dinner."

"But it's still raining, and it's getting dark," she whined. "And the moussaka smells so good!"

"It'll be even better in an hour. It's just a light drizzle now, and Clancy's barely been out all day, have you, mate?" The dog looked up, tilting his head in agreement.

"That's true—I've been hogging you."

It had been a relaxing Sunday. They'd met Lior and his wife at an Ethiopian restaurant on U Street the evening before, and then gone club hopping, something neither of them had done since their undergrad days. They slept late and ambled out to Theo's favorite local coffee shop. Then, when it started pouring, they'd run back to his apartment through the pelting rain. While her clothes dried, Theo had given her the Hoyas sweatshirt he usually ran in. It came down past her knees. He spent a few minutes rummaging in his drawer looking for the shirt before he realized she was still wearing it. A rain shell made more sense, anyway. He shrugged it on.

"Can you take the moussaka out in fifteen minutes? It needs to rest, to let the flavors—"

"I know, I know." Jess rolled over on the sofa and picked up a *New Yorker* from a pile on the floor. "And I'll set the table."

Theo laughed. "Don't forget the candelabra." There was no dining table in his tiny apartment. They'd be eating on their laps.

He stepped out into the rain. The fine mist glistened in wide, arcing billows, like a wind-blown curtain. Clancy danced from paw to paw with anticipation. Theo looked down and smiled. He had the dog to thank for his running habit. He'd never been a runner before he brought Clancy home from that New Haven shelter, but the dog's coiled energy had demanded a release, and once he started running, he realized that his athlete's body had been craving it.

They began slowly and picked up speed as they entered the park. He decided they'd take the valley trail that paralleled the creek along the park's eastern edge. Over the traffic on Rock Creek Drive, he could hear the water, replenished by the day's rainfall, tumbling over boulders. Theo felt his lungs fill and empty, the moist air as exhilarating as a cocktail. Before Jess, he'd never given much thought to his own anatomy. He'd always just expected his legs to do the motions that human legs always have done since they evolved to chase down prey and flee from predators. But she'd made him aware of the mechanics of his bones, the connections of each intricate set of tissues, the nerves traveling through vertebrae to fire along the clusters of muscle. He enjoyed thinking about that now as he lengthened his stride and increased his pace.

The leaves were slippery underfoot and exhaled a fresh, woody aroma as he landed on them. His stride settled into a pleasing rhythm. He was aware of his heart rate, effortlessly increasing to push the blood to his muscles. Ahead of him, Clancy paused to shake off the wetness, flinging sparkles. Along the rim of the park, streetlights blinked on, and the night shimmered. Theo felt the edge of runner's high begin to flood his body with well-being. He picked up speed, feeling his heart working harder as he sprinted up a slight rise of ground. The track narrowed as the rise became a hill, slanting along the creek where it cut deep into the rocks, forming a small ravine. He leaned into the incline until he reached the crest. Going downhill, Theo slowed his pace, watching for tree roots and loose stones. As the light faded, it was becoming hard to see. He realized he should head back soon. There was a bridge over the creek about a quarter of a mile ahead. That's where he would turn for home.

The path took a sharp curve right. Clancy dashed ahead out of sight. As Theo came around the turn, he almost stumbled over the dog, who was standing stock still in the middle of the path, staring down at something in the ravine.

"What is it, Clance? Did a deer go by?"

Clancy whined. Theo came up level and looked down toward the water. About fifteen feet down, a figure—a woman—lay prone against the rocks.

"Ma'am? Are you okay?" he called. She didn't answer. "Miss?" he said again. "Can you hear me?" There was a muddy scar down the bank, marking her skid. She'd either slipped taking the turn and hit her head or passed out in midstride and fallen. He fumbled for his phone to call 911. Then he cursed. No signal.

Theo slid down the bank to her side. Her spare frame was clad in vividly colored technical fiber. She wore marathoner's shoes—a serious runner. Tentatively, he reached for her wrist to check for a pulse. Her skin was cool to the touch—she must have been passed out for a while—but the beat, when he found it, was strong. He breathed out, relieved.

He ransacked his memory for the little first aid he knew. He couldn't see any obvious signs of injury. Her spandex leggings were streaked down one side, where she'd skidded down the bank, but he could see no blood. Her fair hair was cut very short and there was no obvious mark of injury on her head. He recalled something about trying to put an unconscious person into the rescue position—left side, knees bent, helps the blood flow. He hesitated, wondering if he should move her. Then he knelt down and bent over her still body. Gently, slowly, he eased her onto her side. As he tried to bend her legs, she gave a catlike wail. Theo reached for his phone, checking again for a signal. Her eyes fluttered open.

"Ma'am, you fell," said Theo. "Are you—"

At that moment a blaze of white light flared from the bridge, illuminating

Theo as he knelt over the woman. Theo looked up, blinded by the sudden brightness.

"Police! Freeze!" bellowed a voice from the bridge.

Theo lifted his cell phone to shade his eyes from the glare.

And then Clancy's thin howl, shearing the night.

ALEXANDER'S JARRET

Road to Midway
Woodford County, Kentucky

1865

Jarret cantered Lexington through the gathering dark, staying at the barely audible edge of the hoofbeats ahead. The horse seemed energized by the high emotion of the evening's events. Jarret had to hold him back from a full gallop that would overtake their quarry.

The sky was cloudy, the rising gibbous moon offering only sporadic illumination. "We're both blind, tonight," Jarret murmured. Quantrill's gang was keeping to the road, which was fortunate. Jarret was not sure he would have been able to guide Lexington had Quantrill led his men into the woods.

He tried to divine their destination. He had come to know most of the nearby families. They were heading west, so he visualized the map of farms that lay in that direction. Was there a secesh sympathizer among them ardent enough to give sanctuary to men such as these? If so, he couldn't think who that would be. Many families in the county supported the rebel cause; some even had sons fighting in the Confederate army farther south. But those men followed the rules of war. Quantrill's gang were murderers. And Willa Viley was widely respected. Jarret could not think of a local family who would countenance an assault on the old man.

Just then, the moon edged from behind a scallop of cloud and illuminated a pale, lumpen bundle on the road ahead. Lexington's nostrils flared. Jarret eased him to a walk as they came up on it. At first, he thought the bushwhackers had jettisoned a bedroll or dropped a sack of some kind. Jarret peered down as the fabric fluttered.

He slid from the horse. "Captain Viley, that you?"

Viley groaned. He was lying facedown in the dust, just as he'd fallen. He tried to turn himself, but failed and flopped back, helpless.

"Captain, it's Jarret here. Can I help you up, sir?"

Viley reached out weakly and Jarret took the arm over his shoulder, easing the old man into a sitting position. His flesh, where Jarret touched it, was on fire. His face registered the agony of every move.

"Jarret?" he rasped. "How did you—boy, you shouldn't have followed, they want you and that horse of yours. You'd best turn back."

"I know they want us. I heard them—that's why I got Lexington out of there. But I need to help Mr. Scott, and rescue the horses. They made away with six or more of Lexington's get, including Asteroid, and those horses are too good for the likes of them."

"I don't see what you think you can do," Viley rasped. "Where's Alexander?"

"Fighting the fires they lit, I guess. To be honest, I didn't wait round to find out."

"You're a foolish boy."

"I ain't a boy. Sir."

Viley drew a painful breath. He looked at Jarret as if seeing him for the first time. Jarret's eyes glinted in the dark, holding the gaze. Viley's face collapsed and he nodded. "No, you are not. You're . . ." He broke into a fit of coughing and doubled up. "I think I've broken some ribs," he gasped. "I fell off the pony—my grandson's pony—had no choice, only horse on our place saddled up when Quantrill's pack of rats swarmed us. I'm a fool, like you, thinking I could give chase. And now look at me." He coughed again, and blood ran darkly down his beard. "They just left me to die where I lay," he wheezed. "Rode right on over me. Not a conscience left in a one of those devils."

"Do you know where they're making for? Can you think of anyone who would take them in?"

"Judge Sayers, my guess," Viley wheezed. "His wife, Finetta, is old friends with those damnable James boys who ride with Quantrill. I heard one of them—Jesse, it was—speaking of her. Their place is on the road to Taylorsville, between Samuel's Depot and Deatsville. You know the place?"

"I think so—big brick house—the white one—is that it?"

"Yes, that's the one."

"But we have to get you situated first."

A violent cough wracked at Viley. Tears of pain rolled down his bloodied cheeks. "It's no good. I can't mount a horse."

"Don't you say so. I think we're close by the Kirklands' Cane Spring farm. We can get you that far, at least, and the Kirklands can send word to your son."

Jarret asked Lexington to kneel. He lifted Viley and placed him in the saddle. "Just grab onto the mane. This horse won't let you fall." He clicked for the horse to stand. Jarret estimated it was less than a mile to the Kirklands, and when it proved to be just half that distance he was relieved, because by then Viley was slipping in and out of consciousness.

The Kirklands came out armed but lowered their guns and rushed to help once they recognized Viley. As Jarret eased the broken old man off the horse, he grasped Jarret's arm with a sudden burst of strength.

"We shouldn't have done what we did. This horse—it should have been yours. Richard and I—I put him up to it—I showed him the way to get around Warfield. It was wrong. I'm sorry we cheated Old Harry. We never ought to have done that."

Jarret let a tide of anger crest and pass before he spoke. "No good be done thinking on that now. Harry Lewis long past minding." He stood by

Lexington as they carried Viley indoors. He took the bread and the flask the Kirkland woman offered, and then he mounted up and rode off toward Taylorsville.

He steered Lexington off the road before they reached the gates to the Sayers home. Traversing the paddock, he picked a careful way closer to the house. He could see lights flickering in one of the downstairs rooms. And in the woods behind, a small campfire. Perhaps Quantrill and the James brothers were with their friends in the main house while the rest of the band camped out.

He resolved to find a safe hiding place for Lexington and to go forward on foot. He followed the fence line down a gentle hill toward the sounds of a brook. He let the horse drink and then tied him up loosely in a small copse of trees. Then he waited for the moon. When a luminous edge emerged from the clouds, he scanned the pasture, picking out his path. In a moment, it was dark again. That was when he sprinted for the trees.

He melted from tree to tree until he had a vantage point on the campfire. From a distance, he watched the moving figures. He could count only four men. So they'd followed their usual tactics and split into small units to confound pursuit. It would be sheer luck if this was the group that had Scott.

He would need to be patient. He could tell from the slurred voices that the whisky jar was out. As the intermittent moon climbed higher, the drunken utterances grew louder.

An hour passed. Jarret felt his muscles cramping as he tried to remain still. As the air cooled, he felt a heavy dew misting his skin and clothing. Talk ebbed and became sporadic. Jarret risked creeping closer.

He was behind the men now—only two still awake by the dying fire. Another snored. He strained for snatches of their conversation. The men were slurring; it was hard to make out words. It seemed like some long-winded reminiscence of a raid on a dry goods store. Then: "Don't know why we didn't kill *this* Federal right where he stood, like we did them damned Dutchmen shopkeepers."

"Quantrill say he want to trade him for the five got they selves captured over in Mercer County—Jim, Andy, and them others. Federals took 'em up the road to Louisville, fixin' to hang 'em in a big show."

"Well, it don't sit right with me, having to haul his sorry ass."

"Me neither." He yawned, stretched, then struggled up from his squatting position. He staggered away from the fire. Jarret heard the thud of a boot landing in flesh, then a muffled groan.

"You shut the hell up."

Another kick, another groan.

A hissing sound. Jarret realized the secesh was pissing on Scott. The other one laughed at that, drunken guffaws. He struggled to get up, fiddling with his own fly. The two sleeping men did not stir.

The secesh couldn't seem to untie his pants. He was looking down, cursing, as he began to piss himself. Jarret only had to lean forward, grab a hank of his long hair, and pull his head back. He sank his knife into the side of his neck and drew it in a wide arc. The man pitched forward, gurgling. Jarret eased him back down to the ground.

The man standing over Scott's prone form turned. "Jimbo, ain't you—"

But Jarret was behind him, and the question was never asked.

In the flicker of the dying fire, Jarret saw Scott's pale eyes, wide and incredulous as he sawed at the rope binding his ankles. There wasn't time to mess around with the ties on his wrist. Scott struggled to stand as the blood rushed back to his feet. He staggered and Jarret supported him as they faded into the trees.

Only when they were clear of the copse did Jarret pause to cut the ropes around Scott's wrist and pull the filthy gag from his mouth.

"Where are the horses?" Jarret hissed.

"In the barn, but we can't risk . . ."

"We can. We will."

The lights were out in the big house now. They circled the house in case a picket had been posted, but Quantrill must have felt secure that no one knew of this safe harbor. When Jarret was sure there was no guard, he came up to the barn. Carefully, he eased back the door bar.

Inside, a young Black groom startled awake. He scrambled to his feet. Jarret grabbed the boy by the shirt and put a finger to his lips. "You never saw us. We knocked you out cold. Got it?"

The boy nodded. "I ain't gonna hurt you. But I got to make it look like I did, understand?" Jarret pulled out his bloody knife. The boy flinched, his eyes wide. Jarret ran his hand down the blade and smeared the blood on the groom's forehead. Then he pushed past him and went stall by stall. Five of Alexander's stolen horses were there, including Asteroid.

Jarret threw a bridle on Asteroid and the thoroughbred mare, Nanny Butler. Working quickly, he roped the other horses together, tail to neck with a bowline, and led them out of the barn. He'd never ponied so many thoroughbreds before and he prayed they'd have the horse sense to stay calm about it.

"Quick," he said, signaling Scott to mount up on Asteroid. "Ride and find your unit. On that horse, no one can catch you. Lead them back here, clean up this mess, and find out where the rest of our horses are." As he spoke, he jumped on Nanny Butler and drew the other horses up behind.

"Where are you going?"

"To get Lexington."

"And then what?"

Jarret didn't turn.

"North," he said, and led the horses out into the dark.

JESS

The moussaka had been cooling on the counter for more than half an hour. Jess checked her watch. He'd said it would be a short run. "Weird idea of 'short,'" she muttered to herself, slicing a lime. Even though she'd been drinking wine, her slightly irritated state demanded something stronger, so she made herself a gin and tonic and sipped it as she perused the shelves of art books.

One title intrigued her: *You Are an Acceptable Level of Threat.* She reached an index finger into its spine and pulled it down. Banksy. She plopped on the sofa and leafed through it. She checked her watch again. This was borderline rude. Not like him. She put the book back and pulled out a fatter tome about the Museum of Old and New Art in Tasmania. Promising. He seemed pretty enthusiastic about Australia, which was a change from most Americans, whose interest didn't extend much beyond the charismatic fauna. She'd been saving up vacation time so she could take three weeks with her parents in Tasmania the following winter. Maybe she could convince Theo to come with her, if they were still an item by then. Jess's mind wandered pleasantly around an itinerary. Tassie first, then Uluru to see an entirely different Australia—he'd be interested in the Papunya Tula artists—then fly back after a few days in Sydney. If he loved it, maybe they could even move there . . .

She reeled the fantasy back in. She was getting way ahead of herself.

She wandered over to his desk and glanced at some pages of his thesis he'd printed out for editing. He was working on a chapter on Harry Lewis, whom he had identified as the Black trainer depicted by Troye in the painting titled *Richard Singleton with Viley's Harry, Charles and Lew*. She picked up a page.

Evidence exists that Lewis's interest in the racehorse Lexington may have been plundered from him against his will. Willa Viley's own copy of the rules governing the Kentucky Association racetrack bears a suggestive annotation—someone—Viley?—has inked a cross next to the following rule: "No negro or mulatto, to make nomination in any stake, to be run over this course." *Since Viley succeeded in acquiring a valuable interest in Lexington, it is plausible that he used this rule as leverage in order to compel a sale of the horse.*

Jess replaced the page on the desk. She recalled how excited Theo had been to discover that annotated document among Viley's archived papers. It was one of the things they had in common, this enthusiasm for chasing down small shards of knowledge.

The rain picked up again and began to lash against the window. She checked the moussaka. The bechamel topping was congealing, getting cold. Surely, in this kind of rain, Theo would be home any minute—dripping, with a sodden kelpie at his heels.

She would call his cell phone. Why hadn't she thought of that earlier? She hit the numbers on the keypad. Took a breath. She didn't want to sound as irritated as she felt.

The voice that answered wasn't Theo's. Instead of the clipped, Oxfordian "Hello, Jess," it was a flat Baltimore accent.

"Who is this?"

"It's Jess. Who's *this*? Where's Theo?"

"Theo." The voice repeated the name without inflection. "Theo who?"

"Theo Northam. What are you doing with his phone?"

"Is this Mrs. Northam?"

"There is no Mrs. Northam. Who *is* this? What's going on?"

"Ma'am, what is your relationship to Mr. Northam?" There was something in the way he said "Ma'am" that made Jess's head feel light.

"I'm his"—she paused—"girlfriend. What's happened? Has he had an accident?"

Her voice was suddenly feeble. Her legs began to tremble. She sank onto the sofa. Whatever was coming next, she didn't want to hear it. The words came out of the phone: "Interrupted assault. Police-involved shooting. Homicide detective." Jess heard them, but they made no sense to her.

"But he just went out for a run. With his dog."

"Yes. Well. As I said, it's under investigation. Can you tell me the name of his next of kin?"

"Next of kin? You mean his mother?"

"Mother. Or father."

"His father died in Afghanistan. His mother lives in Lagos."

"Lagos?"

"In Nigeria."

"There's no one else—brother, sister?"

"No. He's an only child."

"Then we may need you to identify the body."

"Body?"

"Yes."

Jess felt a big lump of something land on her chest. She couldn't get any air. "What happened?" she asked again.

The detective cleared his throat. It sounded like he was reading. "At seven twenty p.m., an officer in Rock Creek Park interrupted an assault and robbery in progress. The victim was a female Caucasian. When the officer asked the suspected assailant to freeze, the suspect appeared to raise a weapon, at which time the officer responded with lethal fire."

"But what's that got to do with Theo? Did he witness the assault, or something?"

"Ma'am, he was the assailant."

Jess gave a strangled laugh. "Assailant? Theo? He's an art historian. He's a PhD candidate at Georgetown."

There was a long silence.

"Ma'am. Are you presently in DC?"

"Yes, I'm at his place. We were about to have dinner . . ."

"If you'll give me the address. I'll need to take a statement."

Jess, numb with shock, opened the door to the detective a few minutes later. He was accompanied by a woman officer. Both of them were extremely wet. The detective was a thin man, haggard, with restless brown eyes that seemed to be constantly scanning. As his gaze radared over Theo's neat apartment, the vintage-modern furnishings and book-lined walls, his face tensed. The detective and the police officer exchanged glances.

Step by step, he took Jess through the events of the day until the point when Theo left for the run. She heard herself answering his questions, but her mind was in the park, agonizing over what on earth could have happened there.

"The officer at the scene said the suspect was wearing a black hoodie. Is there any reason he would wear black, to run, at night?"

"It was a rain jacket, not a hoodie. He usually runs in this," she said, plucking at the white sweatshirt with its blue Hoyas lettering.

"You said earlier—his parents—Nigeria? Afghanistan? So he's an immigrant? Muslim, maybe?"

Jess felt anger flare through the shock.

"He's American. His father worked for the State Department and was killed in the line of duty in Afghanistan. Star on the CIA wall, for all I know."

She saw the grim look pass between the detective and the officer again. She stood up, shaking.

"We're done here." She was trembling from head to foot. She could barely walk the few steps to the door. "Get out. I don't want you in his home."

The female officer looked to the detective. He nodded slightly and rose. He scribbled something on his notepad, tore out the page, and placed it on the coffee table. "That's the address of the DC Medical Examiner. Next of kin IDs are from ten a.m. to four thirty p.m. I'd be grateful if you could be there tomorrow morning."

Jess closed the door behind them without replying. She leaned her back against it, fighting down a heaving sob. Then she turned, flung open the door, and ran out into the rain, scanning the street for the officers. They were halfway down the block, almost to their car.

"Wait!" she yelled. "Where's Clancy? What happened to his dog?"

ALEXANDER'S JARRET

Road from Midway, Woodford County, Kentucky

1865

North, he had said. But to get there, he'd need to ride west. And to do that, he'd need forged papers. Jarret shook his head, trying to rid himself of the fatigue and fear. He needed to think, which was difficult, picking a way through the dark with so many horses. His mind was filled with the soft, wet give of the knife, the warmth of the flesh under his fist, the graze of the stubble. Men killed one another in war; he knew that. But knowing was one thing. Doing was another thing entirely.

Lexington whinnied as he smelled the other horses approaching. Jarret gave a low whistle so that the horse would recognize him. He let Lexington scent each horse in turn, so he would know they were familiar members of his own herd. He then retied the string to put Lexington in the lead. Before he remounted, he went to the stream and washed the blood from his hands and forearms. He held up his arms in a sliver of intermittent moonlight, but he could not tell if he'd removed all the traces.

He needed paper. He needed a pen. He decided his best chance was to double back to the farm where he had left old Viley. They would recognize him there.

The brothers came out armed, as they had the first time. They were edgy. "We were expecting young Viley, coming for his pa, but then when we heard all them horses we thought it was Quantrill, come back this way to burn us out. They Mr. Alexander's horses?"

"Yessir."

"You rescue them? Well. That's something. You taking them back there?"

"Nossir. Not risking that. Not while Quantrill's on the loose. I plan to bring them to Mr. Alexander's farm across the river. He meant to bring his best horses there if things here got too hot."

The boys murmured together and then nodded. "Our sister will give you some supplies."

In the kitchen, the girl put out a jug of water and Jarret drank thirstily. She made him a sack with a loaf and some cheese. As she set it down on the scrubbed deal table, she took a step back, startled.

"That's not Captain Viley's blood on your shirt, is it?"

"No, miss."

"Did you . . ."

"I had to kill two of Quantrill's men to free Mr. Scott, the Union soldier they had hostage."

The girl twisted her cotton pinafore in her fist. Then she pulled the shawl from around her shoulders and handed it to Jarret. "Cover yourself with this and give me that shirt while I wash that blood off it."

"I'm obliged, miss. How's the old man doing?"

"Poorly. He's done burning up, his fever so hot. I don't think he'll last the night."

"You've sent for his son?"

"One of my brothers went to fetch him. But unless he makes haste—" She turned away as Jarret took off his shirt. She stretched out a hand behind her back to take it from him.

"Miss—could you give me some paper—a pen?"

"Might be. But what for?"

"I need to send word to Mr. Alexander."

"You know your letters then?"

"Yessum."

Jarret did write a note to Alexander, listing the horses he'd recovered and explaining his intentions. But then he wrote two more notes, forging Alexander's signature on each. One set asserted that the Woodburn horses were destined for Grant's army; the other said they were a secret gift to John Hunt Morgan. If he met a Union army unit or a rebel militia, the papers might just save the horses from being commandeered.

Luck was with him: traveling by night, and on backroads, he made it to the river crossing unchallenged. To the bargeman who would ferry them across to Illinois, he told the simple truth: that he was bringing his master's most valuable horses out of reach of the war, to safety on his property in Sangamon County.

Jarret knew the way. He had traveled there in the company of Napoleon Belland not long after Alexander bought the place. He had been charged with choosing a good location for a stable on the farm and instructing the Belland boy in fitting it up to receive horses. But none had been sent, month following month. Alexander's faith in his neutral status had been unshakable. Jarret had come to resent the wasted effort. But he didn't feel that way as he trotted the string of horses through the dark.

Dawn was just breaking over the ridge as they neared the farm. Belland burst out of the farmhouse door, rubbing the sleep from his eyes.

"Finally brought you some work to do," Jarret said, and together they led a small fortune in horseflesh through the gates into the waiting pastures.

A few days later, they met the train carrying a dozen more horses that Alexander had loaded in secret, by night. By the end of the war, most of his horses had been transferred to Illinois, and Jarret had crossed the border into Canada, not as a runaway seeking freedom, but as R. A. Alexander's trusted agent, charged with buying and selling thoroughbreds on his behalf.

JESS

J ess spent the night sleepless in Theo's bed, burying her face in his scent. Without his cell phone, she had no way to contact anyone—not his mother in Nigeria, not any of the friends he'd told her about. She waited for the first gray daylight, then rose wearily and crossed the city to her apartment. In the shower, she turned her face up into the cascading water and wept.

Just before ten a.m., she walked the short distance from her apartment to a building she'd passed a hundred times—a vast, glass-fronted edifice on E Street. She'd barely registered it; just another shiny block in the sprawling DC bureaucracy. She hadn't realized those shimmering glass walls enclosed a palace of sadness.

She handed her ID to the security guard, passed through a metal detector, and was directed into a windowless room. A soft-spoken woman with Fulani braids and gel fingernails decorated with tiny stars indicated that she should sit. The sofa was very new, contemporary, like it belonged in the waiting room of a high-end medical practice.

"I'm going to give you this clipboard. On it, there is a photograph, facedown, of the deceased. When you are ready, please turn it over and, if you can, give an identification."

"Photograph? You mean I don't get to see him?"

The woman shook her head and her beaded braids rattled. "In DC we don't let next of kin inside the morgue. People get emotional. Too many incidents."

Jess had steeled herself for metal drawers, toe tags, a body bag unzipped by a sympathetic coroner. She stared at the clipboard with its little passport-size square. Having screwed her courage to the sticking point to view his body, this seemed inhuman, inadequate.

"When you're ready," the woman repeated softly.

She would never be ready. She willed her thumb to release the clip. She slid the picture down and turned it over. She stopped breathing. There was Theo, his beautiful face. He looked exhausted, as if he'd fallen asleep after some kind of long ordeal. She wanted to caress that face. She touched her finger to the photograph. After a long moment, she handed it back to the starry fingernails. "Yes," she said. "That's him."

After filling in the required paperwork, she walked unsteadily out into the bright morning. The rain had stopped and now the streets were exhaling the musky scent of wet leaves and drying concrete. She hailed a cab and gave the address of the animal shelter.

"Come in, we're expecting you," the attendant said, over a chorus of yaps and barks.

"Expecting me?"

"Yeah. The police called. Said you'd be coming by around this time to pick up the dog."

That, at least, was kind.

"He's been moping. He'll be glad to see a familiar face. Just wait here and I'll bring him out."

The attendant emerged a minute later with Clancy, his body hunched, his tail clenched between his legs.

When she saw him, Jess crouched low. "G'day, little mate," she said softly. His head shot up. She held out her arms and he rocketed into them, whining.

"I know," she said. "I know." She buried her face in his fur. It was matted and hard. She ran a hand through his coat. A dust of rust-colored powder speckled her fingers.

"I'm really sorry, we didn't get a chance to give him a bath. We only have one person here overnight. I was going to do it this morning, but . . ."

"It's blood," Jess whispered.

"Yes. I'm so sorry. The officer who brought him in said he was lying on the body—wouldn't let anyone near it."

"Oh, Clancy," Jess said.

She crumpled on the disinfectant-scented floor, cradling the dog in her arms. The two of them stayed there a long time, whining and weeping. The attendant brought a box of tissues, then a bowl of water, and finally a cup of tea. She placed them on the floor.

Jess reached blindly for the tissues, then the tea. Jess's mother had always sworn by the curative properties of a "cuppa." Not that her mum would have recognized the pale sepia beverage in the paper cup as tea.

Jess thanked the attendant for her kindness, signed the paperwork, and led Clancy outside. His tail gave a single wag as they left the building. Jess leaned down and gave him a reassuring pat. "Oh, mate. You didn't think I'd leave you there, did you? I forgot he adopted you from a shelter. Must've been horrible being back there. We'll go to your place and get your stuff, then you can come home with me. We can be sad together."

It was an hour walk from the shelter to Theo's, but Jess was in no hurry to arrive there. She thought a long walk would do them both some good, and she tried to quiet her mind and focus on the feel of the sun on her skin. When they turned the corner to his street, Clancy strained at the leash.

"He's not going to be there. I'm so sorry, mate."

But somebody was. A young Black woman stood at the door to the graduate apartments, bending over to scan the names on the buzzers. Jess saw her press the button next to Theo's name.

"No use. He's not there."

"Oh, I know. I just thought there might be someone . . . Do you live here? Did you know him?"

Jess said nothing.

"Sorry, I'm Justine Treadwell from *The Washington Post*. I'm writing about the shooting."

"I know your work."

Until she met Theo, Jess had only scanned Treadwell's articles. The neighborhoods and subjects—racial profiling, excessive use of police force—had seemed like things that didn't have much to do with her. Of late, though, she'd read her work more carefully. It was always meticulously reported, full of telling details that brought the people she wrote about into clear focus.

"This must be the dog?"

"He's Theo's dog, yes."

"My colleague, the beat reporter at the scene, said the dog wouldn't leave him. They had to get an Animal Control guy with one of those noose-on-a-stick things to haul him off."

Jess's face crumpled.

"I'm sorry, I shouldn't have—"

"No," she said, rummaging in her bag for a tissue and wiping her nose. "I want to know. I need to understand how this could've happened. I am—I was—" What, exactly? Girlfriend, she'd told the police. But there had been no declarations between them. Their short, intense affair hardly gave her the right to claim anything.

"I was his friend. Would you like to come in?"

"Thanks, yes. I would. I've got this morning's police report, if you want to see it. It's not much, not yet."

Inside, Jess poured Justine a glass of water and sat down to read the terse, single-page report:

MPD Officer Involved Shooting, Rock Creek Park, September 6, 2019

At approximately 7:20 p.m., a uniformed patrol officer of the Fourth District interrupted an apparent assault on a Caucasian female jogger by a Black male. Officer heard the female victim scream, at which time the officer identified himself and called upon the suspect to freeze. The suspect raised an object the officer believed was a firearm at which point the officer discharged his firearm one time, striking the suspect. DC Fire and Emergency Medical Services responded to the scene. The suspect was pronounced dead, the victim was transported to an area hospital for treatment of minor injuries.

The decedent has been identified as 26-year-old Theodore Naade Northam, a graduate student enrolled at Georgetown University.

The officer involved has been placed on administrative leave, pursuant to MPD policy. This case remains under investigation. Anyone with information is asked to contact MPD at (202) 727-9099.

Jess threw the report down on the coffee table. "It's preposterous. There's no way Theo was assaulting anyone. And I'm positive he didn't own a gun."

"Yeah, the investigating officer isn't saying much, but he did admit that no weapon was found at the scene. It's just lucky your man was a Georgetown intellectual and not some kid from Shaw or Deanwood, because they may well have planted one if he was."

"What about the woman? Do you know who she is? Have you interviewed her?"

"Yes, but not much help, I'm afraid. She's got a fractured fibula and contusions consistent with a fall. Has a concussion. Says she can't remember a thing. I'm guessing your friend probably saw her fall or came along just after and tried to help her."

"Yes," said Jess. "That's exactly what he would've done. But what happens now?"

"It'll get investigated, the officer'll be exonerated, and it'll be another statistic in this country's long history of Black killings."

"How can he be exonerated? He shot an unarmed man."

Justine Treadwell shrugged. "The way it usually goes, the cop'll say he *thought* he saw a gun and feared for his life. He's a rookie, apparently—hasn't been on the force a year—so they might use that. But what they have going for them is the woman's concussion. Unless she remembers what happened, no one can prove your man was helping her. They'll continue to claim it *was* an assault."

"But that's bullshit."

"I know. But that's the playbook. Maybe if his father was still alive—from what I've been able to learn, he was a rising star at State. He was acting DCM in Afghanistan when he died and everyone assumed his next post would be an ambassadorship."

"But what about his mother? Can't she . . . ?"

"Nigeria got put on the list of our president's 'shithole countries,' remember? She can't even get a visa. At least, not anytime soon. And she's pretty emotional about it all, as you'd expect. I managed to reach her in Lagos."

"But she's foreign service, isn't she? Surely there's some string she can pull?"

"She *was* foreign service. Different elites in power now and the ex-general she married isn't a favorite with the new regime, apparently."

"How did you find all this out so quickly?"

"Foreign desk. Our West Africa correspondent keeps close tabs on Nigeria—who's up, who's down. The whole Boko Haram thing, trouble in the oil fields . . ."

Jess got up and walked to the apartment's tiny kitchenette. "Can I give you something else? Tea? Coffee? I need something. Maybe gin." No, not gin. Not ever. The minute she thought of it, she felt nauseated. The scent of it would always remind her of that phone call.

"Coffee would be excellent, thanks. I've still got a lot of ground to cover on this story. Even though it probably won't make any difference in the end, at least I can write a profile of Theo and make it just that bit harder for them to brush this under the rug. Will you help me?"

Jess tore off a piece of paper towel, wiped her eyes, and blew her nose. "Of course I will. Everything I know." And then the bleak thought: everything she knew about Theo was, now, all she would ever know.

She had thought they had all the time in the world.

JARRET LEWIS

Park Row, New York, New York
1875

J arret drew the watch from his vest pocket and checked the time. He was early for his noon appointment.

Across the street, sunlight flared off the bright bronze of a newly installed statue. Jarret wondered which grim-faced, potbellied grandee was being honored, so he ambled over to read the inscription. *BENJAMIN FRANKLIN. Printer, Patriot, Philosopher, Statesman.* Jarret thought it an odd order in which to list the man's accomplishments. What would the old man think of this depiction of himself? Robert Alexander had owned a far more flattering portrait of Franklin, an oil painting that hung above the desk in the parlor. Alexander's father had served as the great man's private secretary in Paris.

Printer. Well, the statue did face the building that housed *The New York Times*. He imagined that Franklin would enjoy being in earshot of the presses. As the noon bells began to chime from a nearby church, Jarret turned back to the barrel-vaulted building across the street. Inside the foyer, he could smell the mist of ink in the air.

"Jarret Lewis to see Colonel Sanders Deweese Bruce. The colonel is expecting me."

"Is he now?"

The doorman scanned Jarret. Polished boots, tailored jacket, buff kid gloves, beaver hat, a silken necktie symmetrical as moth wings.

"*Turf, Field and Farm* office is on the third floor," he muttered.

Jarret took the stairs, passing rows of compositors deftly setting blocks of metal type and reporters hunched over desks, scrawling dispatches for the next day's *Times*. The *Turf*'s office was tucked inconspicuously on a floor rented out to several publications.

Colonel Bruce rose from behind a large oak desk. "Jarret Lewis? I have looked forward to this meeting. My condolences, my very great condolences. I hope you feel we did justice, in our obituary?"

Jarret removed his hat and inclined his head. "It was a very fitting tribute." Jarret had read the obituary through a glaze of tears. He had committed the words to memory. *He was as far superior to all horses that have gone before him as the vertical blaze of a tropical sun is superior to the faint and scarcely distinguishable glimmer of the most distant star.* "I did not know the writer—Mr. Simpson, was it?—but he certainly knew how to describe Lexington's quality." He took the seat Bruce pulled out for him and drew off his gloves.

"Such a horse," said Bruce. "Shall we see his like again? Not in my lifetime, that's a certainty. Not only the fastest, but also the greatest sire in history. Remarkable, especially when you think of all his get that never raced, on account of the war. Let me see, what did Tom Scott write for us—" He fumbled with some papers on his desk. "I retrieved this, when I learned that you would visit." He scanned the dense page of newsprint. "'*Lexington transmitted much of his own pliancy of limbs to many of his sons and daughters . . . while some of them, at least, like Norfolk, Asteroid, Kentucky, Lightning*'—my goodness, I'd forgotten what a very long list he gave here, it does go on—" He ran his finger along the type. "Here we are, he finally gets on with making his point: '*have shown themselves nearly his equals in racing powers, will any of them approach his fame as a sire when bred to native Kentucky mares?*' A good question, but personally, I doubt it. It's implausible that one horse could produce so many champions. What was it—sixteen years he led the list?"

"Yes," said Jarret quietly. "Sixteen years as the top stud sire. Even topped the list again this past year."

"Extraordinary. And I understand Alexander was charging five hundred dollars to have him cover a mare? Unheard of!"

Jarret fingered the stitching in the glove that rested in his lap and said nothing. Bruce coughed awkwardly and restrained his ebullience. "They say you were with the horse from the day he was foaled till his dying day, is that so?"

Jarret nodded. "At the end of the war, and in the years since, I have been obliged, by my affairs, to be in Canada for some months each year. But I was with him in the end, yes, just as I was in the beginning."

"When I was informed you planned to visit us, I began to entertain a hope that you might favor us with an account of the great hero in his last days. The appetite for stories about him is unsated. Our readers, you know—they cannot learn enough of him."

Jarret replied quietly. A month later and still it was difficult for him to speak of that day. "I had a feeling that it might be his last summer, so I returned to Woodburn from Canada quite early in the spring. I had my usual business in the state, in any case, but I was able to spend much of my time with Lexington. He was quite well, till the very end—very few of the usual frailties of a twenty-five-year-old horse. We would still ride out every morning. Mostly at the walk, these last years. But he seemed to want the different smells of the farm, the sensation of the changing footings. Once, when I had concluded he was past the need or capacity for such exercise, he took his own bridle off the hook and brought it to me." Bruce, delighted by this anecdote, scribbled rapidly. He looked up, pen poised.

"May I ask what carried him off, in the end?"

"In the end? He just wore out. Nothing was ever gravely wrong with him. He never broke down, and his legs were clean as a colt's up to his last day." Though the horse had a fine appetite, Jarret had spent many patient hours hand-feeding grain, watching the stable hands sweep up the quidded hay the aging horse could no longer chew. "It was on the first day of July that he refused his feed and began to have trouble breathing. He was alert to the end. We buried him on the hill overlooking the green pastures where his mares graze."

"Most appropriate." Bruce flipped a page of his notepad. As the pen scratched across the page, Jarret recalled the waning heat of the July evening, the lushness of the grass, the horse's head heavy in his lap in the shade of the big beech tree. Watching the sightless eyes close. The strange sense of something passing through him as the stallion exhaled his last breath. Such a still, peaceful ending after so much speed, so much danger.

Lost in his reverie, Jarret hardly noticed that Colonel Bruce had stopped scribbling and was gazing at him expectantly.

"Of course, if you'd rather not say—"

"I'm sorry. What was the question?"

"About your future plans, now that the horse—"

"Oh. My plans. I have determined that this will be my last journey to this country. Canada is my home now and my business is centered there."

"Really? You do not intend to return? Surely there are still many oppor—"

Jarret interrupted. "Colonel Bruce, you must be aware of the rising difficulty for men like me in the thoroughbred world. You must know that for some who supported the Southern cause, the war is not over. They deplore their reduced circumstances and do not care to see someone like me finding success. It leads to unpleasantness that I would rather . . . avoid. Even the greatest jockeys, the men everyone delighted to cheer for, cannot now get a decent mount, South or North. And if they do chance to ride, it has become perilous. The White jockeys collaborate against them to provoke falls. A great trainer such as Charles Stewart is relegated to house servant, caring for carriage horses." He felt the anger rising in him. "You do no favor to the turf by not addressing these matters in your journal, Colonel. This sport that once gathered all classes and, yes, colors, will not thrive long if it continues to spit on the talent that built it."

Bruce stared at his hands. Jarret regarded him coldly. He would say his piece. The man needed to hear it.

"You express surprise that I see my future in Canada. Let me tell you: I saw it the day I first crossed the border. I could vote there, you see, when I was still counted three fifths of a man here. It's been some few years I have come back to Kentucky only for the horse. So, now there is no further need." Jarret shrugged. "My wife and child are glad of it."

He thought of Lucinda, radiant in the early morning light, standing on their farmhouse porch as she had waved goodbye, the baby on her hip. Lucinda, born and raised in Canada, daughter of a runaway, as fearless and resourceful as her mother. When he was introduced to her for the first time, he felt as if his entire life had led him to that moment. She had met his passion with an equal ardor and now they had their son, Lucien Lewis. In just two days' time, his beautiful wife and his baby boy would be waiting on the porch to welcome him home. That image cooled his anger.

"I think you know, Colonel Bruce, that I did not come here to be interviewed."

"Quite. Your letter. You saw the notice."

"I saw the notice." Jarret drew a folded sheet of newsprint from his vest pocket and read aloud. "'*One of the best portraits of Lexington was painted by Scott, representing him led by black Jarret, his groom . . . Our friends can examine the painting by visiting us in our sanctum.*' And so, Colonel, though I do not presume to be counted a friend, I am still, I suppose, 'black Jarret,' if no longer a groom, and I have come to your sanctum. May we examine the painting now?"

"Of course, yes. Follow me." They crossed the small newsroom to a wood-paneled library. Over the mantel, the painting of Lexington gleamed. He felt love for the horse rise in his chest. He gazed at the unlined face of his younger self, innocent of the terror that was coming so soon.

So much had happened to the young man in that painting. He still sometimes woke in a sweat, recalling the desperate night ride on the blind horse, the stink of whisky and urine, the slide of the knife. He dropped his head, drew out a pocket square, dabbed his eyes, and struggled for composure. Colonel Bruce, standing a little behind him, extended a hand. It hovered a few inches from Jarret's shoulders before he withdrew it.

Jarret refolded his pocket square.

"What do you hear of Mr. Scott? We corresponded for a time, but I have not recently had a line from his hand."

"I suppose you heard he married at last?"

"A widow woman. Yes, I did hear that. In fact, my last note to him was a word of congratulation."

"That may have been a bit previous. They shared just three months of marital bliss before she returned to her people on Long Island and he resumed his peregrinations in horse country." Bruce chuckled. "He did not choose the pen name 'Prog' for nothing: 'one who wanders and forages.' Well, with the death of Mr. Troye so suddenly last year, one hopes he will 'forage' somewhat more successfully. I think it safe to say he has succeeded Troye as the most popular painter of thoroughbreds in this country."

"I should be glad to contribute to the fruits of his foraging. I have previously had two of Scott's portraits of Lexington in my possession, but I have neither of them now." Jarret thought bitterly of the oil of Lexington as a colt that Scott had painted for him at the Meadows. It had never been recovered from Quantrill's raiders. And then the later portrait, when Lexington first came to Woodburn, the one he had given to May. He wondered if she had needed to sell it, or if her life with Hawthorne had prospered enough for her to keep it. He hoped so. He hoped she looked at it from time to time and thought of him kindly, as he thought of her. Now that he knew what it was to be truly loved, he had no regrets there. Hawthorne's return had freed him to find his way to Lucinda, and for that he was thankful every day.

Now he would again own a painting of Lexington. "I believe you are selling this painting on Tom Scott's behalf?" This one, the best one, would more than compensate the loss of the earlier pictures.

"Well," said Bruce, "Tom's never been entirely clear about that. He sent this painting to us during the war, you know, via a friend of his, a Frenchified colored boy from New Orleans. Fellow was a fine painter himself, so Tom wrote, though I never did have a chance to see his work. Died suddenly—cholera, I think it was? Tom was quite upset, I recall. In any case, Tom was not avid to sell this painting, as was the case with other pieces he sent us. He saw it rather as an argument for his skills and left it in our care to show to those from whom it might inspire commissions. As it has, many times, this past decade. He said to me, 'Sandy, you have my permission to sell it should someone offer a fool's price.'"

Jarret drew a paper from his vest pocket and handed it to Bruce.

"Would that be the sort of sum you think he had in mind?"

Bruce unfolded the paper. His eyes widened. "Well, um, yes, I should say . . ." he blustered. "I thought—your letter—I believed you wished just to view it, for sentimental reasons. You aren't—are you?—proposing to pay this amount?"

"If you look at the note, you will see it is a check drawn on the Imperial Bank of Canada and bearing my signature. So, yes, that is exactly what I am proposing."

"But that's quite a sum."

"And this is quite a painting. As you said, Scott's best work. And even were it not, I have certain reasons, personal reasons, that make it of greater value to me than, perhaps, any other man. Sentimental, you might say."

"Well, then, I am sure, for this sum, Tom would—and your long personal connection, of course . . ."

"Very good. Might I trouble you to have someone wrap it?" Jarret pulled out his watch. "I have a very long train journey ahead of me and I should be very glad to be as far as Albany by nightfall."

"So the painting will go to Canada?"

"To Canada, yes. To my home."

JESS

J ess gave Clancy one last long scratch between his pointy ears, tucked the Hoyas sweatshirt around him, and then closed the door of the crate.

"I hate to do this to you, matey. But it'll be worth it once we get there, I promise."

She took the backing off the government veterinary seal and taped it over the latch as she'd been instructed. It wouldn't be opened until an Australian Biosecurity Officer met the plane, some fifteen hours later. At that point, they'd remove the sweatshirt and burn it. She wasn't entirely sorry. Every time she saw that sweatshirt, it caused her to relive the worst night of her life. She was willing to let it do its final job, surrounding Clancy with a beloved, familiar scent, and then she'd never need to look at it again.

She checked the water dispenser one last time and then reached into her bag for the bulging file of vaccination records, microchip numbers, and import permits. As she passed it to the freight agent, her hand shook. The agent smiled at her kindly.

"Dogs do fine on these flights, really. He'll probably sleep better through the trip than you will, won't ya, fella? What's ya name?"

"It's Clancy," Jess sniffed.

"Clancy," the agent repeated, writing it down in thick black Sharpie on a card that he slid into a sleeve and affixed to the top of the crate: *Talk to me. My name is Clancy.*

"That's for the guys on the ramp. We'll take good care of him, don't worry."

"You're sure he'll be okay?"

"Absolutely sure." Jess let Clancy lick her fingers through the grate and then reluctantly turned away. She felt absolutely miserable as she walked out into the gathering dusk to wait for the shuttle to the passenger terminal.

Two days after Theo's shooting, there had been a demonstration at Georgetown University. Jess had gone to it. Anger and grief simmered in the young crowd. Black activists spoke about police violence and the necessity to fight the rising tide of White House–sanctioned white supremacy. A student from one of Theo's classes broke down as she offered personal reflections on losing a valued teacher. Then his thesis supervisor took the mic. Jess knew the two of them hadn't seen eye to eye. But the professor addressed the crowd with precision and passion, placing Theo in the pantheon of Black intellectuals whose contribution had been stifled and extinguished by racism. At the end, a student read a somber litany: the names of unarmed Black people killed by police. There were names Jess knew well: Eric, Michael, Philando. And then, so many she didn't—Aiyana, Rekia, Ezell, Akai. Each name landing like a blow. Jonathan, Dontre, Laquan, Jerame. Finally, at the end of the list, Theodore Naade Northam. A moment of silence before the crowd began roaring the chant: "We gon' be all right."

Jess left the campus carried on the hopefulness of those young voices, convinced that this time, the police would have to hold Theo's killer accountable.

When the *Post* published Justine Treadwell's profile of Theo—the accomplished Black intellectual, son of a brave diplomat—she was even more certain. But then she made the mistake of reading the comments on social media. She wondered how Justine lived with it: the racist bile directed as much at her as at Theo. She avoided Fox News and right-wing radio, but snatches reached her: *No evidence he wasn't about to rape that poor woman. Only bad guys wear black in parks at night. Super-predator. Young cop just doing his job.*

By the time the police investigation wrapped up, she had steeled herself. The investigators concluded that the officer had reason to believe an assault was in progress and that the assailant was armed. He was exonerated and reinstated. There was a vague recommendation about additional training for police in their first year of service—a pathetic sop that would probably never be acted upon.

Jess checked activists' social media for an announcement of further demonstrations. There, she learned that the evening before, an unarmed middle schooler had been shot in front of his house in Southeast DC, and with his family and neighbors calling fiercely for answers, the community was rallying to support them. Jess carried her rage and grief to the demonstration for the boy. But when the chant went up, Jess's voice failed her. She could *hope* the young people all around her were going to be all right, but conviction was gone.

Later that week, Jess got a call from a number she didn't recognize. It was Theo's friend Daniel. He'd flown from San Francisco to deal with the death bureaucracy on Abiona's behalf, since her visa still hadn't come through. The police had released Theo's personal effects to him. "I found your number in his phone," he said. "I'm clearing his apartment today. I wondered if there was anything you wanted."

"Just the dog," she said. "I'd really love to keep him. Will that be okay?"

"More than okay. All of us—all his friends from Yale—are relieved that Clancy's being taken care of. That dog and Theo . . ." His voice caught.

Jess filled the silence, asking Daniel if he had come across the pages from Theo's thesis. "Because I spoke to his editor at *Smithsonian* magazine about the work he'd done and he said he thinks he can shape it into an article."

"That's great. Yeah, I have it set aside. I read some of it—it's really good work. I'd be glad to get the pages to him."

Jess gave Lior's address to Daniel and was about to hang up when she remembered the horse.

"There is one other thing. Sort of his last wish, I guess." She explained to Daniel about the painting and Theo's plan for it. "It was the last conversation we had, so I . . ."

"I get it. For sure. Come on by."

She rang the buzzer, even though she still had her key. Daniel opened the door. The sofa was already gone, the bookcases disassembled to a stack of planks and a half dozen milk crates. On the wall, the hooks where Theo's bike had hung were empty. Jess extended a hand and touched a dark smudge left by the front tire. Daniel pushed a pair of tortoiseshell glasses up the bridge of his nose. "I barely hit send on Craigslist and my phone exploded with people wanting to buy that bike," he said. He stood surrounded by cartons, most already filled with art books. "The books are going to a high school in Southeast that doesn't have much of a library budget. You never know. Maybe some kid'll get inspired and turn into an art nerd like he was."

Jess struggled to keep her composure. It was hard being in the apartment again, seeing it in disarray.

"I still can't believe it."

Daniel ran a hand through his locs. "Yeah. Right."

She caught the thin wedge of anger in his voice. "Well. I can't."

"He couldn't, either. Whereas I—we—all his friends—can believe it, no problem. Who *does* that? Go help some White girl. In a park. In Northwest DC. At night." He shook his head and dropped another book into the box.

"What else *could* he have done?"

Daniel straightened. "Girl, he should have sped up, kept on running right to a well-lit road, and called some White folk to help her. He just didn't know how he needed to be if he was going to live in this country." He sighed. "We tried. Gave him 'the talk,' like our parents did when we were little kids." He shook his head. "He thought he knew about cops. But the cops he knew in England, ninety percent of them weren't carrying guns. No, make that a hundred percent, the bougie 'hoods where he came up. Art historian, Lord Fauntleroy accent, Yale and Georgetown—none of it was ever going to keep him safe. Like I said, we tried to warn him. But seems like it never sank in. And we weren't here." He glared at her. "You were."

Jess felt the sting of the accusation. "I don't know what you mean."

"Look. It's not your fault you get to move easy in the world. We just can't afford to. Sir Galahad was a White dude. Theo should've been with someone who would've kept reminding him. That's all."

"You're only lucky till you aren't," she said in a small voice.

"Huh?"

"Oh, nothing. Just something my dad used to say. About expecting the world to be good to you."

"Yeah, well. Black people in America sure don't get that luxury."

Jess turned away. She didn't want to break down. She scrunched her fist against her face and struggled for composure.

"Hey," said Daniel, his voice softened. "We're having a memorial, in the spring, at Yale. Alumni weekend. There's going to be a scholarship in his name. You should come."

"I wish I could, but I won't be here by then. After what happened . . ." She trailed off. "I've given a month's notice. I'm going home."

"Australia's a great bastion of antiracism? I guess I missed that news cycle."

"I just feel like there's more chance to change things there. They actually *want* everyone to vote . . ." Daniel shrugged and turned back to the boxes.

"Thanks for telling me. About the memorial. I better let you get on with it."

"Sure. There's that painting, over by the door."

"Thanks." Jess picked it up, then took one last look around. Soon it would just be anonymous grad-student housing again; no remaining trace of Theo's brilliant mind, his vivid life. She placed the apartment key on top of a carton and let herself out.

Across the street, the woman opened the door without undoing the chain. She peered at Jess. A stale smell—cigarettes and mold—drifted from inside.

"You don't know me. I was Theo's friend."

The woman's papery brow creased. "Who?"

"Your neighbor across the street. You threw this out, but he found out it's worth fifteen grand. He wanted you to have it back."

"He . . . he . . . What? Fifteen thousand *dollars*? That old thing? We—my husband, I mean—had no idea. He said it come down to him from his great-granddaddy in the Civil War." The edges of her thin lips turned up in a bitter smile. "If he'd a known how much he could get for it, I don't think he'd have give two hoots about ol' granddaddy. . . . And your friend—that's mighty generous. Where is he? I—I need to thank him."

"Well, you can't," said Jess. "He's dead. Shot in the park by a cop."

"That was *him?*"

Jess's eyes welled. She thrust the painting through the crack in the door. "Here. Take it. And here's the number for the person in Kentucky who wants to buy it." She turned and ran down the steps. She wanted to get away from the woman's pale, pinched stare.

"I'm sorry about your friend," the woman called. "He was very nice, for a—"

"Shut up! Don't say it!" She took off, running blindly.

"—for a student." The woman craned her head around the door and stared at Jess's retreating back.

After that, Jess avoided Georgetown. She moved between her apartment and the lab, working extra hours finishing projects and preparing for a smooth handover. At home, she took Clancy out on long walks and then busied herself paring down her possessions, giving most away.

She'd made the decision to go home before she had any idea what she'd do when she got there. She was thinking about a PhD; something that would redirect her work to endangered species. But when Catherine unexpectedly gave Jess a coauthor credit on her research paper, Jess became the go-to for all those suddenly fascinated by Lexington. Soon, the equestrian community was begging the Smithsonian to lend the skeleton indefinitely to the International Museum of the Horse in Kentucky, where it could be properly displayed: the centerpiece of an exhibit on the history of the American thoroughbred. Jess loved the idea and lobbied for it within the Institution's bureaucracy. Instead of being "Horse," Lexington would be himself again, returned to his birthplace, the star of his own extraordinary story.

In her last weeks as a Smithsonian employee, Jess designed the packing materials that would keep the frail bones safe in transit. Then she traveled to Kentucky to oversee the installation. When she walked into the room where the skeleton was to be displayed, she stopped and stared. Hanging on the wall, already labeled and lit, was the painting Theo had salvaged.

She walked closer and read the text. "Lexington, as a colt, painted by Thomas J. Scott at The Meadows, circa 1851. Given in memory of Theodore Naade Northam."

She turned to the museum director, tears prickling her eyes.

"How did you get this?"

"One of our donors bought it for the museum."

"But how did they know Theo Northam?"

"I don't believe they did. I was told that particular acknowledgment was a special request of the seller. Condition of the sale, in fact."

Jess turned away. The director looked at her with concern. "Are you all right?"

"Yes," she said, swiping at her eyes. "I'm just surprised. To see it again."

"Ah. Right. I heard it was restored and authenticated at the Smithsonian. You were involved with that?"

"Yes," she said softly. "I was involved."

A day later, she was up a ladder, reattaching the horse's skull—a delicate matter of manipulating the tiny, nineteenth-century brass screws—when the museum director led a tall, pale man with long silver hair into the exhibit hall. Jess didn't pay any attention—there had been a stream of visitors—reporters, museum supporters, local VIPs—ever since Lexington's skeleton had arrived. This one, she thought absently, must be a big donor, the way the museum director gushed over him. The guest circumnavigated the skeleton, staring intently, saying nothing as the director laid on the lashings of southern charm. Finally, he turned.

"Shut up, would ya? I just want to look at the bloody thing."

Jess recognized the Australian accent. She pushed the binocular loupes up onto her forehead to get a clearer view. She was fairly sure she recognized him. Mathematician, gambler, art collector. The person whose sophisticated betting system had made him a fortune. He'd won $16 million on a single Melbourne Cup and then spent his winnings building an art museum. It housed his personal collection, everything from Egyptian antiquities to the edgiest contemporary installations, all connected by his fascination with sex and death.

"Why's the bone around the eye socket all buggered like that?"

Jess climbed down her ladder and explained the horse's history and the hypothesis about the deformation. He listened, then turned and walked out without saying anything. The director scurried after him, looking back over his shoulder with an apologetic shrug.

The next day, Jess got an email. He was offering her a commission. Over the years, he wrote, he had collected the remains of more than a hundred extinct animals. He wanted her to prep the bones and articulate the skeletons in a very particular way.

"I want them all fucking. The regenerative act that can't regenerate. The price of the Anthropocene." He would pay her first-class airfare and put her up at one of the riverside apartments that usually accommodated well-heeled visitors to his museum. "My collection includes the remains of a Dawn Horse from Messel. Forty-seven million years old."

She rubbed the tips of her fingers together, imagining the delicacy of the fossilized bone. The Dawn Horse, *Eohippus*, was the earliest antecedent of the modern Equidae. The tiny animals stood only two feet tall and had human-like toes instead of hooves. To study the bones would be amazing; to articulate an *Eohippus* would be a huge challenge. But the project was ridiculous. A frivolous waste of important scientific materials. There was no question: she would turn him down.

But then: a second thought. Perhaps a shocking installation about something as shocking as mass extinction *wasn't* frivolous. Science hadn't moved people. Maybe art could. Theo had certainly believed that. His whole life had been devoted to the proposition that art mattered, that it could change the way we understand the world.

If this crazy offer was for real, she decided, she would do it. For the lost species, and for Theo.

She called the number in the email for his assistant, who was brisk and businesslike. "The studio will be available to you first thing in January. Let me know what special equipment you'll need and I'll get on with ordering it." Jess's voice must have betrayed her uncertainty. The assistant laughed. "If it's any reassurance, I can tell you that this is the least strange thing he's planning."

Jess had traded in the first-class ticket for a business-class one and used the difference to fund Clancy's transport. She'd rented a car and driven across the country in stages, to make the trip easier on the dog, but also to give her a chance to say a slow goodbye to the country that had given, and taken, so much. By the time they reached the ragged desert edge of the LA sprawl, she was ready to go.

As she made her way through the tedium of check-in lines, security lines, boarding lines, she noticed several people wearing paper surgical masks. She wondered if they were being paranoid about that new virus she'd been hearing about. As she stepped from the jetway into the plane, it struck her that for fifteen hours she'd be sealed in a metal tube with hundreds of people. She wished she'd thought to get a mask for herself. It was good she was leaving when she was; if the virus spread, it might get complicated to fly. But then she looked around at all the people cramming their wheelie bags into overhead bins, adjusting their neck pillows, scrolling through the in-flight video choices, and dismissed the idea. Restless humans. You'd never stop them traveling.

She found her seat and began all her own preflight rituals, arranging her space for the long hours ahead. As the plane took off, she glanced at the stranger in the seat next to her. It should have been Theo. They should have been making this trip together. It took her a long time to quiet her mind. When she finally fell into a fitful sleep, the plane was high above the ocean, the turbulent air rocking her like a cradle.

In her dream, Lexington galloped across the red soil of the Australian desert. She could see the long, strong bones that powered his elastic stride, but also the bronze sheen of his coat. He shimmered in the sunlight, each stride sending fans of fine red soil flying into the bright air. All around him, a herd of tiny Dawn Horses gamboled at his feet.

AFTERWORD

Fiction is obliged to stick to possibilities; truth isn't.

Mark Twain

This novel is a work of the imagination, but most of the details regarding Lexington's brilliant racing career and years as a stud sire are true. He covered 960 mares, resulting in 575 foals, a remarkable percentage in itself. Many of these foals went on to be outstanding champions, four of them winning the Belmont Stakes and three winning the Preakness—Preakness himself was a Lexington foal.

In reconstructing Lexington's life, I relied on reporting in the lively turf press of the day. At a time when the country was still heavily agrarian, these newspapers had an immense readership, and even in New York, two of the three leading papers were devoted to horse racing.

It is also true that Lexington's skeleton, once a celebrated exhibit, languished for many years neglected in a Smithsonian attic before being loaned to the International Museum of the Horse in Kentucky in 2010, which is when I first heard of it. At a donors' lunch at Plimoth Plantation, I was seated across from Harold A. Closter, director of Smithsonian Affiliations, who had just handled the delivery. As a horse lover, I became transfixed by the details he shared and resolved to learn more.

This led me to the remarkable story of Thomas J. Scott, whose work was just then being rediscovered thanks to a discarded painting rescued from a neighbor's curbside throwaways by Gordon Burnette, a manager of physical plant at the University of Kentucky. The soiled portrait of a mare and her foal charmed Burnette and prompted him to research the painter. What he uncovered inspired the art historian Genevieve Baird Lacer to catalogue and exhibit much of Scott's known oeuvre in 2010. Her catalogue, *A Troye Legacy: Animal Painter T. J. Scott*, is the best account of his life and work to date.

Details of Scott's Civil War service are drawn from a memoir by his unit's chaplain, Thomas M. Gunn. His relationship with the New Orleans painter and his role in the Woodburn raid is imagined.

As horse racing in America becomes increasingly scrutinized and controversial for its treatment of equines, it is important to appreciate its immense popularity in antebellum life. For the wealthy, both North and South, racehorse ownership was a matter of vast prestige. This thriving industry was built on the labor and skills of Black horsemen, many of whom were, or had been, enslaved. After Reconstruction, the racing industry became segregated and these Black horsemen were pushed aside. White jockeys conspired to put their Black competitors at grave risk during races. Some were forced to travel to Europe to continue their careers; others became destitute. As I began to research Lexington's life, it became clear to me that this novel could not merely be about a racehorse; it would also need to be about race. Horse farms like the Meadows and Woodburn prospered on the plundered work and extraordinary talent of Black grooms, trainers, and jockeys. Only recently has their central role in the wealth creation of the antebellum thoroughbred industry begun to be researched and fully acknowledged.

Descriptions of Scott's missing painting of Lexington being led by "black Jarret, his groom" (especially in *Harper's New Monthly Magazine*, July 1870) prompted me to search in vain for more information on who Jarret might have been, but I could not uncover further references to him by name. There was a typical reference in the *Kentucky Live Stock Record* of Lexington being transported from Natchez in the care of a "Darkie" and on these slim filaments, bolstered by details of other skilled Black horsemen involved in the stallion's welfare, I began to imagine the character in the novel.

The life of Harry Lewis is a little better documented. One of the most exceptional trainers of his era, he was responsible for Lexington's early success, during which period he owned the horse's "racing qualities." I am indebted to Edward Hotaling's *The Great Black Jockeys* (Forum, 1999), in which he notes the annotation in Captain Willa Viley's copy of the Kentucky Association Rules, next to the item prohibiting any "negro or mulatto" from running a horse on that track. It is possible that this rule was used to pressure Lewis into surrendering his interest in Lexington when the horse was sold to a syndicate that included Viley and Ten Broeck.

Katherine C. Mooney's *Race Horse Men: How Slavery and Freedom Were Made at the Racetrack* (Harvard University Press, 2014) and Tera W. Hunter's *Bound in Wedlock: Slave and Free Black Marriage in the Nineteenth Century* (Belknap Press, Harvard University Press, 2017) provided a wealth of historic detail about Black lives of the period. Jessica Dallow's remarkable essay, "Antebellum Sports Illustrated: Representing African Americans in Edward Troye's Equine Paintings," shaped my thinking about depictions of the Black horsemen in art.

Woodburn Farm was raided twice during the Civil War, including by Quantrill's murderous irregulars, who stole Lexington's progeny. Unfortunately accounts of the raids are incomplete and somewhat conflicting. I have fictionalized many aspects of the incident, including the roles played by Jarret and Scott. But it is true that Lexington and many other Woodburn horses were spirited away to safety in Illinois for the duration of the war after the raids.

Martha Jackson's bequest to the Smithsonian did include Scott's portrait of Lexington, an anomaly among the modern-art masterpieces in her estate. I have tried to imagine a reason why the committed modernist might have owned such a painting. While her mother was a champion equestrienne who died following a fall from her horse, I have invented the connection between that horse and Lexington. But Smithsonian records reveal the painting was briefly in the possession of Paul Mellon, and it is true that Jackson Pollock died in the convertible Martha Jackson traded him for paintings. Many details in the novel are drawn from a 1969 oral history interview with Martha Jackson in the Smithsonian Archives of American Art.

As well as Harold A. Closter, I am indebted to many at the Smithsonian Institution for a wealth of research help. Thank you most especially to Darrin Lunde, head of Collections, Division of Mammals, and Eleanor Jones Harvey, senior curator at the American Art Museum. Daniella Haigler, Osteology Prep Lab manager at the Museum Support Center, and her assistant, Teresa Hsu, were magical guides to that vast treasure house in Suitland, Maryland, and the funky corner of it that houses the bug room.

At the Straus Center for Conservation at Harvard University, once again my fellow Aussie Narayan Khandekar provided much help, as did his colleague Kate Smith, Conservator of Paintings.

At the International Museum of the Horse, where Lexington's skeleton is now the center of a magnificent exhibition, director Bill Cooke generously shared years of research on both Lexington and the history of Black horsemen. It was Cooke's years of lobbying that finally brought Lexington home to the Bluegrass. His research into the contribution of Black horsemen continues in the blog africanamericanhorsestories.org. When I looked for a tour guide in the Bluegrass, luck led me to Mary Anne Squires and a true insider's access to the backstretch, breeding sheds, pastures, and manorial estates of Lexington's homeplace. Her husband Jim's account of their unlikely success as breeders of a Kentucky Derby winner, *Horse of a Different Color* (Public Affairs, 2002), is by turns hilarious and horrifying.

Many veterinarians helped me understand horse physiology and their methods of research. I am especially thankful to Renate Weller, professor of Comparative Imaging and Biomechanics at the Royal Veterinary College London; Michael Moore at Woods Hole Oceanographic Institution; Denis Verwilghen, University of Sydney; and Dennis E. Brooks, University of Florida.

As always, I relied on the generous help of librarians. Thank you to Keeneland Library, the Filson Historical Society, and my own indispensable

West Tisbury Library. I am grateful to the American Library in Paris, where I was Centennial Writer in Residence in 2020, a productive time that was unfortunately cut short by the Covid pandemic.

My friend and agent, Kris Dahl, is a marvel, and my long partnership with the whole team at Viking Penguin is a gift. Special thanks, always, to my editor, Paul Slovak, and to Louise Braverman, director of publicity and so very much more.

All of my novels have relied on early readers; for this one they proved indispensable. My dear friends Salem Mekuria, Misan Sagay, and Ed Swan generously and patiently read early drafts and shared insights into contemporary Black experience, as did my son Bizu. I'm lucky to have writers in the family who wield a red pen to great effect. My sister Darleen Bungey, my in-laws Elinor and Joshua Horwitz, and my son Nathaniel were eagle-eyed readers. I also received invaluable input from Fred and Jeanne Barron, Richard Beswick, Jane Cavolina, Kate Feiffer, Fiona Hazard, Allie Merola, and, as always, Graham Thorburn, *mio miglior fabbro*.

My mare, Valentine, and her companion, Screaming Hot Wings, were daily inspirations and offered their opinions in the language of *Equus*.

I started this novel with the encouragement of my husband, Tony Horwitz, the true historian in the family. He hadn't been crazy about my previous novelistic plunge into myth and biblical history but thoroughly embraced my engagement with a more recent period he knew and loved. Often, a pertinent article or a promising source he had ferreted out would land on my desk. Together with Bizu, we traveled to Kentucky, where our research often intersected in intriguing ways as he followed the trail of Frederick Law Olmsted for his book *Spying on the South* (Penguin Press, 2019). Back home, Tony's quips would keep me on task if I procrastinated: "Doesn't look like *Horse* is galloping to the finish line today."

Tony died suddenly on book tour, not long after speaking to an enthusiastic audience at the Filson in Louisville. My partner in love and in life, I miss him every day.

West Tisbury, July 20, 2021

LEXINGTON'S
HISTORICAL
CONNECTIONS

ROBERT AITCHESON ALEXANDER, 1819–1867

Alexander inherited his uncle's Scottish estate and lived there nine years before returning to his birthplace in Kentucky and creating Woodburn, a preeminent livestock breeding farm. He bought Lexington from Ten Broeck while in England in 1856. The horse was already standing stud at a neighboring Kentucky farm. While Alexander traveled to and from Europe studying breeding practices, two of his enslaved men, Ansel Williamson and Edward D. Brown (bought by Alexander at the age of seven), took charge of Woodburn's thoroughbred operations. Williamson trained Lexington's colt Asteroid, who was undefeated in his racing career, and went on to train Aristides, the winner of the inaugural Kentucky Derby. Starting as a jockey, Brown won his first race at fourteen on Asteroid. Later he won the Belmont Stakes riding Kingfisher. Emancipated after the Civil War, both men remained in Alexander's employ until his death, then became successful trainers independently. Brown died a wealthy man in 1906 and was finally inducted into the National Museum of Racing and Hall of Fame in 1984. Williamson's induction followed in 1998. Though a groom named Jarret was painted with Lexington by Thomas J. Scott at Woodburn, I was not able to learn details of his life, so I have modeled the career of my fictional character on these two accomplished horsemen.

RICHARD TEN BROECK, BORN ALBANY, NEW YORK, 1812, DIED SAN MATEO, CALIFORNIA, 1892

"He lived in Clubs and Crowds and Died at Last in His Old Age Forsaken and Alone, but with no Taint of Dishonor Upon His Name" read the headline on his obituary in *The San Francisco Call*. A classmate of Robert E. Lee's at West Point, he left abruptly after just a year and worked with William R. Johnson, the so-called Napoleon of the Turf, from whom he gained expertise that would lead to his success as a racing impresario. As driver of a racing pair, he competed successfully on the racetrack, as well as owning one. The first to bring American thoroughbreds to race in England, he won the friendship of British aristocrats, as well as almost two hundred thousand dollars in purses, before returning to the United States in 1889, broke, unhappily married, and in failing health.

CASSIUS MARCELLUS CLAY, 1810–1903, MADISON COUNTY, KENTUCKY

The son of wealthy planters, Clay was inspired by William Lloyd Garrison while at Yale and became publisher of *The True American*, an emancipationist newspaper. He survived a mob raid on his paper and two assassination attempts, besting his gun-wielding assailants with his Bowie knife. A founding member of the Republican Party, he was appointed by President Lincoln as minister to Russia and is credited with winning the czar's support for the Union during the Civil War. While in Russia, he had an affair with a ballerina, which may have contributed to his divorce, after forty-five years of marriage and ten children, from Mary Jane Warfield.

MARY JANE WARFIELD CLAY, 1815–1900

Mary Jane was an early leader of the suffrage movement whose daughters would become the most well known of the Kentucky suffragists. While her husband was in Russia, she astutely managed their estate, innovatively renovating the White Hall mansion, and profitably selling farm produce to the army.

MARY BARR CLAY, 1839–1924

When her mother was left homeless after divorce, losing the estate she had successfully managed, Mary Barr was appalled by the injustice. She joined the women's rights movement, inspiring her three younger sisters to do likewise. She was elected president of the American Woman Suffrage Association in 1883.

WILLIAM JOHNSON 1809–1851, KNOWN AS "THE BARBER OF NATCHEZ"

Freed from enslavement at age eleven, Johnson became a successful businessman and developed an uncommonly close relationship with Adam Bingaman, on whose plantation Lexington was trained. Johnson, who kept a detailed diary for sixteen years, took a keen interest in horse racing and even dabbled in breeding, with Bingaman allowing some of his own renowned stud stallions to cover Johnson's mares. Johnson held sixteen enslaved people at the time of his death. His house in downtown Natchez is now a National Park Service Museum.

HARRY LEWIS, BORN 1805

Lewis worked as a trainer for Robert Burbridge and Captain Willa Viley, for whom he trained what was then Kentucky's finest horse, Richard Singleton. His expertise allowed him to amass the funds necessary to buy himself out of enslavement, and he went to work for Dr. Warfield as a free man, where he trained Darley, later Lexington, to his first wins, while owning the thoroughbred's "racing qualities." He married Winnie and had one son, Lewis. It may be that the "Lew"—either the groom or the jockey depicted alongside Harry in the Troye portrait—is this son.

JOHN BENJAMIN PRYOR, 1812–1890

A slaveholder (of as many as twenty-seven individuals) and a leading race-horse trainer, Pryor was employed for a time by the prominent Mississippi politician Adam Lewis Bingaman. He is widely credited with Lexington's successful races at Metairie, although at least one of the two occasions on which Lexington injured himself—the colic incident—occurred when the horse was under his supervision. In 1881 he gave an account of the incident in a letter to the *Kentucky Livestock Record* in which he called Lexington "undoubtedly the best racehorse that ever was foaled." Like Ten Broeck, Pryor went to England during the Civil War. He lived there with his wife, Frances, who was Black and probably one of Adam Bingaman's daughters. He trained horses at Chesterfield House in Cambridgeshire and Roden House in Berkshire. He wrote: "I have seen all the best horses run here for five years and seen them run all distances, and feel sure, without prejudice, that Lexington was superior to all horses in England or any other country." When they returned to the United States in 1872, the family settled in New Jersey, where at least four of his sons also pursued careers as trainers.

THOMAS J. SCOTT, BORN TULLYTOWN, PENNSYLVANIA, C. 1831, DIED LEXINGTON, KENTUCKY, 1888

A pharmacy graduate, Scott became an itinerant thoroughbred painter known for incorporating insights into the horse's personality in his portraits. He also worked as a regular correspondent for the newspapers *Turf, Field and Farm*, and the *Kentucky Livestock Record*. During the Civil War he served as a hospital steward in Company E, 21st Infantry Regiment, Kentucky Volunteers: 218 men from the regiment were lost; 152 died of disease. In Washington in 1878, Scott visited Lexington's skeleton at the Smithsonian. He noted several anatomical inaccuracies and wrote: *For the benefit of Mr. A. H. Ward, of Rochester, N.Y., who prepared and mounted the skeleton of Lexington, I would suggest that, as a useful guide, he should always obtain an accurate description of the living animal from those familiar with the form.* Scott married late, in 1871. Though they had four children, Scott and his wife lived together only intermittently, as Scott resumed his itinerant career just three months after the wedding.

EDWARD TROYE, BORN SWITZERLAND, 1808, DIED GEORGETOWN, KENTUCKY, 1874

Troye, the preeminent horse portraitist of his era, taught Scott drawing and painting in the mid-1850s and the two remained close colleagues.

WILLA VILEY, 1788–1865

Viley was a captain in the War of 1812, a farmer, a thoroughbred breeder, and the first president of the Lexington Racing Association. With his brother-in-law, Junius Ward, he was part of the syndicate that purchased Darley from Dr. Warfield. His son Warren had a farm near Woodburn, and Viley was captured there by Quantrill's raiders and rescued only after a harrowing chase and gun battle.

ELISHA WARFIELD JR., BORN ANNE ARUNDEL COUNTY, MARYLAND, 1781, DIED LEXINGTON, KENTUCKY, 1859

Warfield was named by *Thoroughbred Heritage* as "one of the most important early figures in Kentucky racing and breeding" and was a founder of the Lexington Jockey Club. A businessman, farmer, medical practitioner, and professor of surgery and obstetrics, he delivered Mary Todd Lincoln. In 1945, his stud farm, the Meadows, became a residential subdivision of that name in the Lexington suburbs. His graceful sixteen-room brick mansion was razed in 1960.